Praise for Anna

"Durand's Hot Scots series has been loads of fun to read, and [*Irresistible in a Kilt*] is no exception. [...] The author's action-packed and suspenseful plot keeps the reader on their toes, and the grown-up sizzle never disappoints."
Jack Magnus, Readers' Favorite

"[*Lethal in a Kilt* is] full of hot sex, adventure, and so much laughter. I found myself laughing-out-loud at the antics of the Witches of Ballachulish (Logan's sisters) and the hilarious flirting and sexy banter between Serena and Logan. [...] Recommend highly!"
Sharon Clayton, The Eclectic Review

"[*Insatiable in a Kilt*] smokes from the very first pages... Durand's characters are a delight and seeing how they mix business with their increasing attraction for each other is entertaining indeed. [...] Durand's Hot Scots family saga just keeps on getting better."
Jack Magnus, Readers' Favorite

"I loved the Scottish in Ian and the strength of Rae, but the love of one little girl makes [*Notorious in a Kilt*] something to behold."
Coffee Time Romance

"*Gift-Wrapped in a Kilt* is a marvelous continuation of the author's MacTaggart family saga. Durand's story has an entertaining plot, and her steamy interludes are well-written...a celebration of healthy relationships between loving adults written in a tasteful and compelling manner."
Jack Magnus, Readers' Favorite

"I have enjoyed this whole series, but Emery and Rory [from *Scandalous in a Kilt*] have stolen my heart and are now my favorites!"
The Romance Reviews

"An enthralling story. [...] I highly recommend the writing of Ms. Durand and *Wicked in a Kilt*, but be warned you will find yourself addicted and want your own Hot Scot."
Coffee Time Romance & More

"There's a huge hero's and heroine's journey [in *Dangerous in a Kilt*] that I quite enjoyed, not to mention the hot sex, and again, not to mention the sweet seduction of the Scotsman who pulls out all the stops to get Erica to love him."
Manic Readers

Other Books by Anna Durand

Gift-Wrapped IN A KILT

Hot Scots, Book Four

ANNA DURAND

JACOBSVILLE BOOKS **JB** MARIETTA, OHIO

GIFT-WRAPPED IN A KILT

ISBN: 978-1-949406-00-9 (paperback)
ISBN: 978-1-949406-01-6 (ebook)
ISBN: 978-1-949406-02-3 (audiobook)
Library of Congress Control Number: 2018912264

Manufactured in the United States.

Jacobsville Books
www.JacobsvilleBooks.com

Publisher's Cataloging-in-Publication Data
provided by Five Rainbows Cataloging Services

Names: Durand, Anna.
Title: Gift-wrapped in a kilt / Anna Durand.
Description: Lake Linden, MI : Jacobsville Books, 2018. | Series: Hot Scots, bk. 4.
Identifiers: LCCN 2018912264 | ISBN 978-1-949406-00-9 (paperback) | ISBN
    978-1-949406-01-6 (ebook) | ISBN 978-1-949406-02-3 (audiobook)
Subjects: LCSH: Holidays—Fiction. | Man-woman relationships—Fiction. |
    Scots—Fiction. | Americans—Fiction. | Highlands (Scotland)—Fiction.
    | Families—Fiction. | Romance fiction. | BISAC: FICTION / Romance /
    Contemporary. | FICTION / Romance / Holiday. | FICTION / Romance /
    Romantic Comedy. | GSAFD: Love stories.
Classification: LCC PS3604.U724 G54 2018 (print) | LCC PS3604.U724 (ebook) |
    DDC 813/.6—dc23.

Chapter One

Emery

My name is Emery MacTaggart, and I'm the newest member of the American Wives Club, three ladies from the US of A who each married a MacTaggart man and moved to Scotland. I'm not writing this to talk about myself, though. I want to tell you a story. It's about two people who believe nothing can save their love. They're wrong, and I've resolved to prove it.

I adore my sister-in-law, Jamie MacTaggart, because she reminds me of myself in many ways. She has spunk and fire and a cheerfulness I thought knew no end. Gavin Douglas pulled off the impossible, though. He broke her heart and shattered her positive outlook. I know he didn't mean to, but still. It happened. Gavin—brother of Calli MacTaggart, my sister-in-law and fellow American Wives Club member—has never felt at home among the MacTaggarts. I know he can be if he makes an effort. If he does what he needs to do, Jamie and Gavin's love can be saved.

Here comes my story. Well, their story.

After more than a year of intercontinental romance—Gavin in America, Jamie in Scotland, traveling back and forth to see each other—Jamie has had enough. She wants a commitment, and Gavin thought he was ready for it. Ah, that poor, misguided man. Like every man I've ever met, he has no clue how he really feels. The male of the species doesn't go for self-examination. Instead, these guys bumble around until the right woman straightens them out. Ask my hubby, Rory. He's an expert on denial, repression, and the value of a feisty American woman.

Rory taught me all about men who refuse to acknowledge, much less deal with, their fears. I married him four days after we met, and though he believed I'd done it for the money and excitement, I hitched my fate to his because I saw his potential. He's lived up to it and then some. If the most repressed man in Scotland could shed his fears and find happiness, I know Gavin can too.

Getting back to Jamie and Gavin…You might wonder how I know all of these things about their relationship.

"You meddle, that's how."

Strong hands grasped the top of my high-backed chair, hands belonging to the owner of that sexy-as-hell voice. I tilted my head back to gaze up at my husband.

"Hey, Rory baby," I said, snapping the laptop's lid shut. "Are you spying? Reading what I'm typing over my shoulder?"

Rory kissed my forehead. "How else will I know what nefarious plots you're cooking up?"

"This plot's already happening. Too late to stop it."

He sighed. "I doubt I want to know what your plans are for Jamie and Gavin."

"Better leave it to the expert." I patted his cheek, his face upside down to me. "Go get naked and I'll meet you in the office in ten minutes."

"The office again? Every surface in there is hard and sharp, and you're pregnant. We will not have sex anywhere except a well-padded bed until the bairn is born."

"Oh please, I'm not even showing yet." I looped my arms around his neck, pulling him in for a soft, sweet kiss. His hand drifted down to my breast, giving it a light squeeze. I broke the kiss, hissing in a sharp breath.

He snatched his hand away. "Are you all right?"

"A little tender. It's normal pregnancy stuff." I rubbed my lower back where an ache had started. "But you may be right about those sharp surfaces. Let's swap the office for the bathtub, and you run ahead and get the tub filled. I'll catch up in a jiff."

"When you're done documenting your meddling."

"Is it my fault people like to talk to me? I don't get judge-y, like some grumpy-but-sexy people I know and love." I tickled his lips. "I meant you, by the way."

"Judge-y? That's not a word, Em."

I reached around to slap his ass. "Scoot. I'll meet you in the ground-floor bathroom."

Rory ambled out of the sitting room. Yes, we lived in a home that had a sitting room. We lived in a castle, actually, one with four levels but only three floors. Don't get me started on that craziness.

I flipped my laptop's lid open again, fingers poised over the keyboard.

What was I saying? Oh yes. Jamie and Gavin.

The trouble started this morning when Gavin decided to give Jamie what he thought she wanted. Being a man, though, he lacked the self-awareness to see the train wreck looming ahead of him.

Chapter Two

*G*avin Douglas relinquished the soft, warm lips of Jamie MacTaggart with a long sigh, reluctant to give up her sweet flavor one second sooner than necessary. He had to break away now, though. How could he ask a question with her lips fastened to his? Not that he minded the fastening. God, he loved kissing this woman.

He didn't even care about the other people in the outdoor cafe. If they cared about the couple making out in the corner, under the shade of the striped awning, they didn't show it. The Halloween decorations hanging from the awning shielded them even more. The weather gods had gifted them with nice weather today, so they could enjoy the outdoors.

Jamie's cheeks dimpled. "You must have something important to say, otherwise you'd never stop kissing me after a few minutes."

Yeah, their make-out sessions tended to go on for a lot longer.

He loved her Scottish accent, but he loved those dimples even more. The sunshine, muted by the awning, made the green flecks in her hazel eyes glimmer like polished chips of green garnet. He couldn't resist sliding his fingers into her long, golden-brown hair and cupping her cheek in his palm. Her eyes softened, her posture softened, and a pang stabbed into his chest.

Jamie. Perfect, sweet, loving Jamie. She deserved so much better than an unemployed salesman from America.

He just suppressed a wince. Jamie didn't know he'd lost his job. He'd found out only this morning when his boss sent him a damn email to let him know he was laid off thanks to downsizing. What a cliché.

On top of everything else, he hadn't made love to her in three months. Long-distance romance sounded easy, but it generated way more stress than he'd thought it would. All his fault, probably.

"What's wrong?" Jamie asked, her bright smile fading.

"Nothing, I—" *Need to tell you I got fired when all I really want to do is ask you a question.* His gut twisted. "Uh, well, see…"

"You can tell me, whatever it is." She pressed her small mouth to his. "Do you trust me?"

He swallowed hard, but the tightness in his throat wouldn't let up. "You know I do."

"Then tell me. I'm tougher than I look."

Gavin tried, but the words had gotten lodged in his throat.

She sighed, her lips forming the loveliest little smile of understanding. "You think about it while I powder my nose."

"Your nose looks fine to me."

Jamie laughed softly, her melodic voice tickling his senses. "It's a polite way of saying I need to take a piss."

Hearing words like "piss" come from the mouth of sweet little Jamie always struck him as odd. Her three brothers had taught her to curse, in English and in Gaelic. There was no sight on earth like the vision of Jamie MacTaggart swearing a blue streak in another language at her misbehaving older brothers. Aidan was mostly to blame for Jamie's knowledge of wicked Gaelic, but Lachlan and Rory had played their parts too. Her two older sisters, Fiona and Catriona, didn't swear half as much as his Jamie.

"I'll be a minute," Jamie said.

Gavin watched her sashay across the cafe, navigating around tables and chairs, her hips swaying and her luscious ass framed by the swishing skirt of her flower-print dress. When she'd moved out of sight into the cafe's small interior section, he slumped in his chair. Fingering the square lump in his pants pocket, he let his gaze wander to the street. The outdoor cafe overlooked the main street of Loch Fairbairn, the village Jamie described as "cute" and "romantic." When Gavin had asked where she'd like to have lunch, she of course wanted to come here.

He nudged one of the two plates that had gotten shoved to the center of the table. The remains of their lunch littered the dishes.

This town belonged to Jamie's brother Rory. Not literally, but yeah. The Scottish guy all but owned the place since everybody here thought Rory was a superhero. Jamie's second-oldest brother didn't like Gavin, he knew it, and being in the village where the pod people worshiped Rory was bad enough. The guy was a lawyer too—sorry, a solicitor—who could sue Gavin upside down and sideways if Rory decided Gavin was mistreating his baby sister.

Never mind that Rory's little brother had screwed Gavin's baby sister days after meeting her. Sure, Calli married Aidan last year, but come on. And Rory had married a woman for sex after knowing her for a few days. The guy had no right to feel, well, self-righteous about Gavin's relationship with Jamie.

Feeling bitter really sucked, especially when he couldn't figure out why Jamie's brothers bugged him so much. They weren't half-bad guys but being around them irked Gavin for some weird reason.

He leaned his elbows on the porcelain table and rubbed his eyes. What galled him the most was he had to accept a free ticket on MacTaggart Family Airlines to get here. Okay, it wasn't actually an airline. It was a jet owned by Lachlan, Jamie's oldest brother, and often used by Rory. Rory, the solicitor with a heart of steel, had extended the invitation to fly here on his jet. Galling. Demeaning. Confusing, since Rory hated Gavin. This wasn't the first time Rory had flown Gavin here for a visit with Jamie, which made the situation all the more confusing.

"Here I am," Jamie said breezily as she breezed back to the table and reclaimed her seat beside Gavin. "What was it you wanted to talk about?"

He sat up, back straight, chin lifted. Time to charge through the front lines straight into the battle.

"You okay?" Jamie asked, canting her head. Long locks of her hair flowed over her shoulders, and those hazel eyes studied him with concern. "The flight has you knackered, doesn't it? We can talk later."

"No," he said a bit too abruptly. "Now. We should, uh, talk now. I'm going home tomorrow."

Two days with Jamie would never be enough. He wanted her for good, for keeps, not for the occasional weekend.

His mouth went dry, but his hands grew clammy.

"Go on, Gavin." Jamie leaned in, her cheeks dimpling yet again. "I'm listening."

The expectant look on her face made his gut clench.

She wanted a proposal. She'd never told him that, but he knew. Mostly because his sister told him. Calli had punched him in the arm and said, "Ask her to marry you already."

Gavin had come here to do that. He wanted to ask. He'd wanted to pop the question for months, but something always held him back. A week ago, he'd committed to doing it, but his enthusiasm for proposing had fizzled when he got the downsizing email. If he didn't ask her soon, she might leave him. If she found out he was unemployed, she might leave him.

His hand slipped into his pocket like it had a mind of its own, and his fingers curled around the velvet ring box. *Do it, moron. You love her, so do it.*

Did he have any right to do this to her? Ask her to bind her life to his when he had nothing to give in return? A cold panic gripped him, paralyzing his body and mind. Memories barreled through him, as real as the moment they'd happened. Leanne standing in the doorway, the sunshine streaming over her as she hovered on the verge of walking out the front door.

"I need to find myself," she'd said, "and I can't do that with you stifling me. I gave you everything, held your hand through it all, but I can't do this anymore."

Stifling, she'd said. Like he'd held a pillow over her face or something. He'd done nothing wrong as far as he could tell, nothing except stick to the wedding vows. Love, honor, cherish. If Leanne could walk out with no warning, no hint of anything wrong...

What if he'd been the problem after all?

Jamie wasn't Leanne. And he'd changed, hadn't he?

The question paralyzed him again, his muscles stiff and his heart pounding. The ring box felt cold in his hand. Cold and hard and...final.

His throat constricted, his mouth went even drier, like sandpaper.

With no conscious thought for what he was doing, Gavin shoved his other hand in his other pocket and pulled out the other item he'd intended to give Jamie. After the proposal. After she was blissfully happy.

He thrust the credit card at her.

"This is for you," he said, his heart pounding harder and a cold sweat beading on his brow. "It's so you can get miles to use for travel expenses."

Jamie took the credit card between her thumb and forefinger, holding it as if the thing was infected with the Ebola virus. "I don't need miles. We both fly on Rory's jet."

Duh. Gavin knew that, so why had he gotten her the credit card? He'd come up with the moronic idea the card would be a joke—but he'd planned to give it to her after he asked her to marry him.

His fingers, clamped around the ring box, began to ache from the pressure he exerted on it.

In his mind, he'd rehearsed the proposal so many times. All his practice, the speech he'd worked out during the long plane ride, disappeared like a flame doused with water. Instead of a vow to love her forever, the wrong words tumbled from his stupid, stupid lips. "I got one of those credit cards where you earn miles with every purchase. Made you an authorized user on it. This'll, uh, help pay for—expenses. When you visit me."

"You said this already." Her lips quivered. Her eyes glistened with unshed tears, but anger tightened her jaw. "And I reminded you I don't need a bloody credit card. Is this why you brought me here? To a romantic restaurant? This is the important thing you needed to tell me? After eighteen months together, this is all you think I'm worth."

Oh shit. What had he done? Still time to fix it if he brought out the ring box and—

Tears spilled down Jamie's cheeks even as anger flashed in her eyes. "You're an eejit, Gavin. A *bod ceann* and an eejit, and I'm done."

She'd called him a dickhead in Gaelic, and he deserved it.

Fix it now, you moron. "Jamie—"

The love of his life jumped out of her chair so fast it toppled over, then she hurled the credit card at him. It tumbled onto his lap. "I cannae do this anymore, Gavin. It's over."

"What?"

"I'm breaking up with you." She enunciated each word with knife-like precision. "Goodbye, forever."

Jamie MacTaggart stomped out of the cafe, down the street, and out of his life.

Gavin wanted to run after her, tried to get his ass out of the chair, but his entire body had turned to stone, rendering his feet too heavy to move. He buried his face in his hands and cursed himself far worse than Jamie could have even in the worst Gaelic imaginable.

Chapter Three

Jamie MacTaggart sniffled and swiped tears from her eyes as she barreled down the sidewalk, head down, unsure of where she was going. Rory's office was two blocks away. She could go there and…What? Rory had never accepted Gavin.

But her brother loved her. Rory had let her live with him for more than a year and would've let her stay even after he brought home his new wife. Emery was wonderful, but Jamie hadn't felt right about living in their home when they'd just married. She lived with Aidan and Calli now, and their baby daughter, Sarah. Jamie could've talked to Calli about Gavin's credit card, except Calli and Aidan were both at the offices of their construction company today. The office in Ballachulish. Half an hour's drive from Loch Fairbairn.

Tears streamed down her cheeks. She stopped walking and mopped at her eyes with the hem of her shirt. She needed to talk to someone now, not in thirty minutes. Could she drive safely in this state, anyway? Crying. No, weeping was more like it. How had she let this happen again? The first time, with Trevor, had been bad enough. She hadn't thought about him in years, not since she'd realized what a scunner he was. She hadn't thought about him until last week, that was. He'd sent her an email asking how she was doing these days and would she like to meet for coffee sometime since he'd be visiting Inverness on business this week. *Away and boil your head*, she'd wanted to tell him. Instead, she'd deleted the email.

At least no one realized what Trevor had done to her or what a fool she'd allowed him to make of her. She hadn't loved him half as much as she loved Gavin. He'd made an even worse fool of her than Trevor had.

How could Gavin have done this to her? How could she have let him?

A credit card. *Bod an Donais.* Could he honestly think she wanted a piece of plastic? Besides, she and Gavin both flew to each other on the jet Lachlan and Rory shared. Everyone called it Rory's jet, though. With free air travel, why in heaven's name would Jamie need a credit card to earn her frequent-flyer miles?

She lifted her head, and her eyes widened. She'd stopped right in front of Rory's office. Not that she planned to walk in there looking like a pathetic mess, like a pathetic lass who'd lost her boyfriend because he was, apparently, the biggest idiot on the face of the earth.

Eighteen months. She'd wasted all that time with Gavin, and for what? A credit card.

She leaned against the building, out of sight of the sole window on the front of Rory's office. Jamie stayed there, breathing deeply and slowly, until her tears dried and she'd blown her nose five times. Halloween decorations festooned the window on the inside—fake cobwebs, hairy spiders with big eyes, a witch on a broomstick suspended from the window's top edge. Rory hadn't cared for holidays in years, not since before his first wife. Emery, his fourth wife, had transformed him into an aficionado.

Jamie smoothed her blouse and her hair, squared her shoulders, and forced a smile. Jamie MacTaggart forcing a smile. No one would believe it. She was the one who smiled no matter what, who kept a positive outlook no matter what, and here she was faking it.

A credit card, Gavin?

Her heart hurt recalling the incident.

She marched into Rory's office.

The reception desk in the small outer office stood empty, as always, though a figurine of a ghost occupied the desktop. Why Rory had a reception desk but no receptionist, no one knew. Emery probably knew the answer. She knew everything about her husband, even the things he wouldn't tell anyone else. Through the open door to the inner office, Jamie spied Rory hunched over his desk studying papers. Little pumpkins with silly faces painted on them were stationed at all four corners of the desk.

When she tromped inside and flopped into the wooden chair across from him, Rory peered at her over the tops of his reading glasses.

"What are you doing here?" he asked.

"Not sure." Jamie slouched in the chair.

Rory took off his glasses and plunked them down on the desk. "Where's Gavin?"

She shrugged.

"How was lunch?"

She shrugged again.

He frowned. "What's the *bod ceann* done?"

Jamie shot upright in her chair, hands on the arms. "Don't call him a dickhead, Rory."

Even if Gavin had acted like one, she wouldn't have her brother insulting her boyfriend. That was her job.

The brother in question drummed his fingers on the desktop, his lips pursed. "He's hurt you again, I can see it. Jamie, you have no talent for hiding your feelings. Tell me what the b—what Gavin has done, so I can batter him with a caber."

"Would that be the one Emery pulled out of your erse a few months ago?" Jamie couldn't help brightening at the chance to tease Rory. He'd been so serious and sad for such a long time, and it turned out all he'd needed was a good, strong woman to love him with all her heart and soul. Love changed people, but the effect had been lost on Gavin. The thought of *him* made her a little queasy, so she focused on tormenting her brother. "Do you still have wood splinters in there?"

Rory's mouth twisted as he tried not to smile, or maybe scowl, at her. "Cabers are for tossing, you cheeky bairn. Now tell me what Gavin did."

Some people might've found Rory intimidating—the big, braw solicitor who brooked no nonsense from anyone except for his wife, who loved silliness. Jamie had always adored Rory, though, because he'd always looked out for her. The baby of the family had needed protecting, according to her brothers. Lachlan, as the oldest child, had been the referee between all his siblings. Aidan, the youngest brother and second-youngest sibling, had been her best friend and playmate. Rory, the serious one, had served as her guardian. One stern look from him and any laddie who tried to make time with her fled in terror.

"Tell me," Rory insisted gently.

"He—" *Ugh.* How could she talk to Rory about this? She rubbed her palms on her thighs and bit her lip. "Um, where's Emery? I'd rather talk to her."

Rory sank back in his chair, sighing. "Naturally. Everyone talks to my wife."

"She listens without growling or scowling, that's why."

"Hmm." He picked up a pen, twirling it around his fingers. "Emery drove to Ballachulish to help Calli with her office computer." Rory glanced at the clock on the wall. "She's probably done by now and on her way home."

"I'll meet her there."

Jamie rose, and so did Rory. She raised her brows.

He grabbed his keys off the desk. "I'm driving you."

"But my car—"

"I'll ring Aidan and ask him to pick it up." Rory strode around the desk, gesturing for her to exit the room. "You're upset. I'm driving, no arguments."

Resigned to the fact no one argued with Rory successfully, no one except his wife, Jamie followed him out of the office and to his Mercedes S-Class parked along the curb. Much more posh than her old car, for sure.

Her brother stood by the passenger door until she'd climbed in and buckled her seatbelt.

As they drove down the streets of Loch Fairbairn, they passed the cafe.

Jamie tried not to, but her eyes insisted on searching for Gavin there. The table where they'd eaten lunch was empty. Gavin was nowhere in sight, and neither was the pickup truck he'd arrived in, the one he'd borrowed from Calli.

He hadn't come after her.

What had she expected? The man was an ex-Marine. He wouldn't rush after her to beg forgiveness and plead with her to marry him. Not the manly thing to do. Maybe he didn't want that, anyway. She no longer had any idea what he did want from her—or what she wanted from him.

Another man had made a fool of her. Would she never learn?

Jamie slumped into her seat, her head against the window, and watched the miles speed by in a blur.

Chapter Four

Gavin fidgeted in the metal folding chair, glancing around the trailer that served as the offices of MacTaggart Construction. His sister, Calli, studied him from across the metal desk, her arms resting on its fake-wood surface. The sallow light from a desk lamp darkened her flame-red hair and emerald-green eyes.

"Are you planning to answer my question?" Calli said. "Sometime this century, I mean."

"Maybe." Gavin scratched his head. "What was the question?"

Calli gave him a long-suffering look. "Why did you give Jamie a credit card she doesn't need or want instead of asking her to marry you?"

"Oh. That. Yeah." He had no frigging idea how to answer, because he had no clue why'd he'd done it. He'd meant to pull out the ring box, drop to one knee, and pop the question he'd wanted to ask for a year. Longer than a year. Almost since the day they'd met. Acid roiled in his gut at the memory of the heartbroken look on Jamie's face when he'd offered her the credit card. God, he was such a stupid, stupid jerk.

And he had no idea how to fix this. So naturally, he was asking his baby sister for help. With a mental groan, he rubbed his forehead.

"Don't groan at me," Calli said.

Okay, more than a mental groan. Damn, he couldn't control his guttural noises any more than his dumb-ass mouth.

"Tell me the truth, Gav. Do you love Jamie?"

He made a probably rude face at his sister. "Come on, C. Would I be so messed up if I didn't?"

Calli drummed her fingertips on the desk. "Is this about Leanne or Afghanistan? Or both?"

"Neither, not really."

"You're lying." Calli waved a finger toward his head. "Your ears are turning red, which always means you're feeding me a whopper."

Gavin wiped at his ears like he could make them stop screaming *liar liar* with their flaming-red skin. "Kid sisters are supposed to look up to their brothers, not treat them like babies."

She leaned back, hands clasped over her belly. "If you'd stop acting like a schizo infant, maybe I'd stop treating you that way. I love you, Gavin, but you're screwing up your life and I can't figure out why."

He coughed and rapped a knuckle on his thigh in a rapid-fire beat. "I—I don't know why this happened."

Calli scrutinized him with narrowed eyes, her focus so intense a tiny shiver raced down his spine. Sometimes, he felt like she could read his mind, like they were twins with a freaky connection. She was eight years younger, though. Unless their parents bought twin embryos and saved one for later, he and Calli didn't have telepathic mojo.

"I'm going to ask you a question," she said, "and I want you to say the first thing that pops into your head. No thinking, no balking, just say it. Okay?"

This sounded like such a bad idea, but he didn't have much to lose. He'd already lost the woman he loved.

"Yeah, sure," he said. "Whatever."

Calli puckered her lips, canting her head. "What are you afraid of?"

"That Jamie will get sick of me and leave." He dropped his head into his hands, groaning again, sickened by the realization. "She already did that, though. I made her do it."

"I believe that's called a self-fulfilling prophecy."

With his head in his hands and all, he didn't see her come around the desk to kneel in front of him. When her hands settled on his knees, he peeked through his fingers at her. The empathy in her expression chafed his heart. Calli didn't feel sorry for him. She didn't do pity. No, she understood his feelings better than he did.

Great. Some tough guy he was.

"I get it," Calli said, her voice as compassionate as her expression. "I was afraid too when I met Aidan. Remember? You told me, and I quote, 'love isn't rational, you've got to take a chance'. You also told me you were over your divorce, but that's not true, is it? I'm sure you thought you'd gotten past it, until you fell in love again." She tapped a finger on his forehead. "Love isn't rational, and you have to take a risk for it."

"Not fair to use my own words against me." He lowered his hands but kept his eyes downcast, unable to stomach meeting her gaze. "Besides, you're a girl. Things are different for guys."

"Uh-huh," she said. "It's different because men are so totally not self-aware. Emery says women think about their issues and work through them, but the only issues men dig into are their monthly subscriptions to *Playboy* magazine."

Gavin opened his mouth to spout a sarcastic retort but stopped. Calli was the smartest person he knew. Well, tied with Jamie.

A pain throbbed behind his ribs. He rubbed the heel of his hand on his chest, but it didn't alleviate the pain. Jamie. Her name was all it took to make him sick.

"Jamie deserves better than me." He blurted it out before his brain analyzed the statement. Maybe Calli and Emery were right about men and their non-self-awareness. He let his shoulders cave in and his chin drop toward his chest. "I lost my job."

"Oh Gavin, I'm so sorry. What happened?"

He hiked up one shoulder. "Downsizing. Plus, I've been kinda distracted with weekend trips to Scotland. More than enough reason for me to be first in line for the pink slip. On top of that, I spent most of my money on overseas phone calls to Jamie, presents for her, fancy dinners when we saw each other, anything I could think of to keep her happy. Not that it worked out that way."

"The tension with Jamie," Calli said. "It's been building for a while."

"Would you stop being so damn insightful? Jeez, C, let me think for myself."

Calli sat back on her haunches, arms crossed over her chest. "Then start thinking."

He rubbed his jaw because it ached like somebody had slugged him. "How can I marry Jamie when I don't have a job? No prospects, running out of money. She deserves a guy who can take care of her."

"Stop being so medieval." Calli stood, and his baby sister loomed over him in a way that made him feel weirdly small. "Jamie has a job working for me and Aidan. She can support both of you until you find a new job. Besides, all the MacTaggart men have offered to help you find employment in Scotland." She rocked forward, looming over him even more, her expression fiercer than he'd ever seen her. "You keep turning them down."

And here it came again. The brothers. Rory had semi-retired from practicing law, taking on only cases that interested him and mostly for free. Emery, Rory's wife, provided computer troubleshooting services to anyone who needed it, often at no charge. Lachlan had sold his financial consulting business because he no longer needed the money, and these days he and

Erica operated a small farm. They donated fresh produce to the local schools and sold it to everybody else for whatever they wanted to pay. Aidan wasn't rich like his brothers, but he did pretty well as far as Gavin could see.

Everybody did better than Gavin was doing lately. Accepting help from Jamie's brothers—her rich, successful brothers—would make him feel like a stray dog they took in out of pity.

He wanted to get up, but Calli blocked him. Instead, he straightened in the chair and frowned up at her. "Exactly what I need, your Scottish husband and his brothers making me their charity case."

"It's not charity. You are family, and we MacTaggarts help our family."

A wave of cold sluiced through him. She'd called herself a MacTaggart. That made Gavin the last living member of the Douglas clan. With their parents gone...Their cousin, Tara, had married too and joined another family. He was alone.

Calli stepped aside, chewing her lower lip. "Gavin? Are you okay?"

"No, not even a little bit." It was the most honest thing he'd said all day.

"Find Jamie. Talk to her."

He pushed up out of the chair, shaking his head. "You were right, C. I have no goddamn idea what I'm feeling or why. I can't work this out with Jamie, if it can be worked out, until I sort out my own shit."

Calli laid a hand on his arm. "Can I help?"

Gavin rolled his eyes heavenward. "I need therapy from my sister. This keeps getting better."

She nudged his arm with her fist. "You're still my hero, Gav."

He grunted.

"My advice stands," she said. "You should talk to Jamie today. Let her know you'll be sticking around instead of flying back to America tomorrow."

"Since when am I sticking around?"

Calli grinned. "Since I told you to."

"You sure have gotten snarky since you married Aidan. I think he's a bad influence." Gavin swung his arms and clapped his hands together. "I can't afford the hotel anymore, so—"

"Oh please, like that's an insurmountable problem. You can stay with me and Aidan, or with Lachlan and Erica, or..." Her smile turned impish. "You could stay with Emery and Rory."

Gavin threw his hands up. "Uh-uh, no way, no how. Rory would probably sneak a rattlesnake into my bed."

"There are no rattlesnakes in Scotland."

"He'll find something else awful and excruciatingly painful to kill me with, then." He raised one hand to silence her impending comment. "And

I'm not staying with Lachlan or Aidan either. Lachlan hates me almost as bad as Rory does, and you and Aidan have Jamie with you."

"I'll find you a place to stay, don't worry about that." She slapped his arm. "You go talk to Jamie while I call every MacTaggart from the parents on down to the cousins."

Bunking with a MacTaggart, knowing every single one of them loved Jamie and would take her side, sounded like the awesomest plan ever. They *should* take her side, of course. But that didn't make it any easier for him to accept charity from them.

One thing he knew for sure. He could not talk his pigheaded sister out of an idea once she'd decided it was *the* plan.

"Fine," he said with all the resignation of a man sentenced to death row. "I'll go with your plan. Got any idea where Jamie might be?"

"Nope." She poked a finger into his chest. "You get to call Rory and ask him."

Yep, this day just kept getting better.

Chapter Five

Jamie slumped on the sofa in the sitting room of Dùndubhan, gazing out the windows into the walled courtyard of the castle. She didn't really see anything, though. Her focus had retreated inside herself, to the pain in her chest and the burning in her gut and the image of that blasted credit card. What in the world had Gavin been thinking? Did she mean so little to him?

Emery occupied the chair by the window, the one where Rory usually sat. She kept eying Jamie with a strange expression. This was the look Rory said meant Emery was scheming to meddle in someone else's life.

"I've seen it often enough," he'd told Jamie, "when my wife was meddling in my affairs. She does it gently, and there's no stopping her when you become the object of her mission."

Jamie's life was a mess. Maybe she needed someone to gently interfere.

The monster-movie figurines on the windowsills—Dracula, the Wolf Man, the Mummy, and a zombie—might once have seemed out of place in the home of the most uptight MacTaggart. This year, thanks to Emery, Rory had embraced Halloween.

"Go on," Jamie said, "tell me how you think I should get Gavin back."

She didn't like the sharp edge in her voice, but her emotions seemed to have shut down her brain. No one had ever called her tough. Sweet, cheerful, happy, even naive. Never tough.

"Do you want him back?" Emery asked, her spooky-cat shirt glittering in the light streaming through the windows.

Jamie hunched her shoulders. "Donnae know."

"Yes you do." Emery rose and crossed to the table in front of the sofa where she sat down on its shiny surface. "You're a smart girl, Jamie. You know what you want. So, do you want Gavin?"

"I do." Jamie grabbed a pillow and hugged it to her tummy. "And it's awful."

He'd humiliated her and made her feel as pathetic and small as Trevor had five years ago. No, Gavin had made her feel even more pathetic and so small she expected she might fall through a crack in the floorboards.

"Listen," Emery said, "I know what it's like to love a man who's damaged on the inside. Rory didn't want to love me. He did everything he could to make me dislike him, but I saw what he was really doing. It's a protection mechanism. Gavin's doing the same thing, though I know nothing about his reasons. If you really love him, if you want to be with him, you need to help him work through his issues."

"What if he won't let me? I can't force him to tell me all his secrets."

"Force isn't required." Emery said with a devious glint in her eyes. "I found sex to be an excellent tool for loosening up a man's inhibitions—and his mouth."

Jamie flattened her lips, feeling her brows lower. "Ye cannae be serious. I'm to seduce Gavin in hopes he'll open up to me about his problems?"

"Exactly."

"It won't work." Jamie clutched the pillow tighter, head down. "I can't get in the right mood when he's hurt me the way he did."

"Don't try it today," Emery said, her tone implying that was a silly idea. "Stay here with me and Rory for a spell. Relax, take a nice bubble bath in the claw-foot tub, go for walks, whatever makes you feel better."

"Then what?"

Emery tapped her chin, squinting as if thinking hard. "Let me think about it. I'll come up with something."

"I should smack him in the head with a hammer. Nothing else will loosen him up."

"You're hurting right now. Don't make any decisions until you've cooled down."

Jamie let her head fall back against the sofa and moaned. "You're right, I know. But I don't like feeling so…miserable."

"We have that in common. Being unhappy isn't in our nature, so we tend to feel cast adrift when someone makes us miserable."

Emery really did understand. Maybe Gavin wasn't Rory, but Emery's experiences with her wounded husband might prove the best inspiration for Jamie to save her man.

Save him? Och, did she want to do that? Should she do it?

Never a fool again.

A knock sounded at the door, and they both swung their attention to Mrs. Darroch hovering on the threshold of the open doorway. The gray-haired woman lowered the hand she'd used to knock on the doorframe. "Jamie, ahmno sure if ye want to see him but…Gavin Douglas is in the vestibule. He's asking for ye."

Jamie's stomach flipped and flopped and did a pirouette. Anticipation raced over her skin, an electrical current that raised every hair. She should not be excited to see Gavin mere hours after he'd shattered her hopes and dreams. She shouldn't want to see him, but her heart had other ideas.

"Let him in," she told Mrs. Darroch. "Send him here."

Mrs. Darroch left to retrieve the scunner.

Jamie winced inwardly. Even thinking the word scunner in association with Gavin made her a bit queasy. She'd never done well with nastiness. Besides, until recently, Gavin had been sweet and thoughtful. Since they couldn't see each other often—twice a month, maybe—they talked on the phone, Skyped, texted, emailed. He sent her gifts for every holiday. For the American holiday known as Flag Day, he'd sent her a stuffed bear wearing a T-shirt that said "USA" on it and holding a little American flag in its chubby fingers. He sent her real maple syrup from Minnesota on National Pancake Day. Gavin had noted UK holidays too, sending her a tiny, smiley-faced stick man and a picture of a bonfire for Guy Fawkes Day. Cigarette lighters and matches, he'd explained, couldn't be sent via mail. She'd been touched he remembered what she told him about how people burned effigies of the traitor Guy Fawkes on every November 5 and tried to commemorate it with her in his own way.

Gavin paid attention to everything she said. How, then, had he misread her so terribly today?

Emery touched Jamie's knee, pulling her out of her reverie. "I'll be in the kitchen. Call me on the house phone if you need backup. I'd be happy to whoop his ass for you."

Jamie couldn't help smiling, though her lips quivered a wee bit. "Thank you, Em. You're my favorite sister, even if we didn't grow up together."

Emery winked. "I won't tell Cat or Fiona you said that."

"Oh, I've already told them. They don't mind. We all know you're a miracle worker, with the way you turned Rory upside down, shook out his nonsense, and set him right again."

Laughing, Emery shook her head. "That's a strange way to describe it, but not entirely inaccurate. I helped Rory work out his own nonsense. He had to want to do it, like Gavin has to want to fix himself."

She squeezed Jamie's knee and strolled out of the sitting room.

Jamie huddled there, feet tucked under her, pondering the embroidery on the pillow clutched to her belly.

A man cleared his throat.

She glanced up to see Gavin in the doorway, his wary gaze on her. His big body filled the doorway. He bunched his shoulders, his entire body taut and every muscle on display thanks to the close-fitting shirt and jeans he wore.

"Can I come in?" he asked.

"Aye."

He shuffled to the sofa, then hesitated again. "May I, uh, sit here? I could go over to that chair or stand—"

"Bloody hell, Gavin." She thwapped the cushion beside her. "Sit, before I change my mind about letting you in the room."

"Okay." He settled onto the sofa, his firm ass straddling the other two cushions as if he thought she might skelp him if he got too close. "I'm sorry, Jamie. I handled this all wrong."

She snorted. "How should you have handled giving me a credit card I don't need or want?"

He grimaced. "That was supposed to be a joke. Kinda."

Kind of a joke? He'd made a fool of her, that was for sure. She had no idea what to say to him now because anger and pain warred for control of her heart. Skelp him or weep? Neither one would make her feel better.

Gavin laid a palm on the cushion near her knees. "I know we can't go on like this. Me flying here, you flying to America. That's no way to live."

She didn't dare look at him. That might lead to either violence or melting into his arms. Neither option seemed useful at the moment. A coldness infiltrated her, borne of a dread she couldn't quite name. What was she afraid he'd say? Or not say? Something worse than his credit-card malarkey.

"Are you asking me to move to America?" she said. "Or are you offering to move here?"

He fidgeted, his mouth twisting into a pained expression. "Neither. I need time to figure out what I want. What's best for both of us."

"Both of us?" She scowled, powerless to keep from looking straight at him. The muted light glistened on his cinnamon hair, and his pale-honey eyes shimmered with...regret? Oh, she would not feel sorry for him. "You're going to decide for me what's best? I make that decision, not you."

"Sorry. I said it wrong again." He bowed his head, scrubbing his scalp with his nails. "Dammit, I can't figure out how to say it right. I need time, that's all I know. Time alone."

"Without me is what you mean." Though her gut churned, and bile tainted her mouth, she had to ask. "Do you still love me? Did you ever love me?"

He fisted his hands on his lap and glared down at them, his brows cinched together. "I—God, I don't know what I feel anymore."

She jerked as if he'd struck her. He hadn't said he didn't love her, but his words implied it. The cold inside her mutated into ice that seemed to coat her skin and penetrate to the core of her being. She would've expected tears, but somehow, none came. They must've frozen along with the rest of her. She could do nothing except stare at him numbly.

"I lost my job," he said, like the statement explained everything.

Jamie couldn't speak. Or move. Or think.

His gaze zeroed in on her. "I've got nothing to give. No money, no prospects, no goddamn clue why I'm so messed up lately. I've gotta get myself in order before I can figure out how I feel about us. I'm not expecting you to wait around forever. Give me a little time, that's all I'm asking. If you get sick of waiting, you can dump my ass all over again and I won't pester you to take me back."

Dump him? Was that what she'd done today? The ice inside encased her heart, suffocating her soul. She loved him. In spite of what he'd done, she couldn't stop loving him at the snap of a finger.

"Take your time," she said, stunned by the flatness of her voice. "And I'll think about how long I can wait for you to sort yourself. Or if I can."

"Fair enough." He leaned in, though not all the way. "Could I...kiss you goodbye?"

Her pulse sped up. He didn't know if he loved her. He didn't know if he wanted to be with her. Still, she wanted his kiss. She wanted him. It made no sense, but then, feelings often ignored logic. One kiss goodbye. If he decided he couldn't be with her, at least she'd have had this one last moment with him.

Jamie bit her lip and nodded.

Gavin draped an arm along the sofa's back, his hand alongside her shoulder. He scooted closer, his body surrounding her, the scent of him spicy and tempting. Those full lips, the ones she'd kissed so many times before, hovered millimeters from her own. His breath teased her lips, and they tingled with anticipation.

His eyes searched hers.

She slanted in, their mouths brushing against each other, and parted her lips.

"Jamie..." He slid his tongue along her lower lip, drew it between his, and released it little by little, leaving her lip moist and warm. His tongue slipped between her lips only to withdraw. "God, Jamie..."

She pressed her mouth to his, stealing a taste of him between his lips.

With a groan, he gave in. His tongue thrust inside her mouth, and she opened wide for him, starved for the flavor of him and the rough strokes of his slick, hot tongue. She met his swipes with her own, coiling her tongue around his even as her teeth nudged his and their lips crushed into each other. He belted one arm around her to pin her body to his.

A little moan escaped her, swallowed by his mouth consuming hers.

She clenched her fingers in his shirt. Her body softened and heated, excited by the sensation of his hard muscles flexing against her. The peaks of her nipples shot rigid, rubbing on his chest, making her so wet she moaned again.

His free hand plunged into her hair. He tipped her head back, delving deeper into her mouth. The hand on her back rushed down to palm her behind, the fingers kneading her flesh.

Jamie didn't think, couldn't think. She climbed astride him, their mouths still fused and hungry.

Gavin sank back into the sofa, one hand in her hair, the other shifting down to the hem of her skirt and whisking beneath it. She fastened her arms around his neck, devouring him with ever more frantic thrusts of her tongue. He devoured her in return and shoved his hand inside her panties to cup her ass, skin to skin. Her body ached and throbbed and thrummed with need.

So long since he'd touched her this way. So long since he'd taken her.

This jackass broke your heart, a voice inside warned.

With his mouth latched to hers and his body beneath her, she didn't give a damn about anything that had come before this moment. She loved him, needed him, wanted him with a desire so ferocious it annihilated every thought and inhibition.

He swept his hand, still inside her panties, around her hip to the front of her body, palming her mound. With a guttural groan that resonated into her through their joined mouths, he thrust his fingers between her folds to fondle her clitoris.

She rocked her hips into the caress, moaning into his mouth.

Those strong fingers rubbed her clit, delved down to stroke the inner lips of her sex, swept back up to torment her nub. She threw her head back, riding his fingers as if he were inside her, driving her toward climax with deft thrusts of his fingers instead of his cock. Its length rubbed against her thigh, thick and rigid, and though she struggled to take his shaft inside her, she couldn't make it happen while her panties and his hand on her sex combined to block her efforts. He muttered "fuck" and rubbed her faster, harder, compelling her to seize his shoulders and bow her spine. The pleasure, it scorched her from the inside out, throbbing through her flesh and shortening her breaths. She gasped for air, writhed against his hand, and he spread a hand over her back to tug her toward him.

When his mouth sealed over her nipple through her shirt, she cried out.

And then she came. With a sharp spasm, she climaxed against his hand, too breathless to cry out again, too stunned by the suddenness and ferocity of her orgasm. As the pulsating waves inside her dissipated, he pulled his hand out of her panties. They both fought for breath, chests heaving.

She leaned in to kiss him, but he grasped her shoulders and pushed her back, holding her at a distance. A few centimeters, but it felt like an ocean between them.

"I'm sorry," he said, his voice uneven and hoarse. "Didn't mean to—This was a mistake."

Flushed all over, her sex drenched and achy, she couldn't focus on anything he said. Despite her orgasm, she burned for more, for him inside her. Overpowered by the need, she laid her hand over his erection where it bulged in his jeans.

"Gotta stop," he said. "Can't do this, not now."

He shoved her off his lap, to the side so she dropped onto the adjacent cushion, and all but leaped off the sofa. A lump in his pants belied the words he spoke next.

"Don't want this," he said, still fighting for breath. "We'd both regret it later."

Sprawled on the sofa, she gaped at him. Was he off his head?

He knifed a hand through his hair. "I need time. Alone. I'm sorry."

Gavin stalked out of the sitting room.

Jamie sat there, dumbfounded and panting, for several minutes before she marshaled the composure to push up off the sofa and straighten her clothes. What had happened? Why had she let it happen? No surprise there. Gavin was gorgeous and sexy, and she never could resist him. She'd slept with him only days after they'd met.

Maybe that had been her first mistake.

She hurried down the hall to the kitchen.

Emery glanced up from perusing the offerings in the refrigerator. Her smile faded swiftly when she took in Jamie's appearance. "What is it, sweetie? You look like you had a good, hot tumble—or at least a good, hot kiss. But your face says you're devastated."

Jamie sucked in a breath, willing away the tears suddenly brimming in her eyes. "We—It was something between a kiss and a tumble. He said it was a mistake and ran out. Says he needs time alone to think. Doesn't know if he loves me or not."

The tears poured down her cheeks, scalding her skin.

Emery enfolded Jamie in her arms, rubbing her back and murmuring consoling words.

Jamie's anguish lessened gradually, swept away by her sister-in-law's understanding and compassion. Emery did know what it was like to love a wounded man. Maybe Jamie ought to listen to her advice.

When Emery pulled away at last, only when Jamie's tears had dried, she said, "How hot was this tumble-kiss?"

Jamie almost smiled remembering it. "We nearly shagged on the sofa."

Emery grinned. "Perfect. I was right, then. Sex is the key to getting inside Gavin's shell."

"He said he doesn't know if he loves me, or if he ever loved me. He told me he didn't want to have sex with me."

"Is that what he actually said?" Hands on her hips, Emery hit Jamie with a pointed look. "Or is that what you assume he was implying? Men are obtuse, and they rarely say what they mean. They've got to dance around it to spare their manly pride."

Jamie blinked rapidly. "You don't think he meant he doesn't love me?"

"I don't know. Only one way to find out."

Shoulders flagging, Jamie groaned. "I'm not as sexy as you are."

"Baloney. You are a super-hot Scottish siren." Emery tucked a lock of hair behind Jamie's ear. "This is your decision, though. You know Gavin better than I do."

"Not sure that's true. He won't talk about his ex-wife, or his parents' deaths, or his time in Afghanistan." Jamie screwed up her mouth. "How am I supposed to seduce him into sharing all of that with me?"

"It's a tough one, I admit." Emery squinted her eyes, her gaze distant. After a moment, she made an *ah-ha* face and held up one finger. "I've got it. Wednesday is Halloween. Rory and I will throw a party and invite Gavin. I will loan you one of my costumes, a real hot one that will have Gavin panting for you so hard he'll do anything you want. Even spill his guts."

"Emery, that's crazy. I'm not you, I can't do something like that."

"You can, and you will. The question is, are you committed enough to get the job done? I think you are." Emery stepped back. "But it's up to you."

Jamie considered the idea for a moment. Seducing Gavin wouldn't be a trial, that was for sure. Keeping him from taking advantage of her like he had in the sitting room, that might prove more of a challenge. Maybe Emery had a point. Maybe this was a good plan, with a bit of tweaking.

"I'll do it," Jamie said, squaring her shoulders. "I'll make Gavin want me so badly he won't be able to see straight, much less think of reasons to stay away from me. Sex only, no talking or emotional nonsense unless he begs me to listen to his heartfelt apology and confession, followed by a plea for me to marry him."

Emery's mouth opened, but she seemed to have lost her ability to speak.

"Yes," Jamie said with a nod, "this plan is pure dead brilliant."

"That's not quite what I meant," Emery said slowly. "I understand you're hurting, and some payback sounds like a great idea, but sex only? Are you sure you can do that? Screwing a guy without feeling anything, good or bad, is a lot harder than it sounds. I couldn't pull it off when I thought Rory and I were having a one-nighter, and I didn't even know his name at that point."

"I can do it."

Her sister-in-law squashed her lips between her teeth, saying nothing for several seconds. At last, Emery threw her hands up and said, "Okay, if that's what you really want."

"It is."

"You've got my support, you know that." Emery swept an arm in the direction of the doorway. "Now, let's go scarf down ice cream sundaes and hash out the plan for Halloween."

Chapter Six

Emery

That's how it all started. Today, the day after Gavin the deluded man-child threw over his sweet and lovable girlfriend, I lounged in the claw-foot tub in the ground-floor bathroom cuddled up against Rory, his big body framing mine from behind. The recently shaken water lapped against our naked bodies while we enjoyed the languorous bliss of post-coital afterglow. Rory held me with one arm strapped around my waist, his knees bent by necessity. The tub was not designed for a strapping man like my hubby. I leaned my head back against his shoulder and traced circles on his thigh with one finger. The scent of roses tickled my senses, thanks to the bath oil I'd created from the last blossoms of the vine roses in the garden.

Rory wiggled his fingers on my belly. "Your meddling has given us a houseguest."

"Temporarily. Jamie needs a place to chill out and realize she wants Gavin back."

"Have you considered she and Gavin might not be right for each other?"

"I considered it." Twisting my head around, I aimed my sweetest smile at my husband. "But I ruled it out."

"Naturally." He shook his head, smiling at me with affectionate exasperation. "You and Jamie have a secret plan, don't you?"

I hadn't told him about Jamie's sex-only idea because I'd promised her total secrecy and because her brother didn't need to hear about such things. My husband, however, knew me too well to not realize I was keeping a secret. "I won't break my promise to her solely to satisfy your curiosity. Can you live with that?"

"Yes, I suppose I can."

Since he sounded less than certain, and I knew he would worry about his sister, I took pity on my husband. "Jamie got a silly idea in her head, but I'm sure she'll give it up soon enough. In the meantime, I'll look out for her."

"Who will look out for Gavin?"

The question startled me, and I swung my head around to regard him again. A realization rippled through me. "You like Gavin, don't you?"

Rory made a face I'd witnessed many times before—embarrassment disguised as disgust.

I reached behind me to cup his face in one hand. "That's so sweet, honey. You care what happens to Gavin. Don't worry, I'm looking out for him too."

Rory grunted. "Donnae give a hoot about Gavin Douglas."

"Hoot?" A laugh burst out of me. "That's a me word. You're starting to talk like me."

"Please don't tell Aidan I said that word. And stop looking at me like I've gone soft." He adopted a totally fake frown until I faced forward again, then he relaxed and stroked my belly with his long fingers. "What's the next stage in your nefarious plot?"

I gave his thigh a playful slap. "It's not nefarious. And stage two is a Halloween party."

Rory groaned and clapped a hand over his eyes. "A party, Em? Halloween is a ridiculous holiday."

"You said you liked the decorations, and I'd know if you were fibbing." I peeled his hand away from his face. "You were not lying."

He wriggled beneath me and tried to slump down but couldn't with me on top of him.

"Admit it," I said. "You've caught the holiday spirit."

"Maybe I have, but I am not wearing a silly outfit."

"No, of course not." I kissed his palm. "The costume I have in mind is masculine and totally hot."

"Costume? Emery, I said no silly—"

"Don't be a grump. And it's not silly." I slithered around to straddle him, my hands on his wet, brawny chest. "I'll make it worth your while to comply."

He ran his palms up and down my back, molding his big hands to my bottom. "Make it *very* worth my while and I'll consider it."

I shimmied on his lap until he hissed in a breath and then I made him very, very happy—and very, very amenable to my plan. My husband the steely solicitor had one fatal weakness. Me.

Following our sensual interlude in the tub, we walked back to his office hand in hand. At the door, I laid a hand on his arm to stop him. Rory raised one brow.

"When do you think we should tell everyone we're having a baby?" I asked.

"Once we've had sufficient time to enjoy the idea on our own." He kissed my forehead. "We've only known for a week. Patience, *mo gaoloch*."

I loved when he called me his dear in Gaelic.

After he retreated into his office for a call with a client, I wandered down to the great hall to gaze out the large windows at the lawn. After a few minutes, I dialed up Calli to check in with her about the Gavin-Jamie situation.

"I talked to him earlier," Calli said. "For my big brother to come to me for advice, it must be a sign of the apocalypse."

"You're his family, of course he'd come to you. I had a talk with Jamie too." I swirled a fingertip on the windowpane. "I know these two belong together. Do you have any idea what Gavin's problem is?"

"He thinks he's over his divorce," Calli said, "but it's obvious he's not. He wouldn't have acted like such a moron with Jamie if he had gotten over it. The idea of getting married again terrifies him."

"You didn't tell him that, did you?"

Silence, then she coughed. "Kind of."

"Oh, Calli. Why would you do that?" I bumped my forehead into the wall. "Men don't like being told what they're feeling. It's a macho-pride thing."

"Aidan doesn't mind if I explain his feelings to him."

"Uh-huh. And are these sexy feelings you explain for your husband?"

Another silence followed by another cough. "Yeah."

I made a frustrated noise, bumping my forehead into the wall again. "Honestly, Calli, how can a woman married to a naughty man like Aidan be such an innocent?"

"I'm not innocent. But I'm twenty-six, and Aidan's the only man I've ever slept with or even really dated." Rustling suggested Calli was squirming. "Besides, I've never tried to give my brother advice before. I figured if Aidan's okay with it, Gavin should be too."

"Aidan's an unusual man. He has macho pride, but it's less pronounced than in men like Lachlan and Rory—and Gavin."

"I'm sorry, Emery. How bad did I screw this up?"

"Don't worry, it's fixable." I set a hand on the windowsill and leaned into it. "And I've got a plan. Want to help?"

"Absolutely. I'm in."

"It starts with Halloween…"

Chapter Seven

The sun had dipped low in the sky, descending through twilight toward night, by the time Gavin pulled up to Calli and Aidan's house in the pickup he'd borrowed from Calli that morning. No rental car for him. That would've been too comfortable. Given his current financial situation, he had no recourse except to let his sister take care of him.

And Calli wondered why he felt like a useless lump.

Gavin parked beside another vehicle, a rusty old Range Rover, and climbed out of Calli's pickup—a nice, new Ford Ranger she'd gotten her husband to buy because she wanted something American in their lives. Shutting the door, Gavin ambled toward the front door of the modest-size, two-story house. Aidan and Calli had bought it with the money she'd gotten in her divorce settlement when her jerk of a first husband finally released her from their green-card marriage. His baby sister, one of the two smartest people he knew, had married a man she didn't love so he could get citizenship. She'd committed marriage fraud, a crime in the US Gavin hadn't known a thing about it until Aidan came along, and Calli had to reveal all.

Her ex-husband had taken advantage of her kindness in the wake of their parents' deaths. Gavin should've been there for her, to make sure she didn't do anything reckless like that, but he'd been too consumed by his own grief to be any good to her. He'd failed Calli. How could he know for sure he'd handle marriage to Jamie any better? If things got tough, would he fall apart again?

Jamie deserved so much better.

But he couldn't live without her.

The front door of the white house swung open at the instant Gavin reached the wooden steps that led up to the door. Calli walked out, smiling with that sparkle she'd acquired since marrying Aidan.

A strange man followed her out the door.

Gavin scrunched his eyebrows at his sister.

She and the stranger stepped down onto the gravel path that connected with the driveway. Calli asked, "How'd it go with Jamie?"

"Uh…" *I dumped her, after she'd already dumped me, and she dumped me again. So, fantastic, yeah.* His gaze zipped to the unknown man standing beside Calli. "Rather not talk in front of a stranger. No offense, man."

"None taken," the stranger said. His lips spread in a low-key smile that revealed a glimpse of his teeth. Although they were nice and straight, they weren't perfectly white like he'd had work done on them. No, they struck Gavin as natural teeth—unlike Trevor's laser-bright smile. The man had a hook nose that somehow looked rugged on him instead of harsh, and his eyes were as pale blue as Lachlan's. His brown hair resembled Rory's and Jamie's, though with a few strands of gray in it. The man stood almost as tall as the three MacTaggart brothers.

Gavin drew his head back, surprised by a revelation, so surprised he blurted it out before thinking. "You're a MacTaggart, aren't you?"

"Aye," the man said, seeming surprised in return. He proffered a callused hand to Gavin. "Iain MacTaggart, first cousin to the Three Macs."

"The who now?"

Iain chuckled. "The Three Macs. That's what I call the three brothers—Lachlan, Rory, and Aidan. They're a family unit all by themselves. And of course, they think they're the bosses of all the other MacTaggarts, even those of us who are considerably older."

The glint in his eyes and the way one side of his mouth kicked up slightly told Gavin the guy had a sense of humor.

Gavin shook Iain's hand. "I'm Gavin Douglas, Calli's brother."

"Oh, I know all about you." Iain winked and smirked in a very Aidan-like way. "Calli told me you need a place to stay."

She laid a hand on Gavin's arm. "Iain has graciously agreed to put you up for a while."

"Long as ye need," Iain confirmed.

Gavin studied his sister, struggling to figure out her game here. Because, yeah, his sister definitely had an ulterior motive. He hadn't figured out what it was yet, but he'd bet a million bucks he didn't have that Emery was the instigator.

Rory's wife had a whacked-out plan for Halloween, and she'd called Gavin to pester him until he'd agreed to cooperate. He knew only his part of the cockamamie scheme, though he was pretty sure Emery had gotten

Jamie involved too. A recipe for disaster, he thought, but desperation made him, uh…desperate.

"Can I talk to you alone, C?" Gavin asked.

Iain waved a dismissive hand. "Don't worry, Gavin. I'm a neutral third party."

"How can that be? You're related to the three guys who hate me."

The Scot made a dismissive noise rather than flapping his hand again. "The Three Macs are their own little mafia, yes, but don't take them seriously. Everyone in their branch of the family tree sees it as their right and duty to suffocate poor Jamie with overprotectiveness. I play shinty with the Three Macs, but I have no particular stake in Jamie's personal matters."

Gavin glanced at Calli, who smiled a little too brightly. If his red ears gave away his lies, her phony smile gave away her ulterior motives. "You're working with Emery on this, aren't you? Moving me around like a pawn on your chessboard of meddling. What's Iain got to do with it? Is he supposed to report back to you and Emery about what I say and do?"

"No," Calli said, trying a little too hard to sound offended. "I'm helping you find a place to crash, that's all."

Iain raised a hand. "Told ye, I'm a neutral party."

The Scot seemed sincere, and Gavin couldn't blame him for the shenanigans of the American Wives Club. Erica would be involved soon too, no doubt, if she wasn't already. Rory and Lachlan must love this turn of events. They were probably apoplectic over it.

The thought of Rory's response to his wife's meddling made Gavin's lips tighten and inch upward a smidgen.

"Your bags are already in Iain's car," Calli said, pointing at the rusty Range Rover.

"Jeez," Gavin said, "you packed my stuff? Way to be bossy, C."

A baby cried inside the house.

Calli pecked him on the cheek again and turned to go back inside. "Have fun at Iain's. I'll see you Wednesday night at Dùndubhan."

The castle. Where Rory and Emery lived. Where Jamie was staying.

In two days, the castle would host a wacky scheme dreamed up by his sister and her sisters-in-law. Yep, things just kept getting awesomer.

"Let's go," Iain said, clapping Gavin on the shoulder. He led Gavin toward the Rover, to its passenger door. "Relax, laddie. I have no intention of murdering you in your sleep."

"Gee, thanks." Gavin sighed, his shoulders flagging. "I really am grateful for this. Thanks, Iain."

When his new best friend swung the passenger door open, Gavin settled into the seat and shut the door, waiting while Iain strode around to the driver's door and got in. The Rover looked ramshackle from the outside, but the interior was clean and well-maintained. The seats featured pale-tan fabric that seemed almost as good as new.

"Fasten your seatbelt," Iain instructed.

Gavin asked a question while he did up the seatbelt. "Why don't you fix up the outside of this thing?"

"Not worth the bother."

He supposed that was all his host would tell him, and it wasn't really his business, anyway.

Calli had gotten him a roommate. He was staying with a MacTaggart. Sure, Iain swore he had no stake in the Jamie thing, but it still felt weird to bunk with a member of the family headed by two men who hated him and a third who tolerated him but wasn't his bud.

The Rover jounced along the dirt road, its bones rattling. The headlights speared the ever-increasing darkness ahead.

"How ancient is this car?" Gavin asked.

"Not as old as I am," Iain said. He patted the center console. "She'll get us there."

"Can I ask you a personal question?"

"Anything you like. Ask away."

They hit a pothole, and Gavin's teeth clacked together. "What do you do for a living?"

Iain shrugged one shoulder. "I have a PhD in archaeology, and I used to teach at university, but that ended a long time ago. These days, I volunteer at digs on occasion, sometimes with my cousin Catriona. She couldn't make much use of her archaeology degree either, so we commiserate about our lack of higher-level employment."

"You're unemployed?"

"No." Iain said. "I work with Aidan."

"Thought you were a neutral third party."

"I am, yes." Iain leaned back into his seat, holding the wheel negligently with one hand. "I don't care either way if you cozy up to the Three Macs, or if they toss your corpse out in the middle of the nearest muir."

"What's a muir?"

"A moor, laddie. High, flat grassland."

Gavin shot his new roomie a sardonic half frown. "My name's not 'laddie', it's Gavin."

"My mistake. Gavin." Iain spun the wheel with one hand, veering around a squirrel that had dashed out into the road. The little critter scurried away unscathed. "What is your profession?"

Gavin snorted. "At the moment, unemployed loser. Before that, I was in sales."

"Selling what?"

"Restoration services." Gavin gripped the seat as Iain hit the gas and the Rover rocketed over the bumpy road. "People whose homes got wrecked in a natural disaster or flooded by a burst pipe, whatever. I sold them the company's services."

"Fascinating."

"You almost sound like you mean that. Trust me, it was boring as hell." Gavin held on as Iain swerved the car around a corner onto a paved road. "But it paid well. Until they laid me off. Budget cutbacks."

"Now you've lost your career and your woman." Iain clucked his tongue. "Dead awful situation. I know how that feels."

"Losing the job or the woman?"

"Both." The Scot grasped the steering wheel in both hands, easing up on the accelerator. "At the same time."

Iain had told Gavin about losing his archaeologist job. He'd lost a woman too? Gavin had never been nosy, but he couldn't help asking. "What happened with the girl?"

The other man fell silent, his expression grim. He focused on the road ahead like it held all the answers to the world's problems but dangled them an inch beyond his reach. When he finally spoke, the humor had left his voice. "I had been deep into field research, excavations and what have you, but I was offered a teaching position at a private American college. I accepted and moved across the pond. That's when I met her. She was twenty-two, bonnie, clever, and I…fell in love with her. She was a student, though, and such things aren't allowed. Particularly when the teacher is fifteen years older than the student."

For some weird reason, hearing the private story of a man he'd met today perked Gavin up. Maybe knowing a muscle-bound MacTaggart had girl problems made him feel less like the black sheep of this extended family. "You slept with her."

"Sleeping would've been better, less destructive. No, I seduced her." Iain grimaced. "Never saw her again after that."

"It was that bad?"

The Scot shook his head, and a note of misery tainted his voice. "It was perfect, but someone ratted on us. The next morning, I was summarily fired and told to leave the country immediately. I never saw the girl again."

"You still think about her."

Iain gave a sharp nod and cleared his throat. "I've been with other women since, but none of them measures up to her. What a dunderhead, eh? Pining for a woman I made love to once, a lifetime ago."

Gavin sat there for a moment, considering what this man had shared with him. "Why are you telling me about your lost love?"

"As a warning. I gave up on the love of my life because I was ashamed of what happened. Never could get another teaching position, but losing her was worse than losing my career." Iain eyed Gavin sideways. "Don't let your pride keep you from doing whatever it takes to be with Jamie, if she's the one woman for you."

"She is."

Maybe this revelation explained why Calli and Emery had wanted Gavin to stay with Iain. Emery and Calli's master plan might involve Iain showing Gavin the error of his prideful ways. Those women needed to take up knitting or something. Interfering in his love life was god-awful irritating.

"Take my word for it," Iain said. "Losing the only woman who's meant everything to you is not a good way to live."

"Did my sister put you up to this? The male-bonding share-fest, I mean."

"No one puts me up to anything. I do what I please when I please."

"Good to know." In spite of what Iain said, Gavin couldn't shake the conviction the American Wives Club had selected his new roommate for this specific purpose. "How many people know your sad-sack story?"

Iain chuckled. "Sad sack? I suppose I am, at times. Only Aidan knows the story."

Ah-ha. Calli's husband must've told her. His meddling sister had made use of the information to connive a way for Gavin and Iain to meet. Calli had turned into a sneak. Gavin couldn't summon any anger about it, though, because she'd done it out of love. She might've joined a new family and left him behind, but his sister would always want to help him out.

Left behind? Was that how he felt? Twice today, he'd thought of himself that way. Alone. Abandoned. Christ, he was like an orphan begging for attention in the street.

"Remember what I said," Iain told him. "Don't let your pride ruin the best thing in your life."

For the rest of the ride to Iain's home, Gavin chewed on that advice.

Chapter Eight

I nside the tower bedroom on the second floor of Dùndubhan, Jamie smoothed the front of her dress, turning her torso this way and that
to get the full view of herself. She'd never worn anything like this in
her life, never tried to be enticing, because it seemed unimportant. She liked
short skirts, but this was...different. The Greek goddess costume consisted of
one sheer layer of slippery white fabric that glided over her skin whenever she
moved. Though not transparent, the fabric was thinner than anything she
would've chosen on her own. The toga-like style draped over one shoulder,
leaving the other bare, and flowed down to mid-thigh. The hem plunged lower
over thigh.

Emery had selected the outfit. Cat and Fiona had deferred to her, mostly
because they'd come to think of Emery as a sister too.

Jamie glanced down at her feet. Gold stilettos boosted her height by five
inches, with thin gold straps that wound over her feet and up her calves
almost to her knees. A belt fashioned from thin gold rope was slung around
her waist, its ends dangling over her hip.

"I don't know, Em," Jamie said, astonished at her own reflection. "Maybe
it's too much."

"Don't be silly," Emery said, coming up beside Jamie. "It's perfect. Sweet
and sexy, just like you."

"Feels ridiculous." Jamie fidgeted, adjusting the belt. "You're sure no one
can see through this? The fabric is so thin."

"It's diaphanous," Emery said, "not transparent. And you are gorgeous,
Jamie. You'll knock the socks right off Gavin."

A silly image flashed in Jamie's mind, of Gavin's shoes and socks flying off his feet. She choked back a laugh, knowing it stemmed from anxiety. What was she doing? Putting on a sexy frock in hopes of seducing her boyfriend. Ex-boyfriend. Sort-of ex. Gavin needed a break to sort himself, but she honestly had no idea what that meant.

Except he needed time away from her.

Trevor had needed "a break" to "sort his feelings," and it ended with a broken engagement and the worst humiliation of her life. No one else knew what had gone on between her and Trevor, but she knew. This thing with Gavin had ripped open that old wound. She understood the source of her angst but not the reasons behind it.

Jamie took a step backward and nearly tripped over the teetering heels of her shoes. Righting herself, she frowned at Emery. "This is ridiculous. The whole plan, it's dead ridiculous."

"You've been spending too much time with Rory. Ridiculous is his favorite word." Emery plucked up a white cardboard box and removed its lid, revealing more gold-colored items nestled in fluffy layers of padding. "Time to accessorize."

Jamie must've looked mulish, because Emery gave her the same expression she gave Rory whenever he resisted her outlandish plans. The most uptight MacTaggart rarely resisted these days. Emery had brought out sides of Rory no one had ever seen, not even before his ex-wives shoved that caber up his erse.

Outlandish? Jamie mentally cursed herself. She'd used another Rory word. Maybe Emery was right. She had spent too much time with her favorite brother.

No one ever accused Jamie of being uptight, but maybe some of Rory's uptightness had landed on her when Emery swept it off him.

"First," Emery said, lifting out of the box a set of interconnected golden chains. She raised the delicate web to Jamie's head. "Hair jewelry. Relax, it'll look fabulous."

Emery draped the web-like ornament over Jamie's head. The interwoven chains formed a delicate crown secured by a clasp in back and a solitary chain that went straight back over her head to latch onto the main clasp. Next, Emery hooked large gold earrings through the holes in Jamie's lobes. The concentric hoops brushed her neck when she moved her head.

"Last but not least," Emery said, "the arm cuff."

Jamie let her sister-in-law lift her left hand, slipping a gold metal cuff around her wrist. The cuff shielded several inches of her arm, its elegant filigree design vaguely Greek in style. This may not have been the most historically accurate costume, but with the accessories, it made her feel divine.

Emery stepped back, sighing with contentment. "You are a vision of goddess-like beauty."

A faint blush warmed Jamie's cheeks. She spun around, loving the way the skirt flounced around her thighs and kissed her naked skin. The dress didn't allow for a bra, but Jamie had gone without panties too, though she'd kept that fact to herself. Emery still didn't approve of Jamie's sex-only plan. The notion of having Gavin at her beck and call gave her a deliciously shivery feeling in her belly.

And being naked beneath the sheer dress made her feel sinfully decadent.

"Now for makeup," Emery said brightly.

She nabbed a makeup bag and set to applying smoky shadow to Jamie's eyes. Dark mascara made her lashes thicker, rouge highlighted her cheekbones, and glossy red lipstick gave her small mouth a luxurious sheen. Earlier, Calli had painted Jamie's nails—fingers and toes—a glittery shade of gold. Erica had styled her hair, giving it voluptuous waves that cascaded over her shoulders.

A knock rattled the door.

"It's us," Calli called through the wood. "Calli and Erica."

"Come on in," Emery said.

The door swung inward. Calli rushed inside, but Erica needed a minute to navigate the last couple steps. The tower bedroom lay between floors, with stairs leading up to the doorway that opened into the long gallery where the gala awaited.

Music wafted down from the gallery, the bouncy tune of a dance song.

Erica wore a witch's costume, with a plunging neckline and a daring slit along the side of her long, black skirt. Calli had dressed as an Egyptian princess, though her dress also featured a slit that stretched nearly to her hip. Aidan and Lachlan must've been in heaven with their stunning wives dressed to kill.

Calli stopped a few feet from Jamie, clasped her hands under her chin, and gazed at Jamie as if she'd seen a heavenly apparition. "You are so beautiful. The costume is perfect."

"That's what Emery said," Jamie told her.

Erica stopped alongside Calli. "They're both right. It's perfect, and you're the sexiest Greek goddess who ever walked the earth. If anyone asks, tell them you're Aphrodite."

"Oooh," Emery said, rubbing her hands together, "the goddess of love. Good choice, Erica."

The original American wife, Lachlan's beloved Erica, grinned and waggled her eyebrows. "Gavin looks pretty damn hot too, very Bah—"

Emery smacked Erica's arm, without any real punch. "You're not supposed to tell her anything about his outfit. It's a surprise, like hers is for him."

"Sorry."

Calli beamed at Jamie. "He's going to flip when he sees you."

Another silly image flashed in Jamie's mind, of Gavin's shoes and socks flying off an instant before he did a backflip.

"What's funny?" Calli asked.

"Nothing," Jamie said. She took one last look at herself in the mirror. "Am I ready now?"

"You are," all three sisters-in-law said in unison.

Calli and Erica headed back up the stairs.

Emery crooked her arm around Jamie's waist and led her to the door. "Don't worry. This is a great plan. Well, the part about driving Gavin nuts with your sexiness. I'm still not on board with your other idea." At the doorway, Emery gave Jamie's bottom a light slap. "Be yourself and have a good time, okay? I'll go up first, so you can make your entrance."

Jamie nodded, suddenly unable to speak. Her throat had gone dry and tight.

Emery headed up the stairs.

Hauling in a deep breath, Jamie ascended the steps one by one, careful to plant each stiletto-clad foot firmly on the next step before raising the other foot. She gripped the handrails as she went, afraid she might tumble back down into the bedroom if she let go.

The music grew louder and then segued into a slow, sensual tune.

Jamie halted in the doorway to the long gallery. The room occupied the entire second floor, save for the other bedroom attached to the far end. Shimmering metallic balls hung from the high ceiling, their facets glinting as the balls twirled slowly. The night sky appeared inky and fathomless outside the tall windows lining one wall, though the first stars twinkled amid the darkness. Guests and family milled about in the gallery, stealing snacks from the buffet table, dancing in pairs, chatting in small groups. Most of the people here tonight were MacTaggarts—Jamie's siblings, cousins, aunts and uncles, and sisters-in-law, not to mention her parents. The others were family friends invited by her three brothers and two sisters.

Catriona and Fiona caught sight of Jamie and waved, their smiles broadening.

Jamie smiled back but couldn't move enough muscles to wave. Her body had turned to stone as if she'd become a Greek statue.

Don't be a coward, she admonished herself. *Go find him.*

She wended her way along the periphery of the dance floor, glancing around, searching for Gavin.

A man in a tuxedo bent over the buffet table, studying the offerings.

Jamie's heart stuttered. It was Gavin.

She'd seen him in regular suits before, at the weddings for her brothers, but never in a tuxedo. The impeccably tailored suit clung to his muscular physique without seeming too tight. The ultra-black color of the pants, jacket, and bow tie contrasted with the pure white of his shirt, lending the whole outfit an ultra-chic look. Shiny black shoes completed the ensemble. His brown hair was slicked back with a hint of a glossy sheen.

Her tummy fluttered, her heart too.

Gavin Douglas, a man who preferred jeans and T-shirts and only endured formal wear when he was required to, had donned the couture elegance of a prince or a billionaire or…James Bond. That's what Erica had almost said. The ex-Marine had transformed into the sexiest, hottest James Bond she'd ever seen.

Jamie laid a hand over her belly. Lower down, sensations stirred—hot, wet sensations. No sex for three months, except for that brief encounter a few days ago, had turned her into a lust-drunk wanton.

But only for him.

He hadn't seen her yet, focused on the buffet selections.

She longed to sashay over to him, stun him with a sexy ice-breaker of the sort Emery excelled at, but her body was paralyzed again. Jamie sought out Emery with her gaze, finding her sister-in-law at the far end of the room alongside Rory. Their gazes connected, and Emery's lips tightened into a sympathetic little smile.

Jamie tried for a pathetically desperate expression, and it must've worked.

Emery mouthed, "Wait there."

Then she marched straight to Gavin.

Chapter Nine

Gavin picked up a finger sandwich, scrutinized the thin slices of cucumber inside it, then plunked the sandwich down again. Didn't they have any manly food here? With all these testosterone-laden MacTaggarts gathered in this ginormous room, the crowd must've been clamoring for real food. Red meat. A T-bone steak. Hell, he'd settle for bacon.

"The real food is on the other side of the room."

Gavin started, whirling toward the woman who'd spoken to him.

Emery pointed to the other side of the gallery.

He squinted but couldn't see anything, until a break in the crowd of dancers and a glint of light from the sparkly ceiling balls revealed it to him. Another buffet table. Overly muscled MacTaggart men ambled along the table's length, snatching up hearty-looking snacks.

"Didn't see it over there," Gavin said. "Hiding the good stuff, huh?"

"Not on purpose. It's hard to keep the MacTaggarts away from their beef and haggis, though." She glanced back at her husband, who hulked a dozen yards away with his equally hulking brothers. "They're all so big, they tend to dwarf their surroundings."

"And I'm a shrimp?"

"No, sweetie, you're a big, braw man in your own right."

Weirdly, her statement made him feel better. Whenever he got around the Three Macs, he started to feel like the runt of the litter, though he stood six one. Didn't help that each of them wore super-manly costumes. Lachlan was a pirate, complete with a billowing shirt that hung open to the waist, exposing his chest, and a scuffed leather vest to go with his scuffed leather pants. A cutlass hung from his belt, and he had a fake parrot attached to his shoulder, which must've been Erica's idea. No way a man like Lachlan would volunteer for that. Aidan was a firefighter, sort of. He had no shirt, only the fireman pants and suspenders, along with the requisite boots. When Gavin had asked Calli about her husband's outfit, she'd gotten a secretive little smile on her face and said it reminded them both of the night they'd met.

Gavin decided not to press her for details. Some things he didn't need to know.

Aidan held a fireman's hat in one hand. When Calli hopped up on her tiptoes to whisper something in his ear, he grinned and slapped the hat on his head.

His sister, the sweet girl who'd once been too shy to go as anything but a ghost with a sheet over her head, wore an Egyptian costume with the highest slit he'd ever seen. Erica's costume featured a slit almost as high, though she'd dressed as a hot witch.

And Emery…Well, he hadn't quite figured out her costume yet.

She wore a miniskirt kilt, made from the blue-and-green tartan of the MacTaggart clan. Instead of an actual shirt, she'd squeezed into a black-leather bustier with skinny straps over her shoulders. Metal buttons decorated the thing's front side while leather laces cinched it up in back. Black leather boots covered her calves up to her knees, and she'd tied her blonde hair into twin ponytails. A dainty little crossbow hung from a chain on her hip while an equally dainty quiver strapped to her back held arrows with feathery pink fletching. She'd accessorized her outfit with leather wrist cuffs and a plaid scarf slung around her neck, its ends tumbling down her back. A plaid cap, the same blue-and-green as her kilt and scarf, perched atop her head. A fluffy blue ball topped the cap.

Just to make the costume weirder, she wore a crucifix around her neck and had a clear bottle filled with water strapped to her hip, the one not sporting a crossbow. The bottle had a crucifix symbol painted on it.

"Uh," he said, waving a finger in a big circle to indicate her outfit, "what the heck are you supposed to be?"

Emery grinned, her cheeks dimpling. "I'm Emmy the Scottish Vampire Slayer."

"The wha—" He couldn't finish the question, not while she was tapping her cross-adorned bottle of water.

"My holy water," she said. "The last resort, of course. I prefer to nail the vamps with an arrow to the heart. Then—" She made an explosion sound and a matching gesture with her hands. "Poof. They're dust."

"Uh-huh." He glanced toward Rory. The guy wore skintight black pants with tall black boots, and a black shirt-like thing that seemed kind of sci-fi. It exposed his arms and massive biceps. A red cape flowed down his backside, and a hammer thingamajig hung from his belt, its head huge and rectangular. Gavin swore he'd seen something like it before. "What's your husband supposed to be?"

"Thor, the Norse god of thunder." She winked. "As portrayed by Chris Hemsworth, of course. Rory is the super-hot version of Thor, not a cartoon character."

No, Rory MacTaggart wouldn't want to be confused with a cartoon. Still, Gavin couldn't believe the stern lawyer would dress up at all for Halloween. At least now the hammer thing made sense. It was Thor's hammer.

"His hair is brown," Gavin said, "not blond, and it's short."

She shrugged. "Rory will not wear a wig under any circumstances. I don't mind the creative license, though. I love Rory's hair."

No way in hell would Gavin ask why.

So instead, he gestured at her kilt and asked, "That's the MacTaggart tartan, right?"

Emery nodded. "Sure is. Surprised you recognize it."

"Jamie's got a blanket made out of it."

"Speaking of Jamie..." Emery laid a fingertip on his jaw and turned his head slowly with slight pressure. "Your goddess has arrived."

Gavin froze, his gaze locked on the goddess lingering twenty feet away, her shimmering eyes fixed on him. Every flash of the disco balls set her golden-brown hair alight. A short, billowing toga hugged her curves and flared out around her thighs, accentuating her voluptuous figure. Her full breasts rose and fell with every breath, their luscious mounds hidden by the thin fabric that clung to them. He couldn't resist running his gaze over her body, from her creamy shoulders and down past her slim waist and womanly hips to the mouthwatering curves of her thighs and calves. Sky-high heels gave her ankles an elegantly sensual curve.

And her hair. Heaven almighty, it framed her face in sleek, bouncy waves that kissed her shoulders. A sudden urge gripped him, to thrust his hands into that hair and claim her mouth while the silken fall of her hair feathered over his skin.

His cock shot hard.

"My work is done," Emery said, and she retreated.

Gavin hardly noticed because he couldn't tear his gaze away from Jamie. A goddess come to life, ethereal and earthy at the same time. He strode to her, not giving a damn if he bumped into anyone on the way, despite a couple of Gaelic curses aimed at him. All he saw was her, all he wanted was her, and everything else became noise in the background, fading from his awareness as his world telescoped down to the transcendent beauty of her.

He reached Jamie at last, stopping a couple feet away. "Hey."

Way to charm the lady, dumb-ass.

Jamie's red lips curved upward. "James Bond, aye?"

His mind blanked for a heartbeat. "How did you know?"

"Erica almost let it slip, and I guessed when I saw you."

"It was Emery's idea. Pretty dumb, huh?"

Jamie raked her gaze over him, her tongue flicking out to moisten her glossy red lips. "Wouldnae say that."

"You like the monkey suit?"

She nodded slowly. Her pupils had grown large, dark pools within the rings of her hazel irises, and her breasts rose and fell on heavier breaths. Her taut nipples jutted through the fabric of her dress.

He burned to suck those little peaks into his mouth and scrape his tongue over them until she moaned.

Gavin ran a hand over his mouth. "Jamie, you are so damn beautiful."

"Thank you." A natural blush deepened the makeup-created one on her cheeks. "You look very handsome. The most handsome man in the room."

Not the handsomest in the world, he noted. She used to call him that, but after what he'd done, he needed to earn back the right to be tops in her eyes.

What was he supposed to say now?

He glanced toward Emery, to where she had been, but she'd moved out of sight. He spotted Iain, though, who tipped his punch glass toward Gavin in a mini salute. The Scotsman had dressed as a cowboy, with a Stetson hat and silver-toed boots to go with his silver belt buckle.

Iain gave him a thumbs-up. For some weird reason, seeing Iain made him feel better.

"Am I boring you?" Jamie asked.

His attention snapped back to the outrageously hot woman in front of him. He struggled to remember how to talk, but the sight of her scattered his wits. "No, not bored."

Jamie's lovely mouth curved into a smile, her lips sealed. She roved her gaze up and down his body once more, and the fingertips of one hand drifted to her chest, caressing the skin between her breasts in an unconscious gesture. "Emery has good taste in men's clothing."

"Yeah." His voice had gone rough, and he couldn't look away from her fingers and the way they teased her skin. He suffered another inappropriate urge, one so strong it stole his breath, to swoop in and lick her flesh everywhere she'd touched herself.

Jamie moved closer to run her hand along the lapel of his tuxedo jacket. When she detected the bulge beneath it, she slipped her hand inside the jacket to fondle the object nestled near his armpit. In a sultry voice, she murmured, "I love a man with a hard weapon. Even if it is plastic."

"Emery said—" His words got choked off when her hand massaged his chest. He fought for breath, his erection growing almost painful. "She said it was part of the persona. Being armed and dangerous, licensed to kill."

"Mm." Jamie skated her hand down to his waistband, slanting in with her head angled back to gaze up at him with desire in her eyes. "Know what else is part of the persona?"

"What?"

"Shagging a beautiful woman at every opportunity."

Her lips. So close. Ripe, red lips begging to be kissed and nipped and sucked.

Jamie stepped back. "Are you going to ask me to dance?"

"Huh?" He couldn't manage eloquence right now, not that he ever had a talent for it. Her seductive hotness so near him drove out any semblance of reason he might've had left after seeing her in that dress. "Sure. Yeah."

With a hand on her elbow, he guided her out onto the dance floor. She settled a palm on his shoulder while he settled one of his hands on the small of her back and clasped her free hand. Hers was so delicate, so soft, so warm. They wandered among the other couples, their gazes intertwined, their bodies separated by millimeters. Out the corners of his eyes, he noticed familiar pairs twirling past them—Lachlan and Erica, Calli and Aidan, Rory and Emery. His sister waved a hand to get his attention, then gave him an encouraging smile. Stupefied by the woman in his arms, he pulled off nothing more than a curt nod to Calli. When Rory and Emery glided past, the architect of this crazy scheme winked at him. Her husband flashed him a glower.

Yeah, he'd make friends with Rory MacTaggart—in the last minute of the last day of never in eternity.

Jamie swept her hand from his shoulder to his neck, tickling him with one fingertip. "You're frowning."

"Am not." He focused on her, on those beautiful eyes and their glittering green flecks. Her skin warmed his palm through the thin fabric of her dress, and the way her breasts kept brushing his chest was about to drive him insane. If he didn't kiss her soon…He bent his head to whisper in her ear. "Can we go somewhere private?"

She turned her face toward his, her lips grazing his cheek. "Aye."

Oh God, she smelled wonderful. No perfume, he knew that. The natural scent of her permeated his senses, drowning him in the essence of her.

Jamie took his hand and led him through the maze of couples spinning around the dance floor, to the far end of the long gallery. They hurried down the short hallway to the closed door of the guest bedroom. She bit her lip, releasing it slowly as she grasped the knob and pushed the door inward.

Darkness blanketed the room, penetrated only by the milky rays of the moon.

She ushered him inside and shut the door.

The thick wood muted the music playing in the gallery until it became a distant reminder of the party going on outside the door. The festivities seemed like a faint transmission from a faraway planet. They existed inside their own little world, here in this room.

Jamie sashayed to the four-poster bed in the center, its headboard pushed against the far wall. She leaned back against one of the posts, stretched her arms above her head, and wound her fingers around the carved wood. Bending her knee, she braced the stiletto heel of one shoe on the lower portion of the post.

"What will you do with me?" she whispered in a smoldering voice. She traced the tip of one finger down the post, across her throat, down her breastbone until her hand hovered between her luscious tits.

Holy hell. She couldn't want him to—not after what he'd done.

"Gavin," she purred, "don't ye want me?"

Yes, yes, and hell yes. But he wouldn't take advantage of her. She must've downed several glasses of booze before walking into the gallery tonight. He could think of no other reason she'd want to have sex with him. Here. Now. In a bedroom of the castle owned by her brother, who hated him, while a party went on mere feet outside the door.

A party attended by all her relatives and his sister.

Gavin gripped the back of his neck and commanded his dick to cool down. His body disobeyed his orders, but he could at least act like a gentleman. "We should talk, right? Let's go downstairs to the kitchen, have a snack, and hash things out."

"The kitchen?" Her sultry smile widened into a wicked grin. "Aye, let's get out the whipped cream and—"

"No. Talk, that's all." Christ, he was trying to be a good guy. Did she have to keep stroking her chest that way? And her voice…That fervid tone threatened to catapult him over the edge.

"I don't want to talk, Gavin."

His name rolled off her tongue like the song of a siren, luring him to his doom.

She crooked a finger, beckoning him.

Every man had his limits. He was dangerously close to slamming into his and shattering right through them.

Jamie, the temptress, pushed away from the post and strolled to the bedside table. She opened a drawer, palmed something, and shut the drawer again. Her red lips kinked up at one corner with the sexiest look of smug satisfaction he'd ever seen. She sashayed back to the post, leaning back to mold her lithe body to the wood. With one hand, she stroked the bumps and dips in the polished surface of the post. With her other hand, she raised a condom packet to her throat and dragged it down her chest.

He choked on a breath.

"Come here," she purred.

And he couldn't resist her. His feet carried him to her, despite his every attempt to stop this. A matter of inches separated their bodies, and his gaze gravitated to the undulating swells of her lush breasts, the condom packet she grazed over her skin in sensual circles, the pink tips of her nipples visible through the almost-sheer fabric. The expanse of one creamy shoulder, bared by the dress, snared his focus.

I love you. That's what he should've said. *I'm sorry I hurt you, please forgive me.*

No words came out of his mouth.

Helpless to resist the lure of his siren, he pressed his body to hers, pinning her to the post. A tiny gasp escaped her lips. He lashed one arm around the post, around her, encompassing her body. Even in the stilettos, she had to tilt her head back to look at him, and the movement exposed her delicate throat. Her breaths quickened, her breasts bounced on each inhalation. Those lips, the succulent color of ripe strawberries, parted in invitation.

"Please," she moaned.

And he lost his mind.

He tunneled a hand into her thick, silky hair, cupping her nape. Her rigid nipples rubbed him through his shirt. With a long groan, he gave in to the need, crushing his mouth to hers and thrusting his tongue between her sweet lips to devour the flavor of her. She opened wider for him, her body going soft against him, her tongue twining with his again and again. Her mouth was hot and wet, her body warm and pliant. He shifted his arm, the one clamped around the post, to take hold of her hip and tug her lower body into his. The rock-hard erection barely contained in his slacks chafed against her belly, and every last shred of reason disintegrated.

"Jamie," he mumbled against her throat, his lips scraping her tender flesh.

She flung her arms around his waist and bucked her hips into him. "Gavin, please."

As if his body had a mind of its own, his hand raced down her thigh to dive beneath the dress and then whisked up the inside of her thigh until his fingers found—Oh God, the slick heat of her desire, exposed to the world.

"No panties?" he said, his tone verging on frantic. She'd been walking around naked except for the ultra-thin toga dress? Lust pulsated through his entire body, and somehow, his hard-on got even harder.

"Aye," she said, tugging his shirt out of his waistband. "Wanted this. Wanted you. Inside me, please, now, please."

Though a faint voice in the back of his mind urged him to stop, he'd roared straight past common sense into the steamy, seductive waters of the siren. Of her. His Jamie, pleading with him to take her.

"Fuck," he hissed, and it was the last coherent word he spoke.

He tried to nab the condom from her fingers.

She closed her fingers around it. "I'll do it."

Damn. He'd never survive that.

Her fingers found his zipper and freed his aching cock. The soft flesh of her palm skimmed over his skin as she rolled the condom over his length.

A breath caught in his throat.

She frisked her hand up and down his dick.

He pushed her hand away, shoved up her skirt, and grabbed one of her thighs, hooking it over his hip. She locked her arms around his shoulders, breathing hard, her chest sprinkled with a delicate pinkness, her lips swollen from their kiss.

He buried himself inside her body.

"Gavin," she gasped.

The need to possess her, to come inside her hot little body, compelled him to thrust. Hard. Relentless. Faster and faster until their bodies slapped together and her wetness made a sucking sound every time he drove into her. He grasped her breast through the dress, scraping his thumb over the nipple again and again, his need escalating with every little gasp and moan she made. Her stiletto heel dug into his ass. He pounded into her heat, the scent of her need intoxicating, and the bed began to jump with every punishing thrust.

The pressure to come, it mounted inside him, throbbed through his cock.

He let go of her breast and shoved his hand between their bodies, rubbing her clitoris hard and fast.

"Oh God," she whimpered, "I'm coming, Gav—"

Her orgasm wrenched her whole body. Her sex pumped him with wave after wave of powerful contractions. He fought to hold off his climax, desperate to wring every last ounce of pleasure from her first, but the pressure built and built until he couldn't breathe. She cried out, her back bowed, her nails scraped against his jacket. Only when she'd finished, only when her body went limp in his arms, did he pull his hips back and pound into her one last time, punctuating his release with a strangled shout.

Panting, sweat dribbling down his neck inside his shirt collar, he nuzzled her neck. His dick was still inside her. The aroma of sex lingered in the air. Damn, he hadn't meant for this to happen. They'd never done it like this, rutting like wild animals.

He kissed her shoulder, her neck, her cheek. "That was fucking amazing."

"Aye," she said breathlessly, and linked her hands behind his neck. "We fucked. It was amazing. This is how I want things to be between us."

Gavin drew his head back, studying her moonlit face, ethereal as an angel. "What are you saying?"

"You want time and space to sort yourself." She toyed with the collar of his shirt. "You can have it. But I want us to keep having sex."

He must've hallucinated for a second there. No way could she have said what he thought she'd said. "Come on, we need to talk."

"No." She sealed two fingers over his lips. "Until you know what you want, there's nothing to talk about. I want us to get together for sex in the meantime. Only sex."

Either he was being punked or he'd stumbled into an alternate reality. Sweet little Jamie MacTaggart would never suggest hot sex with no strings. She was the kind of girl who needed commitment.

She wriggled free of him, ducking under his arm to stand near the opposite post. Hands on hips, she lifted her chin. "This is what I want. Sex only. Can you handle it? Are you not man enough for an arrangement like this?"

"I'm not that easy to goad," he said, knowing he was a damn liar. Her brothers got under his skin without saying a word to him. And Iain was right. He had, well, kind of a problem with manly pride getting in the way of rational decision-making.

But he wanted her. Despite what he'd said about needing time, he couldn't stand being away from her. What if he never figured out what his problem was? He'd lose her, for sure.

Unless he took her up on this crazy offer.

Sex with the woman he loved, the woman who fired up his libido like nobody else. Nothing but sex. No expectation he'd bare his soul to her, or vice versa. Wasn't this every man's dream? It might've been his, back before Leanne and his parents and everything that came after, but not anymore.

If he said no, she might cut him out of her life.

Gavin cleared his throat, shucked the condom in a nearby trash can, and tucked his dick back in his pants. "Okay."

Her eyes flared wide for a heartbeat. "Really?"

"Yeah." He squared his shoulders. "I'm in. Sex, sex, and more sex with no strings attached."

Jamie stared at him for a moment, unblinking. Finally, she strutted up to him and planted a quick, firm kiss on his mouth. "I'll call you when I want you."

With that, the love of his life traipsed out the door.

Chapter Ten

Jamie shuffled down the hallway into the gallery. Her knees felt wobbly. Her breaths shortened, coming faster. She stopped a few feet inside the huge room, paralyzed by the sight of everyone she knew and loved enjoying the party. They had no idea what she and Gavin had done in the bedroom. Could anyone tell she'd been ravished moments ago? No, of course not. Right?

Bloody hell. She'd begged him to take her.

Cool air tickled her legs and arms and chilled the wetness still gathered between her thighs. She moved her hand as if to tug her dress down, but it had no more coverage to offer. Going without panties had seemed naughty and fun before she enticed Gavin into following her into the bedroom. Now, her lack of undergarments seemed like a shame she'd dumped on herself. And she'd suggested casual sex. *I'll call you when I want you.* She'd said that.

She'd turned into a flipping tart.

But he had agreed to a sex-only arrangement.

A little shiver of arousal tingled through her. Sex with Gavin. Whenever she wanted. It sounded like the perfect situation, but only if she ignored the fact she was in love with him and he'd offered her a credit card.

Jamie drew in five deep breaths, slow and easy, her muscles slackening with each exhalation. The jittery sensation lessened, and her knees solidified. She would excuse herself from the party. No one would mind.

She took two steps toward the crowd and froze again.

A man had nailed his gaze to her. Short curls of his sandy hair framed his face, a boyishly attractive face, the face she'd once held in her hands and kissed.

Trevor Langley smiled, his gray eyes squinting almost as if he'd forced the expression.

Jamie couldn't move. Her feet had mutated into lead. Even her heart seemed to have grown sluggish as if it couldn't acclimate to this new situation. Her ex-fiancé, the one she hadn't seen or spoken to in five years, was striding toward her.

He halted an arm's length away, still smiling.

She gaped at him, rendered speechless by his very presence here, at a family gathering. He wore an outfit from the eighteenth or nineteenth century, like something out of a historical romance novel. His black pants fit snugly over all his muscles and disappeared inside a pair of shiny, knee-high black boots. His hunter-green coat hung long in the back but stopped at his waist in the front, while some sort of frilly scarf draped down from his throat.

Like a Victorian gentleman—or maybe Edwardian, she didn't know the difference—he bowed from the waist and clasped her hand to light a feathery kiss on her knuckles.

"Jamie, what a pleasure it is to see you." Trevor straightened but kept his fingers loosely around hers even as his attention flitted to her bosom where her nipples remained stiff. "And my, you are a vision this evening."

His English accent used to thrill her. Tonight, his voice and his dashing attire had no effect on her except to leave her awash in confusion.

"What are you doing here?" she asked, twisting her fingers free of his.

"Rory invited me." Trevor hooked a thumb inside the ascot around his waist. "I rang him to say hello and to see if he'd help me with a legal matter. I'm buying an old distillery, thinking of turning it into a tourist attraction."

Of course. He'd come to the Highlands on business, not to see her. Not that she wanted to see him. But telling a woman he'd sought her out as an afterthought wasn't the cleverest idea.

The full import of what he'd said caught up with her then, and her mouth fell open. "Rory invited you? To the party?"

"Yes." Trevor took hold of his lapels. "When he offered, I couldn't say no. The chance to see you again was irresistible."

Footsteps clomped behind her.

She glanced over her shoulder, knowing who would be there.

Gavin's brows cinched together over his nose, etching a crease that spawned more lines across his forehead. He shoved his tongue against the inside of his cheek, making it swell outward, his attention glued to the other man positioned in front of her.

The clock in her head banged out the seconds. One, two, three…

Jaw set, Gavin swiveled his gaze to her. The question in his eyes was unmistakable.

"A friend of yours?" Trevor said. He barreled past Jamie to offer his hand to Gavin. "Trevor Langley. I'm an old friend of Jamie's."

Gavin shook the other man's hand, but he watched her as he spoke. "Nice to meet Jamie's *old friend.*"

"I haven't seen Trevor in five years," she blurted out, as if anyone had asked.

Trevor smiled at her again. "Letting her go was the worst mistake of my life. One I hope to rectify."

Something in his voice made her wonder about his true intentions. A sharp edge. One that smoothed out in an instant. Maybe she'd imagined it.

Gavin gritted his teeth, a muscle jumping in his jaw. His gaze drilled into Trevor with the power of a tunnel-boring machine.

"He's joking," Jamie said.

Trevor moved closer to her, claiming her hand. "It's no joke. I want you back, Jamie. No one else has ever measured up to you, and no one ever will."

A wave of cold rushed over her, frosting her skin. Her scalp began to tingle, and she suddenly realized she'd stopped breathing. What in heaven's name was Trevor on about? Five years ago, he'd denounced her as a simple Scottish girl, not posh enough for a man with dreams of grandeur. Her love of the Highlands hadn't meshed with his need to conquer the big city. Her devotion to her family had gone against his desire to whisk her away to London where they'd live the high life together.

He hadn't asked if she wanted those things. He'd assumed she wouldn't go with him, and he hadn't cared about losing her. Since then, she'd realized he'd been right. If they'd really loved each other, they would've found a compromise, a way to merge their lives. He wanted things his way, and she wanted no part of the diamond-studded lifestyle he yearned to achieve.

Now, he turned up at a family Halloween party and announced he wanted her back. He crashed into her life with no warning—invited by her brother.

Jamie scanned the crowd, seeking Rory and Emery. Her brother was deep in conversation with Iain, but she caught Emery's gaze. The vivacious blonde waved to Jamie and glanced away. Jamie, mouth agape and eyes wide, flapped her hand until she recaptured Emery's attention.

Emery gave a sharp nod, rolled her shoulders back, and marched straight toward Jamie.

The kilt-wearing vampire slayer was coming to her rescue.

Her husband trailed after her appearing slightly amused and baffled at the same time. Rory often looked that way around his wife.

Trevor stared at Jamie. Gavin stared at Jamie.

She swallowed hard. All this attention from handsome men should've made her giddy, but instead it left her scratching her arms to chase away an itch that had no physical cause.

Emery wrapped an arm around Jamie, pulling her close in a protective embrace. "What's going on over here?"

"Nothing," Trevor said. "I was talking with Jamie and meeting her new friend."

"Friend?" Gavin all but snarled. "Listen here—"

Rory arrived, and everyone shut up.

Except his wife. Emery said, "Jamie, what happened?"

Jamie shot Rory a sharp glance. "Your husband invited my ex-boyfriend to the party."

Emery compressed her lips into a slash.

Rory had gone stiff and blank-faced. Robot Rory, Emery called him when he was like this.

"Is this true?" Emery asked.

Her husband shrugged one shoulder.

Emery shook her head, part exasperation, part affectionate chastisement. She hugged Jamie tighter to her side and murmured, "Why don't you and I go downstairs and have a chat." In a louder voice, she said, "Rory and I will talk later."

Jamie swore her stoic big brother flinched a wee bit. Only Emery could cow Rory MacTaggart. Well, Emery and Sorcha MacTaggart, their mother.

"What about them?" Jamie whispered into Emery's ear. "Gavin and Trevor. And Rory."

Emery spoke in a commanding voice that made all three men take notice. "Rory made this mess. He can slog through it on his own for a while."

She flashed her husband a smile bright enough to blind airliners in flight thirty thousand feet above their heads. Emery towed Jamie out of the gallery and down the spiral staircase to the vestibule on the ground floor. They hustled through the dining room and out the rear door into the guest wing. Once they'd reached the sitting room, Emery urged Jamie to sit on the sofa. Emery then plunked down on the coffee table in front of Jamie.

Hands on her thighs, Emery sighed. "Tell me everything."

Gavin stood there long after Jamie had left, glaring at the man who'd barged into the middle of his relationship with the only woman he'd ever really loved. Gavin wanted to punch Trevor. Grind his pretty-boy face into the wood floor. He didn't do a damn thing. What if Jamie wanted this asshole back? What if she'd pined for Trevor all these years and Gavin had been second choice?

He didn't know what to believe anymore. Jamie had offered him casual sex. If the sweet girl he'd fallen for could want his body and nothing else, maybe she did have a candle burning for the pretty boy.

Trevor slapped Gavin's arm. "Relax, mate."

Mate? Had the guy seriously called Gavin 'mate'? Like they were good buds. Like they might share a few beers and crack jokes together.

Gavin responded the only way he could. He sucked it up and acted like none of this fazed him.

"What are you supposed to be?" Gavin asked, waving at Trevor's outfit.

"A rake." Trevor grinned, his perfect white teeth bared. "Of the Regency variety."

Regency? Sure, Gavin had a clue what that meant. *Not.* The other part he understood. "You dressed up like an old-timey gigolo?"

"A rake is a libertine, a freewheeling man in the vein of Don Juan or Casanova."

"Like I said, a gigolo."

Trevor stiffened, grasping his lapels. "In the Regency period, a rake was a gentleman."

Gavin snorted. "Come on. Even back then, a rake—" He did his best imitation of the snooty way Trevor had pronounced the word. "—was nothing but a lousy lowlife who preyed on vulnerable women."

"Preyed on?" Trevor chuckled, his tone as derisive as his nose-up expression. "I'm surprised you have such a wide vocabulary. What are you meant to be, then? A waiter?"

"James Bond." Gavin ground the words out between his teeth.

Trevor shook his head with mock pity and tsked. "Bond was British. You are a lowly American."

"Maybe I am, but Jamie's with me."

"We'll see about that." Trevor leaned toward Gavin. "My bank balance measures eight digits. How many shillings do you have to your name?"

"Do you really think Jamie's so shallow you can wow her with your fat wallet?"

"I can shower her with all the things she could never afford. Women value security. I have the connections to make certain she gets anything she wants or needs. I'd wager I could have you locked up in the Tower of London if I wanted."

"The Tower's a museum. You planning to lock me in the janitor's closet?"

"I'm sure you'd feel comfortable in there." Trevor rocked back on his heels. "The point is, I can fulfill Jamie's every wish. What do you have to offer?"

What did Gavin have to offer? Not much. But dammit, he loved Jamie—and she loved him.

"Your silence speaks volumes," Trevor said. He rocked back on his heels, thumbs hooked inside the ascot of his frilly outfit. "Two months ago, I came across a copy of an Inverness newspaper. In the society section, there was a picture of Rory and his new bride at their wedding. You and Jamie were in the background." Trevor tipped his nose up, radiating superiority. "She did not look happy."

He sauntered away, vanishing into the crowd.

For a few seconds, Gavin pondered Trevor's motivations for coming here. Though he'd said Jamie didn't seem happy, he hadn't sounded disturbed by the idea. In fact, Gavin almost thought the guy seemed…pleased.

Nah, he must've misread Trevor.

Gavin tried to shove his hands in his pants pockets, but the slacks of his monkey suit didn't have any. Why couldn't he ask Jamie to marry him? At the critical moment, he'd choked. And now, all she wanted from him was orgasms. Maybe she would prefer a slick British multimillionaire over an unemployed American with emotional hang-ups.

Why else would she have never mentioned Trevor?

A hand clapped down on his shoulder.

"That was a right massacre," Iain said. "You look like you need a drink."

"Not sure it'll help, but what the hell."

His life couldn't fall any deeper into the shithole.

Iain squeezed his shoulder. "Cheer up, laddie. Trevor's a bleeding ersehole and everybody knows it."

Gavin wasn't so sure Jamie agreed with that statement.

He let Iain shepherd him toward the wet bar, but the gnawing in his gut only worsened.

Chapter Eleven

There's a young man at the door for you, Jamie," Mrs. Darroch said. She stood in the doorway of Jamie's room on the ground floor of the castle, eying Jamie with a tight-lipped expression. "It's that Trevor person. Should I tell the wank to leave off?"

Jamie laughed. "Wank? Never heard you use that word before."

"Donnae care for this one. He's…ungentlemanly." Mrs. Darroch sniffed and lifted her nose, making her gray curls bounce. "Causing a scene at the party last night, that's no way to behave. And poor Gavin…"

The housekeeper, who doubled as a mother hen, had adored Gavin from their first meeting. She thought he was "charming" and "clever" and "sweet enough to eat." Mrs. Darroch often pinched and patted Gavin's cheeks, which always made him blush. Despite the fact he'd dumped Jamie, Mrs. Darroch still believed they belonged together.

"Will ye see the w—the young man?" Mrs. Darroch asked.

Jamie slid off the bed and slipped her feet into a pair of slippers. "Yes, I'll see him."

"Donnae sound excited by the prospect."

Was it her imagination, or did Mrs. Darroch look pleased that Jamie was less than thrilled about seeing Trevor?

"He's no Gavin," the woman said, "is he?"

The housekeeper's preference was clear. Every woman Jamie knew encouraged her to take Gavin back—not that he'd asked her to or expressed any interest in reconciliation. Her sisters, Catriona and Fiona, fawned over Gavin. Her sisters-in-law, the three American wives, all thought Gavin was wonderful. Only her brothers expressed no particular opinion about her relationship with Gavin, though Aidan had developed a polite attitude toward his wife's brother.

Gavin believed her brothers hated him. She couldn't subscribe to that theory. Lachlan, Rory, and Aidan didn't hate anyone. They were the best men she'd ever known, except for Gavin. But lately, he'd turned into a bit of a nutter.

"Ye coming?" Mrs. Darroch asked.

Jamie nodded and followed her down the hallway, through the dining room and into the main hallway. At the entrance to the vestibule, Jamie stopped.

Mrs. Darroch headed up the spiral staircase.

The door to the outside was closed. Mrs. Darroch must've left Trevor standing there, instead of inviting him inside. A silent expression of her feelings for the Englishman.

Jamie glanced down at her clothes—a loose-fitting T-shirt, yoga pants, and fuzzy slippers. Well, what did a man expect when he turned up at her door at nine in the morning? Not that she cared what Trevor thought, anyway. Sighing, Jamie crossed the vestibule and swung the door open.

Trevor Langley beamed at her, though the expression seemed a bit forced. "Jamie, you look lovely this morning."

He looked like an advert for men's clothing. The blue of his polo shirt set off the matching highlights in his gray eyes, and his charcoal slacks featured a modern fit that accentuated his muscular thighs. The sun painted his sandy hair in golden hues until they almost glowed like a halo.

"What do you want, Trevor?"

"No pleasantries, then." He leaned against the doorjamb. "Have you eaten yet? I was hoping to buy you breakfast in the village. I saw a cafe that looked perfect."

Her throat tightened. Loch Fairbairn had one cafe, the place where Gavin had offered her a credit card instead of an engagement ring.

"Thank you, no," she said.

Trevor craned his neck to peer around the jamb into the vestibule behind her. "Are you going to invite me in?"

"Not a good time." With one hand on the door, she eased it halfway shut. "Have a safe trip home."

He chuckled. "I'm not going home, love. Not unless you come with me. Didn't I make my intentions clear last night?"

Unfortunately, he had. Right in front of Gavin.

Jamie might've been upset with Gavin for the fiasco at the cafe, but that didn't mean she wanted to take up with Trevor. Once, she'd found him beautiful and alluring, and his accent had tickled her senses. Now, she felt only phantom sandpaper scraping along her nerves.

"You left me," she said, "because I didn't fit into the posh lifestyle you wanted so badly. Looks like you've found it, congratulations."

His brows lowered, and his lips angled down, but the expression vanished in a heartbeat. "You ended our engagement, Jamie, not me."

"Maybe I was the one who said the words, but you made it clear you wanted out." Her hand still on the door, she clamped her fingers over the edge. "I haven't changed. I still want to stay here in the Highlands."

"That's the best part." He straightened and took possession of her free hand. "As I said last night, I'm buying an old distillery here. We could turn it into a tourist attraction, or anything you like. Say the word and it's yours." He raised her hand to his mouth and skated his lips across her knuckles. "I'm yours."

She stifled a derisive laugh. "Come off it, Trevor. You didnae buy a distillery for me. You bought it to add to your bank balance, as if you need more money. I value family and loyalty, not money and status. I have no interest in your project or you."

"Loyalty?" His lip curled. "How does the American pisser give you that? I heard he broke your heart. Can you honestly say you want him?"

Jamie opened her mouth to remind him he'd broken her heart, but she stopped. Had he hurt her that much? She'd been upset, of course, when he walked away from her. But broken-hearted? No, she couldn't claim that. She hadn't loved him enough to feel half the pain Gavin's non-proposal had caused her.

Maybe Gavin thought she wasn't good enough for him. Why else would he string her along for eighteen months?

She tore her hand free of Trevor's. "My relationship with Gavin is none of your business. I do not want you. We will never be a couple again. Nod if you understand."

He sighed and tilted his head sideways. "I knew it would a hard slog to win you back. I'm in this for the duration, Jamie, and I won't give up."

"There's nothing to win or give up. I am not interested, and that's my final word."

With a condescending little laugh, he chucked her under the chin. "I've always admired your spirit."

He ambled toward the driveway.

Jamie slammed the door. The bang reverberated in the vestibule.

Emery appeared in the doorway as if she'd been hanging around in the hall. "Everything okay? Mrs. D mentioned your ex was here. Then I heard the door slam."

"Trevor wants me," Jamie said. She rubbed her forehead where an ache had begun to throb. Between Trevor and Gavin, she had too much manly nonsense in her life. "I told him I don't want him, but he says he won't give up."

"Yeah, he told Rory he made a huge mistake letting you go." Emery waved for Jamie to follow her into the hallway. "Come on, we'll talk in the sitting room."

Jamie let her sister-in-law shepherd her through the dining room and down the guest-wing hallway to the sitting room. Emery sat down on the sofa, patting it in a tacit invitation. Jamie flopped onto the cushion beside her, huddled in the corner.

"Why the bloody hell did Rory invite Trevor to the party?" Jamie asked.

"Not sure. He conveniently fell asleep before you and I finished our chat, and he conveniently has a long conference call this morning." Emery propped her feet on the coffee table. "Don't worry, I'll grill him later. Rory will explain and make it right."

"Make it right? How?" Jamie snatched up a throw pillow and hugged it to her belly. "Trevor's here, and he won't go away. Short of thumping him on the head with a big rock, I don't see a way to change his mind about winning me over. I told him flat out I am not interested."

Emery made a noncommittal noise. "Men can be stubborn, especially when their masculine pride gets the better of them."

"What do I do?"

"Um…" Emery squinted her whole face as if straining her mind in search of an answer. With a brilliant smile, she said, "Well, if you decide on the rock-thumping idea, I'm sure your brothers would volunteer to drag Trevor's limp body over the border to dump him in England."

Jamie dropped her chin toward her chest, moaning piteously. "Not helping, Em."

"Sorry. I'm just not sure advising you is the best course this time."

"Are you joking?" Jamie peeked up at Emery through her lashes. "Meddling is your favorite pastime."

"No, not my number-one favorite." Emery's gaze turned dreamy, aimed at nothing in particular. "My favorite pastime is getting it on with Rory."

"Ech! Donnae talk to me about doing that with my brother."

"You do realize Erica gets it on with Lachlan all the time, and Calli and Aidan do it—"

Jamie hurled the pillow at Emery.

Emery dodged the pillow, and it bounced off the end table behind her to land on the floor. "You brought up the issue of my favorite pastime. I was being honest. Besides, Rory and I have never done it twenty feet away from a family gathering."

Jamie threw her hands up to cover her face and peeked out between her fingers. "Did you hear us?"

"No-no, nothing like that," Emery said. "I deduced the fact based on your flushed and flustered state after you and Gavin snuck off together."

A horrid thought occurred to Jamie, and she sat bolt upright. "Did Rory deduce the same fact?"

Emery waved a dismissive hand. "Oh no, he would never consider the idea. He probably thinks you're still a virgin."

"I doubt that." Jamie relaxed into the sofa. "I told Aidan I'm not a virgin when he caught me buying condoms once. If he knows, Lachlan and Rory know too."

"But they don't want to think about their baby sister having erotic adventures."

No, they wouldn't. Her brothers wanted to know about her sex life as much as she wanted to know about theirs.

Emery hopped to her feet and clapped her hands. "I have the solution."

"To what?"

"Your glut of men." Emery spread her hands. "Rory and I are going to Skye for three weeks. That gives you plenty of time to sort out your love life."

"What?" Jamie sprang to her feet. "How is that helping me? You're leaving me for three weeks."

"Be back in time for Thanksgiving."

"Which is an American holiday. We don't have it in Scotland."

"True," Emery said, "but this family has Yanks in it now. And we insist on celebrating our American holiday of gluttony and giving thanks."

Jamie's shoulders sagged when she thought about this plan. For the bulk of November, she would be alone in this castle while fending off Trevor's advances and who-knew-what from Gavin. "I can't do this alone."

Emery grasped Jamie's shoulders. "You need to work this out on your own. With the house to yourself, you'll have no excuses. You and Gavin can get it on in every room if you want. And you'll be forced to talk to him."

"No talking. I told him I wanted sex only."

Her sister-in-law rolled her eyes. "Oh Jamie, we both know you don't want casual."

"I know, but—" Jamie threw her head back to scowl at the ceiling. "Don't know what I'm doing."

"Which is exactly why you need three weeks without siblings or sisters-in-law interfering."

Jamie shot Emery a dubious look. "How am I supposed to stop my brothers and sisters from poking their noses in?"

"Calli and Erica will keep Lachlan and Aidan in line. And I'll talk to Cat and Fiona."

Rory's wife seemed to have it all worked out. Would three weeks give Jamie time to untangle the mess her life had become? To find out, she'd have to give Emery's plan a go.

"All right," Jamie said. "Go to Skye, and I'll...do something here."

Emery gave her a quick hug. "I believe in you, Jamie. You can handle the situation all on your own."

Jamie considered the idea of having the castle to herself for a moment, then remembered an important fact. "Mrs. Darroch will be here."

"Nope," Emery said. "She's leaving this afternoon to visit her daughter in Caithness."

"Oh." Completely alone? For nearly a month? Gavin and Trevor might drive her insane. "If you come home to find two corpses in the vestibule, have Rory haul them into the woods."

Emery laughed. "That won't be necessary. If you murder your suitors, call Aidan. He'll bring his backhoe and dig the graves for you."

With that, Emery strolled out of the room.

And Jamie was left to ponder two thoughts. One, everyone she knew had a morbid sense of humor. And two, the next three weeks would test her patience, her willpower, and her inner strength.

Two men. Three weeks. What could go wrong?

On the afternoon following the worst Halloween party ever, Gavin got desperate. Iain had told him Aidan said Lachlan heard from Rory that Emery had seen Trevor at Dùndubhan that morning. The MacTaggart grapevine reported the Brit begged Jamie to take him back but she said no. Had she meant it? Or was she thinking about taking up with the English Ass? Jamie had told Gavin she wanted sex, nothing else—from him. Though he couldn't picture her doing him on the side while having a regular romance with Sir Smiles-A-Lot, he could imagine her kicking him to the curb to take up with Trevor.

Any woman would love a smooth-talking rich boy.

With no other ideas, Gavin headed to Dùndubhan to see Jamie. What he would say, he had no clue. Mrs. Darroch answered the door, pinched his cheek, and escorted him into the kitchen.

Jamie was slumped on a stool at the granite island. She poked at a lump of half-melted ice cream in her bowl, her gaze downcast, her expression melancholy.

Gavin wanted to rush over there and drag her into his arms to kiss away her misery. But it was his fault. She might not want comforting from him.

"There ye are, *mo luran*," Mrs. Darroch said as she nudged him across the threshold toward Jamie.

Mrs. Darroch bustled off to do housework or whatever it was she did around here. Gavin had never asked exactly what her duties were since it wasn't his business. Sometimes she seemed like the house mother at a fraternity.

Jamie glanced at him, her spoon going still between her fingers.

"Hey," he said. *Way to charm the socks off her.*

She pursed her lips. "Mrs. Darroch is trying to play matchmaker. Do you know what she called you? *Mo luran.* It means 'my pretty boy' in Gaelic."

"That an insult or a compliment?"

"It's an endearment, Gavin. Means she likes you." Jamie stabbed her spoon into the soft mound of chocolate ice cream. "She never called Trevor *mo luran.*"

Maybe Mrs. Darroch liked him, but he wouldn't count her on his team yet. Everyone sided with Jamie. He wasn't at all sure they were wrong. Still, it made him uneasy being surrounded by an army of hostile Scots bent on destroying him.

If Calli were here, and he'd spoken that sentence out loud, she would've slugged him in the arm and told him to stop being so damn paranoid. She would've been right.

But she wasn't here to rein him in, so he blundered ahead on his own.

"Wanted to talk about last night," he said. "Why didn't you ever tell me you had a serious boyfriend before me? You never mentioned Trevor at all."

Her eyes, always bright with life, turned dull. Her focus retreated into a distance he couldn't see. "He was more than my boyfriend. We were engaged."

Gavin stumbled backward a step. "What? You never told me—"

"I'm sorry. It's not a time in my life I like to dwell on. Things ended badly." She stared down at her ice cream, her shoulders folding in. "I had no idea Trevor would be at the party."

"Yeah, I know." Gavin couldn't prevent his lip from curling when he muttered, "Rory invited him. Interfering bastard."

Jamie leaped off her stool. The spoon tumbled from her grasp to clatter in the bowl. "Rory is not a bastard."

Gavin winced. He seemed to do that a lot lately, probably because he kept screwing up. "Sorry. I meant bastard as, like, sort of a general term for an annoying guy."

"Annoying?" She lodged her hands on her hips. "Rory is my brother. Do I tell you Calli is annoying?"

"Calli isn't irritating. She's sweet and kind."

Jamie rolled her eyes and sighed in melodramatic style. "Calli's a perfect angel, of course. You won't hear a bad word about your sister, but I'm meant to sit here and take it when you insult my brothers."

Where had this conversation gone wrong? The second he'd opened his mouth, that's when.

Gavin shoved both hands in his hair and scrubbed his scalp. It didn't loosen up any common sense that might've been stuck in the back of his brain. "It's not the same. You get along with Calli."

"Have you ever tried to get along with my brothers?" She whapped a hand down on the island. "The answer is no, you haven't."

"I tried, but they hate me."

She threw her hands up and unleashed a frustrated noise. "They donnae hate you. The problem is yours, not theirs."

Gavin couldn't help it. Anger seared his chest and tensed his whole body. "Right, your brothers are the most amazing guys ever to walk the earth. They've got no faults, no prejudices, just layers and layers of awesomeness."

She buckled her arms around herself, head drooping.

He should've shut the hell up, but an anger he couldn't understand drove him to keep going. "Wake up, Jamie. Rory brought in your ex-boyfriend to try to get between us."

Her head snapped up, and though she glared at him, her beautiful eyes shimmered with gathering tears. "Are you implying my brothers are the source of our problems?"

"No, I'm flat-out saying it. They want me gone."

"Ahmno listening to this."

She stormed out the door, her shapely figure dwindling out of sight as she raced deeper into the castle.

Gavin stood immobile at the island. His gaze flicked from the doorway to the ice-cream bowl, back and forth, his focus split by warring needs. Find Jamie and apologize. Hide in here. Chase after her. Run out the front door.

He stood there, stiff and cold. For a long, long time.

Chapter Twelve

The dining-room door slammed shut after Jamie as she rocketed down the hall of the guest wing. Tears streamed down her face. Her eyes burned, and the tears blurred her vision. She clutched at her belly but couldn't stave off the ache there, the one that matched the pain in her chest. Gavin blamed her brothers for everything. How could he say that to her?

She stopped halfway down the hall. Sniffling, she wiped at the tears with the back of her hand. All right, she had to admit Gavin had a reason for laying part of the blame on Rory—but only for last night, not for what happened before that. She couldn't understand why Rory had invited Trevor to the party. What if Gavin was right? What if Rory wanted to chase him away?

If Rory wanted her to reconcile with Trevor, he should prepare for a verbal skelping. For the first time in her life, Jamie suffered an impulse to throttle him. She looked up to Rory, idolized him even. How could he have done such a devious thing to her?

"Jamie, honey, what's wrong?"

She sniffled again, mopping her eyes with her shirt sleeve to clear her vision.

Emery was hurrying toward her. When she reached Jamie, Emery clasped her upper arms and fixed her concerned gaze on Jamie's. "What happened? Mrs. D told me Gavin showed up."

"He says—" Jamie straightened and raised her head. "He told me my brothers are the problem. He thinks they want him gone, and that Rory tried to use Trevor to get between us."

"Rory does have explaining to do." Emery rubbed Jamie's arm. "Don't worry, I'll get the truth out of Rory before the day is out."

"It doesn't matter." Jamie swallowed, though her throat stayed tight. She would not cry anymore, would not act like a silly girl who couldn't control her own life. Not anymore. "Gavin hates my brothers. What does he want from me? Does he expect me to move to America with him and forget my family?"

Emery studied her for a moment, calculation in her gaze. "If you want to know what Gavin thinks, better ask him."

Jamie made an irritated noise that came out as almost a snarl. "I don't think he knows what he wants. When I met him, he was different. Strong and confident and sexy. He took my breath away. And he stood up to Aidan when my rascally brother teased him. Gavin pursued me, despite Aidan moaning about his little sister being defiled, and they even became friends." She screwed up her mouth. "Well, it was more like they agreed to a Cold War truce. The point is, Gavin has become…I don't know what. Not the man I fell in love with. I will not give up my brothers to please him."

She'd almost done that once before to please a man. Never again.

"You don't know that's what he wants," Emery said.

"Can't ask him." Jamie scrunched up her face. "Last night, I told him I want only sex from him, and that I'd call him when I want it."

"Oh Jamie, you and Gavin are such adorable idiots."

Jamie bristled, her spine snapping straighter and stiffer. "Idiot? I thought you were my friend, but you're calling me names."

"No, sweetie, I'm not insulting you." Emery hooked an arm around Jamie's shoulders and gave her a squeeze. "I love you, but like I said earlier, you need to figure this out on your own. In the meantime, maybe I should have a little chat with Gavin. Set him straight about a few things."

Jamie shot her a sidelong look. "How is that me handling this on my own?"

"Think of it as a jump-start." Emery withdrew her arm from around Jamie. "Once I get the engine running, it's up to you and Gavin to set the timing right."

"Please, no automotive metaphors."

"Sorry." Emery thought for a moment, her cogitation visible in the squint of her eyes and the way her fingers drummed in the air. "Here's a better one. Gavin is Steve Rogers, about to step into the scary machine that will turn him into Captain America. You are Peggy Carter, telling him everything will be okay if he takes the leap."

Captain America? Jamie shook her head, though she was more amused than annoyed by Emery's superhero reference. Her sister-in-law loved movies about muscle-bound men in skintight costumes.

"Trust me," Emery said. "Gavin isn't a lost cause."

"If you say so."

"Where did you see him last?"

"The kitchen."

Jamie watched Emery march off in search of Gavin. If he hadn't left already, he was in for an Emery Talk. The woman knew how to meddle without seeming like a busybody, but Jamie had her doubts about Emery's power to persuade Gavin to do...whatever it was Emery thought he should do.

Three weeks alone in this house. Three weeks to sort out this mess.

Bod an Donais.

Gavin was still standing there like a mannequin in a museum when Emery waltzed into the kitchen. She had that knowing look on her face, the one that usually preceded a round of meddling.

He parked his butt on the stool Jamie had vacated. "She told you, didn't she?"

"That you blamed everything on her brothers? Yes." Emery braced a hip against the island a few feet from him. "You poor, deluded man. That's not the way to win Jamie back."

"I can't get her back. Jamie won't talk to me anymore after this. All she wants is a sex slave."

Not that he minded being enslaved to her passion. But still—

"Sex slave?" Emery said, and laughed softly.

He froze, the awareness of what he'd confessed to Emery hitting him like a snowball to the face. Fidgeting, avoiding her steady gaze, he mumbled, "Why did I say that?"

She laughed again, but as always, her amusement never seemed like scorn. Everybody talked to Emery, not solely because she liked to intervene in their lives. She was easy to talk to. Hell, any woman who could get under Rory MacTaggart's skin must have voodoo-level skills.

"Relax, Gavin." She nudged his foot with hers. "Jamie already told me about her offer. I know what she thinks. Now, I want to hear what you think, what you want."

"I want Jamie." He propped an elbow on the island and dropped his forehead into his raised palm. "That's never gonna happen now. She thinks I'm an asshole, and she's not wrong."

"You told her the problem is her brothers." Emery crossed her arms over her chest, giving him a *you're a damn idiot* look. "How did you think that would go over?"

Gavin slouched down, wishing he could disappear into the granite countertop. "I was mad. I heard she'd been talking to her ex, that suave

English douchebag Rory invited to the Halloween party. Rory probably thinks Trevor is the perfect guy for Jamie, way better than me. And the English Ass begged Jamie to take him back. Since she doesn't want me, not the right way, she must want him."

Emery half stifled a laugh. "I think you're interpreting the gossip through the lens of your own insecurities."

Damn, she was right. So damn right it pissed him off. He wasn't angry with Emery, though. He hated himself for having these insecurities and feeling like a loser because he didn't have what the English Ass offered Jamie—financial security, emotional stability, and no baggage.

Trevor Langley was perfect. How could Gavin blame Jamie for preferring him?

Emery sighed. "Acting like a big old asshat won't help you win Jamie back. She doesn't want Trevor, but if you keep pushing her away, she might change her mind. Is that what you want?"

"No." Gavin kicked the wooden side of the island with the toe of one shoe. "I know it's not really her brothers' fault we're having problems, but they don't like me. Jamie needs her brothers to approve of me. I don't understand it. Why do we need their okay?"

"Yes, it's a mystery." Emery's lips kinked into a sly smile. "You don't care at all what your sister thinks of your life choices, do you?"

Gavin wriggled on the stool, lifting his head out of his palm. "You're really annoying, you know that?"

"Why? Because you know I'm right?" She rested a hand on the island, leaning into it. "I'm not emotionally invested in this thing. That's why I can see things you won't let yourself admit to."

"I care what Calli thinks. What's that got to do with the MacTaggarts?"

Emery studied him for a moment, as inscrutable as the Buddha. "Remember how you felt when you showed up at Calli's house to find Aidan living there?"

Oh yeah, Gavin remembered that. His sweet, innocent sister shacked up with a man she'd known for a week. A Scottish man. A guy who walked around half naked like he was the god of sex.

The man who'd seduced his baby sister.

Calli and Aidan were married now. He didn't hold a grudge against Aidan these days, not since he'd realized how much the guy loved Calli and that he'd do anything to keep her safe and happy. Still, he wasn't exactly friends with his brother-in-law.

"I didn't like him at first," Gavin admitted, "but I've gotten used to Aidan. I get why he and his brothers don't like me. Jamie's their baby sister. But I got over Aidan screwing my little sister, so why can't they get over me and Jamie being together?"

"Have you given them a reason to?" Emery tapped a fingernail on the island. "I met you when Rory and I came home, freshly married, and the whole family gathered in the garden to welcome us. You were there, but you hung back. Didn't talk to anybody except Jamie, Calli, and me. It's the same at every MacTaggart family get-together. You hang back and only talk to Jamie, Calli, or me."

"Yeah, okay, that might be true." It was absolutely true, but he couldn't bring himself to say so out loud. "The Three Macs don't exactly go out of their way to make me feel welcome."

"Three Macs?"

"Iain calls them that. Says they're a mafia."

Emery snorted with partially repressed laughter. "Mafia? No, sweetie, they're nothing more than three men who adore their baby sister."

"And hate me."

Her head fell back, and she groaned. "Honestly, Gavin, if you keep saying they hate you, then Jamie will never let you back into her life. It's a package deal, Jamie and her brothers."

He picked at the granite countertop, but like the Three Macs, it wouldn't give an inch for him. "Nothing I can do, then, is there? I've lost her."

"Gavin, stop being so obstinate. You are the interloper here, and as far as the brothers are concerned, you've been jerking their sister around for a year and a half." She speared him with a hard look. "Think about it. Jamie is more than their baby sister. She's the baby of the family, the youngest of six children, the one they've looked out for all her life. Lachlan was fifteen when Jamie was born, and Rory was eleven. With an age difference like that, of course they're overprotective of her. Think of how you feel about Calli and multiply it by ten. That's their relationship with Jamie."

Shit. Emery was right. Gavin had been a jerk for not figuring it out on his own. Not only was he reflecting his own insecurities onto Trevor and the MacTaggart men, but he'd underestimated how much Jamie meant to her brothers. In their situation, he would've beaten the crap out of any guy who treated his sister the way he'd treated Jamie.

"They'll always hate me," Gavin said, all but moaning the statement because he felt hopeless and whiny. "How can they not? I have jerked their sister around. Didn't mean to, but you know what they say about the road to Hell." He gave a bitter laugh at his own idiocy. "I paved enough roads with my good intentions to circle the globe five times."

"Oh, they don't hate you. This is fixable, with a little humility."

"Great, because that's my strong suit."

"Listen up," she said, edging closer to him. "Know what Jamie told me a few minutes ago? She said when you two met, you were strong, confident, and drop-dead sexy."

He aimed a quizzical look at her. "Jamie said drop-dead sexy?"

"I may have added the drop-dead part, but the rest she said verbatim." Emery touched his shoulder. "You swept her off her feet once, which means you can do it again."

"No frigging idea how."

Emery straightened and waved a hand in a get-up gesture. "Rise to the challenge, Gavin."

Grumbling, he got to his feet. "I'm up. Now what, Mistress Yoda?"

"I'm not green and wizened."

"No, you're hot and nosy and way too perceptive for everybody else's good." He rubbed the back of his neck. "I'm open to any nosy advice you want to give."

"You know what you have to do. There's no way you'll ever separate Jamie from her brothers. The question is, how committed are you to winning her back?"

Though he had a sick feeling he knew the answer, he asked anyway. "What is it you think I need to do?"

"You have to bromance the MacTaggart brothers."

Gavin curled his lip. "Bromance? What an asinine word."

"Call it what you like, but the fact remains. You have to win them over if you want to have any chance with Jamie."

He groaned, long and low and rife with all the frustration and resignation he'd experienced since his flubbed proposal. "I'm pretty sure your husband wants to throw me around like a caber."

She shook her head, tsking. "Come on, stop assuming you'll fail. Besides, Rory's a big old teddy bear."

"A what?" Gavin barked out a laugh. "Rory MacTaggart? A teddy bear? He's more like a polar bear stalking his prey across the tundra."

"Take it from me, the only one who knows him inside out." She slanted in a smidgen. "Rory is a teddy bear. Give him a chance, suck up to him good, and he'll show you his warm and fuzzy side."

"Not holding my breath for that one." Gavin twisted his mouth into a rueful expression. "Please tell me he won't, like, hug me or anything."

"Oh no, Rory doesn't hug anyone but me."

"Thank heaven for small mercies." Gavin rubbed his neck again, which suddenly ached whenever he thought about the herculean task of getting buddy-buddy with the brothers. "I'm never gonna be besties with these guys, but I guess I could try harder to make peace."

"Start with Aidan. He's predisposed to accept you, since he's married to your sister. Being nice to you makes his wife happy, and we both know how much Aidan cares about keeping Calli satisfied."

Gavin couldn't deny it. "Aidan has made Calli happier than I've ever seen her. And he'd do anything for her and baby Sarah. I have to give him props for that."

"There's your starting point."

"For what?"

Emery chuckled. "Getting into Aidan's good graces."

Gavin was supposed to tell Aidan MacTaggart he appreciated the way the Scot treated his sister and niece. Sounded easy.

The knot in Gavin's stomach belied that assumption.

He would try. No, he would do it. Whatever he needed to do, however much he had to humiliate himself in the process, he would make peace with the three Macs to please Jamie.

Then and only then might he have a shot in hell of getting her back.

Chapter Thirteen

Emery

I found my husband in his office, the old library attached to the castle tower. Rory reclined in his leather executive chair with it tipped back slightly, his feet on the desk with his ankles crossed, hands folded over his belly. When I walked into the room, his gaze swiveled from the tall windows to me.

He had the good sense to look guilty.

Swinging his feet off the desk, he straightened and coughed. "Emery, I—"

"You've been hiding from me," I said as I tromped around the desk to drop my butt onto his lap. "It's okay. I know you're a recovering uptightness addict. A few slips now and then are to be expected."

He relaxed into the chair and slipped an arm around my waist.

"I may be forgiving you for avoiding me all day," I said, turning sideways in his lap to loop my arms around his neck, "but you're still on the hook for the Trevor thing."

"Trevor thing?" He adopted a look of pure innocence.

"You know what I'm talking about." I leaned in to stare straight into his amber eyes. "Why did you invite Trevor to the Halloween party?"

"He rang me to ask if I'd help him with the legal issues surrounding his purchase of an old distillery." Rory averted his gaze to the desk. "I told him I don't have time. He accepted that answer, but then he asked after Jamie. I may have suggested he come to the party to catch up with her."

"Catch up?" I leaned in more, our noses bumping. "Are you trying to drive a wedge between Jamie and Gavin? Do you even know why she and

Trevor broke up? What did you hope to accomplish with this little invitation of yours?"

"*Mhac na ghalla*, Emery, I was being friendly." He cast me a mulish sidelong glance. "You keep insisting I should be more welcoming."

"Swearing at me in Gaelic won't help. You're the one who decided bringing Jamie's ex to the party was the perfect way to start your friendliness campaign."

"Jamie always said they parted ways amicably. I thought she'd like to see an old friend."

I groaned. "Honey, I know you meant well. But this was a truly knuckleheaded idea."

My husband bristled. "I am not a knucklehead."

"Oh, Rory baby." I stroked his cheek. "All men are knuckleheads on occasion. It's one of the defining traits of manhood."

His lips twisted into a wry smile. "I think I should be insulted, but given my transgression, I feel the irritating need to apologize."

"Yes, apologize to Jamie."

Rory jerked his head back. "Jamie? No, I meant apologize to you."

I tapped his nose, more amused than annoyed by his display of manly embarrassment. "Apologizing to me won't help. You screwed up, so you get to beg your sister's forgiveness."

He grumbled and slumped as much as he could with me on top of him. "Fine, I'll talk to Jamie."

I opened my mouth, but he cut me off with a roll of his eyes.

"And I will also apologize," he said, "to Jamie."

I patted the top of his head. "Good boy."

He rolled his eyes again.

Snuggling into him, I said, "From here on, baby, leave the meddling to me. You suck at it."

Those whisky eyes of his rotated to study me sideways. "What have you done now?"

"Nothing much." I grinned. "Just told Gavin he needs to bromance you MacTaggart brothers."

"What?" Rory virtually screeched, sounding not terribly masculine. "Ahmno being...Donnae want him doing that with me."

"Calm down, sweetie. All I meant was he needs to make friends with you three." I tipped my head to the side. "Did you know Iain calls you the Three Macs, and he told Gavin you're a three-man Scottish mafia? No wonder he's afraid to speak to you."

A smug smile curved his lips. "Serves Gavin right."

I gave him a weak punch in the shoulder. "Behave, Rory. We want Jamie to be happy, and Gavin makes her happy."

He grumbled again, slipping both arms around my waist. "Am I meant to be friendly with him? The man who broke my sister's heart?"

"You broke my heart over and over and over and—"

"I get the idea. That was different."

"Right. Different." I feathered my lips over his. "Pretty sure Gavin never told Jamie to sleep in another room, or told her not to say his name during sex, or commanded her to keep her eyes open during sex, or—"

"Again, I understand your point." He made a petulant face. "I don't do that anymore."

"Nope, you got over it. You're almost freewheeling these days." I licked at the seam of his lips. "If you try to be nicer to Gavin, I'll reward you in many and varied ways."

"You can't keep placating me with sex, Em."

"Sure I can." I took his bottom lip into my mouth and sucked, then released it slowly. "Works like a charm."

"Maybe it does. And maybe I could make more of an effort with Gavin." He slid a hand up my side to cup my breast. "Now show me one of these rewards, *mo gaoloch.*"

Chapter Fourteen

*J*amie spent the better part of the next two days wandering through the castle, avoiding Emery and Rory as much as possible while she brooded about the situation with Gavin. Their rammy had left her with a rock in her gut and a spike of ice in her heart. He blamed her brothers. *They want me gone,* he'd said. It was not true. Lachlan, Rory, and Aidan would never interfere in her life in that way. They protected her, but they would never go so far.

Gavin's words echoed in her mind. *Your brothers are the most amazing guys ever to walk the earth. They've got no faults, no prejudices, just layers and layers of awesomeness.* He believed she saw them that way, but she recognized they had faults.

Did she overlook their flaws? Did she, as Gavin claimed, think of them as her perfect heroes?

No, she didn't. She couldn't. She was an adult, not a helpless girl, and mature women took charge of their own fates.

It was time she did that.

Her plan came to her while she reflected on the view beyond the tall windows in the first-floor hallway. The grass had begun to wither. Thanksgiving would arrive in three weeks, bringing with it the festivities her American sisters had arranged. Gavin would be there. Calli would invite him, for sure, but Emery would want him there too. The woman had become fixated on repairing Jamie's love life.

She loved Emery for it, but still…

If she let the Gavin situation stew for three weeks, she'd turn into a bampot. Emery had suggested she make Gavin crave her so desperately he'd do anything she wanted. Jamie's addendum to the plan had been to declare she wanted sex only, no emotional nonsense. She'd enacted that plan on Halloween, but she needed to take it further. What if she made Gavin want her so badly he lost his ability to think and couldn't restrain his lust? What if she drove him so wild with desire he'd rue the day he announced her brothers were the problem?

Afterward, she would walk out on him. No conversation. Out the door and away.

Could she follow through on her casual-sex scheme? The idea of using her body for revenge, of toying with him that way, made her stomach hurt. And yet...

The thought of seducing Gavin made her body ache in the most wonderful way.

What then? asked an annoying voice in her head. *You make him barmy with lust, walk away, and then what?* Och, she had no idea. She might've been hoping he'd realize his mistake, run after her, and fall to his knees to beg her forgiveness. Or she might've fantasized about him making a grand romantic gesture like Rory had done when he belted out a Frank Sinatra song in the middle of the village square in Loch Fairbairn, then stripped off his shirt and almost stripped off his pants, all to prove to Emery how much he loved her.

Gavin would never do anything like that. Military men didn't make fools of themselves for women.

Back to the plan, then. Make him crazed for her.

And then...She'd figure out the answer later.

Two days later, Gavin lay on the bed in his room at Iain's house. Gavin had cooked dinner for the two of them by way of thanks for Iain's hospitality. The Scot's digs turned out to be a nice, if older, house of modest size on the outskirts of Loch Fairbairn. Gavin thumped the heel of his hand on the cushy mattress. He had no complaints about the boarding arrangements his sister and her cohorts had made for him. Plus, Iain was a cool guy to have for a roommate. Gavin liked hearing about Iain's good old days as an archaeologist.

A knocking emanated from the front of the house, muffled by the distance to Gavin's room and the big wooden door he'd shut for some privacy. Someone had arrived at the house. Since Iain was in the living room, Gavin didn't feel the need to get up and see who their visitor was. Probably one of Iain's conquests. Gavin had heard the rumors in town, the whispers about how Iain had seduced all of the single women in the village and some of the married ones too. Gavin couldn't reconcile the man he'd gotten to know with the version everyone else seemed to see. Then again, rumors could be vicious and completely wrong.

None of the MacTaggarts treated Iain like he was a ruthless cad.

How many women had the guy slept with? Come to think of it, how old was Iain?

Gavin pondered those questions until someone rapped on the door to his room. Hands clasped under his head on the pillow, he lifted his head to squint at the door. "Who is it?"

"Jamie."

He sprang off the bed and bolted for the door. With his hand on the knob, he paused to calm down. Yeah, okay, he was excited to see her. Excited she wanted to see him. But if he ripped open the door and grinned like an idiot, he'd seem like, well, an idiot. Instead, he drew in a breath and exhaled it slowly, assumed a casually interested expression, and opened the door.

Jamie's nibble-worthy mouth curved into a saucy smile.

His attention stalled on her outfit, if it could be called that. She wore a raincoat that stopped an inch shy of her knees. With the top two buttons undone, the coat revealed enough skin to suggest she had not much of anything on underneath. Her hair cascaded over her shoulders in loose waves, and red lipstick accentuated her mouth. High heels elevated her high enough she didn't need to crane her neck to look at him.

His mouth opened, but no words came out. He glanced at the lapels of her raincoat, and the way the coat exposed her breastbone straight down into the space between her breasts.

"Are you—" He lost his voice, flapping his head with his mouth gaping. "Tell me you've got clothes on under that coat."

She caught her bottom lip between her teeth, releasing it gradually while she shook her head.

Though his dick stirred to life, he tried to maintain a casual demeanor. "You're actually naked under that thing?"

"Mm-hm."

He heard a noise from the other end of the hallway, and with the suddenness of a bomb blast, he realized Iain had seen Jamie in this getup.

"Iain saw you?" he said, powerless to keep the shock out of his voice. Shock with a little bit of excitement thrown in. Naked Jamie with nothing but a coat on.

"Don't worry," she said, laying her delicate hands on his chest. "He's my cousin, and besides, Iain is a gentleman."

"But he knows you came in here to, uh…" Gavin struggled for words but couldn't find any to describe what she seemed intent on doing. "What exactly did you come here for? A couple days ago, you were boiling mad."

"Sex only, that's the arrangement." She skated her hands up his chest, and even his shirt couldn't lessen the effect her touch had on him. "We can have fun even when I'm angry with you. No talking. A good, hard shag and nothing else."

Naked Jamie. A shag. His dick shot hard because it loved the idea, but his brain got hung up on the meaning of this.

She stood in the doorway, clothed in only a raincoat.

Gavin seized her arm and hauled her into the bedroom, kicking the door shut. "You show up here looking for a good time, like nothing happened the other day. This is crazy. You can't expect me to be up for this after the fight we—"

Jamie whisked her hands down to his waistband, fingering the button of his jeans. Her other hand drifted lower, exploring the length of his erection in smooth swipes of her palm.

He hissed in a breath. Damn, but the light, teasing touch of her fingers was making all the blood evacuate his brain and head straight for his groin. He couldn't move to stop her, wasn't at all sure he wanted her to stop.

They could not have sex like this. The fight the other day. Her pronouncement of "sex only." Those things made it a bad, bad, bad idea all by themselves. Add in the fact they were in Iain's house with Iain twenty feet away in the living room...

Gavin didn't get the chance to examine those reasons. Jamie ripped open the raincoat, the snaps popping apart, and dropped the coat on the floor. She kicked off her shoes.

Naked. Jamie. Creamy skin. Dusky-pink nipples. His gaze wandered lower to the golden-brown hair at the juncture of her thighs.

He gulped. Hard.

She plastered her body to his, all that soft skin warming him through his clothes. "You want me. I want you. It doesn't have to be complicated."

"Yes, it does." With more willpower than he'd known he had, he backed away from her. "We're not strangers having a one-nighter. This is complicated, Jamie, because we know each other backwards and forwards. I know you have a weird and kind of adorable obsession with bicycles. I know you love to be all girlie, but you also love to get your hands dirty helping Tavish take care of the garden."

The Scottish vixen sashayed up to him, those lush hips swaying, and took hold of the button on his jeans. "Getting dirty is exactly what I want tonight."

Oh shit. How was he supposed to keep resisting her?

He had to resist, period. Letting her coax him into a round of hot sex under these circumstances would be the wrong thing to do.

She wetted her lips with a long, slow glide of her pink tongue.

Wrong sounded awfully good right now.

No, no, no, you idiot.

He raised a hand. "Let's talk about this—"

"Mm-mm." She fanned her palms over his chest and pushed, reeling him backward onto the bed. "No more talking."

Okay, he could've fought a little harder when she pushed him. Her behavior, so unlike anything she'd done before, had caught him off guard. Sure, that was why he'd let her knock him back onto the mattress. It had nothing to do with his throbbing dick or the way her breasts bounced when she shoved him.

He raised onto his elbows, his feet still on the floor. "Jamie—"

"Shh." The vixen knelt between his legs and unhooked the button on his jeans. "Lie back and relax."

Was she nuts? Relax, with her naked and wedged between his legs inches from his hard-on.

He needed to stop this.

Yeah, he'd do that…in a few more seconds.

She unzipped his jeans, slipped her hand inside his boxers, and closed those soft fingers around his dick. Her pupils had gone large and dark. Her lips parted as she withdrew his length from his pants. She drew in a shaky breath, her tits heaving, and all the while her hand stayed firmly around him.

What was going on here? She'd sauntered into the bedroom and pushed him onto the bed, that's what. She seemed intent on—

Jamie laved her tongue over the head of his cock.

He jerked and gasped.

What kind of man lay here in a lump while his girlfriend did naughty things to him?

The really, really lucky kind.

Oh dammit, he couldn't let it go down this way. He tried to sit up, but she closed her lips around him and took his length deep into her mouth, and then he couldn't think. His breaths came shallow and fast, but he managed to croak, "Jamie, wait, let's talk."

She encompassed his girth with her delicate hand and began licking the head.

He was lost.

The irresistible vixen worked him with her hands and her mouth, cupped his sack with one hand while she licked a path up his length, massaged his inner thighs while she suckled him like she couldn't get enough of the taste. Pressure built in his cock, the need to lose it approaching critical, and he knew he had to make her back away. He had no doubt she'd never done this before—though, damn, she was a quick study—and he didn't want her to feel she had to finish him off like this.

"Jamie," he said, his voice raspy and choked, "you should stop before I—"

She removed her mouth only long enough to say, "Not stopping."

Then she swallowed him again, and all his thoughts vaporized.

His body went taut, the breath stolen from his lungs. He fisted his hands in the covers, gasping for air he couldn't take in. A hoarse, strangled cry exploded out of him at the instant he came.

She didn't stop, not until he'd spent himself completely.

Breathing hard, shocked by what his angelic Jamie had done, he gaped at the woman still kneeling between his thighs. "Wow. Jamie. That was... unbelievable."

Her smile was shy, like she couldn't believe what she'd done either.

Gavin levered up into a sitting position and caressed her hair with one hand, admiring the incredible woman before him. "Just when I think I know everything about you, I find out you're a vixen in disguise."

She covered his mouth with her hand. "Haud yer wheesht, or I'm away."

The cute Scottish way of saying she'd split if he didn't shut up.

Her shyness had evaporated, replaced with a bossiness he would've loved—if he hadn't known she was taking command not to be sexy, but to keep him from talking. To keep from getting truly intimate. To maintain a distance between them.

Hell with that.

What had Emery told him the other day? Something Jamie had told her.

She said when you two met, you were strong, confident, and drop-dead sexy.

Jamie wouldn't have said that unless she liked him that way. Emery had sort of implied that's what it meant. Gavin understood Jamie better than anyone, even her brothers, and he trusted his instincts about her. He'd acted like a wuss for too long. He'd let her steamroll him into—well, into a really hot blow job, but still—he'd let her steer the encounter into what she thought was a casual fling.

Enough of that. Time to grab the reins and show her the man she'd fallen for eighteen months ago, the man she'd slept with days after they met.

"That's right," she said in a sexy voice that made his balls ache, "keep being quiet. Means I won't have to leave."

He dived a hand into her hair to cradle her nape. "We're doing this my way now."

"No." She rose in front of him, her beautiful, nude body inches from his face. Chin lifted, she gazed down at him with a haughty expression he recognized as artifice. "My way or no way."

"Uh-uh." He settled his hands on her hips, tilting his head back to admire the view from between those luscious breasts and catch her gaze with his own. "You had your fun. But if you think this can ever be a good time and nothing else, I'll prove how wrong you are."

She rolled her shoulders back. "You've made your choice, then."

The woman he worshiped spun around, clearly intending to head for the door.

He locked his arms around her midsection and hauled her backward and down until she perched on his lap, caged by his embrace, her arms pinned to her sides. Her hair tickled his face. Though she wriggled and made indignant noises, he had the advantage of strength. She stopped fighting and huffed.

Gavin lowered his lips to her throat and chuckled. "You're so cute when you're frustrated."

"You're holding me hostage."

"That's right." He nipped her throat, licked his way up to her ear, and nibbled on the lobe, relishing the way she moaned and melted into him. "Good girl."

"Ahmno a dog." She stomped her foot down on his, but his sneakers cushioned the blow from her bare foot. "Let me go, you big oaf."

He laughed, loudly this time. "Damn, I love it when you're spunky. But I'm not letting go until we've had a talk."

"No talking. I want sex only."

"Bullshit." He nuzzled her cheek. "I'm in control now, and you like it."

Chapter Fifteen

*J*amie started to protest, then shut her mouth. He was right, which galled her. She loved this side of him, the domineering and yet tender man who could propel her to the heights of ecstasy with such ease. If she gave in, he would show her intense pleasure the likes of which she hadn't known in months, the kind she'd never known with anyone except him.

And he knew that.

Bound to his body, with his erection trapped between her back and his front, she had a bloody hard time concentrating. She needed to reassert her sex-only decree. She needed to get up and walk out the door to prove she could resist him and he couldn't tempt her into changing her mind.

Her body had other ideas.

Gavin unshackled her arms, sliding one of his hands over her belly to hold her loosely, plunging the other hand between her thighs to cup her sex. He thrust a finger between her folds and swirled it around her opening. "So hot and slick, ready for me to take you any way I want."

"You should do what I want."

"I will." He parted her swollen flesh with his thumb and forefinger, then raked three fingers up and down her cleft, his touch light and maddening. "I know what you like, what you need, so anything I do is what you want."

Her head fell back on his shoulder, her breaths quickened along with her pulse. She couldn't formulate a response, not with his fingers teasing her skin and his firm body surrounding her. The idea of surrendering appealed to her so much she had to fight against the impulse to spread her legs and rock her hips into his intimate massage.

One of his fingers plunged inside her sheath. His thumb found her nub and massaged around it in slow, powerful circles.

She moaned. Oh, this felt too good to fight.

"Tell me something," he murmured. "Why do you think sex without conversation is going to make you happy?"

His finger, the one lodged inside her, stroked her in places where no one had ever touched her before. She clamped her lips between her teeth, desperate to silence the moan building inside her, the one that threatened to erupt even louder than the first moan. Her eyes drifted half shut, and the guttural expression of deep pleasure emerged anyway.

"What makes you happy," he purred in her ear, his voice so husky and lustful it made her tremble, "is all the things I can do to you. Want mind-blowing sex? I'm your man, but it comes at a price." He coiled his tongue around her earlobe. "Conversation after."

"No," she said, her voice more breathless than she'd hoped. Lifting her head off his shoulder took more effort than she'd expected, but she managed to sit up somewhat straight on his lap. "I've told ye fifty times. Sex, no talking."

"You sure about that?" His hand on her belly swept upward to close around her breast. His thumb raked back and forth over her nipple. When she gasped and arched her back, he pinched her stiff peak. "I'm going to talk while I fuck you. I'll tell you all the dirty things I want to do to you and how good it feels to have my cock buried inside you. I'll tell you—"

"No talking." A tiny moan escaped before she could squelch it. If she could've squelched it. "This isn't the arrangement. Told you I'd leave if...oh."

He flicked his thumb across her nipple at the same instant he rasped his other thumb over her clitoris.

And her traitorous body responded. Her legs fell open, her body begging for more, and she let out a long, throaty groan of intense pleasure.

"You've got two choices," he said, still tormenting her with both thumbs. "Stay and let me deliver multiple orgasms or leave and try to find satisfaction on your own. We both know the do-it-yourself kind can't compare to what I give you."

"So arrogant."

"And you like that about me." He nipped the tender skin of her throat, then laved his tongue over the spot. "Besides, you told me once you love how confident I am, in and out of bed."

Damn. She had said that. Months ago, before he started acting like an idiot.

Worse, she'd meant it. She still did. This side of him, the confident and determined man, had been the version of him she'd fallen for eighteen months ago. His vulnerability had made her fall deeper, but he'd hurt her so badly. Though the credit card had stung, his comments about her brothers had left her reeling, afraid Gavin would turn out to be like Trevor.

He wasn't. She realized that in the logical part of her brain. Her heart, though, had more trouble accepting it.

"What'll it be?" Gavin said. "Multiple orgasms, or stomping out to make a point?"

Resistance seemed like the Mount Everest of willpower. Why should she fight this? She wanted him, he wanted her, and she could go back to her plan in the morning. It wasn't caving in if she made sure he understood the parameters.

"I'll stay," she said, "but nothing changes. Tomorrow, it's sex only or nothing."

"We'll see about that."

"Gavin."

He abandoned her breast to lay a palm on her cheek and rotate her face toward him. For a long moment, they simply drank each other in. Her heart sped up, though the acceleration had nothing to do with sex. She loved him, so much.

Gently, he tipped her head back and lowered his mouth to hers. He kissed her softly at first, exploring her lips with slow sweeps of his own, darting his tongue out to taste her skin, and she dissolved into him, surrendering all her self-control.

For now. For one night.

His tongue forged into her mouth, hot and demanding, teasing the roof of her mouth with light licks only to delve deep and rob her of breath. He cradled her head with his big hand, and his fingers on her sex worked her into a frenzy of need. She whimpered into his mouth, desperate for what he'd promised, what she craved with a reckless hunger.

She clutched at his thighs, the only anchor she could find.

With a rough groan, he broke the kiss. "Don't think I'll let you off this easy."

He pulled his hand away from her wetness, wiping his damp fingers on his jeans.

"What?" she said, sounding as dazed as she felt.

"You're not coming yet, not until I'm ready to let you. Got it?"

A traitorous thrill shimmered through her. "Yes."

"That's my girl."

He sprang up, taking her with him, then spun around and dropped her onto the bed on her back. In one smooth movement, he grabbed the hem of his shirt and whipped it off over his head. A second later, he'd doffed the rest of his clothes.

Lying there nude, flat on her back, she took her time admiring his body. Those broad, muscled shoulders. That sculpted chest. Defined abs that narrowed down to his waist. Powerful thighs made for driving into a woman and driving her insane with pleasure. And oh, she couldn't forget the erection curving up toward his belly, waving as if that engorged length couldn't wait to perform its duty.

Suddenly, she couldn't catch her breath. Wanting him stole all the oxygen from the room, eradicated her thoughts, demolished her self-control. She would do anything to feel him inside her again.

He placed a knee on the bed, keeping his other foot on the floor. Poised there, motionless and breathing heavily, he hovered a foot from her body while his gaze roved over the entirety of her nakedness.

"Ah, Jamie," he purred, swiping a hand over his mouth, "you are so beautiful. I love the way your skin gets flushed on your chest and your cheeks turn that perfect shade of pink." He swung his leg up and over to straddle her calves. His hand closed around his shaft and slid up and down it in languorous strokes, but his gaze stayed squarely on her. "You make me crazy, the way you move, the way you feel, the way you gasp my name when I'm—"

"Stop talking." She bit her upper lip, almost frantic from the opposing needs to surrender fully and to reassert her control. How could she have sex with him when she still didn't trust him not to hurt her again? He would never harm her physically, but emotionally...He'd done a fantastic job of that.

But every time he spoke in that silky voice and told her she was beautiful and perfect...

No, no, no, no. She refused to become a slave to her lust for him, to her love for him.

While he stroked himself with one hand, he reached down with the other palm to caress her inner thigh.

Heat scorched through her from head to toe, threatening to obliterate reason. Again. Just when she'd regained an iota of it. Maybe she could slake her needs without surrendering all her control. Yes, that was a good plan.

She flipped onto her stomach and bent her knees, leaning back to lift her bottom.

"Jamie," he growled, splaying both hands on her behind, "sweet Jamie, you have the finest ass in the world. I'd love to nibble on it." He shoved one hand between her cheeks to palm her sex. "Like an hors d'oeuvre to whet my appetite before the main course."

The obstinate man was still trying to control this.

And his stubbornness made her wetter, hotter, achier.

Not so strong and in command, are ye?

She would be. This instant.

"We do it my way," she said, rocking back until his shaft grazed her backside, "or not at all."

The infuriating man laughed and slapped her erse. "Not how it works, babe. If you wanted a submissive man, you shouldn't have hooked up with me."

She opened her mouth to snap a scathing retort but never got the chance.

He flipped her over, and she fell to the mattress with a *whump* and a bounce. "I get it. You don't want to look at me while we make love, so you can pretend it's nothing but hot sex. I'm not letting you do that."

"You are the most domineering, stubborn, impossible—"

He flopped onto the bed beside her and rolled her toward him until they lay face to face on their sides. One thickly corded arm imprisoned her like an iron bar around her waist. Their position forced her to gaze straight into his simmering, honey-brown eyes, and the heat of him penetrated her skin to warm her on the inside too. His breaths tickled her face, his erection prodded her hip.

"You'll never convince me," he said, his voice soft and tender, "that a sex-only encounter, with no intimacy, will satisfy you. I know my girl, and she's got to have a deeper connection."

Fear. It iced through her, spreading at lightning speed, freezing her muscles so she couldn't move or speak. He was right, and they both knew it. But she could not give in to what the foolish part of her wanted even after the things he'd done and said to her.

She couldn't summon the will to stop him.

He swept his hand down over her bottom and onto her thigh, drawing her leg over his hip.

Cool air teased her swollen, drenched flesh. Jamie swallowed against a lump in her throat.

With his hand lingering on her thigh, Gavin studied her face. His brows cinched into a tight rivet over his nose. "You're afraid of feeling close to me, aren't you?"

She nodded once.

"Christ." He pulled his hand away from her leg to cup her face. "Am I pushing you to do something you don't really want? I thought you were just being pigheaded." He brushed his fingertips over her cheek. "But if I'm making you feel pressured..."

The anguish in his voice and on his face stabbed a pang through her chest. He truly worried he'd coerced her into this. Maybe she had wanted to take control of the situation, and maybe she had valid reasons for it, but if he'd pressured her she would've walked out the door long before he tossed her onto the bed.

She'd made him feel he'd done something wrong, that she didn't want this.

"No, Gavin," she said, "you have never pressured me to do anything. I have been pigheaded because of what's gone on between us. I always want you. I wish I could keep a distance between us, but it's not possible. This one time, we could do it your way."

"Are you sure?"

"I am." She couldn't tear her focus away from his earnest gaze and the pain revealed in his eyes. Yes, this one time...

She hooked her leg around his ass.

He pushed inside her, slowly, delicately, consuming her inch by inch, every sensation heightened by the deliberateness of his movements and the intensity of the emotions they'd shared seconds ago. They made love at a languid pace, reveling in the closeness and mounting pleasure that bonded them in every moment, in every way. She entwined her arms around his neck, wrists crossed behind his head, her fingers in his hair, and she let the joy of coupling with him sweep away everything else. For now, for this moment, nothing else mattered.

They came together, in perfect sync, their cries and moans echoing through the room. It wasn't the most intense orgasm she'd ever had, but it meant so much more than all the others.

Whatever problems they had, whether they wound up together or apart, she knew one thing with complete certainty.

Gavin Douglas loved her.

Chapter Sixteen

*G*avin claimed Jamie's hand, despite the annoyed slant of her lips when he did it, and led her out of the bedroom. She'd slipped into her raincoat again and tugged her high heels on. Her hair was mussed in that post-coital way he loved. He guided her through the living room and out the front door, ignoring Iain's raised eyebrows as they passed by the Scot reclining on the sofa. Gavin eased the door shut. When Jamie moved to walk away, he laid a hand on her arm to stay her.

She aimed a quizzical look at him.

He cradled her face in both hands and kissed her sweetly. Not his forte, but for this woman, he would do anything. He *could* do anything. She imbued him with a certainty no possibility was out of bounds as long as they were together.

Even getting over his issues seemed possible. With hard work. And—*yech*—bromancing.

By the time he peeled his lips away from hers, she'd gotten that glossy-eyed, soft expression. It made him ache in ways that had nothing to do with sex. When she looked at him like that, he knew she loved him. One way or another, he'd earn back her trust. Then, he might deserve her love.

To get her to trust him again might become the most arduous task he'd ever undertaken. After all, it required him to cozy up to the Three Macs.

He skated his lips over hers one more time. "Tomorrow, you can go back to saying 'sex only.' I won't bitch about it, but I won't stop trying to change your mind either."

Oh yeah, he had lots of ideas for how to convince her nothing between them would ever be "sex only." He'd shown her some of that tonight when he made love to her in a way he'd never made love to any other woman. The intimacy of the act had affected him too. While they lay pressed against each other, bound in body and heart, gazing into each other's eyes, he'd realized how much he loved and needed this woman. He'd win back her trust.

Whatever it took.

"Nothing you say," she said softly, "will change my mind."

"I don't have to say a word." He let his hands fall away from her face, his fingertips trailing down her cheeks. "I showed you tonight, and I'll keep on showing you. Whether it's hot and heavy or intimate and tender, sex with us is always more."

Her bottom lip quivered so faintly he almost didn't see it. Her eyes glistened with newly formed tears.

She blinked furiously, snapped her shoulders back, and cleared her throat. "Good night, Gavin."

Jamie pivoted on her heels and stalked toward Rory's Mercedes parked behind Iain's beat-up Range Rover.

"Good night, Jamie," Gavin said. "Call you tomorrow."

She did not look back but climbed into the car and drove away.

Gavin watched until the Mercedes disappeared into the encroaching fog, then he went back inside the house. Iain still lounged on the sofa, one arm draped across the back, his legs stretched out with his bare feet on the coffee table and his ankles crossed. The TV played a documentary show that featured a serious male voice with an English accent talking about ancient Roman weapons. Actors onscreen shouted and clashed swords in a reenactment of some long-ago event.

Iain occupied the exact center of the sofa, and the only chair in the room had magazines piled on its seat.

"Don't have many guests, do you?" Gavin said, indicating the stack of magazines in the armchair with a roll of his eyes. "There's no place for anybody to sit except you."

"You are my first houseguest." Iain scooted sideways to sit at one end of the sofa, making room for Gavin. "Have a seat."

Gavin flopped onto the opposite end of the sofa and propped his bare feet on the coffee table too.

Peripherally, he noticed Iain observing him with an amused expression.

"What?" Gavin asked, swinging his head in Iain's direction. "You look like you know a big secret and you're waiting for the perfect time to drop that bomb on my head."

"Not a secret." Iain turned partway toward Gavin and rested his arm on the sofa back. "It sounded like you and Jamie reconciled. Several times."

Gavin linked his hands behind his head and leaned back. "Sorry if we made too much noise."

"Don't apologize. Glad to see things are working out."

"I wouldn't go that far." Gavin dropped his hands and scratched his cheek. "Jamie still thinks she wants sex only. Not that I mind being her love slave, but I was hoping she'd give up her dopey plan."

"Ahhh," Iain said in a tone that conveyed deep understanding, "you thought shagging her mindless would make Jamie fly into your arms and declare she forgives you for everything and would you please marry her tonight."

"Uh…maybe." Okay, yeah. Part of him probably had hoped for that result.

"Regaining the trust of someone you've hurt grievously takes more than one night and more than rollicking great sex. I have no personal experience with winning back the love of the only woman who matters, but I'm certain it's no easy feat." Iain sighed, and in that moment, he seemed older and graver as if the weight of memories had exhausted him. "I know what it feels like to lose such a woman forever."

"How do you know you've lost your girl forever? Have you tried to find her?"

Iain twisted his mouth into an irritated expression not unlike the one Jamie had made a few minutes ago. "It's been thirteen years. She might be married, have children, or…" He shut his eyes. "Want nothing to do with me."

"Come on," Gavin said, "you convinced me to do whatever it takes to get Jamie back. You oughta try to get your girl back too."

Iain opened his eyes, and his lips quirked. "I'm meant to be your Zen master, not the other way round."

"I'm no wise man, but maybe I can inspire you to go after your girl."

"Afraid I'm too old for second chances."

"Sorry-ass excuses." Gavin canted his head, studying his roommate. "How old are you, anyway?"

"Fifty."

Gavin felt his eyebrows shoot up. "Seriously? You don't look it."

Iain shrugged one shoulder. "Can't say it was clean living that kept me young."

Though Gavin considered asking what Iain meant by that, he decided to let it go. If the guy wanted to share, fine. Gavin had pestered him for enough details, and he wouldn't wheedle Iain into saying more. So, he changed the subject.

"Do you think," Gavin said, "I have a chance in hell of getting your cousins to accept me?"

"Only if you honestly want them to."

"I'll do anything to make it happen."

"Anything?" Iain leaned in, his tone conspiratorial. "Best be careful making vows like that. Rory has an unusual sense of humor."

"Rory's got a sense of humor? Believe that when I see it."

"Oh, you'll see it." Iain sat back, and his lips curved in the faint smile Gavin had come to associate with the odd Scot. "You may wish you hadn't discovered Rory's humorous side once he lets it loose on you."

"Are you trying to scare me? Thought you were on my side."

"I am."

Gavin folded his arms over his chest. "Well, when Rory starts wailing on me because you said he has a sense of humor, I expect you to step in to help me out."

"My brawling days are over."

"You were a brawler?" Gavin regarded Iain with a new appreciation. "Can't picture that. Seems like not much upsets you."

"Doesn't anymore. I've learned through hard experience getting upset has no value."

Gavin reined in his curiosity about Iain and let the comment go. Iain could keep his secrets. They weren't best friends or anything, though he liked the guy.

But he had to say one more thing before he shut his trap.

"You should look for your girl," Gavin said. "You'll never know if you've got a shot with her until you try."

"Aye." Iain contemplated the view out the window, his expression somber. "Maybe I will try. Someday."

Chapter Seventeen

The next morning, Jamie leaned against the vestibule wall watching Rory haul several suitcases out the door and to the Jaguar F-Type convertible waiting in the drive. Emery had gone to the kitchen to get "munchies for the trip."

Rory strode into the vestibule, not even breathing hard after lugging the suitcases. He liked to toss cabers—which Emery called "giant toothpicks," a term that always made Rory roll his eyes—so Jamie supposed all that caber practice had given her brother the fortitude for hauling his wife's overstuffed bags to the car.

"You're ready to leave," Jamie said.

"As soon as my wife finishes raiding the pantry." Rory averted his gaze, grasping the back of his neck, and his mouth twisted at one corner. "Jamie, I, ah, need to tell you something."

Jamie resisted the impulse to smile with no small effort. Only once before had she seen her brother this embarrassed and uncomfortable, and that had been because Emery asked him to dress up as Thor for Halloween. Still, to Jamie's surprise, he'd done it. After three months with Emery, Rory would do anything she asked of him. He loved her that much.

Would anyone love Jamie that much? Gavin couldn't even commit to one continent for her. Though he was staying in Scotland for now, he'd said nothing about staying for good—or asking her to move to America.

Rory cleared his throat. "I shouldn't have brought Trevor here. I'm sorry."

Jamie pushed away from the wall. "Rory MacTaggart apologizing to his little sister? Are unicorns dancing on the lawn too?"

He lifted his gaze to the ceiling and sighed. "These American wives of ours are a bad influence on the MacTaggart women."

"Are you claiming I was a wallflower before I met Erica, Calli, and Emery?"

Though his mouth opened, he seemed unable to produce words. His eyebrows cinched together over his nose.

"Well?" she said, bouncing up onto her toes. "Did you think I was a wuss-face before they showed up?"

She liked using an Emery word, "wuss-face." Her sister-in-law had a wonderfully colorful vocabulary, and the way it stymied Rory was a bonus.

"I—no—that's not—" He glanced around desperately as if praying his wife would turn up to rescue him.

Jamie laughed and slapped his chest with the back of her hand. "That's what you get for inviting my ex-fiancé to the Halloween party. It's the Mac-Taggart tradition of harassing each other."

Rory relaxed, nodding in relief. "Aye, it is. And I deserved that one."

"Yes, you did."

He rubbed his jaw. "I am sorry, Jamie. Emery's right, I'm a knucklehead."

Jamie pinched his arm so lightly he didn't even flinch. "We love you anyway."

Rory pulled a face. He started to speak, but something past Jamie's shoulder caught his attention and he went rock-still for a moment.

A wide and exuberant grin stretched his lips tight and exposed his teeth. His eyes sparkled.

Jamie turned sideways to Rory to see what he was looking at, beaming at, though she already knew the answer. Emery had walked into the vestibule, her arms laden with a cardboard box full of snack-food items.

Rory's wife grinned at him exactly the way he grinned at her.

Jamie's gut churned. They adored each other and weren't ashamed to let everyone see it. Had anyone ever adored Jamie that way? Maybe Gavin did, but his unnamed issues wouldn't let him show it. He might never behave the way her brothers did toward their wives because Gavin wasn't the sort to gush and moon.

Rory rushed to Emery and plucked the box from her arms. He pressed his mouth to hers for a sweet, lingering kiss that made Jamie's skin go cold.

She wasn't jealous of her brother and his wife. She wasn't. That would be childish.

"Are we ready?" Rory asked Emery.

"Yep," his wife said. She glanced to Jamie and gave her that mischievous smile. "Have fun while we're gone."

Fun? Jamie struggled to keep her shoulders from slumping. The next three weeks would be anything but enjoyable.

When had she lost her positive outlook? It had probably flown away on Rory's jet the last time it transported Gavin back to America.

Emery squeezed Rory's bicep, raising her eyebrows as she gave him an appreciative smile. When she ambled out the vestibule door, Rory followed.

He paused near Jamie. In a grave tone, he said, "Stay out of my office and the third floor."

The third and highest floor housed Rory and Emery's bedroom. What did he think Jamie was going to do in there? *Silly man.*

She saluted and clicked her heels together. "Aye-aye, sir."

He shook his head, smiling slightly, and left.

Jamie wandered outside to stand near the drive as Emery and Rory departed in the sports car. As the cherry-red vehicle disappeared from view, Jamie sighed and turned back to the house. The gray-stone castle loomed before her, suddenly seeming like an imposing blockade instead of a home. She'd always liked Dùndubhan. Facing three weeks alone here, though, she got a strange sick feeling in her stomach.

You are not a wuss-face. Time to show Trevor and Gavin they can't push you around. It was time to reassert control over her own destiny.

If Trevor pestered her, she'd tell him to go to hell.

And if Gavin wanted her back, he'd have to fight for it.

Sweat dribbled down Gavin's face and neck. He swiped an arm across his forehead, sucked in a breath, and swung the sledgehammer up for another blow. The hammer crashed down on the stone wall, smashing rocks free and scattering them across the ground. Five days had gone by since the last time he'd touched Jamie. He'd glimpsed her coming and going at Aidan's office, but otherwise, she'd steered clear of him. Their intensely intimate encounter at Iain's house had left her shaken. Gavin understood that, but he refused to sit around waiting for her to summon him.

Every day, he called her. Several times a day. At first, she wouldn't speak to him. Gradually, she allowed a little conversation of the impersonal kind—"nice weather, huh" and the like—and then last night she'd engaged in some lighthearted discussion of her family's antics. Gavin didn't mind hearing about the MacTaggarts' shenanigans, but he would've rather talked about their relationship.

Yeah, it was really ironic. He, the guy, wanting to talk while she, the girl, clammed up whenever he tried to maneuver the conversation toward the relationship zone. Leanne would never have believed him capable of touchy-feely stuff. Maybe he'd changed since the divorce. Maybe Jamie brought something out in him no other woman ever had.

None of that mattered if she wouldn't open up to him.

Gavin swung the sledgehammer again, pummeling the stone wall.

"Feels good, eh?" Iain said, grinning.

The odd Scot held his own sledgehammer, and together, they'd demolished a short section of the old wall. Thirty years ago, a farmer had built this wall as a dry-stone construction, meaning it had no mortar. The guy had planned to pen his sheep with the fence, but he fell on hard times and sold the sheep and the land. A later owner had tried to slap on some mortar after the fact, which wound up creating a mess. The homemade mortar had turned hard as cement. Aidan had hired Gavin and Iain to tear down the wall for the new owner.

Gavin had no doubts Iain had talked Aidan into hiring him. When Iain informed Gavin that Aidan needed their "help," the older man had assured Gavin, "Aidan desperately needs us. It's rather embarrassing, in fact, how much he begged."

Yeah, right. Aidan begging for Gavin's help? Iain had to be kidding, Gavin realized, though he spotted only one sign the guy was pulling his leg. The slight upward tick of one side of Iain's mouth clued Gavin in to the guy's plan. Gavin had decided to call it Operation Get the Pathetic American a Job So He Won't Feel Like Such a Loser. A long name, for sure, but it summed up the situation.

"Don't see how this is helping me," Gavin said. "But it is kind of fun."

Iain set the head of his sledgehammer on the ground and leaned into the handle. "Imagining those rocks are Trevor Langley's head?"

"Maybe." Oh yeah, definitely, but Iain didn't need to know everything. "You sure Aidan's okay with me working for him?"

"As long as you can do the work, he doesn't mind." Iain gazed out across the fields that surrounded the old farmhouse and the remains of the wall. "Do you still feel useless?"

"No." Somehow, whacking rocks energized him with a new sense of purpose and a renewed determination to work out his problems.

Iain took up his sledgehammer and winked at Gavin. "Told ye."

"What you told me," Gavin said, "was that I should get up off my erse and start acting like a man again. Not exactly a pep talk, oh Zen master MacTaggart."

Iain shrugged, swinging the sledgehammer up to rest it on his shoulder. "Never said I was a competent Zen master."

Gavin realized right then and there he would never understand Iain. "You're a weirdo, but I'm cool with that."

Iain shot Gavin an inscrutable smile and rammed his sledgehammer down on a section of the wall.

They smashed rocks for several minutes, too absorbed in the task to have a conversation. Despite the chilly weather, with temperatures that must've been in the upper forties, their shirts were soaked with sweat. The sun peeked out from the clouds on occasion, but mostly, the sky stayed gray and overcast. It had rained a bit earlier, the light and misty kind, but Gavin had enjoyed the cooling effect of the shower. He supposed he'd get a chill if he stopped working hard, so he kept working. Shattering a pile of stones had become therapeutic.

Which was probably what Iain had intended. The guy was sneaky and determined to "help" Gavin "sort of the way Emery helped Rory, but without the naked bits." Gavin did not ask for details or point out he was not uptight like Rory. *Let Iain have his fun*, Gavin decided. The guy seemed to need a project. And maybe, somehow, becoming Iain's pet project would help Gavin figure out where the hell his life had gone wrong.

Rain began to mist down on them again.

Gavin let his sledgehammer's head drop onto the earth, leaning into its long handle the way Iain had earlier. He turned his face up to the mist, eyes closed.

"Enjoying the rain?" Iain asked.

"It's kinda nice." Gavin ran a hand over his closed eyes, then glanced at his coworker-slash-roommate-slash-counselor. "Sure rains a lot in Scotland."

"Today's rain is tomorrow's whisky."

"Not a big fan of whisky. I prefer beer."

Iain wagged a finger at Gavin. "Best not let the Three Macs hear you say that. They treasure their single malts."

Gavin drummed his fingers on the sledgehammer's handle. "Yeah, I'm sure that's why they hate me. I drink beer instead of whisky."

"Never know. Having a wee dram now and then might grease the wheels, so to speak."

"Uh-huh." Gavin seriously doubted guzzling the right kind of booze would smooth out the potholes in the road between him and Jamie's brothers. He glanced at his watch and discovered he'd forgotten to wear it. He asked Iain, "What time is it? My stomach thinks it must be close to lunchtime."

"It is."

"How do you know? You didn't look at your watch."

"Donnae need to." Iain nodded past Gavin toward the old farmhouse surrounded by scaffolding, evidence of its renovation currently underway. "Have a look."

Gavin turned to glance back, and his heartbeat sped up.

In the driveway, Jamie leaned against Aidan's truck while she chatted with her brother. The flowy skirt she wore cascaded over her hips and down past her knees, its pastel colors matching the peasant top that draped loosely over her breasts and down her arms. The sun emerged from the clouds like it had come out solely to see her and touch her with its warm glow, streaming over her hair and painting the light-brown strands with molten gold.

Aidan pointed toward Gavin, though his focus stayed on his sister.

"I don't get it," Gavin said to Iain, though he couldn't look away from Jamie. "How do you know it's lunchtime because Jamie and Aidan are talking?"

"Look closer."

"At what? I don't—" Then Gavin noticed it. Plastic bags slouched on the ground at her feet, bags pooched out by the Styrofoam containers inside them. "Is that food?"

"Jamie brought lunch. She does it every day when she's working in the office."

"She's taking a vacation these days, at Rory's castle. Why would she drive all this way to bring lunch to the gang?"

"Ah, it's a mystery."

The knowing and slightly snarky tone of Iain's voice made Gavin swerve his attention to the other man, but Iain's expression gave away nothing.

"I know you're being sarcastic," Gavin said, "but I'm not getting the joke."

The Scot rolled his eyes heavenward. "How dense are ye? She came to see you."

Gavin's gaze flew to Jamie at the instant she smiled broadly at Aidan, her face lit up by the expression. *So damn beautiful.* Gavin rubbed a palm on his chest where an ache had sprouted.

Aidan picked up the plastic bags and strode in the direction of Iain and Gavin.

Jamie turned, leaning her front side against the truck. Her focus traveled over the landscape until it settled on Gavin. She raised a hand, wiggling her fingers at him in a faint wave.

He raised a hand but couldn't make his fingers move, or any other part of him except his jaw. It decided to go slack. *Way to win back the girl, Romeo.*

She pushed away from the truck and headed for the Mercedes parked behind it.

"If she came to see me," Gavin said, "why is she leaving? She never got within twenty feet of me."

"She saw you, though, didn't she?"

Was that all she'd wanted? To see him? Not to speak to him, no, she wouldn't want that. Sex only, she'd commanded. He knew Jamie too well to believe she actually wanted that, but he hadn't succeeded at gaining much ground in his battle to change her mind.

Maybe it was time for a different tactic.

He had no frigging idea what that might be.

Aidan reached Gavin and Iain and held up the bags of food. "Hungry?"

Iain dropped his sledgehammer and rubbed his palms together. "Fair starved. Smells like fish and chips."

Aidan shook his head at his cousin, his lips tightening into a closed-mouth smile. "Iain's nose may look like a hawk's, but he's got the smelling sense of a bloodhound. He can identify the kind of food from its smell, from thirty meters away."

Iain feigned disgust. "I'd rather be a hawk than a slavering dog."

Aidan told Gavin, "A hawk is more appropriate for Iain because he scavenges food from everyone. Keep your lunch in your lap with your hands over it, or this one'll steal your chips when you're not looking."

"Hawks are predators," Iain informed his cousin, "not scavengers."

"Which explains your attitude toward the lasses," Aidan said with a teasing smirk.

"You're one to talk," Iain said. "What was it they used to call you? Don Juan MacTaggart. At least I follow through, instead of teasing the poor lasses with flirtation that doesn't go anywhere."

"I didnae feel the need to get under the skirts of every woman in the Highlands." Aidan waved the lunch bags in Iain's face. "If you want my food, you should stop insulting me."

The older man straightened and said, with a faint smile, "Naturally, you were the greatest lover in all the United Kingdom. I can't hope to outdo your legend."

Aidan groaned out a sigh, probably at the blatant sarcasm in his cousin's tone. "When you meet the right woman, you'll feel differently about the lasses. A good one will change your life."

"Why settle for one when I can have them all?" Iain joked, but something in his eyes made Gavin wonder if he was thinking about his long-lost mystery girl.

Aidan led them around the remnants of the stone wall to a birch tree behind the farmhouse. Iain took a seat between two large roots of the leafless tree, his back against the trunk and his legs outstretched. Aidan perched on the largest root, using it like a low bench. Gavin dropped onto the grass facing the two of them. While Aidan handed out the Styrofoam boxes of fish and chips, Gavin surveyed the area behind the house.

His spine snapped straight, and he sharpened his gaze on Aidan. Gavin aimed one finger at the hulking object that had caught his eye. "What's that over there?"

Aidan tracked Gavin's finger to the large piece of machinery parked behind the house. With total innocence, Aidan said, "Looks like a backhoe. Imagine that."

"Yeah," Gavin said, his tone acidic, "imagine that. Why the hell are we breaking our backs with sledgehammers when you've got a backhoe?"

Chewing a hunk of fried fish, Aidan rotated his eyes toward his cousin and back to Gavin. "It was Iain's idea."

Gavin veered his sharp gaze to Iain. "Care to explain?"

"Thought the hard labor might do you good," Iain said while gnawing on a mouthful of fish. He swallowed the food, then shoved three chips— what Americans called French fries—into his mouth. He mumbled something made unintelligible by his chomping.

"Sorry," Gavin said, "didn't catch that. Your lame excuse was drowned out by the food you crammed into your trap."

Iain finished off his mouthful of chips, wiping his fingers on his jeans. "You needed a reminder of how to be a real man."

Gavin wolfed down three chips before he could speak without snarling. "Are you insulting me for fun, or is there a point?"

Aidan answered, since Iain was once again stuffing his face until his cheeks puffed out. "You haven't been acting like a man, have ye? Jamie's ex-fiancé turns up, and you let him strut around her like a randy stallion with a mare."

Gavin hissed a breath out his nose and bit off a large chunk of fried fish.

"Aye," Iain said. "That scunner plans to steal Jamie, and you're not doing a ruddy thing about it. You're a military man, aren't you? When did you turn into a dafty?"

"I am not a dafty—and I know that means a fool, by the way." Gavin slapped the piece of fish he'd been holding back into the Styrofoam box. "What am I supposed to do? If she wants him—"

"She doesn't want him," Iain said. "But you have to work for it if you want her back."

Aidan nodded. "Trevor's a scunner of a Sassenach."

Iain translated. "The Englishman is a nuisance of the first order."

Gavin felt oddly triumphant that Aidan didn't like Trevor. But he had to point out, "Rory seems to like the Sassenach."

Aidan gave him an analytical look as if he were sizing up Gavin. "Are you planning to let Rory decide who Jamie's with?"

"He's your brother. Aren't you on his side?"

"Not when Rory's being an eejit." Aidan plucked up a chip and consumed it swiftly. "Don't let it fash you. Emery will sort him out."

Emery. That woman had her nose deep in Gavin's business, but he couldn't muster any resentment about it. He liked Emery. Everyone did. Hard to dislike the only woman—the only person, period—who'd been able to reform the ogre of Dùndubhan. Rory may have lightened up a lot, but he still glared at Gavin at every opportunity.

Iain paused with a chip in his fingers, hovering it between his open lips. He wagged the chip at Aidan. "See what I mean? The tough-as-nails ex-Marine is afraid of Rory. It's terribly sad, isn't it?"

Aidan nodded with mock solemnity. "A shame to see a strong man crumble."

Gavin squashed his lips together and huffed a breath out his nostrils. "I am not crumbling, and I am not afraid of Rory. No way, no how."

"All right," Aidan said. "Go talk to him, then."

The food in Gavin's belly mutated into cold rocks. Not because he feared Rory, but because he feared the result of a confrontation with the man. If they couldn't work out their differences, Jamie would wind up hurt even worse than she was already.

Iain tapped a finger on the chip in his grasp. "Gavin's afraid of Rory, for certain, and he lets Jamie order him around like a slave."

"Very sad," Aidan concurred.

Gavin snatched up a chip and started ripping it up, the pieces fluttering down into the box. "What am I supposed to do? She doesn't want to talk to me about anything serious. She wants—well, it doesn't matter. We can't have a conversation because she won't listen."

Aidan scoffed. "If I'd given up because Calli told me to leave off, I wouldn't be married to her today."

"Why are you giving me advice? Jamie's your sister."

"And I should dislike you because of that?" Aidan chuckled. "I met you before you got involved with Jamie. I know you're not the *bod ceann* you're acting like these days. Besides, my wife is your sister. Calli wouldn't like it if I declared war on her brother, now would she? You are Calli's hero, which means I have to be nice to you even if I think ye need a good skiting with a caber."

Calli's hero? Jesus, that was a pedestal he'd fallen off of years ago, when he'd left his baby sister to deal with the consequences of their parents' deaths.

Gavin tore off a chunk of fish and chomped it to mush in his mouth. At least Aidan didn't think he was a *bod ceann*. That seemed like a good start to their…friendship, he supposed he'd call it. No matter what Emery said, he would not refer to this as a bromance.

One task remained for him to complete with Aidan. He got heartburn thinking about it, but the time had come to bite that bullet, even if it cracked his teeth. He set down his box of food and cleared his throat. "Aidan, I need to say something."

The other man paused with a chip raised halfway to his mouth.

"If it weren't for you," Gavin said, "Calli might still be hiding out in the woods afraid of getting arrested. You've been good for her and good to her. Thanks for that."

Aidan popped the chip into his mouth and ate it before saying, "She's done the same for me. No thanks necessary."

Gavin's phone vibrated. He pulled it out of his pocket and saw a new text message—from Jamie.

Excitement zipped through him as he read the message. *My place @ 8*, it said. Her place? That meant the castle owned by her brother.

Another message popped up. *Rory and Emery left for Skye.*

Every hair on his body sprang to attention. He'd have Jamie all to himself. Maybe he could convince her to give up this stupid sex-only plan. Maybe he could explain…what? The things he didn't understand himself?

He had to start somewhere. She'd invited him over, and he had to go.

See you then, he typed with one finger.

Jamie replied with an emoji of a winking smiley face.

Iain slapped Aidan's arm. "See how he types with one finger? This laddie's a closet Luddite, I think."

"Aye," Aidan agreed with mock gravitas.

Gavin huffed, shoving the phone back in his pocket. "I'm not a Luddite. My thumbs are too big to type with them on that midget keyboard."

They finished their meal while discussing things unrelated to Gavin's relationship with Jamie. Iain kept ribbing Gavin about his phone-typing style, and Aidan invented numerous and creative terms for it, some of them in Gaelic. When guys razzed each other, it meant they'd become buddies.

Task number one, scratched off the list. He'd made peace with Aidan.

Next up, Lachlan.

Piece of cake—not.

After lunch, Gavin and Iain were collecting some gear from Aidan's truck when Rory's Mercedes rolled up the drive with Jamie behind the wheel. She parked alongside the truck and climbed out. Jamie waved a file folder in the air until she caught Aidan's attention.

He strode over from where he'd been discussing things with the landowner. "What is it, Jamie? Thought you went home."

"I did, but this contract came in by email." She handed him the folder. "Thought you should see it right away."

He arched one brow but flipped open the folder. His brows began to furrow as he read the contents. "This could've waited until tomorrow. You didn't need to come all the way out here again."

She rolled her shoulders back, chin up. "Thought you should have it for the morning."

Aidan glanced at Gavin. "Suppose you're right. It was urgent for you to come out here twice in one day."

Jamie punched his shoulder. "Don't be sarcastic with me, Aidan. I was being helpful."

"Why are you checking company emails, anyway? You're on holiday, and Calli's handling everything."

She snagged the inside of her lip with her teeth.

Gavin tried not to smile. Jamie had made up a silly excuse to come back and see him. It was so cute and sweet he wanted to pull her into a bear hug.

"Cannae fool us," Iain said to Jamie. "We all know the real reason you're here, and he's standing right beside me."

Jamie's cheeks turned pink. "Maybe I did want to speak to Gavin. It's none of your business, Iain. Or yours, Aidan."

Her brother and her cousin both smirked.

She flapped her hands at them. "Go away, you dumb galoots."

Iain clapped a hand on Aidan's shoulder, and both men headed off in the direction of the mostly demolished stone wall.

Jamie retreated behind the car, using the Mercedes as a barricade between her and Gavin.

He stalked around the car, coming up behind her.

She spun around and plastered her backside to the driver's door.

Nothing but sex? Sure, he believed that. The way she tried to keep a physical distance between them, in addition to the emotional distance, contradicted her claim. He couldn't resist taking advantage of the opening she'd accidentally given him.

Gavin edged closer and hit her with a suggestive smile. "Hey, babe, what can I do ya for? Or should I say, how long can I do ya for?"

Chapter Eighteen

*J*amie licked her lips, which had suddenly gone dry along with her mouth. With Gavin near enough to touch if she only raised her hand, she couldn't think straight anymore. Her body insisted on warming up, her skin alive with an energy that permeated her right down to the core of her sex. How could he do this to her with one look? By the time he'd her asked how long he could do her for, she'd already been aching for him to do exactly that. Do her. Take her. Shag her upside down and sideways, any way he wanted.

No, no, no. Sex only.

She hiked up her chin and cleared her throat. "I wanted to make sure you'd be there tonight."

It sounded stupid even to her. Why had she traveled all the way out here? Not for the contract. She'd given in to a desperate impulse to see him again.

Gavin's eyes blazed with an unmistakable hunger, and his lips curved into a smoldering expression that melted her insides, especially the nether regions of her body. He inched a touch closer. "Couldn't wait to see me, huh?"

"I—" She floundered for a rational response, but reason had left her a long while ago. Right about the time she'd sworn she wanted nothing but sex from him. Too late to back out even if she'd wanted to. She'd committed to the plan, and besides, he hadn't recanted his statement that he needed space from her. "I was heading this way to, um, visit a friend. Stopped off here to give Aidan the contract."

"Baloney," Gavin said, his voice low and sultry. "You wanted to see me. I'm cool with that."

Cool was the polar opposite of how she felt. Her body had become overheated, her skin sensitized by an odd mixture of chilly air raising the hairs and inner heat racing through her. His big body lingered too close, his molten gaze seared into her. She became acutely aware of his body, of the way sweat pasted his shirt to his skin and accentuated the lines of every muscle. Her attention snagged on the bulge in his jeans. The swelling bulge. She couldn't prevent her tongue from slipping out to wet her lips again.

Gavin groaned with a longing that resonated in his chest. "I love it when you touch yourself that way. Makes me want to lick you exactly the way you're moving your fingers."

She froze, rolling her gaze downward to her own chest. One of her hands had found its way to her breastbone, a hair above the neckline of her blouse. The heel of her hand rested between her breasts while her fingers traced lines up and down her skin. The feathery sensation of her own fingertips heightened her arousal, though she hadn't realized she'd been touching herself. Gavin's presence, the epitome of masculine virility and strength, made her lose control of her own limbs.

"Ah," he purred, smiling with feral satisfaction, "you didn't know you were doing that. Wouldn't you rather I tease you that way?"

Jamie didn't dare speak. It would sound breathless if she did, and he would know how much she wanted him right now. *Bloody eejit, did ye think he couldn't see that already?* Her plan to make him crazed with lust so she could reject him had flown oot the windae along with her bum.

What else could she do? Say something stupid, that was all she could think of. "Sex only. You agreed—"

"I never agreed to that." Gavin sauntered even closer, anchoring his hands on her hips, their weight and warmth a sensual temptation. "It's never just sex with us. I love you, and whenever we have sex, we're always making love. You can say 'sex only' as much as you want, but that won't make it true."

She tried to swallow, but her throat had constricted.

He eased his hands around to her buttocks, molding his strong fingers to her flesh, and tugged to bring her hips into contact with his rigid erection. "You want me. I want you too, so bad I can't think about anything else. No matter how bad I want you, though, it's always more than sex. I know you, I know what you like, I know how to get you hot and how to make you come whenever I want you to." He pinned her to the car, his arousal hard against her belly. "I could make you come for me right here, right now, with Aidan and Iain fifty feet away. I wouldn't even have to take your clothes off. If I want you to come, you'll do it for me."

She fought for breath but couldn't summon more than shallow, quick inhalations. Her bra had grown tight, her nipples rock-hard and straining against the fabric. She burned for him to tear off her shirt and bra, latch his mouth onto her nipple, and suckle the tip until she climaxed.

Instead, she slapped her palms on his chest and said, "Not here."

The breathy tone of her voice sapped the command of its strength. *Damn him.*

He gripped her ass firmly, hoisting her up onto her toes as he rocked her hips forward into his erection. It rubbed against her mound, and even the fabric of her skirt and panties couldn't minimize the sensation. She gasped, her hands fisting in his shirt, unconsciously pulling him closer.

"Mmm, yeah," he rumbled, lowering his face to hers, their mouths millimeters apart. "I like it when you get needy and bossy at the same time. Tell me to stop, then drag me in for a kiss. It's hot, baby, real hot."

"We're not kissing."

"Not yet." He exhaled a heated breath onto her lips. "Say the word, and I'll flip you around, yank down your panties, and fuck you up against the car."

He grazed his lips over hers at the instant he rubbed his shaft into her groin.

She choked back a whimper. *Yes,* she longed to say, *yes, take me like that.* Her voice wouldn't function, and besides, she couldn't give in when he kept saying it was more than sex. She needed to stop this, immediately, and regain her control before they met again tonight. Yes, take back control. That's what she must do.

Gavin dragged his tongue along the seam of her lips.

And every iota of her resolve disintegrated.

He stepped back, robbing her of his hands, his lips, his raging arousal. "See you tonight."

Was he joking? He'd gotten her worked up only to walk away?

Flashing her a wicked grin, he winked. "Sex only."

Before she could muster a scathing retort, he sauntered away from her, seemingly oblivious of the massive bulge in his pants.

She took three long, slow breaths. Straightened her clothes. Smoothed her hair. And climbed back into the car to head home.

Tonight, she would reassert her control. She would.

Your bum's oot the windae again, eh?

Chapter Nineteen

*G*avin rang the doorbell of Dùndubhan and waited. And waited. The sun had set, plunging the world into a darkness broken only by the light positioned above the door and the faint glow of more lights inside the house. The castle. Sheesh, who lived in a freaking castle?

Rory MacTaggart did. Like he was a king or something, looking down on his subjects from the highest floor of the frigging tower.

Gavin groaned. Okay, maybe he did have a weird complex about Rory, about his wealth and his lifestyle. Not jealousy, not exactly. Something more like anxiety.

He had no frigging idea what that meant.

The door swung inward, revealing Jamie.

Gavin somehow clung to a neutral expression even as his cock twitched. She wore a babydoll nightie made of sheer, midnight-blue fabric that billowed around her, its hem barely below her hips. The spaghetti straps that held the nightie up seemed about to tumble off her shoulders. Panels of intricate lace covered her breasts, sort of, though he glimpsed the rosy peaks of her nipples, stiff and jutting against the fabric. Through the gauzy length of the babydoll, he spied matching, minuscule panties as sheer as the nightie, revealing the thatch of cinnamon hairs on her mound.

Jamie leaned her curvy body against the door, waving for him to enter. "Let's go into my bedroom."

He scuffled through the doorway into the vestibule.

She shut the door and sashayed into the hall, angling left toward the dining room.

Gavin couldn't resist admiring her voluptuous hips as they swayed and her round bottom as it moved beneath the flimsy fabric. His mouth watered, and his palms sweated. He hadn't seen her naked in five days. That might explain why he got a raging hard-on every time he came within fifty feet of her and why he'd been having the most erotic dreams of his life. Despite her claim she wanted only sex and her announcement she'd summon him when the mood struck her, she'd been avoiding him. Avoiding intimacy. Avoiding dealing with their problems.

Another irony in this whole mess. For months, he'd avoided intimacy—both the emotional and the physical kind. The more time he spent around Jamie's brothers, the more self-conscious he got and the more difficult it was to get it up in the bedroom. He was finally getting an inkling why her brothers bugged him so much, but he needed to talk it out with his best friend, the only person who understood him completely.

Jamie.

And she wouldn't tolerate conversation.

With Iain's help, Gavin had figured out one thing for sure. He had to cut out the wuss-bag behavior and act like the man Jamie had fallen for eighteen months ago. Act like the man who'd, half jokingly, threatened to murder Aidan for banging his baby sister. The man who'd swept Jamie off her feet.

Sex only with no real intimacy? Screw that idea. He'd proved her wrong five days ago when she tried to keep their encounter impersonal. Still, she refused to give up her lame idea. She left him with one option.

Keep seducing her. Keep forcing her to experience their connection. Keep her in the moment with him at all times, not retreating into her detached vixen persona.

She could keep some of the vixen stuff. He did love her feisty side.

Jamie guided him into her bedroom. She twirled around and fell backward onto the bed, her body sprawled across it and the nightie riding up to reveal a hint of the curly hairs between her thighs, with only a sliver of lacy fabric to cover them. The pinkish light from the bedside lamp sprayed across her golden-brown hair. Her breasts mounded on her chest, plump and succulent, the taut nipples begging to be sucked.

"Well?" she said, wriggling her red-painted toes. "Get to work, Gavin. I called you here for sex, not to have you gawp at me all night."

His cock pulsed. It wanted her. He wanted her. But this sex-only crap had to stop this instant.

Gavin shrugged out of his jacket, tossing it onto the floor. "I know what you think you want. But I also know what you really want. I know you, Jamie, and you can't fool me. I gave you what you really need the last time we were together. You can lie and say it meant nothing, but I know the truth."

"*Bod an Donais.*" She pushed up onto her elbows, and the nightie slipped out of position, allowing one breast to nearly spill out. "Fuck me, Gavin. That's what I want. It's all I want. Hot, screaming sex for twenty minutes, maybe half an hour, and then you leave."

Though her words hit him like a slap to the face, something in her eyes made him stop and study those hazel irises, glimmering in the soft light. Maybe she'd hoped erasing all intimacy and emotion between them would push him to do the right thing, finally. Well, it had worked, he supposed. He'd woken up to the fact he couldn't live without this woman.

No more dafty boy.

He tugged his T-shirt out of his waistband and pulled it off over his head. As the shirt flumped to the floor, he stripped off his sneakers, jeans, and boxers. Naked, he strode to the bed and bent over it to brace his hands at either side of her head, their faces inches apart.

"No," he said.

Her eyebrows and her cute little nose scrunched up. "No? Ye cannae order me to—"

Gavin covered her mouth with his own, silencing her complaint. He raked his lips over her softer, sweeter ones, licking at the seam and nipping at her flesh. She'd gone tense, though her breaths came fast and shallow. When her lips parted, he glided his tongue between them to tease her mouth with light flicks, then he coiled his tongue around hers, slick flesh sliding over slick flesh, and still he didn't touch her with any other part of his body. Only lips. Only tongue. A tiny gasp escaped her lips, and he deepened the kiss with rough strokes of his tongue, catching her exhalation, taking a part of her into him. He plundered her mouth with an animalistic hunger, starved for the taste of her and inflamed by the tickling sensation of her quick breaths gusting out her nostrils onto his skin. He burned to take her but forced himself to hold back.

His dick had gotten so hard, he didn't know how long he could restrain himself.

Until she caved. Until she admitted sex only wasn't what she really wanted.

"Say it," he murmured against her lips.

Jamie made a desperate little noise, halfway between a gasp and a whimper. "Say what?"

"Tell me you want me, not just sex. Admit you want us to talk. You want a relationship, not just a quick wrestling match in the sheets."

"I told you what I need."

He raised his head to gaze down at her, propped on his straight arms. "Tell me the truth, Jamie. Say it now, or I'm walking out that door. I'll come back every day and kiss you into a frenzy, but we won't have sex again until we talk. *Say it.*"

Jamie couldn't tear her focus away from his eyes. Their honey color seemed to glow in the muted lighting. He regarded her in a way he hadn't done in months. With conviction. Certainty. Determination. A hint of tenderness tempered the commanding force of his gaze. Though his erection nudged her belly, hard and thick, he refused to give her what she told him she wanted. Sex. Only sex. Why couldn't he go along with it like any normal man would do? Another man would've been thrilled to have a woman order him to fuck her with no conversation required afterward.

At least, she thought other men would. Since she'd never demanded this from a man before, she had no way of knowing for sure.

Emery had been right that Gavin wouldn't really open up to her unless she plied him with sex first. He'd announced he wanted to talk, after previously announcing he needed time and space from her, but he denied her the one thing she'd sworn she needed—no emotional entanglement, no intimate conversation. After months of avoiding touching her, he'd suddenly shifted back into his old purposeful, irresistible self.

He was confusing the living hell out of her.

Could she trust him not to lose his nerve again? And what about his hostility toward her brothers? None of that had been resolved.

So talk to him, you silly hen, a voice inside urged her.

Not yet. She needed more time to…What? She didn't know anymore.

That kiss. He'd done it on purpose. He'd gotten her so worked up, so turned on and heated up, that she couldn't think. His take-charge attitude had always made her want to rip his clothes off, but when he'd casually stripped naked and bent his muscular body over her, she'd fought a thousand impulses to do naughty things to him. Her body tingled with need, her nipples ached, and the wetness in her sex oozed down the insides of her thighs.

"Sex, please," she said, breathless from the intensity of her arousal. "Talk later. We can talk about whether to talk after we—"

He lunged his head down to nibble at the hollow of her throat. "Mmmm. Say you're done with the sex-only plan, or I'm outta here."

"You're naked, and it's cold outside. You'll catch pneumonia."

When he chuckled, his lips vibrated against her skin. "Thanks for worrying about me, but I'll get dressed before I go." He nuzzled her throat, his breaths hot and sultry. "Besides, I've been working outside all day. Got rained on too, and I survived."

"I'm surprised you took a job with Aidan. He's one of my evil brothers."

"Never said they're evil." His mouth traveled up to her chin, meandering along her jaw. "But I've made peace with Aidan. We're cool."

"What..." Her voice and her thoughts trailed off as he curled his tongue around her earlobe and drew it into his mouth. Her breaths hitched, but she managed to expel words between gasps of involuntary pleasure at his suckling of her flesh. "What kind of work...ah...were you...oh...doing for... mmmm...my brother?"

Gavin raised his face over hers. "Smashing rocks. With a sledgehammer."

She'd seen him at Aidan's job site, but she hadn't known what type of work Gavin was doing. Smashing things? With a sledgehammer? Her mind painted a vivid image of him wielding that tool, muscles rippling, sweat dribbling down his torso. In her fantasy he was, of course, shirtless. She imagined the perspiration droplets rolling down the outlines of his pectoral muscles and her tongue lapping them up, tracing a path up his chest.

"You're so hot for me," he said, his gaze capturing hers, "I can smell it."

She could smell it too. The realization didn't fash her as much as she would've expected.

He closed his eyes and sucked in a deep breath through his nostrils, then let it out while his lips curved into a smile of pure satisfaction. His lids parted, and he drank her in with hooded eyes. "Sweet and musky. Damn, I want to eat you up."

She choked back a pathetic little noise, one triggered by a lust more intense than anything she'd experienced before. Never in her life had she wanted a man this much. Never had she wanted *him* this much. Aye, he'd always been amazing in bed. But tonight, he'd become an unstoppable force luring her down into a warm, silken pool of pleasure.

And he'd barely touched her.

He lowered his body enough to rub his rigid length between her thighs. Somehow, they'd fallen open without her knowledge or consent. His shaft scraped along her cleft, lubricated by the juices her body released in preparation for him. Her panties, so thin and fragile, posed no real barrier. She couldn't help it. She moaned and arched her back, her fingers clenching the covers beneath her.

"Say it," he growled, his cheeks ruddy and his body tight with need.

All those bunched muscles. Ready to move, to act, to consume her body.

"Yes," she almost shouted as the head of his penis nudged her entrance, brushing her silken panties over her flesh. "We'll talk. We'll—oh. We'll do anything you want."

"Anything?" He pushed up on a single arm, straight and taut. With his other hand, he whisked the nightie over her hips, and when she lifted them, he slid the fabric higher until it cleared her shoulders. Tossing the nightie aside, he straddled her. "Better be careful with that promise."

He wouldn't take advantage of her promise, she knew that. Not outside of the bedroom. In bed, he might. And the idea shivered a thrill through her.

"Anything," she gasped as he devoured her nipple. His cheeks caved in from the ardor of his suckling. She tunneled her fingers through his hair. "Please, Gavin. Please."

He crawled down her body, kissing and licking and nibbling as he moved. His hands glided down her arms as slowly as his mouth traveled down her body. His tongue dived into her belly button and flicked side to side. She writhed beneath him, pleading for more with her incoherent noises. How could any woman stay coherent with a man like him torment-ing her body?

With a ravenous groan, he shimmied lower and lower, his hot tongue sampling her skin along the way. His breaths tickled the hairs of her mound, making her back arch and her fingers clench the covers harder. He took hold of her hips and then he moved between her thighs, his mouth poised over her folds. Her clit throbbed, craving his mouth.

She spread her legs wider, her breaths shortening into pants.

He took deliberate breaths, his hooded gaze riveted to her folds, his lips parted. With two fingers, he gently spread her flesh. He puckered his lips to blow a stream of cool air on her slick, burning skin.

He rasped his tongue over her nub.

"Gavin, please, hurry."

"What's the rush?" he said in a low and sensual voice. "We've got all night."

"I'll lose my mind if you donnae—"

He sealed his mouth over her clitoris, whisking his tongue back and forth, scraping his teeth over her flesh. When she bucked her hips, he pressed down with his hands to pin her to the bed. She didn't care how desperate she sounded, moaning and whimpering and begging for more, because his mouth was driving her insane. He lashed his tongue, drew hard on her clit, and released it to drag his tongue down and back up her cleft, then swirled it around and around her hard nub. When he let go of one hip to slip his hand between her thighs and tease her entrance with two fingers, she stopped breathing.

But when he thrust those fingers inside her and his mouth consumed her clitoris, she exploded.

The climax wrenched her entire body, hurling her outside of herself and straight into heaven, the joy of release too powerful to survive. She must've spun right into the clouds of the afterlife, weightless and free, until his lips on her cheek pulled her back into her body. He whispered endearments into her ear, but she couldn't comprehend them.

"Jamie, sweet Jamie," he said, nuzzling her cheek. "My Scottish angel, my heart and soul."

As her breathing slowed and her heart stopped thrashing in her chest, she marveled at the words he murmured to her. Never had he said such loving and unmanly things. He'd called her "babe" a few times, but never his Scottish angel or...What had he said? *My heart and soul.*

His erection raked across her belly.

Though she longed to talk about this change in him, she wanted him inside her even more. They could talk after.

Her heart thudded. She wanted to talk? That orgasm must've short-circuited her brain. Or else it showed her the truth at last.

A wire had tangled itself around her heart lately. Tonight, he had unwound it. Emotion swelled inside her, and she couldn't fight the words any longer. She didn't want to, and she could no longer pretend she needed only sex from him. Giving up her plan, it frightened her. And yet, being with Gavin made her feel safe.

She folded her arms around him and turned her face into his cheek, her mouth near his ear. "I love you."

"I love you too. God, I love you."

He pushed up onto his elbows, shifting his hips until his arousal was nestled between her thighs. She reached down to touch it, but he grabbed her wrist and held it above her head.

"Uh-uh-uh," he said, his lips kinked into a sensual smile, his gold eyes smoldering. "We're doing this my way."

"Then do it already."

He rubbed his cock into her cleft, between her folds.

She arched into him, her mouth falling open.

The hand on her wrist shifted, and he threaded his fingers through hers, clasping her hand while he covered her open mouth with his. Tongues twining. Teeth clashing. Never had he kissed her this way, so deep and carnal it made her sex clench. He chafed his shaft up and down her flesh, his balls grazing her mound, and she gasped into his mouth.

He pulled his hips back and thrust inside her body.

The fullness of him, the sweet pressure of his shaft inside her, stole her breath. She dug her nails into his back, slung her legs around his hips, and silently pleaded for more.

Without relinquishing her mouth, he pumped his hips, driving his length deep only to withdraw until the tip alone lingered inside her. Over and over he drove into and abandoned her body as her breasts rubbed against his chest and he penetrated her mouth in sync with the movements of his hips. *Faster*, she commanded in her mind, unable to speak with his mouth consuming hers. As if he read her mind, he plowed into her faster, harder, bouncing her on the bed.

Another orgasm struck with stunning swiftness, wrenching her body as spasms undulated through her sex, clamping around him even while he kept pounding into her. He swallowed the cry that erupted out of her.

He tore his mouth away at the instant he came apart inside her, throwing his head back to shout a hoarse, wordless cry. The pulsing of his release made her come harder, and she clung to him through the waves of shattering pleasure until he collapsed on top of her, gasping for air. With his chest plastered to hers, she felt his heart pounding as fast as her own.

"Jamie, sweet Jamie." He rolled to the side, hugging her to him. "I want to marry you."

Her heart soared—but crashed down to earth when he spoke again.

"But I can't."

Chapter Twenty

Gavin watched Jamie's eyes narrow and her lips compress. She tried to push away from him, to wriggle out of his embrace, but he held her fast. She needed to understand, and he would not let her run away this time.

"Listen," he said, tunneling a hand into her hair to grasp her nape. "Don't get upset until I've explained, okay? Listen for a minute."

Though her lips puckered, and she hissed a breath out her nostrils, she nodded once.

He gazed into her eyes, determined not to mess up this time. "I've got problems. I know that, but I don't understand why. Thought I was over my first marriage, thought I'd gotten past my parents dying, but I guess I haven't, not really. Didn't think Calli marrying Aidan and moving across an ocean bothered me, but I was wrong about that too. I don't know why that bothers me. It's not Aidan, I'm cool with him. It's…Shit. I don't know, but I have to figure it out before I can marry you. Wouldn't be fair to drag you into my mess."

Jamie's lips relaxed, but she still wore a tense expression. "I'm already in your mess. Hip deep and getting dragged down."

Her words, spoken in a soft voice, smacked him like a brick in the face. She felt dragged down? Christ, no wonder she was hanging out with her douchebag ex. A rich guy who had his shit together must've seemed like a breath of fresh air.

"I get why you feel that way," he said. "I'm sorry. I never meant to get you stuck in this quicksand my life has turned into. Everything was great in the beginning and for so long after that. I don't know why things changed, but I have to figure it out. And I can't do it alone."

Still trapped in his arms, mashed to his body, she couldn't turn away but could only avert her eyes. "You're going back to America, aren't you? To get therapy or whatever help it is you need."

"No. I'm staying put." He swept a lock of hair from her face with one finger. "I love you. I'm not giving up on us until you tell me it's over, for good and forever. Weird as it is, Emery and Iain both helped me see what I need to do. Leaving you was not the answer. Sex only is not the answer. I need help, but not from strangers."

She turned her eyes up to his, hers glistening with the start of tears.

The sight of it made his heart hurt.

He took her face in both his hands. "I need your help. I need you, Jamie, nobody else."

She squashed her trembling lips between her teeth. "What can I do?"

"Not sure. We can figure it out together, okay?" He touched a kiss to the tip of her nose. "If you still want me around. I know this is a lot to ask—"

"Of course I want you." Her smile was faint and shaky, but her voice sounded solid. "But I need something from you too."

"Anything. Just say it."

"Honesty." She sealed his lips with two fingers when he tried to speak. "You made me realize my sex-only idea was stupid, and I love you too much for anything between us to be casual. I'm officially canceling that plan. But you need to tell me the truth, all of it, about your past and your feelings, everything. I know men don't like to talk about things like that, but we can't make a future together if you won't share your life with me. All of it. Not only the good parts. I'll do the same for you."

This was it, he realized. The pivotal moment. She'd given up her goofy plan for him and asked only one thing in return. If he couldn't give her what she needed, they didn't have any future.

His gut wrenched, and his mouth went dry, but he told her the truth. "I want to do that, but I don't think it'll be easy for me."

"All I'm asking is for you to try. Give it your best shot, for us." Her eyes captivated him, so clear and bright, the tears gone. "Can you do that, Gavin?"

"Yes." And he meant it with every fiber of his being. "I might screw up again, but I'll try my damnedest not to."

"Good." She feathered her soft lips over his. "That's all I need tonight."

Though he exhaled a gusty breath, relief washing through him, a sliver of icy doubt stayed lodged in his chest. Never in his life had he opened up to anyone, not completely, not about his deepest fears and most painful experiences. It might be excruciating. It might be exhausting. It might convince Jamie she belonged with somebody else, somebody not messed up beyond repair.

Not beyond repair. He couldn't think that way. No matter how much this hurt, he would give Jamie what she'd asked for.

He would do anything for her.

"Thank you," he said, then he kissed her, tender and slow. "I don't deserve a second chance with you, but I'm damn grateful you gave me one."

"You do deserve it." She laid a hand on his cheek. "And I know you won't let me down again."

Gavin flipped onto his back, scrutinizing the ceiling. "Would you rather I leave and come back tomorrow?"

"What? No." She gave his chest a light slap. "Don't be a bleeding bampot."

He'd spent enough time around the MacTaggarts to know she was calling him bat-shit crazy. And he supposed he had been acting that way. "Should we start talking yet?"

The last word mutated into a big yawn.

Jamie snuggled up to him, her head on his chest. "Tomorrow. I'm sure Aidan had you working hard all day breaking rocks."

"That was Iain's idea." Gavin pulled the covers up over them. "Aidan would've let us use the backhoe, but Iain decided backbreaking work would do me good."

"Seems like it did." She pressed her lips to his chest. "Good night, Gavin."

"Good night, Jamie." He kissed the top of her head.

He felt her body slacken against him and heard her breathing grow shallower. He stayed awake long after she drifted off, content to have her with him but dreading the trials to come. He'd wanted this, to hash it all out with his best friend and best girl, but the reality of it knotted his gut.

Confess everything to Jamie. That would be hard enough.

Get in good with Lachlan and Rory…That would be his epic journey to redemption.

If the two Macs didn't slay him.

The sunrise glowed behind Jamie's eyes as she lay snuggled against Gavin in bed, half awake. Lying here with him while he slept felt so nice she didn't want to move or open her eyes. She rubbed her cheek on his firm, warm chest, loving the scent of his skin and the softness of it compared to the hardness of his muscles. They were back together. Warmth bloomed in her chest at the realization. She hadn't wanted to break up with him in the first place, but his stunt with the credit card had hurt her more than she'd been able to admit even to herself. His statements about her brothers, though, that had devastated her. How could she be with someone who despised her family?

Her sex-only plan had been spurred by her fears Gavin might turn out to be like Trevor. He was nothing like Trevor, and at last she'd accepted that fact. Maybe Rory had done her a favor by inviting Trevor to the Halloween party. Confronting her ex had, oddly, pushed her to confront fears she'd sublimated for too long.

Now, if she could give Gavin a similar cleansing experience...

When had everything turned so wrong?

Gavin got along well with Catriona and Fiona. It was only her brothers who brought out something in him she still didn't understand. Of course, it didn't help that Rory glared at Gavin constantly or that Lachlan treated him like an invader in the MacTaggart clan's kingdom.

If she was completely honest about it, she had to admit her two oldest brothers hadn't been welcoming to Gavin. Lachlan had once told Gavin, "You're in our country now, laddie, best show a little respect." Jamie knew—or maybe hoped—Lachlan had been joking. As the oldest and most overbearing sibling, he often made jokes with a serious expression on his face, especially if he wanted to intimidate the other person. Rory did the same thing, but he'd learned it from Lachlan.

She peeled her lids apart to gaze up at Gavin's sleeping face. His lips had curved up in a slight smile as if he dreamed of sweet things. She propped her chin on his chest. Their relationship had started out so well. Perfect, actually, in spite of Aidan getting a wee bit peevish about the speed at which things had progressed. Like Aidan had any right to be peevish about that. He'd moved into Calli's guest bedroom after a few days and seduced her not long after. When Jamie had arrived for a visit, Aidan had moved into Calli's bedroom to give Jamie the guest room.

Her thoughts rewound to eighteen months ago when she'd first seen Gavin Douglas. Aidan and Calli had just brought her home from the airport to Calli's house in the woods of Michigan's Upper Peninsula. Calli's puppies, Misty and Mandy, had glommed onto Jamie the instant she walked into the house. Since she'd always loved animals, Jamie had knelt to let them lick and climb on her the way puppies did.

Then the sliding glass doors had opened, and Gavin strode into the house.

Her pulse quickened at the sight of him, six foot one and muscular, standing straight and proud, those pale-gold eyes surveying the situation. When he spotted the puppies assaulting Jamie with their love, his brows had furrowed and his mouth fell open a crack.

She rose, smoothing her skirt, and turned to Gavin. "You must be Calli's brother. I'm Jamie, Aidan's sister."

Gavin's furrowed brow ironed out, and he smiled the goofiest smile she'd ever seen. He hustled over to her, nearly tripping over the puppies in his determination to clasp her hand in his bigger one for a lingering handshake.

And oh yes, Aidan watched from a few meters away with his mouth crimping and his eyes narrowing.

"Hey," Gavin said, a touch breathless, his hand still around hers. "Nice to, uh, meet you. I'm Gavin. Douglas. Calli's brother, Gavin Douglas."

Jamie grinned, delighted by his nervousness. Big, strong men rarely let their nerves show. Calli had told her Gavin was a former Marine, so she would've expected him to be stoic. Instead, he grinned right back at her, a bit lopsided, and maintained dominion over her hand.

She loved the feel of his callused, powerful hand enveloping hers.

Aidan rushed forward to seize her wrist and wrest her hand free of Gavin's. Through gritted teeth, he said, "Let me show you to your room."

She let Aidan haul her away but half turned to flash a smile at Gavin, who flashed her that lopsided grin again. As her bossy brother dragged her down the hallway, she heard Calli tell Gavin, "Gee, Gav, looks to me like you're going gushy over Aidan's sister."

And Jamie had giggled, so softly only Aidan heard it.

Her brother, of course, scowled about it.

She'd later learned Gavin was staying in a hunting shack in the woods not far from the house.

For the next few days, she'd seen Gavin only when Calli and Aidan were around, the three of them spending the days together. Every night, Aidan and Calli would retreat into the bedroom they shared, and Jamie would hole up in the guest room and dream about Gavin Douglas's muscles and his smile and his sexy voice.

One day, she and Gavin had taken the puppies for a walk without Aidan or Calli. That's when it had happened. Their first kiss.

Jamie had been holding onto Mandy's leash, the smaller puppy easier for her to handle. Bigger Misty had been pulling on her leash, half dragging Gavin down the trail through the woods. They'd stopped for a rest in a small clearing. The puppies flopped down in the grass, panting but smiling in the way only dogs could. A patch of the bluest-blue sky she'd ever seen was visible above their heads, and a breeze stirred the leaves of the trees so they sizzled like a skillet of bacon.

"I'm starved," Jamie announced, her stomach grumbling from her thoughts of frying meat. "Should we go back to the house?"

Gavin aimed his golden eyes at her, raking his gaze up and down her body. His tongue flicked out to moisten his lips. "In a minute. Something I gotta do first. Can't wait one more minute for it."

"For what?"

He strode up to her, the dog leash firmly in his left hand, and slung his right arm around her waist to pull her snug against his body. "For this."

At the instant his mouth covered hers, she stopped breathing. Her pulse raced. His lips explored hers tenderly at first, then pressed hard against her lips, stealing her breath and sending her pulse into overdrive. Her eyes drifted shut, her body softened against him. When he lapped at the seam of her mouth, she opened up to him without hesitation, relishing the sensation of his tongue rasping over hers.

She moaned, grasping his upper arms.

He plunged deeper, claiming her mouth as if he'd never relinquish the contact, swirling his tongue around hers, teasing the roof of her mouth. His hand wandered to her behind, cupping her in a possessive way that had her wriggling her hips against him.

The dog leash tumbled from her grasp.

Jamie pushed away from Gavin, lunging down to snag the leash. "Oh! I almost let Calli's baby get away from me."

"Nah," Gavin said. "Mandy wouldn't run off without Misty."

Her cheeks felt hot. Her whole body, in fact, felt hot—and achy in the most wonderful way.

Gavin's mouth slid into a sensual smile. "Why don't we try that again?"

"Um..." She struggled to catch her breath, but he lingered centimeters away from her, destroying any hope she might've had of regaining her composure. "We should get back to the house. Calli will be wondering if we've kidnapped her puppies."

They had returned to the house then, though Gavin held her hand all the while.

Later that day, a trip to a gift shop had left Aidan mildly annoyed because, according to him, she and Gavin had "flirted like teenagers and almost had a poke right there on the floor." He was exaggerating. Maybe she and Gavin had flirted, but that was all. Grinning and touching each other's hands did not equate to having sex on the floor of a tourist shop.

Besides, Aidan actually was having a poke at Gavin's sister on a nightly basis. He had no call to criticize Jamie's flirtations with Calli's brother.

That's when the unfortunate incident happened.

Calli and Aidan had taken off for a night at a motel to have "private" time. Though Jamie and Gavin could've done anything they wanted that night, they'd done nothing sexier than holding hands. Since their first kiss, they'd had little time alone to try that again. Jamie had wanted to try. Badly. She'd begun to wonder if Gavin didn't.

Until the morning after their night alone in Calli's house. He'd slept in the hunting shack, despite Jamie suggesting he could sleep in Calli's room. He'd made a strange face at the suggestion and said, "She and Aidan are—well, you know. In that room."

Having sex, he'd meant. It made him uncomfortable to think of his baby sister enjoying carnal relations with anyone, but especially with Aidan.

After breakfast, Jamie and Gavin sat down on the sofa to talk. The chatting lasted about two minutes. He'd leaned in close, his breaths ghosting over her lips, and said, "I think it's damn well time we tried that again."

She knew what he meant. Her skin tightened at the suggestion, and a tingling in her scalp spread down to her breasts.

"Aye," she said. "We should."

He scooted closer, stretching one arm across the sofa's back behind her. She angled sideways to face him, her knees bent and her belly quivering with excitement. Their one kiss had left her burning for more.

Gavin clasped her upper arm gently, urging her to lean in as he slanted toward her.

Their lips touched.

A spark—she swore to God it felt like a real spark—crackled on her mouth, shooting straight down her body through her breasts and down to her sex. A breath rushed out of her, and her lips opened. He parted his own lips to inhale as if drawing her breath into him, and he ghosted his mouth over hers, back and forth, his breaths a whisper on her skin. Her eyes drifted closed, anticipation a heady current arcing through her. His fingers tightened ever so slightly on her arm. She sagged toward him, and her hands contacted his chest, firm and warm beneath his shirt. Her fingers curled into his flesh when he flicked his tongue out to tease her top lip.

He sealed his mouth over hers.

She sighed against his lips, sliding one hand up to his neck, and higher, to his nape. He slipped his tongue between her lips to torment her with slow, gentle glides that had her moaning and mashing her breasts to his chest, thrusting her hand up into his hair to cradle the back of his head, even as his exploration of her mouth grew more heated, more passionate. She opened wider for him, and he ravished her with an abandon that stole her breath, her thoughts, her inhibitions.

The hand on her arm found her breast. He scraped his thumb over her nipple.

She gasped into his mouth, shocked by a jolt of raw pleasure.

The front door burst inward.

Jamie and Gavin jumped at the same time, their lips torn from each other. Jamie flung a hand up to her mouth, partly to hide her swollen lips, partly in shock at the thunderous expression on Aidan's face. Never in her life had she seen easygoing Aidan so upset.

Gavin's look of phony innocence did not ease Aidan's anger.

Here in her bedroom in Rory's castle, Jamie touched her lips. They tingled from the memory of that day. Yes, Aidan had been angry, but he'd mostly been embarrassed to have caught his baby sister "sucking face" with Calli's brother. That's what Calli had called it when Aidan stormed into the house and she tried to calm him down. Jamie stifled a laugh when she remembered the events after Aidan and Calli walked in on her and Gavin. Aidan's not-so-righteous indignation had crumbled when Calli accidentally referred to her house as Aidan's home too. Calli's flub had changed the tack of the conversation, steering it away from Jamie and Gavin and their make-out session on the sofa.

The interplay between Aidan and Calli had been entertaining, but also enlightening. Jamie learned a lot about man-woman relationships by watching her brothers interact with, and bollocks it up with, various women. Now that her brothers had found their fairy-tale loves with Calli, Erica, and Emery, Jamie tried to learn from how they interacted with their wives compared to how they'd treated them before they admitted they'd fallen head over heels for the Americans.

Lachlan had broken Erica's heart, but she forgave him because he finally shared his secrets with her, secrets he had never told anyone else. Even Jamie didn't know what drove Lachlan to fear love. She did know, because everyone had heard the story a dozen times or more, that Lachlan literally fell to his knees and begged Erica to take him back.

Aidan had told Calli he would win her heart, and he had, but Calli then broke his heart, terrified to trust anyone after being stuck in a marriage of convenience for so long. Aidan forgave her because she finally opened up to him and shared her fears.

Rory had seduced Emery into a marriage of convenience but refused to love her, then let her walk out on him rather than express his true feelings. Emery forgave him because he finally opened up to her about his past marriages, telling her things no one else had ever known or would ever know. He'd nearly stripped naked in the town square of Loch Fairbairn to show Emery he loved her enough to risk any sort of humiliation to win her back.

Jamie was starting to see a pattern here. Her brothers and their wives got together, for real and for good, by opening up about their pasts and their fears. She needed Gavin to do the same for her, and she needed to do the same for him. The idea of talking about her time with Trevor, of ripping open those old wounds, shot a spike of cold straight into her chest.

She couldn't ask Gavin to expose his deepest fears and secrets if she wouldn't do the same.

"Why are you frowning?"

Gavin's voice snapped her out of her thoughts, and she started. "What?"

Eyes half open and sleepy, he dragged his fingertip over her bottom lip. "You're frowning. Why?"

"Thinking about the road ahead."

He yawned noisily, blinked several times, and then pulled her up and onto his body, their faces aligned. One large hand settled on her buttock while the other fanned over her back. "It'll be a bumpy one, but we can get through it. I'll do whatever it takes to keep you."

She squirmed when his hand on her bottom kneaded her flesh. Flashing him a saucy grin, she said, "Would you strip naked in the town square in Loch Fairbairn?"

His mouth crimped in a half-repressed smirk. "The way I heard it, Rory didn't actually get down to the buff."

"Not the point."

"I know." He swirled his palm on her back. "I'd strip naked and streak through Inverness if that's what it takes. Hell, I'd even hug Rory and smack a wet one on his cheek."

Jamie laughed. "Rory would blow his top."

"Totally worth it, even if he skelps me."

"Skelp? I didn't teach you that word."

He pinched her behind, making her squeak. "I learned that one from Iain."

"Should I worry about you making friends with Iain? He's a notorious rogue."

"You called him a gentleman that night when you showed up to blow me."

Though her cheeks warmed at the memory of that night, she wasn't embarrassed. Remembering it made her want to try that again. Instead, she answered the question implicit in his statement. "Iain is a gentleman, mostly, but he has a checkered past."

"Seducing every woman in Loch Fairbairn? I've heard that rumor."

"Might be more than a rumor." She poked his side. "Don't get any ideas of following in his footsteps either."

"No way," Gavin said, hugging her to him, his hands on her shoulder blades, "I've got all the woman I can handle. And I've got an important question for you. What should we do today?"

Jamie tried to shrug but couldn't, what with her body crushed to his. "Donnae know."

"We're spending time together, for the next few weeks. Lots of time." He swept a hand up to her nape, easing her mouth closer to his. "We can do anything you want."

"Anything?" she breathed against his lips.

"Yes. Anything."

She pretended to consider the options, tapping her tongue on the bottoms of her top teeth. "Bicycling."

He pulled a face. "Biking? That gives men cancer of the balls, you know."

"No one knows that for sure. Besides, you can get a special seat to reduce the possible risk." She slid a hand down to his hip, inching it toward his groin, though her body blocked her from reaching the part of him she longed to fondle. "Do you think I'd let you endanger my favorite part of your anatomy?"

He grunted when she ground her body against his erection. "Ah...You win. Biking it is."

"Thank you, Gavin."

"Can't deny you anything when you're on top of me."

She pushed up so she sat astride him, hands on his chest. "Ahm needing to have mah way with ye."

"I did say we'd do anything you want today."

And they did—starting in bed.

Chapter Twenty-One

They drove into Loch Fairbairn in Rory's Mercedes and rented two bicycles at a shop in town. Gavin liked the quaint village in spite of knowing everyone here treated Rory like a superhero, the solicitor who saved them from legal disasters, often without charging a cent. Or a shilling. Or whatever they called it here in Scotland. As part of his plan to get in good with the Three Macs, Gavin kept reminding himself not to grimace every time a village resident waxed poetic about the awesome, amazing, godlike Rory MacTaggart.

Okay, Gavin could admit he still had a problem with Rory. Couldn't explain what it was yet, not completely, but he'd come to the conclusion it wasn't jealousy. He didn't want Rory's life. But sometimes—yeah, fine, often—he felt a weird kind of inferiority complex about Jamie's brother. It didn't help that she worshiped Rory.

Despite his initial skepticism about a bike ride, he found himself relaxing and enjoying it as he and Jamie pedaled their way around the village and then out along a bike trail that skirted the perimeter of the loch that had given the town its name.

"What does the name mean?" Gavin asked while they coasted along a straight stretch, the glassy loch on the right, and on their left, the hulking shape of the mountain that backed Rory's property.

"The name of the loch or the mountain?"

"I meant the loch, but yeah, the mountain too."

Jamie flashed him a smile so sweet it made his heart clench. "Fairbairn means beautiful child."

"And the mountain's name?"

"Beann Dealgach? I think it means mountain of the thorny place."

Gavin tried but failed to stifle a snorting laugh. "Figures Rory would live at the bottom of a mountain called the thorny place."

Jamie frowned, though for only half a second.

"Sorry," Gavin said. "Old habits are hard to bump off, even with a howitzer."

They continued in silence, admiring the scenery, savoring this time in each other's company without anyone else around. When a cute little bird flew by near Jamie's shoulder, she grinned and laughed in a tinkly way that made Gavin's belly do dumb things. He wanted to kiss her but couldn't do it while they were careening down a gently sloping hill.

"Could we stop for a while?" Gavin asked. He nodded toward the soft-sided cooler strapped to her bike. "My stomach's growling for that lunch you packed us."

"Sure," she said with another smile, this one softer and twinkling in her eyes.

They veered off the path onto a grassy area under a stand of trees and propped their bikes against the largest of the elms. In the shade of the tree, Gavin spread out the fleece blanket they'd brought. He lowered his body onto the blanket, legs outstretched, and patted the fleece in invitation.

Jamie sat cross-legged beside him. Her jeans hugged her curvy figure, and the bright-yellow top she wore clung to her breasts without being too tight. He loved knowing how those breasts fit nicely in his hands, not too big and not too small. Her hair spilled over her shoulders, and he longed to slide his fingers into the silky waves.

While she brought out the food items in the cooler, Jamie asked, "Do you have PTSD?"

"Jeez, you could beat around that bush a little bit first."

"It's time for honesty, Gavin." She handed him a sandwich inside a plastic bag, gazing steadily into his eyes. "That means being direct. Do you have PTSD?"

"No. I was screened for it when I came home from Afghanistan, but I'm okay." He unzipped the plastic bag and extricated the sandwich from it, eying the food with less interest than a moment ago. The time had come to share uncomfortable stuff with Jamie. His stomach went sour, so he set the sandwich on his thigh. "I saw stuff over there, watched my friends get blown up, but I dealt with it. Helped I had an awesome family at home to keep me grounded."

"Your parents were still alive then?" Her tone remained mild, her expression too. She plucked up a plastic bag and brought out a sandwich.

"My parents died after I came home." He picked at the crust of his sandwich. "When I was overseas, I Skyped with Calli and my parents almost every day. They'd send me care packages too. Calli was in college then, but she always made time to chat or text or email. She even wrote me actual letters, it was so sweet."

"Your sister loves you very much." Jamie gave him a kind smile. "You really are her hero."

He considered his sandwich, squirming because he suddenly couldn't get comfortable. "I don't deserve to be her hero. I let Calli down so badly. If I'd sucked it up and kept it together, she would never have married that creep Rade."

"She doesn't blame you."

"Well, she should."

Jamie took a dainty bite of her sandwich and chewed it up before speaking again, though her gaze never wavered from him. "Have you spoken to Calli about this?"

"Sort of."

"I'm fluent in Gavin-speak," Jamie said in a lightly teasing tone. "I know that means you haven't told Calli how you feel."

"I'm a guy, what do you expect?" He focused on the sandwich balanced on his thigh, unable to meet her gaze and see the sympathy and concern in her eyes. He nabbed the empty plastic bag and crumpled it in his hand. "I'd rather not talk about my sister anymore."

"Aye, you'd rather not." She set down her sandwich and wriggled her butt to get closer to him. When she leaned in, waves of her hair coasted over his cheek. "We need to talk about all of it. Calli, your parents, your wife, my brothers. Everything."

Gavin bit off a big mouthful of his sandwich, gnawing on it as an excuse not to get into this discussion. Ham and cheese with dill pickle and spicy mayonnaise was his favorite, but today, it tasted like cardboard. She was right. Ignoring the problems had only made things worse. He had to deal with all of it head-on.

He swallowed the bite of food, but it hit his stomach like a cold stone.

"Okay," he said, returning the sandwich to his thigh. "You're right. We need to talk about it, but I've never been good at, you know, that opening-up-and-sharing crap."

"Maybe you'd have an easier time of it if you stopped calling it 'that opening-up-and-sharing crap.' If you really want our relationship to work, you have to tell me everything."

"I get that, I do." He scrutinized the grass between his feet. His gut twisted, his stomach boiled with acid despite the cold lump inside it. "Calli tried to get me to talk about this stuff years ago, right after our parents died. I couldn't do it then, and I'm not sure I can do it today."

"You're not talking to your sister. This is me, the woman you say you love." She laid her hand over his where it rested on his thigh, where his fingers curled into his flesh. "If Rory could tell Emery about what happened with his first three wives, things none of the rest of us know, then you can tell me about this."

He bristled at the mention of Rory, and a snarky comment rose in his throat. Gavin bit it back. Much as he hated it every time Jamie used her brothers as examples of perfect boyfriend behavior, snapping at her about it wouldn't help anything.

Pulling in a deep breath, he tried to fortify himself for the ordeal ahead.

He focused on their hands, his beneath hers, warmed by her soft skin. Could she understand if he told her? She'd never lost anyone. He was glad she didn't have to go through that, but it made this harder to explain. Sharing his weakness, admitting to being a messed-up jerk who abandoned his little sister...He didn't want Jamie to see him that way.

Gavin shook off her hands. "Isn't that enough for today?"

Jamie snapped bolt upright. "Enough? You haven't told me anything."

"Told you how I bailed on my sister. You think that was easy to say?"

Her shoulders relaxed, her mouth too, but she still seemed unhappy. "No, of course not. And I appreciate you sharing that with me, I do. But you said yourself it's not the root of what's going on with you. Please tell me the rest."

Gavin averted his gaze to the loch, his throat suddenly tight.

"Please," Jamie said. "It's important, Gavin, important for us."

She was right, and he knew it.

His gut hurt like it had razor wire twisted around it. His mouth had gone dry, but his hands were clammy.

Jamie splayed a palm on his cheek, her fingertips tickling his ear.

He couldn't look at her. Couldn't move. Couldn't hear anything except the pounding of his pulse in his ears.

She spread her other palm across the opposite cheek and exerted the lightest pressure necessary to encourage him to turn his face toward her. When their eyes met, she gazed at him with a love and compassion that tore at his heart.

"Please tell me," she said, her voice soft and sweet.

He pulled in a shaky breath. "After our parents died, I abandoned Calli. She needed me, and I ran away."

"I'm sure you're exaggerating."

"Listen, I didn't just abandon her emotionally. I ran away to Detroit." He shut his eyes, knowing Jamie might not be so understanding once she heard the rest. "Leanne, my wife, she tried to talk me out of it, but I had to get away from everything, I couldn't deal with it. I begged Leanne to come with me to Detroit. I had a friend there, somebody I served with, and he let us stay in his house while he was visiting family in Florida. I didn't even call Calli for a month. By the time I bothered to go home, two months after the accident, she'd already dealt with everything. I didn't find out until last year she'd married that creep Rade so he would pay all the bills that fell in her lap after our parents died."

Jamie withdrew one hand but kept the other on his cheek.

He leaned into her touch, grateful for the support. She had always supported him, in every way, even when he strung her along for eighteen months only to botch his proposal. He had to keep talking, to help her understand—to help him understand. The more he said, the more he got the feeling his parents' deaths had affected him more than he'd wanted to admit.

For Jamie, for himself, he forged ahead. "I'd been back for eight months when the accident happened. One minute my parents were here, the next they were gone. No warning. No reason for it. Dad lost control of the car, nobody knew why, and they slammed into a tree. Died instantly. It was a total shock, like getting sucker punched and thrown off a cliff. I mean, I can't even explain how I felt right after I heard about it. Numb. Off balance. Kept thinking it wasn't real, and I'd wake up any second to find out everything was okay. But it wasn't."

Jamie stroked his skin with her fingers, her palm still flat on his cheek. "I'm so sorry, Gavin."

"We got another shock after that. Turned out my dad got laid off, and he and my mom had been on their way to Wausau for a job interview when the accident happened." Gavin closed his eyes, wishing the warmth of Jamie's hand could banish the coldness of the memories, but it couldn't. "They'd been in debt, big time. Never told me or Calli. They must've thought they'd get things sorted out, and we'd never need to hear about it. All that debt...They were behind on their mortgage payments too, so the house had to be sold. I wanted to help pay off the debts, and Leanne agreed we should give Calli all the money we had in our savings account. It wasn't enough. I had no idea what Calli did to settle those debts."

"She chose not to tell you. It wasn't your fault you didn't know."

"Yes it was." He opened his eyes, boring his gaze into hers. "I'm her big brother. I should've taken charge and protected her. All Calli told me was she found a way, and I was too selfishly caught up in my own grief to ask questions. She married a man she didn't love, got handcuffed to him for five years, all to pay off our parents' debts. For years, my baby sister was terrified of getting arrested for marriage fraud and I had no frigging clue. I didn't want to see it. Calli should hate me. I failed her."

Jamie combed her fingers through his hair. "That's not what Calli says. She understood why you couldn't handle things. She feels guilty for not taking the time to help you through the ordeal."

Gavin jerked his head back. "Calli what? No, that's crazy. Why would she feel guilty?"

Jamie closed her hand over his. "She never told you she felt that way, did she? Oh Gavin, you and your sister need to have an honest discussion. You're both holding on to guilt for things that weren't your fault."

"Did she use the word ordeal? I mean, did she really think my problems were worse than hers?"

"Talk to Calli." Jamie touched her lips to his. "I think it will help both of you."

Sure, talking to his sister sounded easier than making friends with Rory, but it wasn't. He loved Calli, but they'd never been best friends. He hadn't known she got roped into a green-card marriage. He hadn't known that was how she paid off her student loans and the rest of the debts. Gavin had given her everything he had in the bank, but it hadn't been enough. And like the coward he was, he'd wired her the money instead of going home to help her out.

"Tell me about your wife," Jamie said.

Oh yeah, there was another subject he didn't want to get into—especially right after he'd confessed to being a total jerk and a loser. He evaded the question the only way he could think of, by asking Jamie one.

"Later," he said. "First, how about a little quid pro quo? What's the deal with you and Trevor?"

She yanked her hand away. "Ahmno interested in Trevor."

"Not what I was asking." Gavin slanted forward, planted a hand on the ground beside her hip, and stared into her hazel eyes. "You were serious about him. What happened? And why didn't you ever tell me you'd been engaged before?"

Chapter Twenty-Two

*J*amie averted her gaze to the loch, hoping the glassy surface and the dark waters beneath would entrance her so she wouldn't have to answer Gavin's question. This unusually warm fall day had seemed like the perfect opportunity to spend more time with him, to talk about their problems, to reach some kind of conclusion about their future together. Naturally, he had to bring up the one topic she did not want to discuss.

After everything he'd confessed to her a moment ago, how could she not lay bare her own secrets? She'd avoided this topic for eighteen months, going so far as to omit her relationship with Trevor from any discussions of her past.

"You can tell me," Gavin said, sounding as sincere as he looked. "Come on, please, trust me. I'm not mad you didn't tell me, but I'd like to know why."

Oh, when he gave her that look and spoke in that voice, she wanted to cuddle up on his lap like a puppy and let him rub her belly all day long. Let him soothe away her fears. Let him make her forget they had any problems to sort out.

"I didn't tell you," she said, speaking slowly, the only way she could keep her voice calm, "because I'm ashamed of it. Ashamed of what I became for him."

Gavin didn't speak. He listened, with no anger or disappointment evident on his face, nothing but empathy visible there.

His understanding only made her feel worse.

She folded her hands on her lap, fingers woven together, and concentrated on her hands while she spoke. "I've never told anyone what happened with me and Trevor. Not even Cat or Fiona. Nobody knows. They all think

I got bored with Trevor and ended things. I can't blame them for thinking it. I used to say I wanted to fall in love at every opportunity until I finally found my Prince Charming." She huffed at her own idiocy. "Silly and self-centered, isn't it?"

"No, not at all." Gavin reached out to touch her knee but pulled his hand away before making contact. "You told me the same thing when we first met. I loved the way you were so open to love, not afraid at all. I kind of envied that about you."

Though she kept her head down, she swung her gaze up to peek at him through a fall of her hair. "Why would you envy that? I play with men, knowing full well I'll never really love any of them."

"Baloney. You're the sweetest, most loving person I've ever known."

"Except for Calli." Was that a hint of bitterness in her voice? She couldn't be jealous of Gavin's relationship with his sister. Jamie loved Calli like they were sisters too.

Gavin tugged at his shirt collar. "Let's revisit that subject later. I want to know about Trevor."

Though he still spoke with a gentle tone, he'd tensed his jaw, almost gritting his teeth. After a second, he relaxed with a visible effort, blowing out a breath. She couldn't decide if he was angry about her Calli comment or anxious about hearing the story of her time with Trevor Langley.

Maybe both.

Jamie couldn't look at him when she spoke. "I met Trevor five and a half years ago. He came to Scotland on holiday to celebrate graduating university. We ran into each other at the store when I was buying lip balm and he was looking for sunscreen. I showed him where to find it, and we got to talking. He was charming and clever, attractive and well-spoken. Of course I wanted to fall in love with him. He seemed like a prince straight out of a fairy tale. He even had a title, Sir Trevor Langley."

"Seriously? The English Ass is titled. Figures."

"English Ass?"

"That's the title I gave him. It's way more appropriate." Gavin tickled her cheek with his fingertip. "You could've been Mrs. Sir Langley."

"I would've been Lady Langley, but I didn't care about that." She decided to ignore the slight growl in his voice when he spoke Trevor's title or his name. The English Ass, as Gavin had named him, enjoyed lording his title over everyone who didn't have a title. Never mind that as a baronet he wasn't even a member of the peerage. He still felt superior about it.

"Go on," Gavin said. "You can tell me about Sir Smiles-A-Lot."

The tiniest laugh bubbled out of her. Gavin's creativity in assigning derogatory nicknames to Trevor made her happy. How strange.

"After three weeks together," Jamie said, "I told Trevor I loved him. He said he felt the same. Since he'd overstayed his two-week holiday, he invited me to go home with him to England to meet his family. I'd been to London a few times visiting Lachlan when he lived there, but that was years before. Trevor had a flat in Greenwich, but his widowed mother and extended family lived in the country. I couldn't pass up the chance to see the English countryside."

"What's his family like?"

"Stuffy. They asked what my father's title is. When I said we call him Da, well, Trevor's mother wasn't amused." Jamie picked at her jeans, remembering the expression on the woman's face when Jamie had dared to make a joke to Trevor's mother. "The Langleys don't have a sense of humor. Trevor was different around his family and friends, more haughty and upper-crusty. He apologized to his family for my lack of family title or social rank. He bloody apologized. Asked them to grant me leeway because I'd been raised in the boonies of Scotland."

Yes, she remembered that bit very clearly. Trevor had made her family sound like a clan of heathens who slathered on blue paint every day and rampaged across the English border for a lark.

Gavin didn't say anything, and she appreciated that more than he could know. Sharing all of this was harder than she'd expected.

"I stayed two days at his family's estate," she said, "then I asked Trevor to take me back to his flat. He did. Everything went well between us after that, mostly because he never took me to see his family again. We alternated visiting each other over the next few months. Sometimes I'd go to London, and other times he'd come to Scotland. He seemed to love the Highlands as much as I did. I tried to love London, but the city wasn't for me. I never told him that, though. We had good times together, but he preferred not to spend much time with my family. I didn't argue about it. In fact, I spent more days with him than with my sisters or brothers."

She glanced up at Gavin, expecting to glimpse annoyance on his face. After all, she'd admitted to forsaking her family to make Trevor happy. She'd refused to give up her family for Gavin. Maybe she hadn't explicitly stated it, but Gavin was clever enough to deduce the truth. Still, he watched her with a calm expression, his focus intently on her with no trace of irritation.

Unease trickled through her, little drops of discomfort that cooled her on the inside. She picked at the grass, plucking one blade at a time then discarding each.

Why wasn't he angry? She'd avoided her family to make Trevor happy, but she insisted Gavin must get along with everyone including her brothers. He ought to rail at her.

He lay back on the grass, braced on his elbows, the picture of serenity.

Jamie ripped a clump of grass from the earth, crushing it in her fist. "Why are ye sitting there like that? Donnae ye see? I gave up my family to make Trevor happy."

"Yep, I got that part."

"Why aren't you shouting at me?"

He pulled his head back, chin tucked. "When have I ever yelled at you?"

Never, of course. Even when he got angry, he didn't shout.

"I'm sorry," she said, glaring at the clump of destroyed grass in her palm. "I know you wouldn't speak to me that way, but you must be upset at hearing what I did for Trevor. I hardly saw my family for months. Back then, I was finishing my degree at university, but I would come home often. Once I got involved with Trevor, I rarely came home."

Gavin took a bite of his sandwich, chewing slowly, his attention always on her.

She scratched her arm, afflicted with a sudden, deep itch. "Five months into our relationship, Trevor proposed. I said yes without hesitation, without thinking about it. Being married sounded wonderful, everything I'd dreamed of since I was a little girl."

Her skin crawled, and Gavin consumed another bite of sandwich.

Jamie slapped her hand on the ground. "Donnae ye have anything to say?"

"I'm letting you tell your story." He set down his sandwich. "Thought that was the right way to handle the situation. Keep my trap shut and let you talk."

His tone stayed mild to match his expression, though he seemed a touch befuddled.

She mumbled noises that didn't quite become words. What did she want from him? Anger? A passionate outburst against Trevor? She had no idea.

Gavin sighed and sat up, one hand flat on the ground to prop up his body. "I know you two broke up. Why don't you tell me what went down?"

"A month after I said yes," she told him, "Trevor announced I had to cut all ties with my family, quit university, and become a proper English lady. I would be a lady, officially. Lady Langley. He seemed to think I should be grateful he'd chosen me for the honor. Finally, I put my foot down. I would not give up my entire life for him when he gave up nothing in return. That's when he told me he'd made a great sacrifice for me. He'd asked a Scottish bumpkin to marry him."

Gavin's jaw tightened, and a muscle jumped there, but he stayed silent.

"For the first and only time in my life," she said, "I stood up for myself. I called off the engagement."

"Bet the English Ass loved that."

She made an irritated noise. "He'd told me I was good in bed but immature, the way I clung to my family. He'd made a terrible mistake, he said, believing a fling could become a relationship. It was time for him to find a more appropriate lover."

Gavin's eyes became slits, his mouth set in a dangerous line. He looked fit to throttle her ex-fiancé.

A thrill raced through her. She shouldn't enjoy knowing her current lover wanted to pummel her former lover, but she did.

"I found out," she continued, "Trevor had been pretending to like the Highlands, pretending to care about the things that mattered to me, planning to transform me into the kind of woman a baronet deserved. Like he was Henry Higgins and I was Eliza Doolittle." A hissing growl blustered out of her nostrils. "He made a fool of me."

After she'd ended the engagement, Trevor had felt the need to shame her. She remembered his words like he'd said them yesterday.

"Little Jamie," he'd said in a cloying tone, "I've had a rollicking time in bed with you, but sex is all we ever had. Your family has no title, no ancestral lands, nothing but a love of whisky and revolting sausage made from sheep stomachs. Did you honestly believe I enjoyed choking down haggis to make you happy? And your family, they are the worst sort of bumpkins I've ever met."

Bumpkins. Her family. No one had ever called them that in her life.

He hadn't ended there, though. "I've asked you many times to come live with me in London, but you won't leave the bleeding Highlands. You are a child, Jamie, and I doubt you'll ever wrench yourself away from your mother's apron strings. And your brothers..." His mouth took on an ugly slant. "As long as you cling to them, you will never grow up. I need a real woman, one worthy of sharing my title. You are not the one for me. You are not even a woman, but a wee lassie who has no conception of what love is."

Jamie told Gavin all of this. The words spilled from her lips like a spigot had been torn off and water gushed out of it. When she'd finished, she was staring numbly down at her lap while wringing her hands.

One of Gavin's hands settled over hers, stilling her anxious movements.

If she glanced up at him, she might burst into tears.

"You must have really loved him," Gavin said, his voice soft and gentle.

"What?" She lifted her head, searching his face. "Why would you say that?"

"Because you were willing to give up your family for him." His hand on hers stiffened. "I know how much your family means to you, so you must've really loved Trevor."

More than you love me. She heard the unspoken ending to that statement. He couldn't believe it, though. He knew how much he meant to her. But would she give up her family for him? A huge part of her wanted to give him anything to keep him in her life, but she couldn't do it. Not again.

She took a few breaths before responding. "I'd convinced myself I loved him, but I was wrong. I've always loved the idea of being in love, but I never had a serious relationship until Trevor. I treated romance as a pastime, something to do for fun. Falling in love at every opportunity." She scoffed at her own tagline. "That's over. I'm done trying to please everyone else. I know what I need, and I won't settle for less."

"What exactly are you saying?"

"My family will always be important to me."

He kept his hand over hers, but he twisted his mouth into a half scowl. "I'm doing the best I can with your brothers. Me and Aidan, we're cool. Figure I'll try Lachlan next and save Rory for last."

"Because you hate him."

With a groan, he jerked his hand away. "I don't hate Rory. I hardly know the guy."

"You haven't tried to know him." She crossed her arms over her chest. "You expect me to accept Calli will always be your priority, but you can't even bother to speak to Rory."

"Calli is not my priority. She's my sister."

"Who can do no wrong." Jamie realized she was overreacting and behaving like a bitch, but she couldn't stop the words from tumbling past her lips. "Where do you live, Gavin? You said you're staying but didn't say for how long. Are you moving to Scotland?"

"We can talk about that later."

"Because the answer is no. You hate Scotland like Trevor did."

"I—" He flapped his arms. "I'm here, aren't I? I'm staying so we can work this out. I'm trying to make nice with your brothers. What more do you want from me? I haven't heard you say you'd be willing to pick up stakes and move to America to be with me. Seems like this is a one-sided thing. It's your way or no way."

She opened her mouth to say something she would probably regret as soon as she spoke it, but he cut her off.

"What are you willing to give up for me?" he demanded.

"Give up? I made that mistake once," she said. "No man is worth giving up my family, my home, my dreams. I wanted to become a schoolteacher, like Iain used to be but with children instead of college students. I never did find a teaching job. Trevor thought working with 'sniveling brats' was beneath me. Beneath him, actually. I let him rule my life. Everything I did was for him, to make him happy, to be good enough for him. If you can't accept me, accept my family, then we have no future together."

"Your brother stole my sister. I lost my family, but you won't even consider making a sacrifice for me."

"Stole your sister? Aidan and Calli fell in love."

"Yeah, and she had to move to Scotland to be with him. She made the sacrifice, not him." Gavin grabbed his sandwich and hurled it into the picnic basket. "Erica moved here for Lachlan. Emery moved here for Rory. I'm starting to see a pattern with the MacTaggarts. They seduce Americans away from their families to become part of their Scottish cult."

"Cult?" Jamie leaped to her feet. "Is that what you think of my family?"

Gavin jumped up too. He opened his mouth and then shut it, bowed his head and then scrubbed his face with both hands. When he raised his head again, he looked stricken. "God, Jamie, I'm sorry. We're both emotional after the things we told each other, but I don't know how this conversation got so messed up. We have issues about our families. That's not something we can work out today, it'll take time. You're right, I need to talk to Calli and figure out some things. But you need to figure out a few things too, like why you need your brothers' approval so much."

The conversation had taken a sudden and unpleasant turn. Maybe he was right. Confessing their darkest secrets had left them emotionally raw, and they'd taken it out on each other.

What if they couldn't sort this out? The question haunted her.

He took a tentative step toward her. "I love you, but if we can't work through this stuff, you're right. We won't have a future."

"I know."

Neither of them moved for a moment, their gazes bound to each other. Then they packed up their picnic and got back on their bicycles.

Nothing had changed, but somehow, everything had.

Chapter Twenty-Three

*G*avin lay on his back on the bed, breathing hard, recovering from the incredible sex he'd just had with the incredible woman lying beside him. After their argument a couple weeks ago on the shores of Loch Fairbairn, they'd avoided mentioning their families. He didn't bring up Calli, and she didn't bring up her brothers. They hadn't resolved anything, but they'd taken time to enjoy being together. He followed her through the shops in the village, amazed and enchanted by the way she got so excited over trinkets and T-shirts with goofy sayings on them. When she'd spotted a Christmas tree ornament in the form of a bicycling Santa Claus, Jamie had jumped up and down giggling. Literally. She jumped up and down.

He'd bought her the ornament. How could he not? She'd been so adorably thrilled with it.

"Bicycles and Christmas," she'd told him. "My two favorite things. After you, of course."

That she still called him her favorite thing gave him hope. That she still wanted to have sex with him seemed like a miracle.

For once, he'd convinced Jamie to come over to Iain's place, since the odd Scot had gone out for the day to spend time with "a lass" he wouldn't name. The guy seemed to hook up with a lot of women, so maybe he didn't remember this one's name.

No, Gavin didn't believe that. Iain talked a good game, but the story he'd told about his long-lost love left Gavin with the impression Iain had lost interest in playing the field. It seemed more likely Iain had one lover he saw occasionally, or maybe he fibbed about his amorous pursuits and hadn't been with anyone lately.

Since Gavin and Jamie had the run of the house tonight, and Iain's permission to "have at it with no restrictions," they'd enjoyed themselves in every room except Iain's bedroom. Their last stop had been the guest room where Gavin had slept for the past few weeks.

Eyes closed, he crawled his hand across the bed until he found Jamie's hand. Twining their fingers, he sighed from the contentment of basking in the afterglow of making love to the woman he loved.

"Mmm," Jamie moaned. "See, I was right? Sex without talking is better."

And just like that, she doused his contentment with a bucket of ice water. They hadn't discussed their problems since the day of their second dust-up. He'd come to think of it as The Rammy, a named event like the Battle of the Bulge. He also thought of it in Scottish terms as part of his goal to blend in more with the country where he'd taken up residence. Two weeks had flown by with the two of them talking about lighter topics and steering clear of the weightier issues. He still hadn't approached Lachlan or Rory to make peace with them. He'd let himself luxuriate in the sweet pleasures of spending time with Jamie, though in the back of his mind he always knew the hammer would fall sooner rather than later.

Trevor still hung around her like a mangy, disease-ridden wolf determined to spread his contagions. Gavin had considered renaming the English Ass to something more appropriate, like Patient Zero. Contaminating the world with his ass-ishness.

Jamie must've loved the jerk more than she'd claimed. Why else would his rejection have left her so wounded she couldn't trust Gavin not to abandon her too?

Thinking of the English Ass reminded him of a question he'd been too chicken shit to ask so far. Time to man up.

He rolled onto his side, toward Jamie, and couldn't resist taking a moment to sweep his gaze up and down her luscious body. Those gorgeous tits mounded on her chest, their stiff peaks jutting. He longed to swoop in and suckle them, but he'd had a reason for turning over to face her.

She inhaled a deep breath, lifting her breasts.

What was the reason? He'd had a question or something...

"Already up for another round?" she asked, her cheeks dimpling with a sweetly naughty smile. She flipped onto her side, one hand tucked under her cheek on the fluffy feather pillow.

Iain had great pillows. And super-soft sheets. Gavin wondered if they were silk, which made him wonder if the guy had more dough lying around than he'd let on. Gavin's musing lasted half a second before he suddenly remembered why he'd rolled over to look at the beautiful, sensual woman lying beside him.

"Are you sure you're not still in love with Trevor?"

"Why would you ask me that?"

"You called him your Prince Charming," Gavin said. "Being with him was your fairy-tale fantasy come to life. You've never said things like that about me."

"Maybe I don't say things like that when you're in the room."

Not exactly an affirmation she ever did spout girlie silliness about him. He shouldn't care, but somehow, her lack of confirmation stung worse than if she'd denied it.

"I'm noticing," he said, " you haven't denied you're in love with Trevor."

She pushed up on one elbow, her breasts dangling in his face. "I am not in love with Trevor Langley. Satisfied?"

"Guess so."

She squinted at him. "Are you still in love with your ex-wife?"

Gavin sprang up, half sitting, held up by one arm. "What? No, of course not."

A breath rushed out of her, sagging her shoulders. "Then why won't you tell me anything about your marriage?"

"Nothing much to tell." No excuse, he knew that. He sat up all the way, facing the foot of the bed, and bent one knee to rest his arm on it. "I met Leanne three months before my unit was deployed to Afghanistan. I asked her to marry me a week before I shipped out, and we flew to Vegas to get hitched the next day. It seemed like a good idea at the time."

"You loved her."

"Thought so. I mean, she was sweet and fun to be with, but she always had this restlessness about her. Like she was never satisfied with what she had." He ducked his head, plowing a hand through his hair. "I was gone for six months. Leanne emailed me every day, sent care packages, and we Skyped a lot. Everything seemed fine. When I came home, I got out of the Marines and started looking for a job. Leanne was working, so she told me to take my time and find the right job for me. Thought I'd get something fast, but eight months later, I still hadn't found anything. That's when my parents died."

Jamie leaned against his back, her skin on his, her cheek on his shoulder.

He sank back a little, loving the feel of her body against his. Even the comfort of Jamie couldn't overwhelm the discomfort of reliving the worst time in his life for the second time in less than two weeks.

"I still remember like it was yesterday," he said softly, "when Calli called to tell me about the accident. She was crying and could hardly get the words out. I told you what went on after that. Leanne stuck by me and nursed me through it all. If she hadn't been there…"

He shook his head, shutting his eyes.

Jamie wrapped her arms around his torso, cuddling tighter against him.

"I fell apart," he said, unable to keep the self-loathing out of his voice. "Leanne kept me going, she's the only reason I wasn't holed up in bed with my head under the covers. I always thought I was strong, but I found out I wasn't at all. Leanne took care of me, but Calli had to do everything else. Make funeral arrangements. Talk to a lawyer. Do the probate crap. You know the rest."

He should've moved away from Jamie, not let her comfort him, but he couldn't budge an inch. He'd never explained how he felt about all of this. Didn't want to tell her now. She deserved to know the whole truth, though.

Afterward, if she'd rather be with Trevor, he wouldn't stop her. She deserved a real man who could take care of her when terrible things happened.

Scratch that. He'd do whatever it took to stop her from going back to Trevor—but he'd feel bad about it. He'd rather be a selfish prick than live without her.

"By the time I woke up and manned up," he said, "six months had gone by. Leanne left me not long after. I couldn't blame her, not after all the drama I put her through. She said I was stifling her, and she needed to find herself in New York. Walked away and never looked back. I got a job in Minneapolis to be closer to Calli. We didn't talk about our parents. After she got her master's degree, she moved to Michigan for a job."

Jamie's chin stayed on his shoulder. "And you were alone."

"Yeah."

"Were you lonely?"

He rubbed his neck. "Uh, yeah, I guess. Some tough guy I turned out to be."

She pressed her lips to his neck. "Are you expecting me to be disgusted with you?"

"If I'd been a real man, I wouldn't have let my sister get roped into marriage fraud. That's a real crime, you know."

"Everything worked out." Jamie girded her arms tighter around him. "Calli met Aidan, and they're very happy together."

"I know. I'm happy for her, but—" He clapped his mouth shut. No way would he say those words, the ones he'd thought when he was talking to Calli a few weeks ago.

"You feel like Aidan stole your sister."

"Sort of. I know it's dumb, but...well..." *Shit.* He had to tell her. Enough keeping his stupid thoughts to himself. Talking was supposed to be cathartic, right? "I'm the last living member of the Douglas family. I'm alone."

Jamie crawled in front of him, twisting around to face him. "You are not the last member of your family. There's Calli and baby Sarah. And your cousin, Tara."

"Calli's a MacTaggart now, and Tara got married too. I'm the last one."

"Gavin—"

"It's true, Jamie." He dropped his chin so low it nearly bumped his chest. "Calli has a new family. She moved to Scotland for Aidan, to become a MacTaggart. Everyone I've ever loved has abandoned me."

Jamie splayed a hand over his cheek. "I haven't."

"Not yet." He laid his hand over hers on his cheek. "But if I can't make your brothers happy, we don't have a future together. You said that."

She opened her mouth, seeming like she was about to speak, but stopped.

Yeah, there was nothing left to say.

Chapter Twenty-Four

Thanksgiving sneaked up on Jamie. She woke up one morning, and the day was here. Though Lachlan and Erica celebrated the American holiday, and Calli and Aidan did too, each couple commemorated it in private. Today would be the first MacTaggart family Thanksgiving, in honor of their newest American addition, Emery.

MacTaggart family Thanksgiving? Jamie cringed inside. A week ago, Gavin had confessed to her he felt abandoned and alone, not a part of a family anymore. She'd wanted to assure him it wasn't true, but she couldn't. His sister had left America to marry a Scotsman, and she planned to apply for citizenship as soon as she became eligible. Gavin had good reason to feel abandoned.

Still, she should've said something that day. She should've told him he didn't need to please her brothers because she loved him enough to give up her family to be with him. A part of her balked at making that sort of promise again. She'd been willing to give up everything for Trevor, and he threw it back in her face. She loved Gavin so much more than she'd ever cared for Trevor. If he threw her away…

Had she ever told Gavin how much he meant to her? She'd declared they had no future unless he got along with her brothers. Why had she said that?

Jamie halted with her hand on the knob of the bedroom door. The sounds of family chatting and laughing she'd heard earlier drifting down the hall of the guest wing from the sitting room and the dining room had ceased. Everyone must've tramped upstairs. The dining room hadn't been large enough to accommodate the entire family, so they'd made use of the great hall.

Gavin would be here soon.

Her pulse sped up, excitement fluttered in her chest. She wore her favorite outfit, the one Gavin loved, a flower-print frock with red pumps that matched the tiny red flowers in the print of the dress. The cold and gloomy weather today had inspired her to slip on a cardigan, but she left it hanging open to reveal the low, but not too low, neckline of her dress.

Her question to herself a moment ago echoed in her mind. Though she'd told Gavin she loved him, she didn't think she had ever explained the depth of her feelings for him. Saying three words meant nothing unless she backed them up with the whole truth. He thought he was a coward, but she was the one too afraid to speak up. About her feelings for him. About her desire to be with him, no matter what. About her brothers.

She ought to have told them long ago to stop badgering Gavin. She could take care of herself, thank you very much. Why hadn't she said those words to them? Never before had she been afraid to speak her mind, not even to Rory. Now, she couldn't do it. She'd told Gavin standing up to Trevor had been the first time she'd done such a thing. Though she spoke her mind often, she'd always let her brothers defend her from scunners and cads. These days, she had trouble expressing herself to Gavin, to her brothers, to anyone except Emery.

Well, she could at least summon the nerve to leave this bedroom.

Jamie flung the door inward and marched into the hall.

Mrs. Darroch nearly collided with her.

With a yelp, Jamie veered to the side and slapped a hand on her chest. "Oh, you surprised me."

"Sorry, dearie," the housekeeper said. She pinched Jamie's cheek. "Your man is here. And he looks very braw today, I must say."

"Gavin? Where is he?"

"The darling boy insisted on waiting in the vestibule."

Why on earth would Gavin do that? He'd spent the better part of the past three weeks in this house with her. Of course, today the entire clan was in attendance.

Including her brothers.

No, he wasn't afraid of them. She would never believe that.

"Thank you," Jamie told Mrs. Darroch, and then she rushed down the hall, through the dining room and down the main hall straight to the vestibule.

Gavin waited near the outer door, standing straight and tall, dressed in a dapper gray suit and shiny black loafers. He'd gone sans tie, his shirt collar unbuttoned. Even the colorful garland of paper turkeys and glitter-dusted fall leaves hung over the doorframes and windowsills couldn't detract from his masculine style.

Mrs. Darroch had been spot on. He looked dashing. And sexy as hell.

Jamie crossed the vestibule to greet him. "Happy Thanksgiving."

The greeting came out a touch breathless, but she didn't care. He took her breath away when he stood before her like this, proud and masculine, his lips curved up the slightest bit in a way that suggested he knew exactly what he wanted.

His slight smile broadened into a wickedly sexy grin. "Happy Thanksgiving, Jamie. You look good enough to eat. Who needs turkey when I can feast on you."

"Are you ready for the family? They're all here." A stupid thing to say, but she couldn't think properly with hormones inundating her from her brain to her sex.

"I can handle them." He hooked an arm around her waist and pulled her snug against him. "Maybe we should express our thankfulness to each other in private first."

Oh, yes. That sounded wonderful.

Jamie flattened her palms on his chest, leaning in, her mind and body set on tasting that mouth, the one kinked in an erotic smirk.

Footsteps clomped down the vestibule stairs.

Gavin's brows shot up, but then relaxed as he focused on the person on the stairs.

Jamie twisted around in Gavin's embrace.

Aidan had stopped on the last step, a few feet away from Jamie and Gavin. He pinched his lips together, clearly trying not to laugh. "Ah, Lachie sent me to find you two. Emery and Rory will be bringing in the turkey any minute now."

"Oh," Jamie said, tearing herself away from Gavin.

Her brother sighed with enough melodrama to win him an award for worst actor on earth. "You two managed to avoid helping with the preparations. The rest of us had to lay out the silver and china all by ourselves."

Gavin feigned irritation with equally bad acting. "I'm sure it was real hard to get the job done with only a gazillion of you MacTaggarts around to help."

It was true, Jamie realized with a start. Aidan and Gavin had become friends.

She bounced on her toes, smiling at each man in turn.

Aidan waved for them to follow. "Come on, or you'll miss the meal."

Gavin clasped Jamie's hand and led her up the stairs behind Aidan.

As they mounted the stairs side by side, Jamie glanced at Gavin sideways. He acted like nothing had gone on between them two weeks ago, but she supposed he didn't want to ruin Thanksgiving by bringing up their rammy.

Yesterday, Trevor had knocked on the door of Dùndubhan. Mrs. Darroch had answered the summons and promptly retrieved Jamie from the sitting room where she'd been thumbing through a boring legal journal to avoid thinking about Gavin. It hadn't worked, of course. When Mrs. Darroch tromped into the room, her chin high and wearing her best disapproving look, Jamie had known what the housekeeper would say.

"*He* is here," Mrs. Darroch told her.

Jamie set the journal on the table, sliding forward until her feet cleared the sofa and touched the floor. "Who?"

"Him. The scunner who wants to come between you and your *leannan*."

Trevor would be the scunner, and she couldn't argue the man had become a right nuisance lately. Her *leannan* would be Gavin, though Jamie wasn't sure if he was still her sweetheart after the rammy they'd had. Though they'd enjoyed good times together since, the issues raised by their argument hadn't been resolved, or mentioned at all, since that day.

Jamie rose with an unladylike groan. "Guess I'd better see him. Where did you leave Trevor?"

"In the vestibule." Mrs. Darroch spoke the statement as if she would never have left Trevor anywhere else.

"All right," Jamie said. "I'll deal with Trevor. Thank you, Mrs. Darroch."

"If you need help getting rid of the scunner, give a shout. I'll be in the kitchen."

With that, Mrs. Darroch exited the sitting room.

Jamie wandered through the house to the vestibule where she found Trevor leaning against the railing of the spiral staircase. He had one hip cocked, one arm draped over the railing while the other arm hung loose at his side.

"There you are, lovey," he said when she entered the vestibule.

"I'm not your lovey." She halted barely inside the door with the width of the entryway between them. "What do you want today?"

"To make an offer."

She didn't even try to hold back her annoyed grumble. "We are not getting back together. I'm with Gavin."

"I'm not here about that."

A sense of impending disaster weighed down on her as she wondered what he was here to discuss, what kind of offer he intended to make. She ought to shove him out the door and order him never to come back. She'd done that repeatedly, though, and he kept coming back. Her curiosity got the better of her this time.

"Why are you here?" she asked.

"I told you, to make an offer." He held up a hand to silence her before she spoke again. Pushing away from the railing, he ambled across the vestibule to her. "I've mentioned to you I'm buying an old distillery. The sale went through, and I am now the owner of the former Loch Fairbairn Whisky Works. I intend to refurbish the property and reopen it as a tourist attraction, a museum of Scottish whisky history."

"Bully for you."

He reached for her hand.

She yanked it away.

With a soft laugh, he shoved his hands in the pockets of his khaki pants. "I want you to be my general manager."

Jamie blinked rapidly, certain she'd misheard him. "What? I know nothing about running a museum. You should ask Iain or Catriona, they're the historians in the family."

"I'm asking you."

She took a step back since he'd edged closer, too close. "I'm not qualified."

"Yes, you are." He gave her an exasperated smile. "Honestly, love, you underestimate yourself. You are the office manager for MacTaggart Construction. You're also clever and hard working."

"I do paperwork for Aidan. I wouldn't know what to do with a museum."

"You'll figure it out."

He leaned in, aiming for her lips.

She smacked a hand on his chest and pushed him back. "No, Trevor. No to the kiss, no to the job offer, no to you in general."

He sighed, shrugged, and moved toward the door. With his hand on the knob, he paused to glance back at her. "Think about it, Jamie. The offer will be open indefinitely."

Before she could inform him to close that offer this instant, he swung the door open and stepped outside.

"What the hell are you doing here?" snarled a familiar voice.

Jamie rushed to the doorway.

Gavin stood tall and imposing on the gravel path to the house, several feet away from Trevor. The ex-Marine wore his best steely glare. It outperformed even Rory's flintiest expression.

The Englishman, positioned between Jamie and Gavin, aimed a genial smile at the American even as he backed up half a step. "Good day, Gavin. Jamie's all yours—for today. I'm sure she'd love to tell you about the offer I've made her."

"Run back to your cesspool," Gavin said. "That's where slime belongs."

Trevor sniggered as he strolled past Gavin and thumped his shoulder.

Once the English Ass had left in his Bentley, Gavin stalked up to her where she lingered in the doorway. The sunlight shimmered behind him, casting his face in shadows.

"What the hell does he mean about an offer?" Gavin asked.

"Trevor offered me a job working at the distillery he bought, the one he wants to turn into a museum."

"Did you take the job?"

"Of course not."

He turned sideways, and the light slashed across his cheek. One golden-brown eye ignited in the sunshine. "Don't turn it down on my account. If you want to work with Trevor—"

"I don't. Not ever. Understand?"

"Maybe you should. He'd probably pay you a shitload of money."

"Why would I want a load of shit from anyone?"

"You know what I mean." He hunched his shoulders. "I'm grateful Aidan gave me a job, but we're shutting down for the winter. That means I'm unemployed again. If Trevor can give you a good living, you should take it."

This had been Trevor's plan, she suddenly realized. Her ex wanted to cause trouble between her and Gavin by making Gavin feel inferior.

"I am not working for Trevor." She grasped Gavin's face and forced him to look at her. "I don't trust him, for one. He says he's not trying to get me back, but I don't believe it. And I would never betray you by accepting a job from my ex when he's determined to come between us. I don't care if you're skint. How could I be upset about that when you spent all that money sending me gifts? Besides, money doesn't make a man, and you are ten thousand times the man Trevor is."

A muscle ticked in his jaw. He held motionless, his gaze drilling into her.

She spoke in the most authoritative voice she could muster. "I do not want anything to do with Trevor."

With a crisp nod, he said, "Good to know."

Gavin swept her into his arms and carried her to her bedroom. For the next hour, he made her forget Trevor Langley even existed.

Jamie's thoughts returned to the present, in which Gavin held her hand for the journey up the staircase. They hadn't spoken after the Trevor incident. Gavin had made love to her with an odd intensity like he needed to brand her with his body. Afterward, he kissed her cheek and left.

Today, he showed up in a good mood, smiling and holding her hand.

She would never understand men.

Aidan ushered them out of the stairwell and into the great hall. A long wooden table occupied the center of the room with the MacTaggart clan arrayed on either side of it, seated in high-backed wooden chairs with posh silver and china in front of them. Mrs. Darroch sat at a smaller table positioned near the tall windows, babysitting the bairns with help from her new love, Tavish the gardener. Lachlan and Erica's son, Nicholas, perched in a high chair with his feet dangling while Mrs. Darroch cradled baby Sarah, Aidan and Calli's daughter, in her arms. A bassinet had been placed beside the table in case Sarah needed a nap. Tavish, on the opposite side of the small table from Mrs. Darroch, wrangled Madison and Mackenzie, Emery's twin nieces.

A plethora of ornaments decorated the room. The American Wives Club had insisted on festooning the great hall and the table with harvest-oriented decor and Thanksgiving-specific items too. More garlands like the one in the vestibule draped over the windows and hung from the sides of the table. Baskets placed at intervals on the table held fake but realistic decorations—fall foliage, pumpkins, apples, pine cones, and a tiny scarecrow at the center of each arrangement. The tablecloth featured fall-colored plaid.

"Take your seats," Aidan said, waving toward two empty chairs.

On opposite sides of the table, three chairs away from each other.

Jamie gave her brother a questioning look.

Aidan shrugged. "Emery thought it would be fun to jumble us up. That way, we'll have to be sociable with everyone."

Emery would cook up a scheme like this.

While Aidan took his seat, Gavin made his way around the table to the seat designated with a folded card that had his name scrawled on it in elegant script. Two chairs were empty—the one at the end, across from Gavin and one spot over, and the chair at the head of the table.

Jamie sank into the seat designated as hers, right next to Aidan's chair. She had a sinking feeling in her stomach, a recurrence of that sense of impending disaster. Emery had gotten up to something, and Jamie wasn't sure she wanted to find out what.

"Our first Thanksgiving, eh?"

She looked up at the man who'd spoken.

From his seat directly across the table, Iain nodded at her. His lips twitched upward the slightest bit. "Relax, lass. We won't starve like the Mayflower pilgrims did in their first winter."

"Not starvation that worries me."

He threw a significant glance in the direction of Gavin and the conspicuously empty chairs at the end of the table. "Imagine it's the seating arrangements fashing you."

Emery and Rory were the only ones not here, which meant the empty seats belonged to them. Emery had positioned Gavin close to Rory with only one chair between them. Jamie surveyed the length of the table, noting the seemingly random placement of each adult. To her left sat Cole, husband of Emery's sister, and beyond him Jamie spotted her father and her sisters. On the other side of the table, beginning at the far end, she counted Erica's father, Calli, Emery's father, Erica, Iain, Emery's mother, Erica's mother, Gavin, and Sorcha MacTaggart. The matriarch of the clan caught her daughter's gaze as Jamie reached the table's end in her visual survey.

Her mother winked.

Jamie had no bloody clue what that meant.

She continued her survey, skipping over the empty chair at the head of the table and the one next to it on this side of the table. Beside Emery's empty chair, Lachlan was engaged in conversation with Hadley, Emery's sister. Aidan sat between Jamie and Hadley, though he gazed longingly at his wife seated near the opposite end of the table.

Aidan sighed with mock wistfulness. "Why did Emery have to put Calli way over there? Cannae kiss my wife while we celebrate our first family Thanksgiving."

"You'll survive," Jamie said, giving him a sarcastic pat on the arm.

Iain nodded with mock solemnity. "Aye, and some of us don't care to watch you ravish your wife right here on the table."

As the men launched into pseudo-taunts about their love lives, Jamie's attention drifted down the table to Gavin and the ominous empty chair at the table's end.

"Don't worry about Rory," Erica said from her position at Iain's right. "He won't wreck Thanksgiving. His wife would not be happy about that, and Rory values Emery's happiness over everything else."

True, but Jamie couldn't shake the unease that had taken root inside her.

A sharp whistle pierced the din of conversation.

Every gaze swerved to the doorway.

Rory held a silver platter with a giant turkey on it while his wife removed her fingers from her mouth, her whistling having done its job.

Aidan raised his hand. "Is that one bird enough for twenty-one people and four bairns? Donnae know about you, Rory, but I'm famished."

"No you're not," Calli said. "You ate five waffles for breakfast, not to mention all the sausage patties and bacon."

Her husband lifted his shoulders, attempting to spread his hands but unable to do so without smacking Jamie and Hadley. "It's a holiday."

Emery whistled again. "We've got two more turkeys in the oven. Don't worry, Aidan, you can stuff your face until your wife is too disgusted to touch you."

Aidan and Calli spoke in unison. "That will never happen."

Rory was frowning.

Emery whispered something in his ear, and he perked up. He ferried the platter to the far end of the table and set it in front of his place setting. Then he pulled out Emery's chair, pushing it in once she'd settled onto the cushioned seat. She aimed an adoring look at him, and he reciprocated with the exact same expression.

Rory claimed his seat at the head of the table—and shot Gavin a sharp look.

Oh aye, disaster ahead.

Chapter Twenty-Five

The first bird had been gobbled up, and the second bird brought in with the same ceremony as the first, when the trouble started. Gavin tried to mind his own business throughout the meal. He chatted with Mrs. Teague, Erica's mom, and Mrs. MacTaggart, the clan matriarch. Why Emery had placed him between the two moms, and directly across from Lachlan, he had no idea. He would've been more comfortable sitting next to Iain. Lachlan studied him occasionally, even smiled a couple times. With all the conversation din around them, though, he and Lachlan had trouble speaking over the wide table.

So, he gabbed with the moms.

The longer he talked to them, hearing stories about Erica's life before Lachlan and the MacTaggart brood's shenanigans, the more antsy he got. It shouldn't have bothered him after all these years, but all this family time reminded him he had no family anymore. His parents were gone six years. Calli had joined the MacTaggart clan more than a year ago.

He nibbled at his food, but his stomach didn't seem inclined to accept any of it.

One of the rug rats—he couldn't see which, but Nicholas seemed like the prime suspect—lobbed a yeast roll at the adults table. It bounced off the top of Aidan's head and landed on Jamie's lap. She yelped and giggled. Cole, Emery's brother-in-law, snagged the roll and tore off a big mouthful.

"It wasn't my kids," Hadley, Emery's sister, proclaimed. "They're little angels."

Calli piped up with, "Sarah's too little to pick up a roll, much less throw one."

Everyone looked at Erica.

She pretended offense. "Oh that's right, blame Nicky. I'd like to see the evidence incriminating him. I think Lachlan did it."

Erica scowled at her husband, but the twitching of her lips exposed her humor.

"It was Iain," Lachlan countered. "He knows how to throw bread like a boomerang."

"Do I?" Iain said with that mildly sardonic tone Gavin had come to know as signature Iain. "I'm a magician then, eh, Lachie?"

Laughter and more good-natured taunts followed.

Gavin set down his fork, unable to eat. Families teased each other. Families traded jibes and shared meals. He glanced at Emery, and she winked. Whatever that meant. She was a little weird.

When he'd first arrived at the castle, he'd been in a damn good mood. Jamie had greeted him with a brilliant smile that melted his heart. Then, she'd thrown her arms around him. Yeah, that was a great start to Thanksgiving.

Sure, yesterday he found Trevor here trying to make time with Jamie. She wasn't having any of it, though. The quickest glimpse of the English Ass made him really, really annoyed. Finding out the guy had offered Jamie a job, that had him grinding his teeth. And suddenly, an urge to prove she was his had overpowered him. He'd dragged Jamie to her bedroom and fucked her like she'd vanish into thin air if he stopped, making her come so many times she'd been dazed afterward. Maybe it had been stupid manly pride, or maybe a desperate need to reclaim her.

Not that she'd ever belonged to him. He didn't want to own her. He wanted her, period.

Which meant getting in good with her brothers.

And Lachlan was studying him again.

He couldn't have a real conversation with the guy in this situation. Too much noise, too much of a crowd. What he needed to talk about with Lachlan required privacy. He really didn't need gossip about him sucking up to the Three Macs to spread across this table.

Gavin glanced to the right, past Mrs. Teague and Mrs. Granger, Emery's mom.

Iain nodded at him, his mouth seeming stuck in that subdued smile he so often wore.

Nodding in response, Gavin speared a slice of turkey from the nearest platter and plopped it onto his plate. Time to try food again.

"Mr. Douglas."

The deep voice of Rory MacTaggart boomed through the great hall, and everyone fell silent—even the rug rats at the kids table.

Gavin took a deep breath and swung his attention toward the lord of the castle.

Rory raised his brows. "Enjoying the turkey?"

"Sure, it's good." Gavin poked at the slice he'd put on his plate, despite not wanting to eat. "You can call me Gavin."

"I believe Mr. Douglas is more appropriate since we have business to discuss."

Gavin couldn't help it. He stared at Rory like the man had grown horns. The big, red, spiky kind. What was the guy up to?

"Family business," Rory said.

Emery sharpened her gaze on her husband, her eyes slitted.

Rory ignored her, his focus squarely on Gavin. "What are you doing with my sister, Mr. Douglas?"

Gavin flattened his palms on his thighs, fighting the impulse to gape at the man. How did a person answer a question like that? He had no frigging idea.

So of course, he blurted out something dumb. "Jamie's my girlfriend."

Rory picked up his knife and twirled it between his fingers, the light glancing off its polished silver surface. "You hurt her badly. What makes you think you have the right to call her your girlfriend?"

"Excuse me?" Gavin bristled, and dammit, though he tried to rein in his temper he failed. Those two words came out razor-sharp.

"What precisely are your intentions with my sister?"

Jamie's brother might as well have scraped a metal brush up Gavin's spine. Gavin snapped ramrod straight, his jaw set. "I love Jamie, and frankly, my intentions are none of your business."

Calm down, he chastised himself. *Get a grip and don't let this guy rattle you.* That was exactly what Rory wanted, and it was damn hard to ignore the taunts. He had to do it, though, for Jamie.

Gavin took a slow breath and exhaled out the anger.

"Is that so?" Rory said in that infuriatingly level tone. He clapped the knife down on his plate. "You won't marry my sister, but you've been fucking her in my house."

Before Gavin could react, Sorcha MacTaggart smacked her palms down on the table. "Rory Niall MacTaggart, shame on you. There are children in the room."

Gavin swore one corner of Rory's mouth kicked up in amusement.

"Mrs. Darroch," Rory said without glancing at the housekeeper, "why don't you and Tavish take the children to the sitting room?"

Though she frowned at Rory, Mrs. Darroch murmured to Tavish and the two of them hustled the kids out of the great hall and down the stairs.

Lachlan cleared his throat. "Rory, why don't we try to calm down."

"We?" Rory arched one brow at his older brother. "This conversation doesn't involve you, Lachie."

Emery nailed her husband with a hard look, her eyes squinted and her lips compressed. Gavin wouldn't have been surprised to see smoke curling up from her ears.

Rory smirked at his wife and sneaked a hand under the table.

Emery jerked, then relaxed as her expression softened.

Gavin decided he did not want to know what Rory was doing to his wife under the table.

Sorcha MacTaggart latched onto her son's ear and yanked him toward her. "Rory Niall MacTaggart, you apologize to Gavin this instant."

He flashed his mother an exasperated frown. "This is between me and the American, Mother."

"Then why are ye starting a rammy in the middle of Thanksgiving dinner? Ye've made it everyone's business, and I donnae like it one bit."

"Rory," called a fatherly voice from the opposite end of the table. Niall MacTaggart wore the same kind of unperturbed expression as his son. "You're ruining the holiday meal our American daughters have arranged and looked forward to for weeks."

"This isn't—"

Niall cut his son off with a wave of his hand. "Your wife wanted this dinner."

Rory glanced sideways at Emery, then averted his gaze to his lap.

Holy shit. Rory had gotten shamed by his daddy.

It lasted about three seconds.

Rory jerked his head up and fixed his flinty gaze on Gavin. "I have a right to question the man who's using my sister. An American, no less."

"Hey!" multiple voices shouted simultaneously. All the Americans in the great hall, except Gavin, had voiced their displeasure at the implied insult—and the Americans outnumbered the Scots in this room.

Gavin thumped his fists on the table, rising halfway out of his chair. "Enough of this bullshit, Rory. You don't hate Americans. You hate me. So deal with me, MacTaggart, and say what it is you really want to say to me. If you've got the balls to."

Rory leaned back in his chair like the lord of the manor addressing a peasant. "Do you think you're good enough for my sister? Trevor Langley has a title and money."

"You b—"

The *thwack* of a chair striking the floor reverberated in the great hall, and a feminine voice hollered, "Haud yer wheesht, ye bleeding bawbags!"

Everyone swerved their attention to Jamie. She'd jumped up so swiftly her chair had tumbled over backward. Her cheeks crimson with emotion, she flapped her arms and alternated glaring at Rory and at Gavin.

"Nobody decides for me," she said, "who I'm involved with. Trevor is a scunner, and I donnae care how many titles he has. He could be the Prince of Wales and I wouldnae want him."

Rory opened his mouth, but his baby sister silenced him with one finger jabbed in his direction.

"Donnae be flapping yer gums, Rory," she snapped. "Gavin is my boyfriend until I say otherwise, and you have no say in it."

Again, Rory opened his mouth.

"Haud yer wheesht," Jamie said. "Ahmno finished."

Rory raised his hands, palms out, surrendering to his sister.

Why did it seem like Rory's lips inched upward at the corners? And was that humor in his eyes?

Had Rory planned this whole incident to make Jamie finally stand up to him?

Nah, that was crazy.

Rory rested his elbows on the arms of his chair and steepled his fingers. His lips definitely kinked that time.

Jamie failed to notice. She was on a tear, and nothing would stop her.

Damn, she was hot when she got pissed off.

"For the record," Jamie told her brother, "who I shag is none of your business, Rory. You fuck your wife in every room in this castle, and the outdoors, and the backseat of your Mercedes when it was parked in downtown Loch Fairbairn."

Lachlan and Aidan burst out laughing.

"She's got ye there," Aidan said. "My wife and I are witnesses, along with half of the villagers. I had to cover Calli's eyes. She's too innocent to see that sort of debauchery."

Rory's expression blanked. "We were parked in an alley."

"But ye weren't quiet about it," Aidan said. "Your wife's screams could be heard in Ballachulish."

Emery grinned. "We did have fun that day."

Rory's hands fell to his lap. Rather than seeming embarrassed, though, he smirked. "Emery is rather vocal in her passion."

His wife poked him in the side. "Like you aren't."

Jamie pounded her fist on the table, rattling silverware all the way down to Rory's end. "Quiet! I'm talking to Rory."

Silence.

"I'm listening," Rory said.

Jamie straightened, smoothing her dress and tugging her cardigan back into position. "I am with Gavin. When or if we get married is our decision, not yours. I love him, and you will not chase him away. Not if I have anything to say about it." She jabbed that finger at Rory again when he seemed about to speak. "And I do have a say. The only one that matters. Keep your opinions to yourself, Rory. Gavin is my boyfriend until I decide otherwise."

She held her ground, unmoving, her gaze nailed to Rory.

No one spoke for a minute, maybe longer.

Then Rory sighed and said, "As you wish."

Jamie's eyed widened for a fraction of a second like she couldn't believe she'd won the argument. "Thank you."

Another minute or so elapsed with Jamie not moving and everyone growing uncomfortable, fidgeting in their seats and exchanging confused glances.

"Are you planning to stand for the whole meal?" Rory asked mildly.

"No." Jamie chewed her bottom lip. "But I need a piss."

She trotted out of the room.

Gavin hesitated for about a second before he excused himself and took off after her.

And he swore Rory smirked.

Chapter Twenty-Six

*J*amie raced down the stairs and straight to the ground-floor bathroom. She did need to pee but not as badly as she'd let everyone think. She'd needed to escape. Thanksgiving dinner had mutated into a right rammy between Rory and Gavin, and she had told Rory off. Sure, she'd stood up to him before, but not like this. And for too long lately, she'd let everyone else tell her what to do. The time had come to assert herself. To *re*assert herself.

Christ, what had she done?

After relieving her immediate need, she loitered in the enormous bathroom. The claw-foot tub took up most of the space. Everyone knew Emery and Rory had a poke in that very tub the morning after their second wedding, the public one they'd staged for their families though they'd been married for weeks already by then. The MacTaggart and Granger mothers had insisted on a real wedding since their first ceremony had taken place in a magistrate's office with no family present.

The families got an earful that morning.

Rory, the man who'd cherished privacy more than anything and despised making a spectacle of himself, had noisily taken his wife in the bathroom. He'd done more since, seeming to have no shame about where and when he kissed, fondled, or had a poke at his wife.

If Rory, the uptightest of the uptight, could overcome his past and find happiness, maybe there was hope for Jamie and Gavin.

She needed to tell him that—and more.

"Thought you needed a piss."

Jamie squeaked and whirled toward the doorway.

Gavin leaned against the jamb, a thumb hooked in the waistband of his slacks, his lips curved in that sexy way that made her tummy flutter.

"I did," she said. "Took care of it already."

"Good." He raked his gaze up and down her body, his gaze heating up and his voice turning smoky. "You're really hot when you get mad and yell at everybody."

Her tummy fluttered again, and her body warmed. "Not everybody. Just Rory."

"You told all of us to shut up, and you called me and Rory bawbags." His mouth quirked, his eyes sparkled golden in the muted light of the bathroom. "It was the sexiest thing ever."

"I'm glad you're here," she said, struggling to ignore the tingling between her thighs, spreading outward to suffuse her body. He shouldn't look so good, more edible than the turkey dinner. "Rory is an erse. A big, overbearing erse."

Gavin chuckled, low and deep. "I agree, but I'm beginning to think he has ulterior motives."

"Like what? Making me want to skite his face with my chair?"

He chuckled again and pushed away from the jamb to saunter toward her. "I'm not sure what he's up to, but I'm going to find out. First, I'm talking to Lachlan. Then, I'll talk to Rory and get him to fess up."

She held motionless, immobilized by his proximity as he halted centimeters from her, his face angled down so he could lock those glittering eyes on her. She clasped her hands over her belly. "You don't need to do that anymore. I should never have said we have no future if you can't get along with my brothers. I love you, Gavin, and I want to be with you no matter what."

"I love you too." He tucked a lock of hair behind her ear, then trailed his fingertips down her throat. "I get it now. Family is important, and I'm going to do whatever it takes to become a part of this one."

"But I'm saying you don't need to—"

He placed a finger over her lips. "I need to do this for me. I haven't been myself for a while, and that has to change. This might sound weird, but tonight, arguing with Rory, I felt more like me than I have in a long time. It felt...good."

She pulled her head back and rolled her eyes up to gaze into his. "You liked having a rammy with Rory in front of everyone?"

"Yeah. Weird, huh?"

Jamie let her hands float up to his chest, her palms settling over his firm muscles. "I'm yours, Gavin. You have nothing to prove to me. I've never loved anyone the way I love you."

He stopped blinking, his lips parted.

"I didn't understand," she said, "how much my break-up with Trevor had affected me. Not until we started having problems. I think I was using my brothers as a buffer between us, to keep you at a distance in case you left me the way Trevor did. If you had done that, it would've hurt so much more. I don't know if I could've gotten over losing you. I might have overreacted to the credit-card debacle, but I'd been expecting you to say something else and it hurt when you didn't." She'd expected a proposal, but she didn't want to say that and have him think he had to ask her today. "I started to worry you might be like Trevor, but that was my fears getting the better of me. You are nothing like him. You are a good man."

Gavin laid a hand on her cheek, holding it there for a moment before he dove his fingers into her hair. "I've never loved anyone the way I love you either."

"I won't leave you, Gavin. Even when I broke up with you, I couldn't stay away." She turned her face into his arm and kissed his wrist. "Calli didn't leave you, and I won't. Your parents didn't want to abandon you. Your wife sounds like a selfish twat to me. I hope you know I'm not like that."

"Of course I do," he said. "To be fair, Leanne had good reason to walk away. She's the kind of woman who needs to be taken care of, but she wound up taking care of me instead. She stuck it out as long as she could. I don't blame her, and wherever she is, I hope she's happy."

"She could have been kinder in the way she left you."

"Maybe, but I think she did the best she could."

"You're a good man, Gavin, to forgive her like that."

"It's time I let go of the past." He eased closer, his hand sliding deeper into her hair until his palm spread over the back of her head. "You're an incredible woman, Jamie. I know you won't leave me. I belong with you, wherever that is, and I want to become a part of your family. They accepted my sister without any reservations. I could've tried harder, especially with your brothers." He flashed her an impish smile. "I think your mom likes me, though. She called me *gràidh*. That's a good thing, right?"

Jamie gave him an impish grin in return. "It means darling in Gaelic. Mom must like you almost as much as Mrs. Darroch does. You're very popular with the women in the MacTaggart family."

"There's only one who matters."

He touched his lips to hers in a tender kiss rife with a deep longing and a deeper affection. In his kiss, she experienced his feelings for her, everything he'd held back before, and she couldn't stop from infusing her own emotions into the fusing of their lips.

She clenched her fingers in his shirt, plastering her body to his, craving more.

"Jamie," he whispered against her lips. "My sweet Jamie."

"Please," she breathed. "I need you."

He plunged his tongue between her lips, and the kiss exploded into a ravenous melding of their lips and tongues. The silken glide of his tongue intensified into powerful lashes, robbing her of breath and sanity. Liquid heat burgeoned between her thighs, bringing with it a heaviness that settled low in her belly and triggered a deep, hungry ache. He slung an arm around her waist to bind her to his body even as his other hand, already buried in her hair, clutched the back of her head more firmly. He slanted her head back, and she opened her mouth to him even more, without hesitation, relishing the sensation of his tongue penetrating deeper, the flavor of him arousing her so intensely she moaned and flung her arms around his neck.

Groaning, he whisked his hand down and dived it under her dress to grip her bottom.

He tore his mouth away from hers, looking down at her with surprise. "No panties? This is becoming a habit, eh?"

"I was hoping for a repeat of yesterday, and I wanted to be ready for it." She slipped a hand inside her bra, extracting a condom packet. "I came prepared."

He fanned his long fingers over her ass, tugging up until she balanced on the toes of her shoes. "You were sitting there all through dinner with no panties on. Damn, if you'd told me that when I got here, I would've dragged you into the nearest private room an hour ago."

"We're here now."

"Yeah, we are." He shoved his other hand under her dress, and with both palms on her behind, he scooted backward until he could kick the door shut with one foot. "Let's outdo Rory and Emery. Let's fuck in every room in the house, starting with this bathroom, and then move on to the outbuildings."

"Aye, let's do it."

He spun them around and backed her up to the wall. "Need a hand undoing my pants."

"Mm, I'd love to lend a hand." She snaked her fingers between their bodies, found the button of his slacks, and unhooked it. With two fingers, she yanked the zipper down with a sharp *zzzzt* an instant before the ripping sound of her fingers tearing open the condom packet echoed through the space. She rolled the condom onto him swiftly. As she closed her fingers around his erection, she murmured, "Want this."

"Yes, ma'am." He choked when she stroked his length. "You look like an angel, but you're a hungry little sex demon."

"Best feed me, then."

He hoisted her legs up to his hips. "Hold on to me."

Gazing into his eyes, darkened by passion, she knew she would never let him go. She locked her ankles behind his taut buttocks, her arms still linked around his neck.

With one punishing thrust, he consumed her to the hilt. "Ah...you're so hot and wet."

"You make me this way." She gasped when he pulled out partway, then drove his shaft deeper inside. "Only for you."

He slapped his palms on the wall at either side of her head and pumped into her, fast and rough, crushing her to the wall. Her wetness made a sucking sound with each of his thrusts, in time with his grunts, the sounds mingling and reflecting off the walls. Flesh slapped against flesh. The fabric of his slacks scraped against her inner thighs, but the sensation only heightened her need. She bucked her hips into his pistoning movements, clutching him tighter with her legs, her every breath a harsh gasp.

Gavin stopped.

Jamie made a disgruntled noise, her thoughts clouded by a haze of lust. "What..."

Breathing hard, he grazed his lips over hers. "I haven't told you what I'm thankful for."

"Can we do that later?"

He pecked a kiss on the tip of her nose. "I'm thankful for you. Every day. You're the best gift I've ever received, and I will never take you for granted again."

She squirmed, feeling every inch of his rigid cock inside her, and her clitoris throbbed with the driving need to come. "Stop talking. Get back to fucking."

"In a sec." His mouth slid into a lopsided grin. "Will you marry me?"

"You're asking me now?"

"Uh-huh." He swirled his hips, grinding his shaft into her body, teasing a whimper out of her. "Will you marry me, Jamie?"

"Yes, aye, yes."

He grinned with all the carnal hunger of the sex demon he'd called her. "Thank you, babe. You won't regret it."

"I—"

She lost her voice and her breath when he pounded into her, pinning her to the wall and bouncing her body on his cock with each wild thrust. She couldn't squelch the cries that exploded out of her, and his throaty yells reverberated off the tile walls. Her climax struck so suddenly and with such power it ripped a scream from her throat even as her body gripped him, pulsating and milking his shaft until he came inside her, his release a hot jet of pure ecstasy.

"Gavin," she whispered, dissolving into him, gasping for air.

He let his head fall to her shoulder. "God, Jamie, you're amazing."

As her thoughts cleared, a realization spurred her to lift her head and push his off her shoulder. When he looked at her, she gave his cheek a half-hearted slap. "You bastard. Proposing to me in the middle of sex?"

"Yeah, I did that." He kissed her quick. "You wanna take back your answer?"

"No, not in the least."

She couldn't take it back. Marrying him was everything she'd wanted since the day they'd met.

A tentative knock rattled the door. "Um, Jamie? Are you in there?"

"*Mhac na ghalla*," she hissed under her breath, then turned her head to shout at the door. "Emery?"

"Yep, it's me." Emery hesitated. "We're about to have dessert. Rory wanted to track you two down, but I had a feeling I should do it. I'm assuming Gavin's in there too."

Emery must've heard them. Nobody standing outside the door could've missed the racket they'd made. And *bod an Donais*, here she was with Gavin's cock lodged inside her while she talked to her sister-in-law through the door.

"Go on back to the great hall," she said. "We're coming."

A snort suggested Emery was stifling a laugh. "I'm sure you are."

Footsteps indicated Emery had left the vicinity.

Gavin disengaged from her body, robbing her of the delicious heat and firmness of him. He set her down on her feet and steadied her when her shaky legs threatened to buckle. Giving her bottom a little pat, he said, "Better get back to the festivities, hmm?"

He looked far too pleased with himself.

Then again, she must've looked equally satisfied.

She wilted into him. "You might have to carry me."

"Yes, ma'am." He disposed of the condom, zipped up his pants, threw the door open. Scooping her up in his arms, he carried her out into the hall. "Should I put you over my shoulder?"

"Don't you dare." She wriggled in his arms. "I was joking, Gavin. Put me down."

"Not yet."

He lugged her through the vestibule and took the steps two at a time—strictly to show off, no doubt. When they reached the threshold of the great hall, he deposited her on her feet.

She faced the family gathered around the table and saw…Rory smiling.

Not a grin or even a full smile. His mouth formed a subdued expression of knowing and self-satisfaction like he'd done something grand and nobody knew about it because he wasn't going to tell.

What was her brother up to?

Rory wouldn't let on until it suited him. His plans had something to do with Gavin, that much was clear.

Her fiancé slapped a hand on her ass and gave her a little push. "Hurry up. We've got news to share."

Chapter Twenty-Seven

Emery

That's how it went down according to my sources. People like to talk to me, what can I say? I listen and don't judge. Thanksgiving dinner continued after that without incident, everyone smiling, joking, and sharing stories. Even Rory relaxed after that, and his mommy told me about the time he tried to mediate a settlement between a puppy and a cat. He'd been eight years old at the time, and his efforts failed. Rory insisted it was the only time in his life that he lost a case. Based on the twinkle in his eyes, I decided he was fibbing.

Not that I cared if he didn't always succeed. Everybody failed now and then, and everyone made mistakes. That's a lesson Gavin and Jamie learned the hard way. The blissful couple had announced their engagement after dessert. The whole gang congratulated them, even Rory.

The clan have all gone home now—except for Jamie, who's still in residence at Dùndubhan along with her houseguest, Gavin. They hightailed it upstairs after making swift excuses the instant the last MacTaggart—Aidan, naturally—departed the premises. Rory and I had retired to our bedroom on the top floor. I slipped my satin nightie on over my head, feeling the slippery fabric glide over my skin while the torrid gaze of my husband steamed over me from behind. I knew this because I could see him in the mirror on the dresser.

Even I can't see out the back of my head.

I approached the bed where Rory lay on his back, buck naked, the length of his gorgeous body stretched across the length of the bed. He'd pulled back the covers and joined his hands under his head on the pillow. All those toned muscles and that lightly tanned skin made my mouth water. I always got lustful when Rory was nude. And when he was clothed. And when I talked to him on the phone and couldn't even see him.

Okay, I could admit it. I was incurably addicted to my husband.

"You know the rule," Rory said, "about wearing nighties to bed."

"That's one rule I enjoy. You get to strip me in any way you want." My husband could be very creative, one of my favorite things about him.

He frisked his hand over the mattress beside him, drawing big circles on it. "Come, *m'eudail*. Or rather, climb into bed so I can make you come."

A dirty trick calling me his darling in Gaelic. He knew I loved it. Undaunted, I planted my hands on my hips. "Oh, so you think you're getting lucky tonight after that display during our very first Thanksgiving dinner?"

Rory feigned innocence even better than Aidan. "What display?"

He knew damn well he had explaining to do. Serious explaining.

I braced a knee on the bed's edge, which caused my nightie to ride up and expose all of my thigh. Rory's gaze snapped to my groin, concealed by the satin. I set my palms on the mattress and leaned forward, knowing full well the nightie would sag and give him a clear view of my breasts. I was never above using lust to make my husband confess.

"You're going to tell me," I said, "why you picked a fight with Gavin. I think I know the answer, but I want to hear you say it."

"I'm sure you've figured out the answer, since no one knows me better." He scooted over a little, draping an arm above my pillow, an invitation to cuddle up to him. "Come here and I'll tell you, since you insist on having me speak the words."

Powerless to resist a cuddle with my hubby, I lay down on the bed beside him with my head cradled in the hollow of his shoulder. When he tucked me under his arm, I sighed with a kind of contentment I'd never known before Rory.

"Okay," I said, "I'm where you want me. Time to spill."

He stroked a fingertip up and down my arm. "I didn't pick a fight with Gavin for his sake. I did it for Jamie. She needed to stand up for herself and take the situation in hand. She's relied on me, Lachlan, and Aidan to handle her problems too many times. Jamie is a grown woman, not a child, and she doesn't need our interference anymore. But she wouldn't tell us so." He made a shoving gesture with his other hand. "I gave her a wee push."

"A *wee* push?" I laughed and gave him a playful slug in the side. "You ticked her off so good she called you a bleeding bawbag. You told me before 'bawbag' is a reference to a man's testicles, and it's not a compliment."

"True. But extreme measures were required."

"Because you wanted to make sure she really loves Gavin, so she won't make another Trevor mistake."

"Aye." Rory kissed my forehead. "I realize you prefer a softer approach to problems, but sometimes a manly method is best. We are dealing with a man after all. The rammy with Gavin helped him too. He stood up to me, and he finally proposed to Jamie."

"While they were having sex in the ground-floor bathroom." I traced circles on Rory's tummy with one finger. "I suppose that's a step up from being handed a marriage contract in a suite at a five-star hotel after a one-night stand and being told you're signing up for sex slavery."

"Sex slavery? I seem to recall you seducing me repeatedly."

"Had to. Sweetie-pie, you were totally pent up."

"I'll concede the point." Rory cast me a sideways glance. "You know I always wanted you, not the contract."

"Yes, baby, I know." I sat up, and his hand skated down my back to land on my hip. "Please tell me your harassment of Gavin is over and done with. You got him riled up, he talked back to you, end of story. Right?"

My husband squished his lips together, eyes squinted.

"Oh Rory," I said with a gusty sigh. "Why won't you leave the poor guy alone? He adores your sister, and Calli vouches for him being a good man. So does Aidan. I know this isn't meanness because you are not mean. What gives?"

He ran his hand down my thigh with the languor of a man savoring his wife's body even while engaged in a serious conversation. "You meddled first, Em. It's only fair I have my go at it."

"Not an answer."

"You told Gavin he needed to..." Rory winced as if speaking the word pained him. "You told him to 'bromance' me, Aidan, and Lachlan."

I straddled his lap so I could stare down at him properly. "How do you know that? Were you eavesdropping?"

"No, Iain told me." He grasped my hips. "Gavin discussed the issue with Iain, and Iain thought I should be warned."

"Here I thought Iain was trustworthy." I shook my head. "Turns out he's a gossip like the rest of you."

"Iain was certain Gavin wouldn't mind." Rory pinched me lightly. "Are you calling me a gossip?"

"The men in the MacTaggart family blether way more than the women."

"Hmm." Rory drew my hips forward until I could feel his arousal beneath me. "Did ye never think Iain might've done Gavin a favor?"

"I'll consider that when I interrogate him."

Rory chuckled. "Heaven help the man who annoys my wife. Iain's fifty years old, Em, and nothing upsets him."

"Must be something that does, but I'll figure him out later." I dragged my nails down Rory's chest. "Tell me what you're planning for Gavin."

"I'll tell ye, *mo gaoloch*," he said with a smirk, "after I make you scream several times. We've got to get one up on Jamie and Gavin, after all."

"Give me a hint first."

My husband considered the request for a moment, his expression pensive. "Gavin is the sort of man who needs to prove his mettle in a physical way. I've made arrangements to give him the chance."

"Not sure I like the way that sounds." I rose onto my knees to tower over the naked, aroused Highlander beneath me. "Guess I'll have to torture you for the details."

He skimmed his hands up and down my thighs. "I enjoy your torture."

"Me too." I bent forward to dangle my breasts in his face. "When can we tell everyone we're having a baby?"

Rory groaned and rolled his eyes. "I'm getting the idea you'll be the sort to wake everyone at a four a.m. on Christmas morning."

"Not everyone. Only you."

"I see." He threw his arms around me and rolled us both over so I lay trapped beneath him. "Donnae be in such a hurry, Em."

I soon forgot all about the Gavin problem and convincing Rory to share our good news. My husband had a way of erasing my memory.

When he finally told me his plan, I had to agree it had merit.

Gavin had a plan of his own, though he didn't yet realize it meshed with Rory's scheme.

Chapter Twenty-Eight

C old rain pattered on the roof of the Range Rover as Gavin pulled up in front of the house Calli and Aidan shared. Two weeks had gone by since the Thanksgiving incident. Iain had let Gavin borrow his Rover but only after giving him a hard time about procrastinating. The older man implied—okay, said it outright too—that Gavin was afraid to talk to his little sister. Maybe he was afraid, of what she might say, how she might react to what he said, how their relationship might change in the aftermath.

Gavin groaned. Aftermath? This wasn't a tornado bearing down on them.

Why did it feel that way, then?

He had to say these things to Calli even if she thought he was a total wuss and a pathetic loser afterward. He needed to work things out with Rory too, but he was procrastinating even more with that task.

An Aston Martin sat parked in the driveway behind Calli's truck.

Gavin stopped behind the uber-expensive car and shut off the engine. He knew of only one person around these parts who drove an Aston Martin. Lachlan was here. *Great.* Gavin had hoped to talk to Calli today and deal with Lachlan tomorrow—or the next day, or the day after that. Jeez, he really had turned into a pile of wussy mush.

No more.

He pulled the hood of his raincoat over his head, flung open the Rover's door, and slammed it behind him as he bolted for the door to Calli's house. The cottage was a decent size, though nothing in comparison to Rory's castle or even the farmhouse owned by Lachlan and Erica, which hardly qualified as huge. Iain's house was modest like this one. Gavin felt more comfortable in normal-size houses. Big ones made him feel like he had to be careful where he stepped and watch out for delicate, expensive knick-knacks he might accidentally knock over and break. His parents had owned an average house in an average neighborhood, with an average minivan too.

Nothing wrong with average. He wanted that. A normal, happy life.

Soon, he'd get what he wanted. He'd have Jamie for his wife.

Now, if he could find a steady job…

Gavin knocked on the door.

Voices murmured on the other side of the door, somewhere deeper inside the house, and Gavin recognized Calli's laughter. A squeal pierced the big wooden door. Baby Sarah was awake.

Silence followed, except for the clapping of footsteps drawing closer.

The door swung inward, and Calli smiled. She had Sarah clasped to her bosom, the baby's little face aimed over her shoulder. Gavin had a good view of the back of his niece's head. Beyond that, he glimpsed Christmas garlands outlining every door, with colorful lights embedded in them.

"Hey," Calli said. "This is a nice surprise."

"Uh, sorry, I should've called first." He always, always did. But not today. He'd been afraid if he told Calli he needed to come over and talk he'd lose his nerve.

Calli waved a dismissive hand, holding onto Sarah with the other arm. "You're family. You can stop by anytime."

He suppressed a wince at the word family.

Leaning sideways, he peered around Calli into the house beyond. "Where are Misty and Mandy?"

"The girls are having a play date with Casey."

"Dogs have play dates? Go figure." He twisted his mouth into a wry smile. "Aren't you worried Erica's big boy dog will get fresh with your little girls?"

"Casey is neutered, Gav. And he's a gentleman."

"Never say the word neutered around a man, C."

She angled sideways and flapped a hand in a hurry-up gesture. "Get inside before you turn into a walking puddle."

He hurried over the threshold, and while Calli shut the door, he hung his raincoat on a hook on the entryway wall.

"Is it Aidan?" Lachlan called from the direction of the kitchen.

"No," Calli hollered. "My husband doesn't ring the doorbell, Lachlan."

"Oh. Aye, of course."

"Duh," Calli muttered with a shake of her head and a soft little laugh.

She turned and led Gavin down the hall.

Baby Sarah caught sight of Gavin and cooed, smiling and stretching out one tiny hand to him. He let her have one of his fingers, and she curled her tiny ones around it, gripping him with surprising strength for such an itty-bitty tyke. Sarah gurgled.

"Are you talking to Uncle Gavin?" Calli said. She glanced over her shoulder at him. "See? Your niece misses you."

Guilt weighed down on him like a two-ton boulder.

"Sorry," he said. "I know I haven't stopped by much since I've been in Scotland full time. It's partly your husband's fault. He had me and Iain working constantly for a while there."

"Uh-huh." She threw him a knowing, and faintly amused, look. "I'm sure you're awfully busy with your fiancée too. The way I hear it, Iain has to vacate the premises whenever Jamie comes a-calling or else he won't get a wink of sleep."

"Bullsh—" Gavin cut off his curse when Sarah squeezed his finger and gurgled again. Whether or not a baby could understand his bad language, he didn't feel right swearing in the vicinity of a kid. So, he amended his statement. "Baloney. Jamie comes over because Iain's gone out to see his fu—" *Oh shit.* He'd almost said the phrase fuck buddy in front of his niece. "To see his special lady friend."

Iain didn't seem to have girlfriends. He had women he screwed. Or maybe just one woman. Gavin hadn't quite figured it out yet, but Iain swore he did not have relationships.

Calli raised her brows. "Special lady friend? Everyone knows about Iain's *friendships* with the local women. He's notorious for it."

"I don't think he's as big a man-whore as everybody thinks. Not anymore, at least."

The odd Scot had told Gavin as much. The guy didn't like playing the field anymore, which was why Gavin had the impression Iain went out to have fun with one and only one woman, though he didn't seem to have serious feelings for her.

Calli led Gavin into the kitchen where Lachlan lounged on the far side of the wooden table Aidan had made as a wedding present for his wife. Iain made stuff too. Gavin wasn't handy at all, couldn't even fix a plugged drain. These MacTaggarts made him feel kind of useless.

Except when he was sledgehammering a rock wall. Yeah, that had felt damn good.

Lachlan half rose from his chair. "I should leave. Don't want to intrude."

"Actually," Gavin said, "I'd like to talk to you after me and Calli have our talk. Would you mind hanging around for a while?"

"Not at all," Lachlan said, settling back into his chair.

Calli scrunched her brows at Gavin. "We're having a talk?"

"If that's okay."

"Of course it is." Calli turned to Lachlan. "Could you watch Sarah while we talk? She's been fed and changed, so she'll probably go to sleep."

"I wouldn't mind at all," Lachlan said. "I'd love some time with my niece."

Sometimes Gavin forgot Lachlan and Rory were Sarah's uncles too. Jamie was her aunt. It seemed kind of weird to be engaged to his niece's aunt.

Not like they were related to each other. No such thing as a sister-in-law once removed.

Good thing, since he had no intention of giving up Jamie.

Calli handed Sarah over to her other uncle and ushered Gavin down the hall to the living room. A Christmas tree occupied one corner of the room, near a window, its branches decked out with lights and garlands and festive bulbs. A red blanket with green holly leaves printed on it covered the sofa, and a little sprig of mistletoe dangled from the top of the window's frame.

His sister took a seat on the sofa, gesturing toward the cushion beside her.

"Sit down," she said, "and tell me what's up."

He lowered his body onto the cushion, balancing near the sofa's edge. *Way to project a relaxed and confident attitude.* He couldn't help it. The idea of what he needed to talk to Calli about made his jaw tense.

First, he needed to say something he'd said to his sister once before in his entire life—last summer, when he'd found her living with Aidan and got seriously worried about her. Back then, he'd spoken the words in passing. Today, he needed to speak them with conviction.

Gavin cleared his throat, shifting on the cushion. "I love you, Calli. You know that, right?"

Calli fiddled with her shirt sleeve, her gaze darting away before settling on him again. "Sure, I know that. I love you too."

A pang pierced his chest like a needle driven into his heart. "We never say stuff like that. I mean, in our family we never did."

"Doesn't matter. It's nice to hear, but I know you care even if you don't tell me." She laid a hand on his knee. "You're always there for me. That's what counts."

"Not always."

"What are you talking about?"

"I let you down, big time. After Mom and Dad died, I made you handle everything." He scrubbed a hand over his mouth. "I showed up for the funeral and then I left again."

"You'd hadn't been back from Afghanistan long. I understood why you couldn't handle things."

He hesitated for a moment, summoning the nerve to confess the whole truth. "I wasn't messed up about Afghanistan. I know that's what you've always thought, and I let you go on believing it. But I didn't have PTSD. I was okay until we lost Mom and Dad." He grasped the back of his neck, bowing his head, unable to keep looking at his sister. "I fell apart because of them. You should be pissed at me for how I abandoned you. If I'd been there for you, maybe you wouldn't have married that sleaze who wanted a green card. You wouldn't have spent five years living in fear of getting arrested for marriage fraud. What happened to you is my fault."

"Bullshit."

The sharpness in her voice made him jerk his head up to meet her green eyes. "You've got to take your blinders off, C. Stop making excuses for me. I fell apart. I'm not a big, tough bastard. I'm the guy who let his baby sister get corralled into a green-card marriage so she could pay off the debts I should've been paying."

"Our parents' debts." Calli seized his hand, refusing to let go even when he tried to wrestle free of her grasp. "Listen to me, Gavin. Mom and Dad should've told us they were having financial problems, but they didn't. I should've known better than to accept Rade's offer, but I did. I married a man I didn't love so he could get citizenship. That was my bad decision and mine alone. I have never and will never blame you."

"You should. If I'd taken out a loan or something, I could've paid—"

"Stop it. You are not to blame for my mistakes." She held up one finger when he opened his mouth to speak, silencing him. "Losing Mom and Dad was such a shock it messed us both up, and we did the best we could at the time. Regrets are pointless."

Appraising his sister now, Gavin had the weirdest feeling he was seeing her for the first time. Really seeing her. She was strong and resilient and amazing. The past had no hold on her anymore because she'd let it go. He needed to do the same.

"You're right," he said, laying his other hand over hers, the one that still clasped his. "I need to stop punishing myself for what I might've done better six years ago. And I'm really grateful you're my sister. You're one hell of a woman, Calli, and I'm so proud of you. Mom and Dad would be too."

The start of tears glistened in her eyes.

Wetness gathered in his too. Must've been allergies. Guys didn't cry.

Calli pulled in a deep breath and let it out slowly. "Tell me what else is going on with you. I've never known you to let anyone get you riled up, but you let Rory get to you on Thanksgiving."

Okay, here came the really embarrassing part.

Gavin sucked it up and forged ahead. "I'm pretty sure Rory did that on purpose, but I don't know why. It worked because I've been feeling... abandoned."

Her brows scrunched up again. "Abandoned?"

Swallowing hard, he grimaced. "Yeah. Mom and Dad are gone. Leanne left me. You married Aidan and emigrated to Scotland."

"I emigrated first, then I married him."

"Whatever." He tried again to pull his hand away, but she held fast to him. He diverted his attention to the rug under his feet. "You took off for Scotland so fast. And before I knew it, I was hanging out with the MacTaggarts, feeling like a grimy toad invading the Garden of Eden."

Calli snorted, desperately trying not to laugh.

He flashed her a halfhearted scowl. "I'm confessing embarrassing shit, and you're laughing at me?"

"A grimy toad?" She let go of his hand to slap hers over her mouth. Tears gathered in her eyes again, though not from strong emotion this time. No, she was struggling not to laugh hysterically. After a moment, she got hold of herself. "You're not an invader."

"I feel like one." He slung an arm over the sofa's back, rubbing his forehead with his raised hand. "I told Jamie her brother stole my sister. Stole my family."

Calli's mouth opened, but she seemed incapable of speech.

His sassy little sister rendered speechless? He'd thought he'd never see the day that happened.

"I know it's stupid," Gavin said, "but that's how I feel sometimes. You left for Scotland in such a hurry—"

"You encouraged me to come here and get Aidan back."

He'd done that, sure. At the time, it had seemed like the right move. Push his sister to go after the man she loved. "I wanted you to be happy. But after you married Aidan, I started to feel more and more like an obsolete appendage."

"First, you're a toad. Now you're an appendage?"

He decided to ignore her snarky comment because if he stopped to give her a sarcastic response he might lose his nerve.

"You don't need me, Calli. Maybe you never did." He drummed his fingers on the sofa's back, studying the weave of the fabric to avoid his sister's gaze. "You have a new family. You've got new brothers and new sisters, new parents too. You became a MacTaggart, and I became an orphan. I am the last living member of the Douglas family."

She said nothing for a moment, though he sensed her attention on him. He scratched his neck, but the prickly sensation of his sister assessing him wouldn't go away.

"Look at me, Gavin."

He forced himself to do that and found her gazing at him with an expression of...love. Sympathy. Understanding. And he suddenly got a twinge in the back of his throat.

"Yes, I took Aidan's name," she said, "but I will always be a Douglas. I'll never forget Mom and Dad. I'll never forget you either. We're family, no matter what."

"I get that, I really do." He sighed, closing his eyes for a second. "I've wanted to marry Jamie since the day we met. Never believed in love at first sight, but with her, I felt it. Couldn't work up the courage to ask her because I was afraid she'd leave me too. Seems like everybody leaves me. Mom and Dad, you, Leanne. The people I love go away. Then I met the MacTaggarts, and I kind of developed an inferiority complex, I guess. Their family is so strong, so tight, and they took you in without reservation. Over the past year and a half, I've seen how much Jamie's brothers mean to her. Blaming them for my problems with her was an easy out. If it's their fault, then I don't have to face up to my inner demons."

"But you have," Calli said. "You're engaged to Jamie, and you told me all this stuff that must've been so hard to talk about."

"I still have to make peace with Lachlan and Rory. I know that."

"Jamie doesn't care what her brothers think. She made that clear on Thanksgiving."

"Sure, but they're still her brothers." Gavin gusted out a sigh. "I owe it to Jamie to get along with her brothers. Can't spend the rest of my life arguing with Rory. Whatever it takes, I'm going to get in good with them."

"I know Emery told you to bromance the brothers."

"Ugh." Gavin threw his head back. "If I never hear that stupid, made-up word again, it won't be soon enough."

Calli laughed, the sound light and melodic, the sound of real happiness. "Whatever you call it, you've gotten it done with Aidan. Not that he was much of a nut to crack. My husband has to like my brother since he knows how important you are to me."

That pang came back, sharper and deeper than before. It wasn't a bad feeling. No, he got this pang because his sister really loved him, and he was grateful beyond words to have her in his life.

When had he turned into a sap?

Hell, he'd ooze sap from every pore on his body if it meant he could make the two most important people in his life happy—Jamie and Calli.

To win over Rory, he'd have to can the sap and bring out his man arsenal. Whatever the stoic solicitor wanted to put him through, he'd do it. Anything. Absolutely anything.

Gavin looked at his sister. "Are we cool?"

"We've always been cool. This is your journey, and I'll support you any way I can."

"Don't think you can help me with Rory." Gavin glanced over his shoulder toward the doorway. "But first, I need to talk to Lachlan."

"Rory's not as bad as you think, but Lachlan is definitely a softer target."

He'd never thought of Lachlan MacTaggart as soft, but he got her meaning. Lachlan would be more open to the idea of not murdering Gavin.

Calli stood, and Gavin did the same. She hopped up on her toes to give him a firm hug. He held on to her a few seconds longer than he'd intended to and then he let go.

In a lot of ways.

She pushed him toward the door. "Go. Get it done."

He led the way this time and walked into the kitchen to find Lachlan making silly baby talk to Sarah. The kid was giggling and gurgling. Calli retrieved her daughter and left the room.

Gavin pulled out the chair across the table from Lachlan.

The Scot watched him without expression.

He dived in headfirst. "You once told me to show a little respect. Well, here goes."

Chapter Twenty-Nine

The conversation lasted eighteen minutes. Gavin timed it with his watch. He'd expected his efforts to take longer. He'd also expected Lachlan to act like Rory, standoffish and kind of hostile, but instead he acted more like Aidan. Lachlan watched Gavin with a slight smile on his lips, one arm resting on the table, one foot propped up on the other knee. He sat like that for several seconds—several silent, interminable seconds—before Gavin realized he'd have to start the conversation.

Duh. He'd asked for this, which made it his responsibility to start things off.

"First off," Gavin said, "I'd like to apologize for not being real friendly. It's totally my fault I haven't gotten along better with you and Aidan and Rory. I'm sorry."

Lachlan's brows lifted. "You're claiming full responsibility?"

"I am. Yes."

"Apology not accepted."

"Wha—" Gavin glanced around like he might figure Lachlan out by studying the air molecules in the kitchen. What did he have to do to make nice with this guy? Stay calm, that's what, and let the Scot torture him for as long as it took. Gavin sighed and leaned back in his chair. "Fine, I deserve that. I'm an ass."

Lachlan chuckled. "I'm not accepting your apology because you have no need to apologize. We're all to blame here, Gavin. Aidan always liked and admired you, though I doubt he'd ever admit that to you. Rory and I, on the other hand, weren't particularly welcoming when you visited Scotland for the first time for Aidan and Calli's wedding."

Yeah, Gavin remembered the way Rory had glared at him the entire time. Lachlan had introduced himself and his wife and baby son but otherwise had ignored Gavin. Things hadn't gotten better after that. Like Emery had pointed out, Gavin hung back during family gatherings. He didn't talk to anybody except to exchange pleasantries.

"It was my responsibility," Gavin said, "to try to fit in with your family. I screwed the pooch on that one, didn't I?"

"We all bollocksed things. Our wise American wives set us straight."

"You mean Emery meddled and got Erica and Calli roped into it too."

Lachlan chuckled again. "Aye, that's the way of it."

"Iain got sucked into it too. Guess Emery's got your whole family wrapped around her little finger. That woman's got nerves of steel."

"Which is why she's the only one who could ever get through to Rory," Lachlan said. "And that is why we all adore Emery, and why we let her meddle in our lives. She's headstrong, but she has a heart of pure, twenty-four karat gold."

"So does Jamie."

"Emery and Jamie are alike in many ways." Lachlan paused, his smile flattening out. "Jamie is different in one important way. She had three over-protective brothers interfering in her life. When she was a wee bairn, she needed us to look after her. Jamie's matured into a fine woman, and we haven't been willing to accept she doesn't need us anymore. Not in the same way, at least. I think we've stifled her, but the consequences didn't reveal themselves until she met you."

Gavin had no idea what to say to that, so he kept quiet and let Lachlan go on.

"Aidan was always Jamie's best friend, her confidante," Lachlan said. "But Rory and I were the ones who took on the task of protecting her. I was fifteen when she was born. I was at university when she started school. Rory was four years behind me, and our age difference with Jamie made us view her as a bairn always, even when she'd grown up and graduated university. What started out as protectiveness turned into two overbearing brothers who couldn't accept their little sister had become a capable, intelligent woman."

"I get that. My sister is eight years younger, and I've always been protective of her. Didn't like it when she took up with Aidan."

Lachlan nodded. "But you made the effort to become friends with him. Rory and I haven't done the same with you." He shifted in his chair, clearing his throat. "I had a talk with Jamie yesterday. She told me how Trevor treated her when they were together. I had no idea the bastard had made her so unhappy, but when she told me about it, I realized Rory and I are partly to blame. We smothered her with our protection. She never needed to stand up for herself, and so she let another overbearing man trample her."

Jesus, was that what Jamie had done? Gavin hadn't thought about it in those terms. Hearing about Trevor had made him want to deck the guy repeatedly, pummel him to a bloody pulp, grind his face into the ground until he choked on dirt. But he hadn't considered the possibility Jamie had been afraid to stand up to Trevor. Gavin had always seen Jamie as a bright light, glowing from within, strong enough to stay cheerful no matter what. How could he not have seen her fears?

Oh, he should've guessed. Jamie had never complained about their intercontinental relationship, not until he'd delivered the worst prelude to a proposal in the history of the world. Only then had Jamie asserted herself and informed him she was sick and tired of their jet-lagged relationship.

Lachlan looked Gavin straight in the eye. "You accomplished what none of us ever allowed to happen. You got Jamie to stand up to Rory. When my brother gave his outrageous performance at Thanksgiving dinner, Jamie called him a bleeding bawbag and she meant it."

"She called me a bawbag too."

"Jamie may have said bawbags, plural, but she was speaking to Rory exclusively. I've never heard her shout at anyone, much less express so much anger and passion." Lachlan pointed a finger at Gavin. "And she did it for you."

She had. God, watching Jamie lambaste her brother, her cheeks pink from the intensity of her emotions, the sight had taken Gavin's breath away. She was incredible, and she was his.

He rested his arms on the table and leaned in. "I'd like us to be friends. Not just for Jamie, but for Calli too. Is that possible?"

Lachlan held out a hand. "Consider it done."

Gavin shook Lachlan's hand. "Thanks, man, I appreciate that."

The Scot relaxed into his chair. "I imagine you'll be talking to Rory next."

"Eventually."

"Remember, Rory engineered that rammy on Thanksgiving. He wouldn't tell me why, though I can guess. You might want to consider the possible reasons."

"I know."

Lachlan drummed his fingers on the table, his mouth slightly puckered, studying Gavin with an analytical gaze. "May I give you a word of advice?"

"Sure, why not."

"You need to make a commitment, for Jamie's sake."

"We're engaged."

"I meant a geographic commitment." Lachlan spread his hand on the tabletop. "Either ask her to move to America with you or commit to living in Scotland permanently."

"Oh, that." Gavin sat back, hands on his thighs. "I'm staying in Scotland. Decided that the day Jamie dumped me."

"I assume you have a visa."

"Didn't need a visa to visit the UK. I need one now?"

"Yes, you'll be needing a visa if you don't want to be deported." Lachlan pointed a finger at Gavin. "Best talk to a solicitor about that."

Gavin slumped his shoulders because he knew exactly what Lachlan would say next.

"We've got one in the family, you know."

"Thanks for the solid kick in the ass," Gavin said. "Point taken. I need to talk to Rory, about a lot of things."

His need for a visa gave him an excuse to talk to Rory. He could broach the subject of Jamie and whether he and Rory could ever become friends after that. Gavin would settle for being polite acquaintances with the guy. He didn't expect Rory MacTaggart to ever become his best bud.

Gavin rose, Lachlan did too, and they shook hands to say goodbye. Calli appeared then, with Sarah on her shoulder, like she'd been listening outside the kitchen doorway. Gavin couldn't believe his little sister would do that. She'd probably stopped by to see if the men had finished their confab yet. Gavin hugged Calli again, which made her giggle nervously. Well, he couldn't blame her. In all his adult life, he'd hugged her a grand total of twice, both times today.

Right then and there, he resolved to hug his sister more often. His niece too.

He tickled Sarah's tummy and kissed the top of her head.

After leaving Calli and Aidan's house, Gavin headed back to Iain's place to prepare the big surprise he had planned for tonight. For Jamie. To make up for everything and start fresh.

To show his future wife how much she meant to him.

And tomorrow, he'd tackle Rory.

Not literally. Probably.

Jamie knocked on the door of the largest room at the Loch Fairbairn Arms. When no answer came, she knocked harder, rattling the wooden door. The knob featured an old-fashioned key lock, not an electronic keycard reader. This was Loch Fairbairn, not Inverness.

The door lock disengaged with a click, and the door eased open a few inches.

One of Gavin's eyes peered at her through the gap. "You're early."

"I'm fair sick of waiting in the lobby, listening to a ninety-year-old woman blethering about her gout."

"Lucky for you, I'm ready early." He scanned her up and down. "Where's the blindfold?"

Oh. She'd forgotten that requirement for this evening. Gavin had insisted on complete secrecy about what he had planned for tonight, but he'd been explicit in his instructions that she wait in the lobby for fifteen minutes and that she wear a blindfold when she came to the room. She dug the length of silky pink fabric out of her purse, holding it up for Gavin to see.

"Put it on," he said. "Can't let you in until you do."

She draped the blindfold over her eyes and secured it in back.

He took her hands, guiding her inside the room. When they reached the bed, he helped her sit down on it.

"I've got a lot to make up for," he murmured in her ear, his voice low and deep, a sensual rumble that awakened her body. The dark, spicy scent of his cologne enveloped her. "I plan to do as much of it tonight as I possibly can."

"Can I take the blindfold off yet?"

"No." He nibbled her earlobe, flicking his tongue over it, then dragged his mouth down her throat, making her shiver with a delicious hunger. His lips quivered on the skin above her collarbone when he said, "Trust me, babe. This is all for you."

"Gavin—" Her voice abandoned her when he thrust his tongue out to forge a wet, hot trail down her chest until his head was nestled between her breasts, pushing down the neckline of her blouse.

He splayed his hands on her back, sliding them down to her bottom. "Mm, you smell so good."

"Unh." She couldn't form words, couldn't form thoughts, couldn't do a blessed thing except melt into him.

"But we're doing this the right way." He pulled his head away, his hands too, and whisked the blindfold off her head. "How do you like your surprise?"

She straightened, hands on her lap, and admired the scene around her. Candles flickered on the dresser and the bedside table, casting shimmering light on the room. A wheeled cart, draped with a white tablecloth, held dishes concealed under covers and a bottle of champagne bookended by a pair of glass flutes. Gavin had stepped back several feet, granting her a full view of him. He wore a tuxedo and shiny black shoes, and he stood with his shoulders rolled back and his head held high, his face clean-shaven.

"Is that the same tuxedo you wore on Halloween?" she asked.

He fingered the lapels. "It is. You seemed to like it."

"Oh, I do." Her breasts tightened the longer she looked at him, so handsome and sexy in his black suit and bow tie. "Can I tear your clothes off yet?"

Gavin laughed. "I love your enthusiasm, but I've got something else planned first."

While he headed for the food cart, she twisted around to examine the bed. The blindfold lay beside her. He'd pulled the thick quilt down to the foot of the bed where it lay neatly folded beneath her. The blanket had been tossed aside so it covered half the mattress. She ran her hand over the sheets, surprised by their silky texture. She'd never stayed at the Loch Fairbairn Arms before, and she'd had no idea how luxurious their accommodations were.

"This is a lovely room," she said, for something to say. Her skin tingled with a nervous excitement, and she'd gnarled her fingers in her skirt.

"I got the biggest room at the best hotel in Loch Fairbairn."

"This is the only hotel in the village."

He glanced over his shoulder to flash her a sly grin. "Then it would be the best one, wouldn't it?"

She craned her neck in an attempt to peek around his body. "What are you doing over there?"

"You'll see." He returned his attention to the cart. "Can I trust you to close your eyes and not peek? Or should we put the blindfold back on?"

With a sly grin of her own, she snatched up the blindfold and tied it in place.

"That's my girl."

And she was his. Completely. Willingly. Forever.

The carpeting muted the sound of his footsteps as he approached her, and the rustling of his clothing told her he'd knelt in front of her. He clasped her hands, his warm and roughened by the manual labor he'd done lately. She didn't mind at all. The thought of those rough palms on her naked skin rippled a hot shiver through her body.

He kissed her knuckles one by one, then set her right hand back on her lap, keeping her left hand in his. "I love you, Jamie. There's nobody else for me, not now, not ever."

When he tore the blindfold off, she blinked at the sudden change.

Gavin knelt on one knee, his steady gaze on her. In his right hand, he held a small, velvet-covered box with the lid flipped up to reveal a diamond ring. "Jamie MacTaggart, will you marry me?"

"You already asked me that, and I already said yes."

"While I had my dick inside you." He raised the ring to her eye level. "You deserve a genuine, romantic proposal. What do you say?"

"Yes. Again."

He plucked the ring from the box and slipped it onto her finger. "Now it's official. You're stuck with me, your ball and chain till death do us part."

"I like your balls. They're mine and only mine from this day forward."

Gavin picked her up, carried her to the side of the bed, and laid her down on the soft sheets with her head on the fluffy pillow. He devoured her with his eyes, admiring her body with a heated haze in his eyes, his attention exciting her skin with every sweep of his gaze.

She started to sit up.

He sat on the bed's edge, one hand on her knee. "You've inspired me to go talk to Rory tomorrow."

"How did I do that?"

"You encouraged me to talk to Calli, which wound up with me talking to Lachlan after that." He squeezed her knee. "And Lachlan convinced me I need to talk to Rory. It was like one big circle of pestering from the Mac-Taggarts."

Jamie levered up into a sitting position and placed her hand over his on her knee. "We do it because we love you."

"Lachlan loves me?" Gavin made a disgusted face. "Do I have to hug him now?"

"No," she said with a half-stifled laugh. "And don't tell Lachlan I included him in the group of MacTaggarts who love you. Don't tell Aidan either, he'll tease Lachlan about it forever. Aidan still calls Rory 'sweetie-pie' because Calli mentioned that Emery mentioned Rory's a sweetie-pie."

"That's one convoluted grapevine you guys have there." He slid his hand up her thigh, carrying her hand with it. "I might need some hot sex to reinvigorate me, so I have the energy to deal with the guy who goaded me into an argument at Thanksgiving."

"He did the same to me."

"I know, and tomorrow I'll find out why." He switched his hand position, holding hers beneath it on her own thigh, and moved their hands together until his fingers and hers grazed the hairs of her mound. "Tonight, I plan on celebrating our newly reaffirmed engagement. With lots of moaning and gasping from you. For hours and hours and hours."

For the rest of the night, he proved he hadn't been exaggerating. They made full use of the spacious suite at the Loch Fairbairn Arms—hour after hour.

Chapter Thirty

The next morning, Gavin drove Jamie back to the castle. The place was drowning in Christmas decor, everything from Santa Claus statues that danced and said "ho-ho-ho" to sprigs of holly and decorated trees on every floor. Gavin kissed Jamie goodbye in the vestibule. She headed into the ground floor to her bedroom, to change into fresh clothes. Though she'd offered to be his wingman—"wing-lassie," as she'd put it—during the meeting with Rory, Gavin had politely declined the offer and made her promise to stay away from Rory's office. Gavin didn't need his fiancée's help in dealing with her brother. He could handle this on his own, though he loved Jamie even more for wanting to stand beside him. This was one battle he had to fight alone.

He leaned out the vestibule doorway to watch her sashay down the hall, her round little ass swaying in time with her hips. Waking up with her this morning, with all those curves draped over him and her hair tickling his chest and his cheek, he'd experienced something he'd never known in all his life.

Absolute contentment.

Jamie veered into the dining room, out of sight.

Sighing with deep pleasure, he turned toward the spiral staircase. His gaze traveled up the steps toward the first-floor landing. Rory's office awaited him up there. He'd called this morning to ask if Rory had time to speak with him, and the guy had agreed without any argument or snide comments. He'd simply said, "Be here at ten a.m."

While Gavin drove the Mercedes—oh yeah, he got to drive Rory's car—Jamie had called Emery to tell her about the engagement ring. Emery's shriek had erupted from the phone's speaker and rattled Gavin's ears. Jamie had shrieked in response, all but deafening him. He didn't care. Seeing Jamie so happy made him happy. Ecstatic, actually. He hadn't seen Jamie like this in way too long. The old, ebullient Scottish lassie had returned. *His* Scottish lassie.

Footsteps on the stairs jerked him out of his reverie.

Trevor Langley waltzed down the spiral staircase, halting at the bottom. He aimed a smug smile at Gavin.

"You again," Gavin said. "Damn, you're worse than athlete's foot."

"Finally worked up the nerve to talk to Rory?" Trevor said. "I've been speaking to him for an hour. He doesn't seem at all frightening to me, but then, I'm not an American."

The English Ass said "American" like it was the worst insult imaginable. Well, to an arrogant prick like him it must seem that way. After all, no one on earth could compare to Sir Trevor Langley, at least in Sir Trevor Langley's eyes.

For the first time since Gavin had met the schmuck, he didn't feel the least bit irked by Trevor's insults. "That's right, I'm an American and proud of it. Winston Churchill's mother was American, you know. Isn't he, like, a hero to you Brits?" Gavin chuckled. "Your half-American icon."

Trevor's eyes narrowed. "Rory's investing in my business venture. That means he'd rather have me around than you. I'll have Jamie too, once she realizes her beloved brother prefers me."

Gavin made a derisive noise. "How dense are you? Jamie's my fiancée."

"She'll call it off, that's what she does. She strings men along until they're caught in her spider's web, then she cuts them loose."

"You're not even worth the effort to argue with." Gavin pushed past him to move onto the second step. "You're pathetic, man. Just pathetic."

Gavin started up the stairs.

Trevor's snickering echoed in the vestibule. "Jamie's a tease, Gavin. She loves a good shag, but commitment isn't her style. Once the novelty wears off, she'll be on the hunt for a new bloke to fuck her like the slag she is."

Fury exploded through Gavin, scorching and unstoppable.

He whirled around, vaulted the three steps to Trevor, and slugged the English Ass in the jaw.

Trevor staggered backward, floundering to grab the staircase railing to keep from tumbling to the floor. Half hanging from the railing, he massaged his jaw and glowered at Gavin.

"You'll pay for this," the English Ass snarled.

Gavin stalked toward the man and bent over to spear the guy with his best steely glare. He spoke in a hushed voice imbued with menace. "If you ever talk about Jamie that way again, I'll pummel you into the ground. Do you hear me? Stay away from her, stay away from this house, and go home to England where you belong."

He seized Trevor by the collar of his shirt, hauled him to the door, and yanked it open.

"Go," Gavin growled.

Trevor's lip curled. "You'll regret this. I have friends in very high places."

"Get out," Gavin snarled. "Walk or crawl, I don't care. But get yourself out the door in the next two seconds or I'll throw you out like the garbage you are."

Trevor scrambled outside on hands and knees.

Gavin slammed the door. The windows rattled.

Movement in the doorway to the hall attracted his attention.

Jamie hovered in the doorway, eyes wide, mouth open.

"Christ, Jamie," he said, scrubbing a hand over his face. "I'm sorry. I shouldn't have—"

She rushed across the vestibule, flinging her entire body at him.

He caught her, the feminine scent of her enveloping him. "You're not mad, I take it."

"Mad?" With her arms clamped around his neck and her feet dangling above the floor, she pulled her head back to meet his gaze. "I could have sex with you right now, here in the vestibule with Rory waiting upstairs. No one has ever done anything like that for me."

"Not even Rory, your knight in shining armor?"

"No, Gavin," she said, her voice fierce. "You are my knight in shining armor. Thank you."

"All I did was punch one damn irritating son of a bitch."

"You chased him off. And you did it for me." She mashed her mouth to his in a quick, hard kiss. "You're my hero, not my brothers. You."

A throat-clearing noise from up the stairs made them both crane their necks.

Rory towered above them on the first-floor landing, his expression neutral. "Are we having our meeting, or would you rather skite your fist on Trevor's face again?"

"Hmm," Gavin said, "that is tempting, but no. I'll be right up."

With a curt nod, Rory disappeared into the first floor.

Gavin set Jamie down on her feet, gave her ass a quick squeeze, and kissed her forehead. "You don't need me to protect you, but it's nice to know you appreciate it if I do."

"I love you even more for it."

He strode up the stairs with the love of his life gazing after him like he'd turned into Superman. A minute later, he walked into Rory's office, the old castle library furnished with a huge wooden desk. Rory reclined in a leather executive chair behind the desk.

"Sit," he said, gesturing toward one of the lesser chairs in front of the desk.

Gavin took a seat. "About what happened down there…"

"I'm certain Trevor Langley deserved it." Rory tilted his chair back slightly. "Frankly, I would've loved to do that myself."

"Thought you liked the guy. He sure thinks you do. Told me you're investing in his new business."

Rory grunted. "The man is an erse and an eejit. I listened to him prattle on and on for an hour, telling me about the wondrous opportunity I have to invest in his dimwitted scheme to turn a tiny, ramshackle distillery into a tourist mecca. If he assumed my silence indicated interest, he's mistaken." Rory turned his eyes heavenward and exhaled a long sigh. "I hadn't realized what a right bore the man is. When he was with Jamie, I rarely had contact with him. I can't imagine how my sister could've agreed to marry him."

"She made a mistake. I'm sure he can be suave when he wants to."

"Yes, he can." Rory rubbed his forehead. "He fooled me at first."

Holy mackerel. Rory MacTaggart had admitted to Gavin, the American interloper, that he'd made an error in judgment. Maybe the tide had turned, but he could still drown if he didn't step carefully. "Look, I wanted to apologize for not being real friendly to you and your brothers. I'm sorry. Could we maybe start over?"

Rory studied him without expression for several long seconds.

"I suppose," Rory said at last, "we could do that."

"Thanks, man, I appreciate it."

Rory's lips ticked up at the corners, but he didn't quite smile. "I owe you an apology as well. I haven't been particularly welcoming to you, and what I did at Thanksgiving must've seemed odd to you."

"Yeah, but I get the feeling you had a reason for doing that."

"I should explain."

Gavin held up a hand. "Let me go first. I know it seems like I've been stringing Jamie along, but I wanted to marry her the day we met."

"An inclination I can understand." Rory hooked one ankle atop the other knee and began to rock his chair gently. "I proposed marriage thirty-six hours after meeting Emery. But I'm sure you've heard the stories about our arrangement."

"Kind of hard to miss it splashed all over that dinky little tabloid. What was it called? The Loch Fairbairn Enquirer?"

"Loch Fairbairn World News. Fortunately, the vile toad who owned it has moved on to greener pastures in Liverpool." Rory smiled with a vengeful satisfaction Gavin could relate to. "I hear Graham Oliver has taken up pig raising. Knee-deep in the shit, as always."

"Poetic justice? Gotta love that." Gavin relaxed into his chair, feeling less anxious with Rory sitting there in such a relaxed pose discussing the jerk who'd wronged his wife and gotten his comeuppance. "I used to think you hated me."

"And now?"

"I don't think you hate me, but I can't figure out what you're up to." Gavin paused to think about what to say next, how much he needed to share with Rory. "Look, I've figured out lately why I couldn't make a commitment to Jamie even though I wanted to be with her. I felt like your brother stole my sister, stole my family, and I was like an orphan chucked out on the streets. It was easier to blame you and your brothers for my problems with Jamie than to admit I'm a lame-ass moron who felt abandoned. I shouldn't have done that. I'm sorry."

He hadn't realized how embarrassing his confession would be until the words came out of his mouth. His skin crawled, and his throat had gotten tight. He fought the urge to scratch until he drew blood, but the longer Rory sat there staring him down the harder it got to keep from scraping his skin raw. He'd informed one of the most stoic and confident men on earth that he'd felt like an abandoned orphan. Maybe he should give in to total humiliation and start sucking his thumb.

"That must have been difficult to say," Rory told him, "especially to me. I admire your courage."

Admire? Courage? Gavin must've misheard the guy.

"Yes," Rory said like he'd read Gavin's mind, "I've admitted to admiring you. A wee bit. Donnae let it go to your head."

Rory's mouth curved upward into a...*Holy shit.* The guy was smiling. The closed-mouth expression represented the first time ever Rory MacTaggart had done anything other than glare at Gavin. He considered pumping his fists in the air and hooting, like a goofy victory dance, but he tamped down the impulse.

He had no illusions they'd become friends. Yet.

"None of my loved ones," Rory said, "has ever emigrated to another country. Catriona lived in America for a time, and so did Iain, but those were temporary changes. I suppose I can't understand what it would feel like to have one of my sisters move across the pond permanently."

"I didn't realize how much it would affect me until it happened." Gavin drummed his fingers on the arms of his chair. "It was more than Calli emigrating. I came here and met her new family, all these MacTaggarts who have a kind of bond I've never had with my sister, and I realized I wanted that. But I thought it was too late. Seeing all you guys with your parents... Well, I'm never going to have that. I can change things with Calli, though, and that's what I'm trying to do."

Rory tilted his head to the side, analyzing Gavin. "Has no one told you?"

"Told me what?"

"Your sister talks about you incessantly. She regales us with tales of her heroic brother and his exploits in the Marines, not to mention the childhood stories."

Gavin touched two fingers to his brow, struggling to wrap his mind around the idea. No such luck. His brain couldn't encompass it. "Calli...She talks about me?"

"Yes. She worships you."

Sure, he'd told Calli the PG-13 stories about what he experienced during his stint in the Marines and his tour in Afghanistan. He left out the gory stuff. And the ribald stuff. She'd always listened, but he'd thought she was humoring him and really had no interest in his military days.

He'd misunderstood a hell of a lot.

"Your sister may have emigrated," Rory said, "but she hasn't left you behind."

Rory was being nice. Rory. Nice.

Gavin resisted the urge to glance around and see if Rod Serling was standing in the corner about to narrate this episode of *The Twilight Zone*.

One word Rory had said triggered his memory. "Speaking of emigrating, Lachlan said I probably need a visa. He said you might be able to help me with that."

"I can."

"Uh, so, will you give me a hand? I'd really appreciate it."

"Yes, I will."

"Thank you."

Rory smiled for the second time in the past ten minutes. "I can't let my sister's fiancé languish in immigration limbo, can I?"

"Guess not." Gavin waved a finger from himself to Rory and back again. "Are we good?"

The smile faded into an inscrutable expression, and Rory bent forward to rest his elbows on the desk. He steepled his fingers under his chin. "It isn't over yet."

And there went the floor, plummeting away from him into the center of the earth. So much for getting on solid ground with Rory.

Still, Gavin had to ask. "In what way?"

"I love my sister very much." Rory squinted at Gavin, his gaze flinty. "I will take whatever measures are necessary to ensure her well-being and happiness."

"Me too." He didn't know what the guy was building up to, but he sensed he wouldn't like it. *Stay cool*, he reminded himself, *don't let Rory get to you again.* "What is it you're trying to tell me?"

"How far are you willing to go to prove your worthiness?"

Worthiness? Gavin swallowed a snide retort, clamping his hands on the chair's arms. So much for Rory admiring him.

The guy had said it was only a "wee bit."

And here came the big, honking weight of the rest of Rory's opinion of him.

"Don't assume," Rory said, lowering his hands, "you understand my motivations. Only my wife truly understands me, and she approves of my, as she calls it, 'silly manly nonsense scheme.' In fact, she helped me plan it."

Of course she did. Emery had her mind set on meddling, her way of showing she cared about the outcome. Gavin decided he ought to be more grateful to her, though, considering that Rory without Emery had been a real ogre. Since he found his fourth wife, the guy really had changed. A few months ago, would Rory have let Gavin into his house for a man-to-man talk? No, he probably would've mowed Gavin down with his Mercedes.

So yeah, Gavin was grateful for Emery's meddling.

He let go of the chair's arms, some of the tension dissolving. Whatever Rory had up his neatly pressed sleeve, Gavin could handle it. "Do I get to know what this scheme is?"

"Naturally." Rory surged up from his chair. "This afternoon. Two o'clock."

"You're making me leave and come back later? To pass some test for you?"

"Precisely." Rory balanced his fingertips on the desktop. "But the test is not for me."

"For Jamie."

"No."

Gavin clapped his jaw shut to keep from huffing at Rory. The guy was driving him bonkers. "The test is to convince you I'm worthy of your sister."

Rory's lips twitched like he wanted to smile but held it back. "I told you, it's not for me either."

"Well—" A tiny huff escaped before Gavin squelched it. *No frustration, remember?* He took a deep breath and let it out slowly. "Do I get to know who I'm proving myself to?"

He couldn't believe Aidan or Lachlan would care about putting him through some cockamamie test.

Rory walked around the desk to Gavin's chair, gazing down at him from high above. "The reasons for all of this will become clear this afternoon. Do as I ask, and you'll be glad you've done it."

He offered Gavin his hand to shake.

Gavin hesitated for only a second, then shook Rory's hand. It was a quick, firm gesture.

The deal was done. Whatever fate awaited him this afternoon, Gavin would accept it without bitching. He'd swallow any pills Rory handed him, even poisoned ones.

For Jamie, he would do anything.

The office door pivoted inward, and Emery waltzed into the room with a Santa hat balanced on her head at a slight angle and jingle-bell earrings tinkling. Her T-shirt featured a cute kitten snuggled under a Christmas tree. She slipped an arm around Rory's waist, gazing up at him with unmistakable adoration. "How'd it go?"

"We have an appointment for two o'clock."

Emery glanced at Gavin. "Don't worry, it'll be fun."

Fun? Gavin didn't know if Rory's idea of a good time would prove healthy for him. To be fair, though, he didn't know Rory very well and vice versa. He'd resolved to change that, and apparently, Rory would give him that chance after this mysterious test.

Anything Rory threw at him, he could handle. Even if it involved a tutu and singing in falsetto. Every second of ridicule would be worth it to give Jamie what she really wanted—for Gavin to get along with her brothers.

To become a part of this family, he'd have to pass The Test.

"Jamie's waiting for me," Gavin said. "Nice to see you, Emery. Rory, I'll see you at two o'clock."

Rory nodded. "Mrs. Darroch will instruct you where to go once you arrive."

Emery regarded him with an unsettling interest, like she had inside information she wouldn't divulge to Gavin.

At the doorway, Gavin paused to glance back at Rory. "Mind if me and Jamie borrow the Mercedes for a few more hours? I want to take her shopping in the village."

Emery clapped her hands and grinned. "Shopping! Fun. She'll love that."

Rory shook his head at his wife's enthusiasm, his lips taut with a humor he didn't try very hard to repress. "I promise to take you shopping tomorrow, Em."

"Oh goodie." She clapped again. "I love to blow my hubby's money."

"And your hubby," Rory said with a hint of sarcasm, "loves to watch you blow his money."

Rory had changed a heck of a lot, Gavin realized. Once upon a time, in the pre-Emery days, Gavin had joked that Rory ought to unchain his wallet and live a little. Rory had responded, "I save money, I don't spend it frivolously." Post-Emery, the guy let his wife buy whatever she wanted, no matter how much it cost. Hell, he encouraged Emery to spend his dough.

Still gazing lovingly at his wife, Rory said, "Take the Mercedes for as long as you like."

His wife made an O with her lips and hopped up on her toes. "I have a better idea. Gavin and Jamie should take the Jag."

Rory's eyes narrowed, but then he relaxed and nodded. "A fine idea."

Gavin opened his mouth but couldn't cobble together words. A fine idea? Lending the Mercedes was one thing, but the Jaguar Rory had given his wife as a wedding present?

Rory leaned back across the desk, without releasing his wife, and retrieved a keyring from a drawer. He tossed the ring to Gavin.

Still dumbfounded, Gavin fumbled the catch. The keyring hit the floor, and he scooped it up. The ring held one key emblazoned with the Jaguar logo.

"Thanks, man," Gavin said. "Jamie'll love this."

"I'm sure you won't enjoy it at all," Rory said with a glint of humor in his eyes and on his face.

"Oh no," Gavin assured him, "I'll enjoy it. This is awesome. Thanks, you guys."

While Emery hopped up and down and clapped some more, Gavin walked out of the office headed for the vestibule where the only woman he'd ever really loved waited for him.

And later, whether he liked it or not, he'd find out what "test" Rory had planned for him.

Chapter Thirty-One

J amie tried to watch television in the sitting room, but all she did was zip through the channels over and over, her mind refusing to focus on anything for more than a few seconds. What was happening upstairs? Would Rory and Gavin reach a truce? What if they didn't? She would side with Gavin, no matter what, because that's what couples did. At least, that's what her brothers and their wives did for each other. If Lachlan had disliked Emery, Rory would've told him to jump into Loch Fairbairn on a cold winter's day.

If Rory couldn't accept Gavin, Jamie would tell Rory to jump in the loch. Maybe she'd shove him in herself.

Reading magazines hadn't distracted her either, so she finally gave up and returned to the vestibule to sit on the steps and wait.

"Have you been sitting there the whole time?"

Jamie leaped up at the sound of Gavin's voice, spinning around to see him coming down the stairs. "How did it go?"

Gavin strode down the steps at a leisurely pace, tall and strong and gorgeous. "Rory's helping me out with the visa thing."

"He is?" Jamie's heart took flight, flittering like the wings of an ethereal butterfly. Rory had offered to help Gavin. He wouldn't help someone he disliked. "That's wonderful."

"It's good news, yeah." Gavin stepped down to stand beside her on the vestibule floor. "I think I made some strides there, but Rory asked me to come back at two o'clock to take part in some kind of test."

"A test?" Jamie wrinkled her nose, not sure she liked this development. "Does Emery know about this?"

"Yep. She's all for it."

If Emery thought this "test" was a good idea, Jamie supposed it must be okay. Rory's wife would never let him do anything nasty if she had any warning, and Rory never was nasty, anyway. Except on Thanksgiving. Even then, she'd sensed he'd started a fight for a reason, not solely to be rude. Another test? For her or for Gavin? Both, maybe.

"Let me talk to Rory," she said, turning toward the stairs. "I'll find out what he's on about."

"No, Jamie." Gavin took hold of her upper arms, forcing her to face him. "I can handle this. If your brother needs to test me, I'll do it. I want to be a part of this family, which means I have to make the effort."

"Even if it's embarrassing?"

"Yes, even if."

"We have more than three hours until you meet Rory again. What should we do?"

"Got a plan for that." He whipped a keyring out of his pocket, the Jaguar logo tag dangling from it. "Rory and Emery lent us the Jag. Thought we could go Christmas shopping in the village. What do you say?"

She couldn't help it. She squealed and hopped up and down on her toes. "Yes! Yes! I need to buy presents for all my sisters—Cat and Fiona, and the American Wives Club."

"Guess I better buy something for your brothers too. In the name of sucking up."

His smirk and the sparkle in his eyes made her heart swell. The old Gavin was back, for good.

No matter what Rory did this afternoon.

Gavin hustled her out the door to where the Jag was parked in the driveway. He hooked the keyring around his finger and twirled it. "Wanna drive?"

"Me?" Jamie flung herself at him, arms around his neck, and peppered his face and mouth with a flurry of quick kisses. "Lachlan won't let me drive his Aston Martin. Now I get to drive a Jaguar? Yes, I'd love to."

She kissed him harder, her pulse quickening as their mouths opened and their tongues tangled. He hoisted her off her feet, his hands under her bottom, and deepened the kiss even more. When he set her on her feet again, she was breathless and flushed.

He pinched her bottom and handed her the car key. "It's all yours, babe."

Jamie snagged the key. Gavin swung the driver's door open to let her slide in behind the wheel. The seat felt so nice with its soft, buttery leather. Adjusted to fit Emery, the position of the seat suited Jamie perfectly too. She turned the key in the ignition and then sat there for a moment listening to the engine purr like a kitten.

Time to awaken the beast.

She shifted the Jag into gear and floored the accelerator. The engine roared, and the sports car shot through the massive gateway to rocket down the long drive through the woods.

When they bounced over a pothole, Gavin said, "Slow down, Jamie. We want to be alive when we get to Loch Fairbairn, not a couple of meat sacks plastered to the seats."

Jamie laughed, having more fun than she had in ages, but she eased up on the accelerator.

Gavin flashed her a look of affectionate exasperation. "I learned another new thing about you. Jamie MacTaggart is a speed demon."

She laughed again. "I see why Emery loves this car."

"You can let loose again when we get to that straight stretch on the road to the village." He laid a hand on her thigh. "Think I might've created a monster, though. A sweet, sexy little demon with a hunger for speed."

"That's not all I'm hungry for." She stroked the steering wheel the same way she liked to stroke every part of him. "Emery swears this car is an aphrodisiac. I think she's right."

"Mm, yeah." Gavin shifted his hand to her inner thigh. "How do you think Rory would feel about us getting it on in his wife's car?"

"He'd have a seizure. But after what he did on Thanksgiving, it would serve him right to have his car defiled."

"Emery wouldn't care."

"No, she wouldn't. And this is *her* car, even if Rory did pay for it."

Gavin skated his hand higher up her inner thigh. "Find a secluded spot to pull over, then you can take a different kind of ride."

"I do love the feel of a powerful machine at my command."

She stopped the car in the middle of the driveway. The trees and distance from the house ensured no one would see or hear them unless Rory or Emery decided to take the Mercedes for a drive. Maybe Jamie should've worried about that, about being discovered in the midst of riding her favorite machine, but she didn't give a damn.

Gavin groaned when she shimmied out of her panties while still in her seat. When she got to her knees and swung over to straddle him in the passenger seat, his breathing grew labored and his erection blossomed.

He unzipped his pants and freed his shaft.

She lowered her body onto his length, slowly, deliberately, loving the sensation of his hardness penetrating her.

"Jamie," he groaned. "Let's defile this car good."

And then they did. Three times.

Miraculously, afterward they still had time left for Christmas shopping.

After two hours of shopping with Jamie, Gavin understood why Rory liked letting his wife burn through his wallet. Watching Jamie pick out presents for the MacTaggart women made Gavin happier than he'd imagined it could. She got so excited every time she found the ideal gift for one of the ladies, and she literally jumped for joy when she discovered the "absolutely dead perfect" gifts for her brothers. Gavin picked out presents for the guys too, even for Iain, though he had no idea if they'd like the gifts. He didn't know them very well. Though he'd vowed to remedy that situation, he doubted it would happen before Christmas.

He took the chance they'd hate what he gave them. That was a holiday tradition too, right? Getting things you didn't want from well-meaning friends and loved ones.

At one point, Jamie had held up a bright-green shirt with a picture of Santa Claus on it and said, with a mischievous little smile, "Why don't you wear this to meet Rory this afternoon?"

Gavin grabbed the shirt, holding it up to his chest to show her how it looked. "It's my color, right?"

"Oh aye, green goes with your eyes."

"They're brown."

She patted his chest, her hand smack on Santa's face. "And green complements the brown."

"If you say so." He slung the shirt over his arm. "I'll take it."

Her eyes widened, the green flecks in her hazel irises shimmering in the sunshine streaming through the shop windows. "You will?"

"Yep." He flipped through the rack of Santa shirts until he found the right size, then held it up to Jamie's chest. "You need one too."

Delight lit up her face, and his chest swelled and warmed from the inside.

He pecked a kiss on her lips. "The Santa shirts are my treat. What else can I splurge on to make my fiancée keep smiling?"

"Lunch." She glanced at the clock on the wall above the sales counter. "We've got time to have a piece at the cafe."

The word cafe made his mouth go dry. "You mean, uh, the place where I—where we—"

"Aye," she said with a bright smile. "The cafe where you shattered my heart into tiny little shards and blew them away with the wind."

He sighed and shook his head. "Okay, I deserve to get razzed about that. But are you sure you want to return to the scene of the crime?"

"Yes. We need to exorcise that curse once and for all."

Turned out by "exorcise" she meant they'd make out and feed each other like one of those sickeningly lovey-dovey couples he'd always hated. Today, he didn't care if every couple in the cafe started cooing and spooning pudding into each other's mouths. He didn't care who might see him doing those kinds of goofy things with Jamie.

She introduced him to Scottish craft beer, which turned out to be pretty darn good. After enjoying fish and chips—not the most romantic food, but very satisfying—they finished off their meal with crème brûlée made with Highland cream liqueur. The luscious dessert got Jamie in a luscious mood, and he loved her that way.

They made out while waiting for their drinks. They made out while waiting for their meal. They made out before and after dessert. Hell, they made out during dessert too. The Cafe of Doom had been rechristened the Cafe of Love.

Jamie had changed into her Santa shirt in the car right after they'd left the shop where they bought the shirts. She shrieked and giggled when he whipped off his shirt and replaced it with the Santa Claus one. Nope, she hadn't seen that coming.

She let him drive the Jag home.

As they got nearer and nearer to Rory's castle, Jamie kept eying Gavin's shirt while chewing on her lip.

Finally, he asked, "What's the matter?"

"Don't you want to change your shirt?"

"Nope. I'm good."

Her delicate brows rose, and she stopped blinking. "You are going to wear a Christmas shirt when you meet Rory for the big test?"

"Yes I am."

The surprise on her face—shock, actually—teased a laugh out of him. "I'm way past caring what your brothers think of me. I want to be friends with them, but they'll have to accept me as I am, Santa shirt and all."

Jamie leaned over and kissed his cheek. "I adore you, Gavin Douglas."

"I've got a thing for you too, in case you hadn't noticed."

Her sweet laughter tickled his senses and his heart.

Whatever might go down this afternoon, he had no more worries about losing Jamie. Nothing, not even her stern older brother, could take him away from her ever again.

Chapter Thirty-Two

Rory

I walked into the kitchen, halting a few centimeters inside the doorway to admire the vision of my wife bent at the waist in front of the open refrigerator door. She had one hand on the door, the other one thrust inside the refrigerator while she rooted about for lord knew what, probably something decadent and filled with lush cream and rich, dark chocolate. Her erse jutted up, her tight pants accentuating the lush curves and the separation between those tempting cheeks.

Emery wiggled her behind.

Bod an Donais, that body. I couldn't stop myself. I strode up behind her and splayed my hands over her rump.

She twisted her head around to flash me a naughty grin as she held up a package of eclairs. "Hungry?"

"Famished." I gave her backside a light squeeze. "Ahmno looking for that kind of food. Ahm craving the taste of you, *m'eudail.*"

My wife straightened and spun around, pasting her soft body to mine, her hands on my chest. "How did the meeting of manly men go?"

"Gavin agreed to come back this afternoon. He doesn't know why." The feel of her breasts mounded against my chest made thinking bloody difficult. I would've rather torn her clothes off. "Could we talk about Jamie and Gavin later?"

Emery tapped one finger on my chest. "Are you sure this big event is necessary?"

I groaned, realizing my hopes of ravishing my wife had been dashed. I wanted to fuck. She wanted to talk.

As usual, she understood my feelings before I did.

"We haven't had sex in almost twenty-four hours," my irresistible wife said. "I know how you get when you're sex deprived. I hope you didn't take it out on Gavin."

"Maybe next time you should sit on my lap while I talk to my sister's fiancé." I reached down to palm her behind. "Not that I'd be able to think that way."

Emery looped her arms around my neck. "I'm letting you do your silly macho thing with Gavin. After this, you owe me one."

"Anything you want, my wicked little angel."

She shimmied her hips. "Anything?"

My cock throbbed with a need only her body could quench, and I hissed, "Aye, anything."

"I want to tell everybody about the baby."

"Wouldn't it be wiser to wait—"

Her hips moved again, the sensation maddening, and she wagged a finger at me. "No more procrastinating, Rory. I know you've still got a minor hang-up about expecting things to go wrong, but nothing will. You've got me, forever. And soon you'll have this baby, our baby. Everything is perfect, let's share the good news."

She was right as always. Thanks to her love and belief in me, I'd shed most of my inhibitions about enjoying life—and all of my sexual inhibitions—and I'd come to accept I deserved the good things that came to me. I deserved Emery. Even if I didn't, though, I would never give her up. Not a chance in bleeding hell. She was mine forever.

It seemed only fair since she'd owned my heart and soul from the moment we'd met.

My wife boosted onto her toes and let her lips skim mine. "I get why you're putting Gavin through this test thingy, and it's almost sweet."

Emery had understood as soon as I'd told her. She'd done for me the same favor I was attempting to do for Gavin, though in a vastly different way. I'd needed a feisty woman to force me to accept love again and prove to me I deserved it. Gavin needed a different sort of proof.

If I could change, if I could come to like my wife calling me "sweet" and "adorable," then Gavin could certainly overcome his final hurdle to happiness.

And yes, caring about the happiness of the American who'd broken my sister's heart was a new experience for me. I had no doubt I'd been meant to find Emery. Maybe I'd also been meant to use my newfound outlook on life to help someone else.

Emery caught her lip between her teeth and traced a fingertip along my jaw. "About the baby…"

I stifled a groan when she rolled her hips into me, her softness meeting my hardness. "Christ, woman, yer a wicked angel for certain. Och, aye, we can tell the whole world about the bairn."

"Thank you." She unhooked the button of my pants. "You get a reward for being so good today."

Her fingers dragged the zipper down millimeter by millimeter.

I hooked a finger under her chin to make her look up at me. "What if I'm better later?"

"After I watch you do that test thingy," she said, her voice turning sultry, "I'm positive I'll be so hot for you it'll be a miracle if we make it into the garden before I throw you to the ground and ride you like a cowgirl on a bucking bronco."

I slid a hand into her hair to cup the back of her head. "I'll hold ye to that."

My wife spent the next hour rewarding me in many and varied ways. I rewarded her creativity in every manner I could think of, as much as I *could* think with my naked wife sprawled on the kitchen island in front of me.

I was the luckiest bastard on the planet. Not only did my wife please me in the bedroom—and the kitchen, and the garden, and the bathtub, and everywhere else in the house and out of it—she also pleased me with her unwavering faith in me. She trusted my judgment about the test for Gavin.

Mere hours from this moment, the battle would commence.

Chapter Thirty-Three

When Gavin turned up at Dùndubhan that afternoon, he discovered a boatload of cars parked inside the walls on the gravel area behind the castle. More cars lined the driveway outside the walls, leaving barely enough room for Gavin to get the Jag through the gate. He located the last unoccupied bit of real estate inside the compound and stashed the car there.

Gavin and Jamie had bumped into Calli and Aidan in the village, and the couple mentioned they were heading this way to attend the mysterious event. Even his damn sister wouldn't clue Gavin in to the nature of the "test." Not even one tiny hint.

The sound of the passenger door opening yanked Gavin back to the present.

Jamie leaped out of the Jag, bending over to duck her head inside long enough to say, "I want to speak to Emery before the whatever-this-is starts. Are you all right on your own?"

"Sure, I'm a big boy." He gave her a sardonic half smile. "I can tie my own shoes and everything."

Jamie rolled her eyes the way Rory often did. "Sure you don't want to change your shirt?"

"Positive. This big boy can handle any amount of MacTaggart family harassment."

"I know you can." She shut the door and trotted toward the house.

He waited until she'd gone inside, mostly because he enjoyed the view of her backside. When the vestibule door closed behind her, he climbed out of the borrowed sports car. He really needed to buy his own wheels, considering he'd resolved to live in this country. Somehow, he'd make that happen. For Jamie. For their relationship. For their future.

No more shying away from humiliation. Iain was right, the path of pride led to nowhere. If he wanted a life with Jamie, he had to go straight down the road to potential disgrace and be prepared to prostrate himself before Rory the Magnificent, the superhero of Loch Fairbairn.

Cheers erupted from behind the castle compound, outside the walls.

What on earth was going on out there?

Rory had said Mrs. Darroch would tell him where to go. Gavin headed for the main door of the house, the one Jamie had disappeared into a minute ago. He pushed the doorbell button, knowing it would ring inside the kitchen. He expected to wait a few minutes for Mrs. Darroch to make her way to the door.

Two seconds after he rang the bell, she swung the door open.

"Gavin, *mo luran*," she said with a warm smile. "Rory told me to expect you. Everyone's out on the green."

Everyone? How many people had been invited to witness his humiliation?

Suck it up and do whatever it takes, remember?

He squared his shoulders. "The green. That's outside the walls, right?"

"Through the garden, out the door behind the hydrangeas."

"Got it."

"Have fun. And good luck, *gràidh*."

"Thanks."

Gavin marched through the garden, past the now-withered plants that in summer created a lush and colorful paradise within the garden walls. It was December, but a minor heat wave had raised the temperature into the fifties today. At the back of the garden, he found the old door in the castle wall, heaved it open despite the thing fighting back, and stepped out onto the expanse of wilting grass. The small field was known as the green, though it earned that moniker only in the summer. A multitude of MacTaggarts loitered around the periphery, some near the wall, others gathered near the left-hand end of the field.

Cabers, essentially tree trunks without their branches, lay in a pile on the opposite side from the wall.

Gavin halted a few feet outside the door, his attention snagged by the man facing the crowd with his back to the green. He held onto a four-foot-long wooden handle attached to a metal ball. A hammer, Gavin realized. Lachlan MacTaggart was engaged in the sport known as the hammer throw.

Lachlan began to swing the hammer, whirling it in a big circle from low to the ground up above his head. His heels came up off the ground with each upswing. On the fourth rotation, he released the handle, and the hammer flew through the air to smack down at least fifty feet away.

Cheers. Clapping.

Erica gazed at her husband like he'd hurled the sun into the sky for her. She trotted up to him, flung her arms around his neck, and raised onto her tiptoes to plant a whopper of a kiss on him. He hugged Erica, and their kiss turned more passionate.

A catcall echoed across the green.

Every MacTaggart male wore a kilt fashioned from the clan tartan. The Three Macs and Iain wore blue T-shirts, while four other men wore red T-shirts, and the rest wore different types of shirts. Teams, Gavin realized. The blue and red shirts indicated two teams competing.

Gavin caught sight of Aidan standing a little ways from Lachlan and Erica, his arm around Calli, who held Sarah to her shoulder. The baby studied her surroundings with what seemed like a mixture of confusion and excitement. Calli was grinning and elbowing her husband, no doubt trying to get him to shut up. Aidan could out-gab the gabbiest women.

When Lachlan and Erica finally separated, they moseyed toward the crowd at the end of the field.

Aidan called out to his oldest brother. "Bit off today, eh, Lachie? Used to throw twice that distance. Gotten soft in your old age."

"I'm letting Rory win today," Lachlan said, smirking at someone behind Aidan. "He's newly married and needs to impress his bride."

That's when Gavin spotted Rory. He stood at the front of the crowd with Emery beside him. Well, "beside" was kind of a misnomer. Dressed in a mini-skirt kilt made from the clan tartan, she had her body plastered to his side with both arms slung around his neck—and she was nibbling his throat. In addition to her kilt, Emery wore a sparkly red shirt emblazoned with an elaborate image of Santa in his sleigh with eight reindeer towing it across the sky while on the ground woodland critters observed. Though she'd changed her shirt since this morning, the same Santa hat perched on her head, no doubt held in place by bobby pins given its precarious tilt. The jingle-bell earrings had been replaced with big earrings shaped like round ornaments. A necklace consisting of flashing red-and-green lights draped around her throat.

Emery didn't give a damn what anyone thought of her. Gavin sometimes envied her for that freedom.

Not anymore. He had no shame either, and he would do anything to get in good with Rory if that was the price of making Jamie happy.

Rory gave his wife a lingering, steamy kiss and then disentangled himself from her, looking for all the world like he would've loved to do her right there in front of the whole family.

The presence of kids might've been all that stopped him. Not that it had on Thanksgiving.

Superhero Rory sauntered across the green to where the hammer had fallen when Lachlan chucked it. Rory snatched up the large, and no doubt very heavy, hammer like it weighed nothing. Hammer in hand, he strode back to the starting line, delineated with white chalk.

Now or never, Gavin told himself. He rolled his shoulders back and marched toward Rory.

The solicitor was swinging the hammer left and right as if gauging its weight. He froze when he noticed Gavin approaching.

Rory raised his brows and let the hammer hang at his side with his fist clenched around the handle. "You're early."

"Thirty seconds, maybe."

Checking his watch, Rory said, "Ninety seconds. We'll call it on time. Are you ready for the test?"

Gavin surveyed the green, taking in the throng of MacTaggarts before settling his attention on Rory again. "Let's do it."

Rory swung the hammer up between them and let it fall again. "That's an odd choice of attire for a Highland games tournament."

With a shrug, Gavin hooked his thumbs in the pockets of his jeans. "You got a problem with holiday spirit?"

"On the contrary, I appreciate the history and tradition of Santa Claus." Rory thumped the hammer on his palm. "And I admire your bravery in standing before the entire family dressed that way."

Gavin nodded toward Emery. "Your wife is dressed like a Times Square billboard on Christmas Eve."

"Emery is the bravest person I've ever known."

"No argument here." Gavin folded his arms over his chest, partly obscuring Santa's face. "Whatever you need to do to me today, go on and do it. I'm in this one hundred percent."

Jamie raced out of the garden door to Gavin, breathing hard like she'd run to get here. "I missed Emery in the house. Has the test started yet?"

"Not yet. Your brother's too busy mocking my Christmas spirit."

Rory twirled the hammer. "If ye cannae handle a bit of mocking, ye'll never survive in this family."

"Oh, I can handle it."

Jamie's eyes flitted from Gavin to Rory and back again. "Gavin, I told you before, you don't have to do this for me."

"I'm doing this for me." Gavin looked Rory square in the eyes. "Ball's in your court."

Rory squinted at Gavin, twirling the hammer in a circle again, almost like a gunfighter.

The action was supposed to intimidate Gavin, but he was so beyond intimidating these days. He'd come to terms with his past, with Jamie's patient and loving help, which left one task on his to-do list. Make peace with Rory. It would be done today even if Gavin wound up bloodied and disgraced.

Emery sprinted up to her husband, laying a hand on his arm. "Put down the dangerous implement, please."

Rory cast her a sidelong look, one brow arched. "Why? He seems to want me to skelp him good."

Emery sighed and leaned in to press her body against his. She murmured, "If Rory baby wants to get lucky tonight, he'd better stop threatening to beat his sister's soul mate into a bloody pulp. That's not part of the test."

Rory baby? Gavin snickered. Tried not to, really, but he couldn't help it.

Okay, maybe he hadn't tried *that* hard.

Rory's lips twisted into an approximation of a smile—a reluctant one. He dropped the hammer onto the ground.

Emery kissed his cheek. "Good hubby."

Her "hubby" rolled his eyes, barred his arms over his chest, and faced Gavin. "You said anything I want."

"That's right."

Peripherally, Gavin spied Jamie's worried gaze trained on him.

Rory's lips arched upward in an expression laced with menacing glee. "The games it is, then."

"Don't forget," Emery told her husband, "Gavin's never thrown a hammer or tossed a caber before."

"He said he'd do whatever I want." Rory picked up the hammer. "This is what I want. Are you suggesting I go easy on him because he's an American?"

Rory must've realized the instant he said it he'd made a grievous mistake using the word American as an insult. His wife punched him in the arm, though the action proved ineffectual. Her slender hand couldn't make a dent in her husband's massive bicep. Still, Rory aimed a chagrined look at her.

Emery whispered something in his ear.

His lips formed an expression Gavin could describe only as supreme amusement mixed with steely menace. This must've been what Iain meant when he said Gavin might wish he hadn't come up against Rory's sense of humor when the man finally unleashed it.

Rory MacTaggart wanted to demean Gavin by whooping his ass at these cockamamie games. Fine, Gavin would let him. Maybe he'd even score a few points against the superhero solicitor.

Gavin thrust a hand out to Rory. "You're on."

Rory clasped his hand and gave it a single firm shake. "And you're in for it."

Chapter Thirty-Four

*J*amie seized Gavin's shirt and hauled him close to her, nailing him with what she hoped passed for a stern look. Rory did those better than anyone, and she'd modeled her current expression after his calm but deadly stares. She gave Gavin a hard shake that barely moved his body. "Are ye cracked? You've never done the Highland games before, and Rory's beaten Lachlan and Iain at this. Several times."

Peripherally, she noted Rory's overly pleased smile. Pleased? No. Cocky, he was. She battled warring urges to throttle sense into Gavin and to throttle respect into Rory. She loved her brother, but she worshiped Gavin—in the way a strong woman could worship her man without becoming a lovesick moron.

Jamie tried for another shake with no more effect than the first. "Well? Are ye cracked?"

Gavin's eyes narrowed. He bent his head to spear her with a look as intimidating as any of Rory's, though Jamie was not cowed by it. She knew Gavin well enough to realize he would never shout at her.

In a calm and resolute voice, he said, "I am not crazy, and I can do anything your brothers can. Or your cousins. Or your ex-fiancés. Hell, I'll fight any jerk who tells me I don't deserve you because I know we're right for each other."

Her heart lightened as if it might float out of her body. She loved hearing him say they were right for each other, but she couldn't stand by and let her brother pummel her fiancé into the ground.

Earlier, she'd told Gavin she knew he could handle any harassment from Rory. She'd meant it, but Rory seemed hell-bent on turning a simple tournament into a battle royal.

She pulled on Gavin's shirt, compelling him to slouch over until their faces approached so close their breaths reflected off each other. In a softer voice meant only for him, she said, "I know you're a braw, strapping man. You have nothing to prove to me."

"I know that." He kept his voice low too, their conversation private despite the throng of onlookers. Even Rory wouldn't be able to hear them, and she suspected Gavin realized that, based on what he told her next. "I have to prove myself to Rory. Don't like it, but dammit, I swore to myself I'd do anything to make you happy. Your brothers mean a lot to you, especially Rory. I know what it's like to have an interloper come in and sweep your sister off her feet, take her away to another country."

"You said you don't want to go back to America."

"I'll go anywhere you want." His tone had become tender, his expression too. His eyes, so near to hers, seemed to glow in the sunshine with a warm, golden hue reminiscent of the sun. "If I have to let Rory beat the shit out of me to earn his respect, I'll suck it up and keep going as long as I can, until I pass out or he gives up. That's how much I love you."

Jamie gazed into his luminous eyes, sensing a fire burned just below the surface. The fire matched his resolute tone when he'd said he loved her that much. Enough to endure a beating. She couldn't believe Rory would do that, but her brother definitely wanted to push Gavin to see how long he'd put up with humiliation before his temper got the better of him.

Rory didn't know Gavin. If he did, he would've realized Gavin never lashed out unless somebody gave him a bloody good reason, something more than macho nonsense. Gavin kept his cool. Gavin kept his focus on the mission, and he never wavered from his end goal.

She was his goal. Winning over Rory was his mission.

"Let me do this," Gavin said in a fierce whisper. "I've gone through worse for less reason. You are worth any amount of pain."

Tears stung her eyes. No one had ever loved her that much.

She released his shirt and grasped his face, towing him in for a kiss. She made it her mission to outdo the steamy kisses of Rory and Emery, and Lachlan and Erica. She crushed her lips to Gavin's, and when he opened his mouth to her, she locked her arms around his neck and ravaged him with a passion she'd never allowed herself to exhibit even in private, much less in front of her entire family. He answered the strokes of her tongue with coiling lashes of his own, demanding more, and she surrendered everything to him.

He latched his arms around her, groaning into her mouth so softly and sweetly no one could've heard it.

Aidan whooped.

She knew it was him because Lachlan shouted, "Aidan, whose side are ye on?"

The humor in Lachlan's voice was unmistakable.

"The side of true love," Aidan quipped with that tone of faux innocence he'd mastered.

Rory growled. "Are we having the games or watching you ravish my sister?"

"Let them have their fun," Iain called out.

Gavin released Jamie, brushed his thumb across her bottom lip, and straightened. "Game on, MacTaggart."

Jamie angled sideways to Gavin so she could see Rory.

Her brother picked up the hammer and twirled it by its leather strap. "You take the first run. I wouldn't want to embarrass you from the start."

"Of course not," Gavin said, striding forward to snag the hammer from Rory. "It's better if I show you up first. Your wife can lick your wounds for you, *Rory baby.*"

Jamie expected a muscle to jump in Rory's jaw, but instead, he raised his eyebrows. His lips twitched with a hint of humor.

"Need a wee bit of instruction?" Rory asked Gavin.

"Watched you do it once," Gavin said. He slapped Rory's shoulder. "If an old man like you can pitch this thing, so can I."

"Think you can beat my mark?"

Rory pointed down the green toward a little orange flag planted in the earth with a little wooden stick. There were two flags, actually. Lachlan must've thrown first, like he usually did.

Gavin seemed unfazed. "Yours the closer one?"

Rory chuckled with that threatening glee he loved to use as intimidation. "It's the farther one, laddie."

He pointed again, and she tracked the path his finger drew across the green.

The flag must've been thirty meters away. A hundred feet or so to the Americans gathered with the Scots here on the green.

Jamie bit the inside of her lip. Could Gavin best Rory? Well, Gavin had sworn he'd endure any amount of shame for her. Losing at a manly Scottish sport, maybe that would encourage Rory to be nicer to Gavin.

But she really, really wanted Gavin to win.

She retreated to wait in between Aidan and Lachlan and the American Wives Club.

Gavin took up his position at the starting line, his back to the green, the crowd in front of him. Everyone glued their gazes to the American. Beside Jamie, Aidan and Lachlan leaned in close to each other and murmured things she couldn't make out, holding up fingers as if counting something. Lachlan held up five fingers. Aidan raised ten. They shook hands and aimed their gazes at Gavin.

Were they betting on Gavin's odds of beating Rory? When Aidan glanced at her, she gave him a tight-lipped look she hoped conveyed the fact she didn't like her brothers making wagers about the man she loved.

Aidan hiked up his shoulders and spread his hands.

Gavin wore a determined expression.

Jamie clasped her hands under her chin, tapping her foot on the grass, the anticipation almost too much to bear.

Iain waved to Gavin. "*Aller Anfang ist schwer.*"

Gavin froze in the midst of raising the hammer. "Are you speaking German?"

"Aye. It means every beginning is hard."

"Uh…thanks. I think."

Iain held his hands parallel to the ground, fingers spreads. "Keep the heid, mate."

Gavin looked baffled.

Jamie's cousin strolled up to their group, smiling and nodding at Erica, Calli, and Emery before slapping the backs of her three brothers.

When he patted Jamie's arm, she smacked his chest. "Donnae be rattling Gavin before his hammer throw. Are ye wanting him to lose? He has no idea what 'keep the heid' means. Why didn't you explain it means to stay calm?"

"He grasped the gist of it. My gesture of steady hands got the point across."

"You made him flustered right before his first hammer throw." She tapped a finger on his chest. "You may be a million years older than me, but that doesn't mean I won't batter you for this."

He gave her a lazy shrug. "You can if you like, but I think you're underestimating Gavin. He's made of stern stuff."

"I know." She clamped her hands together under her chin again. "I don't want him to be embarrassed, though Rory would love that."

"Don't underestimate your brother either." Iain hooked an arm around her shoulders and tugged her close. "Women don't understand the ways of men and vice versa."

Jamie decided not to argue with Iain anymore. He never got upset about anything, so she was wasting a good bluster on him. Instead, she let her cousin keep his arm around her while she watched the love of her life do whatever was necessary to win over her brother.

Disaster. Massive. Looming.

Gavin grasped the hammer's handle. He hefted it a couple times, his eyes widening briefly as if he were surprised by the weight but not dissuaded by it.

"Twenty-two pounds," Rory hollered. "Too much for you?"

"If you can take it, I can."

"We'll see if you can beat twenty-seven point three meters."

Gavin hauled in a deep breath.

He swung the hammer above his head, whirling it in a big circle around and around. Once. Twice. Three times. His biceps bulged with the effort, his face was strained. On the fourth circuit, he twisted his torso while his feet remained planted in place and hurled the hammer across the green.

It sailed. And sailed.

The scene seemed to unfold in slow motion while Jamie watched the hammer flying through the air. Her pulse pounded in her chest and thundered in her ears. She didn't breathe or blink or move a muscle until the hammer struck the earth.

Past the orange flag that marked Rory's throw.

Iain jogged out across the field pulling a tape measure after him. Her sister Fiona held the other end of the tape measure while Iain broke into a sprint to reach the spot where Rory had landed his hammer.

Hoisting the tape measure over his head, Iain announced, "Twenty-eight point four."

Jamie shrieked and bolted for Gavin, shedding Iain's arm, tackling Gavin with such energy he staggered backward a step. Gavin laughed and hugged her to him. She could hardly believe it, and he seemed hardly able to believe it either. He'd thrown a twenty-two-pound hammer.

And he'd outdone Rory.

Iain jabbed an orange flag into the ground to mark Gavin's throw and snatched up the hammer, trotting back to the starting line. A drawn-out zipping noise broke the silence when Fiona reeled the tape measure back into its housing.

Gavin set Jamie down when Rory stalked up to them.

Rory eyed Gavin up and down, then looked him straight in the eye. "Nice throw."

Jamie supposed that was as close as Rory would get to admitting an American had beaten him at his own game. She smacked a wet kiss on Gavin's cheek.

Rory thumped one fist into his other palm. "Games aren't over yet, laddie. One more round with the hammer and then we'll have a go at the stone put and the caber toss."

"Sounds like fun."

Jamie and Gavin backed away to let Rory take his second shot. Once Iain handed over the hammer, Rory swung it fast, letting out a loud grunt as he released the hammer, sending it flying over the green. It touched down nearly even with the flag marking Gavin's first throw.

Iain hustled out with the tape measure, planted a flag, and shouted, "Twenty-nine even."

With a smug smile, Rory faced Gavin and made a sweeping gesture, inviting Gavin to take his next turn.

Iain jogged up with the hammer.

Gavin whirled the thing high and fast as if mimicking Rory's speed. He let the hammer fly, and it soared over the green to thunk down almost even with Rory's flag.

Jamie bounced on her toes, impatient for Iain to make the measurement.

At last, he stabbed the flag into the ground and announced, "Twenty-nine point seven."

She leaped into the air, cheering so loudly everyone gawped at her. She didn't care. Gavin had won another round.

Her gaze landed on Rory, who held his wife close against him. He wore a faintly satisfied smile, which struck Jamie as odd. Rory wouldn't be satisfied with losing. He disliked losing in the games as much as he disliked losing in court.

Rory noticed her watching him, and his mouth curved into an enigmatic smile.

Ohhhh, he was up to something for sure.

While Iain slapped Gavin on the back and the pair engaged in an animated conversation, Jamie tromped up to her brother.

She poked Rory in the chest. "Did you let Gavin win?"

"Why would I do that?" No one did deadpan like Rory.

"Don't play innocent with me." She poked him again. "I may be younger and shorter, but I know how to get what I want from you." Jamie glanced at Emery, then back to Rory. "I'll get your wife to make you tell me the truth."

Emery laughed. "You're on."

Hands on her hips, Jamie bounced up on her toes to nearly level her gaze with her brother's. "The truth, Rory. Did you let Gavin win?"

His wife wriggled in his arms until she had her front plastered to his side. "Spill, baby. Is Jamie onto something here?"

Rory switched his attention back and forth between the two women demanding answers from him. After a few seconds, he sighed and lifted the shoulder not currently occupied by his wife. "I considered the idea but discarded it. Gavin beat me with his own strength and determination."

Jamie angled her head to study him. "Then why did you look so pleased with yourself?"

He lifted that one shoulder again.

Emery rubbed her palm on Rory's chest while she looked at Jamie. "Might as well give. He won't say anything more until he feels like it." She gazed up at her husband with a sweet smile on her lips. "Or until I torture it out of him. But we need privacy for that."

Jamie was glad when Iain and Gavin approached. She was happy for her brothers and their wives, but sometimes she needed a break from their wedded bliss.

Her focus snapped to her left hand and its third finger. The diamond ring glittered in the sunshine. Would she and Gavin behave like her brothers and their wives?

A strong hand closed around hers.

She raised her eyes to Gavin.

He kissed her hand. "I did okay, huh?"

"You did great."

Rory peeled his wife away from his body. "You're not done yet, Douglas. It's the stone put next."

Oh lord. Would Rory never relent?

Gavin pecked a kiss on her cheek and whispered, "Don't worry. I've got this."

And she prayed he did. Their future depended on it.

Because if he couldn't win over her brother, they would have to elope. If he still wanted her after enduring Rory's trials.

She had a sinking feeling in her stomach that her brother had plans.

Chapter Thirty-Five

*G*avin realized the true depth of his love for Jamie during the arduous trials Rory put him through during the so-called games. The other MacTaggarts rallied around to watch and cheer and pipe up with sarcastic comments, but to their credit, they ribbed Rory as much as they ribbed Gavin. Maybe the whole clan didn't dislike him, but he wasn't here to please them. He endured this insane spectacle of machismo to convince Rory he deserved Jamie.

Event after event, on and on.

Whatever it takes, he kept reminding himself. And then he'd catch a glimpse of Jamie, her face alight with pride and love, and he'd dig in his heels for the next competition.

The stone put. They heaved sixteen-pound rocks using a technique similar to the shot-put. Gavin won that event. Next, the weight throw. A block of metal weighing almost thirty pounds, attached to a wooden handle by a length of chain. His shoulders ached after three rounds of that event—and Rory bested him.

Score: Gavin, two. Rory, one.

No room for pride here. Gavin sucked it up and kept going, even when Rory's wife flung herself at her husband and kissed him so wildly some of the crowd blushed.

Why didn't those two find a room? They owned a castle with more rooms in it than Gavin could count on both hands.

Next up, weight for height. They each slung a rock that must've weighed fifty pounds over a horizontal pole. After each round, the pole was raised until, finally, only one of them remained.

To his credit, Rory didn't crow about his second win. He congratulated Gavin on a good match.

Score: Gavin, two. Rory, two.

Then came the caber toss.

Rory hefted his caber from the ground to an upright position without any help, despite the fact the caber was thirty feet long. He heaved it end over end across the green until it whacked down fifty feet away. Gavin, loath to seem weaker than Rory when so much was at stake, insisted on hoisting his caber the same way Rory had done. He almost dropped it once but waved away Iain when his friend seemed determined to assist.

Gavin lifted the caber and heaved it into the air.

Fifty-two feet.

Score: Rory, two. Gavin, three.

When Rory offered Gavin his hand, Gavin accepted the firm shake. Rory seemed as spry as ever, but Gavin resisted the impulse to massage his aching muscles. He liked to think of himself as in good shape, but he'd overlooked the caber-tossing practice in his workout regimen.

"You've done well," Rory told him without inflection. "But we have one more event."

More? Gavin suppressed a groan. *Doing this for Jamie, remember?*

If he couldn't walk tomorrow, maybe she'd give him a full-body massage. There were perks to getting stove up.

Rory raised his arms straight up in the air and hollered, "Tug-of-war!"

Gavin's jaw slackened, and he stopped blinking. Was Rory serious? The two of them playing tug-of-war like kids on the playground?

Not quite, as it turned out.

During the lull when Lachlan and Rory went to fetch the rope for this event, Aidan explained that normally the two teams of MacTaggarts took up opposite ends of the rope, four men on each side. But with Gavin here, they would change up the rules. It would be the Three Macs versus Gavin, Iain, and Tavish the gardener. Seriously. The gray-haired guy who tended the rose bushes would fill out Gavin's team.

Rory had his two huge brothers on his side.

And Gavin had the gardener.

When they took up their positions along the rope, Gavin glanced at Tavish. The old guy was nice and all, but he looked so small compared to the Three Macs.

Iain noticed Gavin eying the gardener. He leaned in close to Gavin and whispered, "You have a bad habit of underestimating people, yourself included."

"Therapy later," Gavin hissed under his breath. "Beat Rory now."

"Beat Rory? Not worried about Lachlan or Aidan anymore, eh?" Gavin grumbled.

Catriona moseyed to the center of the rope between the two teams. She raised an orange flag high above her head. "Ready. Set. Go!"

She slashed the flag downward.

And the battle began.

Pulling. Grunting. Feet slipping. Heels digging in. Pulling. Pulling. Muscles stretched to the limit. Teeth gritted.

The Three Macs gained a few feet in their direction.

"Harder!" Gavin shouted to his teammates.

Iain had his whole face squinted, leaning back so far he would've tumbled over if not for the tension of the rope holding him up.

And Tavish, that sly old coot who had seemed badly outmatched for this tournament, hardly broke a sweat while yanking the rope back and back and back, gaining ground with each pull.

Gavin shook off his astonishment and hauled on the rope.

They gained. And gained.

Rory had his teeth bared and gritted, sweat dribbling down his face and soaking his T-shirt. The Three Macs got dragged forward. Lachlan slipped and let go of the rope, rolling out of the way just in time to avoid Aidan stomping on him.

Iain fell next, though Gavin had a sneaking suspicion the guy let go on purpose. He knew this battle was ultimately between Gavin and Rory.

Aidan gave up too, seemingly for the same reasons as Iain. He flashed Gavin a grin, then nodded to Tavish.

The gardener relinquished his hold, leaving only Gavin and Rory to fight this battle.

Gavin sucked in a breath and yanked with all the strength left in his battered muscles.

Rory's knees buckled. He hit the ground on his butt, a shout exploding out of him, his chest heaving.

The sudden release of pressure sent Gavin reeling backward, but he threw his arms out for balance and stayed on his feet.

Flat on his ass, Rory peered at Gavin with an unreadable expression. After a moment, when they'd both caught their breath, Rory clambered to his feet, marched straight to Gavin, and held out his hand.

Gavin shook it, half expecting the guy to tackle him to the ground.

"Congratulations, you won," Rory said. He grasped Gavin's wrist, hoisted it high in the air, and shouted, "The champion of today's games is Gavin Douglas."

The MacTaggarts cheered.

Calli raced up to Gavin and hugged him fiercely. "I'm so proud of you."

He couldn't help puffing up his chest a little. His baby sister was proud of him.

Jamie barreled toward him, and Calli moved out of the way. Jamie leaped onto Gavin, winding her arms around his neck with her feet dangling above the ground. She kissed him on the cheek, the nose, the forehead, the cheek again, and finally the mouth.

He held her tight. *Victory.* But would Rory give Gavin the one thing he couldn't win in any tournament?

When Jamie at last dropped back onto the ground, Gavin kept his arm around her.

Rory approached again, his face a mask of stoicism. "We don't have a trophy for you, but I have something I think you've been wanting more than a trinket."

Gavin held his breath.

Jamie clenched her fingers in his shirt.

Rory clasped Gavin's free hand in both of his. "You have my blessing, Gavin. Welcome to the family."

Gavin grinned so big he thought his face might split open. "Thanks, man."

Slanting in, Rory murmured, "I lent you my secret weapon."

"What's that?"

Rory rolled his eyes in the direction of the gardener. "Tavish."

Gavin had no frigging idea what to say to that. "Uh, thanks."

"Not that you needed it," Rory said, "but my brothers are heavyweights in the tug-of-war competitions, and I thought to even out the odds."

Gavin waved to snag the gardener's attention. "Thanks for the assist. You rock, Tavish!"

The gray-haired man shrugged, seeming slightly embarrassed.

A sense of accomplishment like none he'd ever known before swept through Gavin. He'd won the games, but more importantly, he'd won Rory's approval. And he had Jamie at his side. This day was perfect.

Murmurs and surprised sounds rolled through the crowd. The throng parted around a figure pushing his way through the gathering.

Trevor Langley halted ten feet from Gavin, Jamie, and Rory.

Gavin stiffened. "What the hell are you doing here?"

"I've come to fight you," the English Ass said. "Rory might let you win, but I'll make you work for it."

"Not interested," Gavin said with a dismissive wave.

Trevor stomped closer. "I won't leave until you fight me. Any game you like."

Would this asshole never go away? *Sheesh.*

"Or perhaps," Trevor said, his lip curling as he surveyed Gavin, "a man in a Santa Claus shirt is too soft in the head and the body to handle a real competition."

Jamie's fingers clinched Gavin's shirt tighter. "What are you hoping to gain here, Trevor?"

The English Ass sniggered. "To show you what a useless wanker this American is. As I said, any game you like, Douglas."

Rory exchanged a look with his brothers, who loitered several yards away with their wives and Emery. Lachlan nodded.

"I have a suggestion," Rory told Trevor, "for an appropriate contest."

"What is it?" Trevor asked, seeming a bit wary.

Good. Gavin liked the scumbag unnerved.

Rory clapped a hand on Gavin's shoulder and winked at him, then turned his attention to Trevor. "Haggis hurling."

Chapter Thirty-Six

Rory gestured for Gavin to join the crowd. Iain stepped aside to make room for Gavin amid the many MacTaggarts. Meanwhile, Rory and Lachlan conferred in hushed voices about the impending haggis-hurling match. Lachlan, his expression tight, listened with intent interest as Rory explained who-knew-what. Lachlan nodded, then waved for Aidan to approach. After more hushed and serious conversation, Aidan sprinted toward the castle wall and vanished through the garden doorway.

Trevor waited halfway between the wall and the crowd, set apart, sneering at no one in particular.

"What's going on?" Gavin asked Iain.

"Setting up the match," Iain explained. "Aidan must be gathering the supplies. They'll need some haggis, of course, and it must be cooked. A platform is usually required too, with whisky barrels as the common choice."

"I have to stand on a whisky barrel?"

"Yes. I hope you have a good sense of balance."

Gavin observed Lachlan and Rory, who still conversed but seemed more relaxed now that they'd sent their younger brother to fetch the necessary items. "You said the haggis has to be cooked. Does that mean Rory was planning this all along? I don't mean like he's in league with Trevor, but he must've thought about doing some haggis hurling. Right?"

Iain scratched his chin and nodded slowly. "Rory believes in being prepared. If he thought he might want to hurl haggis, he would've made sure to cook some beforehand."

"All part of his test for me."

"Take it as a compliment," Iain said, smiling in that Iain-like, subdued way. "Rory never bothered to test any of Jamie's previous boyfriends."

Gavin figured he ought to be flattered, but Trevor's appearance had turned this simple test of his determination into an all-out war. If Trevor won this goofy haggis-hurling thing, the English Ass would crow about it forever and probably move to Scotland exclusively to keep on crowing about it, even though the guy hated this country. What was Trevor's game? Not haggis hurling. He had something way slimier up his sleeve.

Aidan trotted out the garden doorway, steering toward his brothers. The youngest of the Three Macs carried a small whisky barrel in one hand while he carted a plastic sack over the other shoulder. Two lumps weighed down the sack. When Aidan reached his brothers, he set the barrel on the ground and dumped the sack beside it.

The brothers engaged in more hush-hush discussion.

Lachlan gave a sharp nod and retreated to where his wife stood with their son in her arms.

Aidan said something to Rory that made the solicitor's brows shoot up. Rory almost smiled, then slapped his brother on the shoulder. Aidan hustled over to his wife and child.

Calli waved one finger to catch Gavin's attention. She gave him a thumb's-up sign and mouthed, "Good luck."

He mouthed, "Thanks."

Jamie wended her way through the crowd to Gavin. She planted a quick but firm kiss on his lips, and said, "Beat him. In any and all senses of the word."

"Will do."

She took up a position beside Emery, and the two women linked their arms.

Rory cleared his throat loud enough to make everyone fall silent. "Gavin Douglas, come forward. Trevor Langley, come forward. The haggis hurling is about to commence."

Gavin and Trevor approached Rory, and both eyed the whisky barrel.

Trevor smirked.

A lot of nasty words popped into Gavin's head, but he stopped short of spewing them. There were kids in the vicinity. Besides, he wouldn't give Trevor the satisfaction of pissing him off.

Instead, Gavin cracked his knuckles and said, "Let's do this."

Rory dumped the contents of the plastic sack, picked up a haggis, and tossed it to Gavin. "The American goes first."

Trevor's mouth pinched into a petulant expression.

Gavin didn't bother suppressing his self-satisfied smile. He had no qualms about liking the Englishman's annoyance.

"Stand on the barrel," Rory said, "and hurl away."

"Man, you better be careful saying that to an American. We have a different idea about what hurling means."

Rory glanced at Emery where she waited beside Lachlan and Erica. "I'm aware of that."

Gavin hefted the large, rock-shaped sausage in his hand, testing its weight. "Aw, even a girl could throw this. Guess that means Langley's in trouble, seeing as he's in the kiddie weight class."

Trevor's nostrils flared, his lips warped into a nasty expression.

Okay, yeah, Gavin could admit he *really* liked pissing off the English Ass.

Gavin stepped onto the barrel, elevated maybe a foot off the ground. He bent his knees for stability, trying to gauge how much the barrel might move. Satisfied he wouldn't tumble over backward, he drew his arm back as if pitching a baseball.

He hurled the haggis.

The lump of sausage plopped down a good distance away.

Iain raced out to measure the distance. "Twenty-eight point one."

Cheers erupted behind him, and he heard Calli shouting, "Go, Gavin!"

Someone whistled. Probably Aidan.

Gavin hopped off the barrel and spotted Jamie with her fingers in her mouth, preparing to whistle again. Not Aidan after all. Emery's mom had taught Jamie how to whistle that way at Thanksgiving. Jamie gave up whistling and clapped furiously, her face alight with joy.

He winked at her.

Trevor stalked past him, bashing his shoulder into Gavin's on his way to the barrel. He threw Gavin a nasty glare.

Sir Pissy snatched up the other lump of haggis and flung it.

The barrel teetered, and Trevor tumbled ass-first to the ground, letting out an explosive grunt.

Everyone watched the haggis fly through the air to whump down on the grass.

Iain jogged out to measure. "Twenty-six point three."

Trevor scrambled to his feet, hair mussed, eyes wild. "We do it again."

Jeez, the guy sounded as frazzled and desperate as he looked.

"You lost," Gavin said, trying to sound conciliatory. "Get over it and move on."

By the expression on Trevor's face, Gavin knew the guy understood he'd meant Trevor lost more than the haggis-hurling match.

Trevor stabbed a finger in Gavin's face. Spittle sprayed as he hissed, "We go again. And again. And again. Until I say we stop. A Langley does not lose anything to a bloody American."

"Enough is enough," Gavin said. "I flung a frigging sausage to make you happy. I don't owe you anything, Langley, and I'm done playing your juvenile games."

"Langleys do not accept defeat or degradation."

Rage distorted Trevor's perfect features.

With an epiphany that hit him like a bolt of lightning, Gavin finally got it. Trevor had never tried to woo Jamie, though he claimed to want her back. He'd harassed her even after she told him off—more than once. The jerk had done everything he could to make both Jamie and Gavin miserable, to drive a wedge between them. Splitting them up had seemed way more important to Trevor than winning back his so-called lost love. When he'd called Jamie a slag, that should've tipped Gavin off. Part of him just couldn't believe anybody could be such a slime.

Wrong. Trevor Langley was made of slime. The putrid, puke-green kind.

"You're not trying to win Jamie back," Gavin said. "You want revenge on her for having the nerve to dump your ass five years ago."

Trevor glowered at Gavin, teeth grinding, breaths gusting out of his nostrils.

"Go home," Gavin said. "And find a good therapist."

A roar erupted out of Trevor. The man hurled his own body at Gavin.

With one arm, Gavin deflected the Englishman's assault and sent him tumbling to the ground.

Trevor lay there flat on his back, dazed.

Aidan piped up. "With all the work you've been doing for me, you've got more than enough muscle to skelp that scunner."

"I don't want to beat him up," Gavin said. "He's not worth it."

Trevor pushed up onto his elbows, brows furrowed. His attention swerved to Aidan, and the Englishman flattened his lips.

Gavin scrutinized Trevor, hit by a sudden certainty the guy was up to something. Nobody got that kind of look on his face unless he was plotting.

A smile of pure satisfaction spread across Trevor's face.

Oh, that was not good. Not good at all.

The English Ass struggled to his feet, dusted himself off, and nodded as if he'd reached a decision. "You're right, Douglas. My task here is done."

Trevor Langley rushed through the garden gate and disappeared.

Everyone watched him go. Then, one by one, they all focused on Gavin.

He hunched his shoulders. "Don't ask me. I've got no clue what that guy was talking about."

"Forget Langley," Rory said. "We have a prize for you."

"You don't have to do that."

"It's already done." Rory nodded to Lachlan who trotted off through the garden door. While his brother disappeared inside the castle walls, Rory fixed his inscrutable gaze on Gavin. "You are an intelligent man. I'm sure you've deduced the reason behind all of this—except for our unwanted visitor's behavior, that is."

Gavin stayed silent for a moment, considering the test and Rory's actions leading up to today. "I have an idea, but I'm not positive about it."

Rory waved a hand in a go-on gesture. "Share your deduction."

"Well," Gavin said, stuffing his hands in his pockets, "I can't figure out why, but it seems like you've been trying to make me man up and stop acting like a dumb-ass, to get me to face up to my fears and get over them."

"Very good." Rory rested one foot atop the whisky barrel. "Anything else?"

What the hell. Gavin had no reason not to forge ahead and blurt out everything he'd figured out today. "At first, I thought it was Calli's sneaky idea to have me stay with Iain, a guy who let the love of his life get away. Then, I decided it must've been Emery. Now, I'm thinking it was your idea."

"Another wise deduction," Rory said. "Emery had wanted you to stay with Lachlan and Erica, thinking my brother might tell you how he overcame his fears. I steered my wife in the direction of Iain because I believed he had the story that would help you the most. Iain never shared the details with me, but I suspected the local gossip had it right, at least the fundamentals of it. You weren't afraid because of a bad marriage as Lachlan and I were. You had different fears that threatened to derail your relationship with Jamie. Iain seemed the perfect friend for you."

Emery hurried up beside her husband, hooking her arm under his. She spoke to Gavin. "I had no idea at first why Rory wanted you to meet Iain, but I knew he must have a good reason. When I finally wheedled it out of him, I was very impressed with my hubby's sneakiness. He's come a long way from the repressed solicitor who couldn't admit he had feelings for me. Now, Rory MacTaggart meddles right along with me."

Rory laid a hand over Emery's where it curled around his bicep. "My wife swears she never meddled until after she married me." He gave Emery a sarcastically reproving look. "I think she might have massaged the truth a bit."

His wife poked him in the side. "I never needed to meddle until I met you. If I hadn't shoved my nose into your business at every turn, we never would've stayed married."

"Yes," Rory said, gazing at his wife with an almost dreamy expression, "you always know what's best for me, *mo gaoloch.*"

Jamie sidled up to Gavin, resting her head on his upper arm and looking at him the way her brother was looking at his wife. Gavin kissed the top of Jamie's head.

"I'm assuming," Gavin said to Rory, "the bromancing thing was all your wife."

Rory feigned a wince, his mouth twisted in mock disgust. "Only Emery would come up with an idea sure to make any man feel like a jessie."

"No one would ever mistake you for a weakling," Emery said, nudging her husband with her whole body. "My idea worked, didn't it?"

"Aye, it did." Rory bent to kiss his wife full on the mouth in a lingering lip-lock. "I will never again doubt the wisdom of my darling wife."

Lachlan jogged out of the garden doorway straight to Rory, handing him a soft-looking package wrapped in plain brown paper. "Here it is. Should we have a formal ceremony for this? Dunk his head in holy water, maybe?"

Rory sighed. "No, Lachie, it's not a baptism."

His older brother squinted at him with feigned indignation. "Maybe I should dunk your head in holy water, to exorcise the demon that makes you keep calling me Lachie when ye know I'll skelp ye for it."

"Nah, Lachie," Aidan chimed in, "you're no rabid wolf. You're a fluffy little puppy, especially when your wife smiles at you."

Emery laughed. "And Rory's a big old teddy bear. What about you, Aidan? Calli, what sort of unmanly thing is your husband when he thinks nobody's watching?"

"Donnae trick my wife," Aidan said, "into calling me anything but a randy bull."

Calli grinned. "He's a bunny rabbit. Sweet and soft and adorable, and lovely to pet."

Gavin couldn't help laughing softly even as he told Rory, "Your family's weird. Sounds like you're all into bestiality."

"Not in the least," Rory said. He slapped Gavin on the back. "You're a part of this family now, so if we are perverts, you're one too."

"As long as Jamie doesn't call me a trout, I'm okay with it."

"No," Jamie said, "you're a wild mustang stallion."

Lachlan made a rude noise. "Why does Gavin get a macho animal for his alter ego, but the rest of us are puppies and kittens?"

"Because ye are, Lachie," Rory said. He offered the paper-wrapped package to Gavin. "Your prize for overcoming your fears and earning a seat at the MacTaggart clan's table."

Gavin peeled away the brown paper. When he realized what he held in his hands, he glanced up at Rory, then back down to the item. Lifting the folded fabric, he studied its colors—blue and green with threads of orange.

"This is—" Gavin cleared his throat and straightened. "Is this the Mac-

Taggart clan tartan?"

"It is. And that is your kilt."

"My...kilt?" Gavin blinked some more, having a hell of a time grasping what was happening. "You're letting an American wear your family's tartan?"

"Yes." Rory cast a suggestive glance at his wife. "I let my wife wear my kilt, after all."

Jamie squeezed Gavin's arm. "This means you're one of us. You have a family, Gavin."

He wasn't an orphan anymore, that's what she meant. He hadn't thought of himself that way in a while. The more he worked to get in good with the Three Macs, the less he felt like an abandoned child all alone in the world. He'd always had Calli, even after she moved to Scotland. Nothing would ever take her away from him, not in the ways that counted. He'd acquired a bunch more sisters and brothers too.

Most important of all, he had Jamie.

He bent to murmur so only she could hear. "What would you think about starting our own branch of this family tree as soon as we're hitched?"

The smile that lit her face illuminated his heart too. "I'd love that."

"Come," Rory said in a booming voice meant to reach every last Mac-Taggart gathered on the green. "Let's go to the great hall and celebrate our newest clan member with plenty of whisky and, as my wife would say, lots of gooey goodies."

Gavin draped the plaid kilt over his arm and led the woman he loved through the garden door. Everything was perfect, more than he could've hoped for a couple months ago, and yet one thought niggled at him.

What was Trevor plotting?

Chapter Thirty-Seven

Gavin got his answer four days later when a letter arrived in the mail, delivered to Iain's house and addressed to Gavin. The letter came from the Home Office, a department of the UK government. Gavin didn't quite understand everything the Home Office did, but he knew they had domain over immigration matters.

He read the letter three times, growing more numb with each pass.

After the third time, he stumbled into the living room and fell onto the sofa. The paper crinkled, and he glanced down to find he was crooking his fingers into the letter. He barely registered the fact Iain had walked into the room, even when the other man sat down beside him.

"What is it?" Iain asked. "You look ill."

Gavin held the letter out to Iain. "Administrative removal."

Iain frowned, etching lines across his forehead. He took the letter and read it. "You're being deported? That can't be. There's a process, you get a chance to defend yourself, but this says you have no recourse except to leave voluntarily or wait to be deported."

"Yeah," Gavin said, his voice barely a whisper. "I violated the immigration laws by engaging in work while claiming to be on vacation in the UK. I misrepresented my reasons for being in the country."

"Talk to Rory. This is a mistake."

"You can't fight the government, in any country."

"So you'll sit here slipping into a coma instead of trying to fight?" Iain smacked the letter down on Gavin's lap. "Bloody hell, you're giving up without even making sure this is legitimate. What happened to the man who overcame his fears and committed to a life with the woman he loves? Don't slide backward down the hill ye just climbed."

"I'm guilty. I did what they said, I worked for Aidan after telling the government I was here on vacation, visiting Jamie." Gavin stared at the wall without seeing it, without seeing anything. "I didn't know it mattered. That's no excuse, though. I screwed this up."

"No, you didn't." Iain hissed out a breath. "Someone reported you. Nothing else explains this."

"Doesn't matter."

Iain watched Gavin for a moment, then jumped up and retrieved a glass of whisky from the liquor cabinet against the wall. He sat down again and thrust the drink at Gavin.

"Drink," he said. "Gain a bit of liquid clarity."

"Getting drunk won't make things clearer." Though he spoke those words, Gavin accepted the glass and downed the contents in one gulp. The whisky burned in his throat, scouring away the shock second by second. Would he lie here in a lump and accept his fate without fighting?

Hell no.

Someone reported him. Iain had to be right about that. Who?

The shit hit the fan three days after he won acceptance from Rory and became a MacTaggart. Three days after he proved to himself he was no wuss anymore. Three days after he bested Trevor Langley in a round of hurl-the-haggis.

Of course.

Gavin sat forward and slapped the whisky glass down on the coffee table. "It was Trevor. He did this. The bastard likes to brag about his family's connections, and he was super pissed when I beat him at haggis hurling. He wanted to punish Jamie by shaming me and getting Rory to denounce me. It didn't work, so he found another way to wreck everything for her—and for me."

"Talk to Rory." Iain got up and waved for Gavin to do the same. "Don't sit there stewing about it. Get off your erse and go see your solicitor."

Gavin heaved himself up off his ass and heeded Iain's advice.

An hour later, he sat across the massive desk from Rory in the library office of Dùndubhan.

Rory held the letter in one hand while rubbing his chin with the thumb and forefinger of his other hand. He contemplated the words on the page for several minutes before speaking.

"You don't want to allow them to deport you," he said at last, placing the letter on the desktop. "If they do, you'll be banned from the UK for ten years."

"How do I avoid that?"

"There is a process, but whoever wrote this letter has made a mockery of the rules." Rory tapped a finger on the letter. "You've been given a deadline to provide evidence of why you shouldn't be subject to administrative removal, but the deadline was yesterday. The letter is dated the day before, but naturally, you didn't receive it until today. And the letter states no appeal will be allowed."

"I noticed. Is that legal?"

"Unfortunately, yes." Rory tapped the letter again. "The only recourse you have at this time is to leave the country voluntarily. Doing so will prevent deportation and the ten-year ban on returning. You'll be allowed to come back in one year."

"A year?" Gavin gripped the arms of his chair as his head started to wobble. No, it wasn't actually wobbling. Only felt like it was. "I can't come back for a year. That's…Could Jamie visit me in America?"

"Yes." With one finger, Rory spun the letter on the desktop. "It won't come to that, though. I will find out who orchestrated this and how."

"It was Trevor, had to be."

Rory sighed, his focus on the paper. "I agree, but we need proof. I suspect he circumvented the system, possibly by illegal means, but proving it could be difficult."

"You're saying I'm screwed every which way."

"No, I'm saying it will take time. I have an investigator I trust, one who works out of London. We will uncover the truth of this and get you reinstated in the UK with a family visa." Rory slanted forward, elbows on the desktop, his expression sternly determined. "You have my word on that."

"I appreciate it." Gavin took a long, slow breath and let it out bit by bit. "How long will I have to stay in America?"

"Hard to say. I'll do whatever it takes to ensure this matter is resolved as swiftly as possible." Rory pushed away from the desk, his chair wheeling backward. "In the meantime, you need to return to America."

That was how, the next day, Gavin wound up standing on the tarmac at the Inverness airport with Rory's Gulfstream jet behind him and Jamie in front of him. Saying goodbye to her made his gut twist and his eyes burn, but he had to believe he'd come back soon. One English asshole couldn't derail their life together. What kind of happy ending would that be?

Jamie sniffled, dabbing her eyes with a balled-up tissue. "This isn't fair."

"Life isn't sometimes." He pulled her into his arms, her head tucked against the hollow of his shoulder. "This is temporary. Rory's working on getting things straightened out."

"I should be going with you." She pushed away from him, her lips quivering even while she tried to scowl. "Can't believe I was so stupid, letting my passport expire."

"You thought I was staying for good, we both did." He took hold of her hand, kneading her palm with his thumb. "Besides, you were distracted by other things. If this is anybody's fault, it's mine. I'm the reason you had so much on your mind you forgot about your passport."

It had expired ten days ago. Fixing the passport situation would take time.

"You'll come visit me soon," he said. "And Rory will get the other stuff sorted out, you'll see."

"We were supposed to have Christmas together."

He hauled in a breath, but his eyes watered anyway. Must've been grit or smog or something irritating them. Yeah, sure, his eyes were watering due to irritants. In the privacy of his thoughts, at least, he could admit he teetered on the verge of crying. Him. The tough guy.

Losing Jamie would tear him up from the inside out.

Not losing her, he reminded himself. He could never lose her.

"If Rory can't fix this," she said, those beautiful, bleary eyes locked on him, "I'm emigrating to America."

"Won't come to that." He rested his forehead against hers. "But thanks for the offer, babe."

"Not an offer, a promise. I'm with you, wherever we have to go to be together."

"Ditto."

"It's only fifteen days until Christmas."

"We'll celebrate it together." He tried to believe that, had to believe it, but he didn't know. Trevor had money and a serious jones for revenge.

"Gavin—"

He took her face in his hands and kissed her, deeply, passionately, infusing the act with all the emotions roiling inside him. "See you soon."

Then he walked up the air stairs and into the jet.

Back to America. Back to a lifeless existence.

Alone.

Chapter Thirty-Eight

*F*ourteen days until Christmas. Jamie sleepwalked through her daily life, returning to work at Aidan's company, filling out paperwork and answering phone calls, pretending to be cheerful when she talked to customers though she felt her heart withering away inside her chest. How could she still breathe and walk when a dead thing had replaced her heart?

Rory insisted he was making progress on "sorting what the bastard did" to screw up her life. Gavin had been forced out of the country because of her, because she'd broken up with Trevor five years ago.

"It's not your fault," Emery told her on the thirteenth day before Christmas. "For the bazillionth time, Jamie, no one is to blame except Trevor Langley. He needs a nice, long stay in a resort for the emotionally deranged. Preferably one in Antarctica."

They sat in chairs at the kitchen table in Calli and Aidan's house. Calli occupied the chair beside Emery while Erica had taken the seat at the head of the table, directly opposite Jamie. The American Wives Club had declared they would cheer her up by whatever means necessary. Cat and Fiona, seated across from Calli and Emery, rounded out the gathering.

"Would the lot of you stop trying to make me feel better?" Jamie said. "I won't feel anything close to better until Gavin comes back."

"How about a stripper?" Calli suggested. "Ogling a naked man always improves my mood."

Erica exhaled a long-suffering sigh. "The only naked man you've ever seen is Aidan. Of course his nudity perks you up."

Rory's wife got a sly look on her face. "I'm feeling a bit down today. Calli, why don't you have Aidan come in here and strip for us."

"Ech!" Jamie exclaimed. "He's my brother, Emery. Ahmno watching him...do that."

"Neither am I," Fiona said.

"Count me out too," Cat agreed.

Emery threw her hands up in surrender. "Sorry, I forgot for a second. But I did get Jamie to do something other than moan and mope. Righteous disgust is a step up."

"It is," Erica agreed.

Disgust was the only thing that broke through Jamie's malaise. Her brothers and sisters kept eying her like she might collapse into a lump of weeping gelatin on the floor at any moment. Rory insisted she stay with Aidan and Calli instead of "haunting the castle like a forlorn spirit." Staying with Aidan and Calli hadn't helped. Sure, she had more company and less room to sequester herself in a dark corner. She got to play with baby Sarah too, but none of it helped.

She wanted Gavin.

Trevor wouldn't let her have what she wanted. Somehow, he managed to derail her every attempt to renew her passport. The paperwork got lost, repeatedly. Then it got misplaced, buried in a pile of papers on the desk of the wrong person at the Home Office. Last she'd heard, someone was reviewing her request. That had been yesterday. Even the fast-track option took a week.

Phone conversations and text messages with Gavin didn't fill the hole in her chest. Not even when he texted her a picture of him in the kilt Rory had given him—the kilt and nothing else. The sight of his muscular chest should've bolstered her spirits, but it only made her long to have him with her, pressing that body down on hers right before he stripped off the kilt and made love to her for hours.

She cried for ten minutes after seeing the picture.

On the twelfth day before Christmas, a package arrived for Jamie. Aidan brought it to her in the living room. He didn't even smirk when he set the box on her lap.

"It's from Gavin," he said. "I'll leave you to it."

"No suggestive jokes? Or nosiness about what's in the box?"

Aidan shrugged. "I hope whatever it is makes you feel better."

Oh God. For Aidan to treat her with sensitivity meant she was worse off than she'd realized.

Tears gathered in her eyes as she ripped the tape off the box and folded back the flaps. Inside, nestled among crumpled bits of newspaper, lay a box wrapped in colorful Christmas paper. A large gift tag was attached to the box. She read the note scrawled on the tag in Gavin's masculine hand.

"Happy first day of Christmas," he wrote. "Day one is supposed to be a partridge in a pear tree, but I don't know what a partridge is or where to get one. Not sure why one would live in a pear tree, either. Instead, I got you the next best thing. Call me after you open your present."

Jamie ripped the paper off the box and tore it open. Tears stung her eyes anew as she lifted out the two items inside, a pair of plush toys, one an avocado and the other a black-and-white bird. The half avocado had a smiley face on its brown pit. She hugged the toys to her chest, burying her face in them, hoping to find a hint of Gavin's scent on them. They smelled like nothing in particular.

Still hugging the toys, she grabbed her phone and dialed Gavin's number.

"Hey, babe," he said when he answered. "Did you get the package?"

"Aye." She blinked to clear the tears from her eyes, but new ones emerged in their wake. "I love the gift. An avocado and a bird. They're so sweet, Gavin. You are so sweet."

"You hate pears, but I remembered how much you liked avocados when we had guacamole at my favorite Mexican restaurant in Minneapolis."

"Never had one before then." She petted the little stuffed bird. "What sort of bird is this? I don't recognize it."

"It's a chickadee. They're American birds. I see them in the tree outside my bedroom window." He exhaled a weary sigh. "Didn't think I'd be stuck in this apartment again, alone. Got used to being your sex slave."

She nuzzled the plush chickadee. "I miss you, Gavin."

"I miss you too, Jamie, so bad. Won't be long till we're together again."

"Need my slave back soon."

"Maybe later we can try phone sex. I hear it's hot."

She giggled. "Emery swears by it. She says a woman shouldn't let a man forget what he's missing when he's away."

"I know exactly what I'm missing."

The intensity in his voice made tears spring anew, and they rolled down her cheeks.

"Wish I could talk longer," he said, "but I have to get to work. Gotta pay the bills while I'm stuck here."

"You shouldn't have to work at a fast-food restaurant. That's what Trevor would want, you beaten down."

"I'm not beaten down." He paused, and when he spoke again, his voice was stronger, imbued with an iron resolve. "I'll do whatever I have to do, even scrub the bathroom floors of a burger joint where kids have barfed up chicken nuggets and fries. This won't be forever, and no work is beneath me. A job's a job. I'm fine with it."

A couple months ago, he'd been ashamed to tell her he lost his job. Now, he gladly took a menial job to stay afloat. He really had changed. Or rather, he'd rediscovered the man he'd been before his fears got the better of him.

Every day after that, she received a new gift from Gavin. He reinterpreted "The Twelve Days of Christmas" to give each day's present a new spin. For day two, he sent her two chocolate turtle candies—the kind with caramel and pecans inside—and taped each candy to the breast of a small, plush dove toy. Three French hens? He gave her three plush chickens wearing berets. Calling birds? She got four more chickadees, each holding a tiny mobile phone. Each gift came with a handwritten note from Gavin.

When she received the box for day five and read his note, she burst into tears and sobbed for fifteen minutes, until Calli found her and insisted she go out to lunch with the American Wives Club.

Five golden rings, that was day five. He gave her gold-colored plastic toy rings. The note simply said, "Only four because you get the fifth on the day we say 'I do.' All my love, Gavin."

Lunch with the girls had to be relocated from a public venue to Erica and Lachlan's house for privacy. Every time someone mentioned Gavin, she started crying again.

Gavin's gifts kept coming, but the days and the presents blurred together. Though she tried not to be a pest, each new gift made her want Gavin back more, and she had to call Rory to ask about the progress of Gavin's case.

"It's progressing," Rory said in that annoyingly even voice he used with his clients. "Relax and enjoy the holidays. All will be settled soon."

She wanted to believe him. She needed to believe him.

Every new day without Gavin eroded her belief that anything could work out.

On day eleven without Gavin, Aidan and Calli dragged Jamie out of bed at six a.m. Calli instructed her to "dress up nice" because she was going to an important meeting. Though Jamie pressed for more information, neither Calli nor Aidan would tell her anything else. They all but shoved her out the door and toward Rory's Mercedes. Rory and Emery had pulled into the driveway seconds before Jamie was ejected from the house.

Once in the backseat of the Mercedes, Jamie began firing questions at them.

They wouldn't crack either. She had no talent for wheedling information out of anyone.

Emery twisted around in her seat to glance back at Jamie. "Take it easy. This is a good surprise."

"Not in the mood for early morning surprises." And yes, she sounded a bit grumpy. She *was* a bit grumpy after getting ousted from her bed with no explanation. Growling out a sigh, she asked Rory, "How is the visa issue coming along?"

"Hush, Jamie."

"Don't tell me to hush, Rory. You haven't wanted to tell me one bleeding thing this whole time, so excuse me for being irritated with you."

"It's better than you crying nonstop."

Jamie sank back into the seat and glared out the window. Kidnapped by her own brother and his wife. If they were taking her for an intervention because they'd gotten tired of her melancholy mood, she'd run them over with this car.

"Here," Emery said, thrusting a plastic cup at her. "Have some coffee. It'll wake you up."

Grumbling, Jamie accepted the coffee and sipped it through the small opening in the cup's lid. Hot but not too hot. With cream. Emery knew how Jamie liked her coffee.

By the time they reached their destination, Jamie had perked up—but only a little.

Their destination turned out to be Dùndubhan.

Jamie sat forward, peering between the front seats at the castle visible beyond the windshield. "Why are we here? If you wanted me to move in with you again, you didn't need the cloak-and-dagger routine."

Rory arched an eyebrow at her.

Emery spoke. "Go inside. Your surprise is waiting in the vestibule."

"Ahmno moving until ye tell me—"

Rory covered her mouth with his hand. "For once, do as you're told without questioning it. Go inside, Jamie. Now."

"Fine," she mumbled through his hand. She swung the rear door open at the instant he removed his hand from her mouth. "You'll be paying for this later, Rory."

He smirked. The blasted man smirked at her.

Emery gave her a knowing smile.

Dear God, they were the strangest couple on the planet.

Jamie climbed out of the car and headed for the vestibule door.

It was flung open from the inside.

And there, framed by the doorway, stood Gavin.

She shrieked and bolted for the door, tackling him and lavishing kisses over every inch of his skin she could reach while suspended in his arms. He claimed her mouth, raking his tongue over hers, holding her so tight she could hardly breathe. When he plunged deep inside her mouth, she completely lost the ability to breathe or think.

When their mouths separated, and Gavin plunked her down on her feet, she twisted her head around to shout to Rory, "I forgive you."

Then she kissed Gavin again.

Chapter Thirty-Nine

Emery

I perched on my husband's lap with my legs crosswise to his and one arm around his neck. Rory had asked me to join him for this meeting with Gavin and Jamie, but I hadn't expected him to ask me to sit on his lap. Helping to save a relationship seemed to have made him very cuddly. On top of that, he wore a contented smile.

Gavin seemed bemused by Rory's mood, while Jamie kept grinning. That might've been brought on by the fact her fiancé had returned to her, legally and for good.

Jamie slapped her hands on the arms of her chair. "Is someone going to tell me what on earth happened? Is Gavin visiting or here to stay?"

"To stay," Gavin said, clasping one of her hands. "I'm never leaving you again."

Her tension seemed to flood out on a whispery exhalation. "Are you sure you can stay? They won't deport you? I don't understand any of this. How did you get your administrative removal reversed?"

Rory cleared his throat to gain the couple's attention. "First, you should know Trevor Langley will not bother you again. He's been arrested."

Gavin looked supremely pleased as he had yesterday when Rory informed him of the news. The two men decided to surprise Jamie with Gavin's return, though I'd voted for telling her right away. If I were Jamie, I would've wanted to hear the news as it broke. The men had convinced me, though, to let Gavin surprise her with his return this morning. It had sounded romantic, and Jamie had been thrilled beyond measure.

"Arrested?" Jamie said. "How? For what?"

Rory looped his arms around my hips, his hands linked. "Trevor conspired to pervert the immigration system. He bribed an official, a family friend, to arrange the administrative removal order by claiming Gavin lied about his reasons for entering the United Kingdom. When Trevor overheard Aidan saying Gavin had done work for him, Trevor used that as the basis for his claims. If he'd stopped there, the scheme might've succeeded. However, he took it a few steps too far, fabricating evidence Gavin had worked for not only Aidan, but Lachlan too. That was the mistake that undid him."

Jamie leaned back in her chair, a little smile of understanding on her lips.

Gavin's mouth warped into a confused expression. "You still haven't explained the details to me. Jamie seems to know why including Lachlan in his claims undid Trevor, but I haven't got a clue."

Rory chuckled in that softly menacing way that made me so hot for him. "Lachlan keeps detailed records for one thing, and for another his past clients include some of the most influential people in the UK." Rory glanced at me, his eyes alight with the joy of squashing a criminal dirtbag. "One of Lachlan's former clients is the brother-in-law of the Home Secretary."

Gavin chuckled now with the same kind of menacing joy Rory had evinced a moment ago. "I think I'm gonna like this story."

"You will," Rory said. "One of my former clients also works at the Home Office. He helped me with another problem a few months ago, and I contacted him again. He joined forces with Lachlan's contact and the Home Secretary to sort out the tangled web Trevor had woven around himself. The Home Secretary was so offended by Langley's actions, he not only canceled the removal order for Gavin, he also fast-tracked Gavin's fiancé visa application. By year's end, Gavin will have his official leave to remain in the UK."

I couldn't help myself. I threw my head back and shouted, "Woo-hoo!"

Jamie sprang up and shouted her own "woo-hoo," then flopped onto Gavin's lap in the same position in which I occupied Rory's lap. Gavin grinned at his fiancée.

Rory kissed me. "Should we tell the rest?"

"Of course. It's their big Christmas present."

"Perhaps we should wait until Christmas Eve."

I bumped my nose into his. "Don't torture them. If you don't make the announcement, I will. You have five seconds. Four, three…"

Rory faced Gavin and Jamie. "Emery and I have bought a house near Ballachulish. For reasons that will become apparent very soon, though not today, we wanted a smaller home. We will no longer be living at Dùndubhan."

Jamie cocked her head at her brother. "But you love it here."

"I bought this house for reasons that no longer apply."

He'd bought it because he wanted to hide from life, overwhelmed by the sadness of two failed marriages. His third marriage had ended in this castle, and I understood why he wanted a fresh start. Besides, we had a practical reason for wanting a smaller place. Easier to keep track of our children.

"You're selling the castle?" Jamie asked.

"No," Rory said. "We're turning it into a museum."

Gavin nodded his approval. "This place would make an awesome museum. You could put cool swords on the walls and maybe a suit of armor." Gavin's mouth curved into a sly smile. "Or a mannequin wearing the Mac-Taggart clan tartan."

Rory pulled me closer, his own smile one of contentment. "I was thinking of a live model to wear the tartan."

"Oh sure," Gavin said. "That'd be cool too."

Jamie aimed a questioning gaze at her brother. "Have you told everyone about this?"

"No, only you and Gavin." Rory pecked my cheek. "My wife had an excellent idea, and I agreed it's the proper solution."

"Don't drag it out forever," Jamie said. "Tell us."

Rory looked at me and tipped his head in a way I knew meant he wanted me to finish the explanation.

I turned my attention to Jamie and Gavin. "We want you guys to run the museum. You'd live here in private quarters that would be off limits to visitors, and you'd have full control over the running of the place. We trust you two to do this."

"That's right," Rory said. "Gavin can be the live model for the Highland warrior exhibit. All the MacTaggart men have agreed to grant Gavin honorary Highlander status."

Gavin's eyes had gone wide. "Wow. That's...amazing. You seriously want us to be in charge?"

"We do," Rory said.

"Absolutely we do," I said.

"Do you realize," Jamie said, "Trevor claimed he wanted me to run a museum for him."

"He was a liar," Rory said without a hint of rancor. "Emery and I are making a genuine offer out of love and respect for you and Gavin."

"Why us?" Jamie asked.

I answered this one. "Because we trust you, one hundred percent. You'll do an awesome job."

Gavin seemed unconvinced. "I don't know anything about museums or Scottish history."

"Jamie knows enough for the both of you," Rory said. "And you were a salesman for many years. Make use of that experience to draw in visitors. A former Marine can tackle any task."

"Thanks for the vote of confidence."

Rory looked at Gavin and Jamie in turn. "You'll do it, then?"

"Yes!" Jamie exclaimed. She vaulted off Gavin's lap and raced around the desk to throw her arms around Rory's neck. She kissed his cheek. "Thank you, thank you, thank you."

My husband's lips quirked. "You're welcome, Jamie."

She rushed around the chair to kiss my cheek too. "Thank you so much, Emery."

I waved her away. "Okay, enough thanking. We know you're grateful, and you're embarrassing Rory."

He drew his head back in righteous indignation. "Ahmno embarrassed. I donnae get embarrassed."

"Not lately, but you have in the past." I didn't need to remind him of the second night we'd spent together, the night after our one-night stand that turned into way more, the night when he wouldn't let me sleep naked. He'd been so adorably embarrassed by the idea that I'd taken pity on him and slept in his shirt.

"Hmm," Rory said, "that hasn't happened in months. I've become desensitized to your habits."

"Desensitized? That's one way to put it."

The other way to put it, the accurate way, was that he now pouted if I tried to wear any kind of clothing to bed, even a skimpy nightie. We both enjoyed the way he divested me of my garments.

Jamie skipped back to Gavin, standing beside his chair with her hands on his shoulders. "Are we done? Or do you have more announcements?"

"Not today," Rory said. "We're done. Go lock yourselves in the guest room and shag all day and night."

"Sounds like an order," Gavin said. "I'm good at following orders."

He sprang from the chair, swept Jamie up in his arms, and carted her out of the library. The door clicked shut behind them.

"That's one happy couple," I said. "Don't you feel good knowing we helped them find their happy ending?"

"Yes," he said, "but our news makes everything else seem unimportant."

I combed my fingers through his hair. "At least you've recovered from yesterday's shock."

He caught my hand, guiding it down to his cheek, pancaked beneath his bigger palm. "If our bairns are anything like you, we'll have our hands full."

"Gotta have something to keep you busy during your semi-retirement years."

His expression turned pensive. "Helping Gavin made me realize how much you've changed my life. I'm a very lucky man to have a woman like you, Emery."

"I'm pretty lucky too." I gave him a teasing smile. "Got me a rich man who's fantastic in bed."

He rolled his eyes.

"You're an amazing man, Rory." I nuzzled his cheek. "We're both lucky to have found each other, and our kids will be lucky to have us."

My hubby and I held each other for a long time. On Christmas, we would tell everyone our good news. It seemed like the perfect time to do it. Our days of meddling had come to a close.

Well, almost…

Chapter Forty

*E*veryone gathered at Dùndubhan for Christmas like they had on Thanksgiving. This time around, though, Emery didn't randomly seat people. She let each couple sit beside each other, with the exception of her and Rory since Rory once again occupied the head of the table. A trio of large turkeys on large platters sat evenly spaced along the table's center awaiting the feast to come.

Gavin found himself situated between Jamie and Emery with Rory smiling at him from the end of the table beside his wife. Yep, Rory was aiming a genuine smile at Gavin. He'd gotten used to this new friendliness from the formerly stern solicitor. Gavin's soon-to-be brother-in-law had even slapped him on the back when Rory and Emery greeted him in the vestibule earlier. Gavin had managed to squeeze out the proper response, in spite of his shock, when Rory grinned and boomed "Happy Christmas" with enough enthusiasm his words reverberated in the stairwell above them.

Jamie had grinned too, and despite her giggling, shouted "Happy Christmas" with slightly less volume than Rory had achieved.

Voices from further up the spiral staircase had hollered the same greeting.

Everybody was beyond happy today.

Gavin couldn't stop smiling either or laughing at any silly joke told by anybody. He'd thought he'd lost everything and might never see Jamie again, much less marry her. Though she'd vowed she'd move to America to be with him if Rory couldn't undo what Trevor had done, Gavin hadn't wanted to think about that possibility. Her family was in Scotland. So was his—both his sister and the new family that had welcomed him into their clan. After finding his place in the world, he didn't want to give it all up because of one English prick.

Luckily, the English prick lost the battle and the war.

Gavin had rejoined the MacTaggart clan and the ranks of the blissfully happy.

Even the sole single person at the gathering, Iain, joked and laughed. Nothing much bothered Iain, as Gavin had realized over the past couple months. Despite Iain's unshakable demeanor, Gavin got the impression one thing did unsettle the odd Scot—his lost love, the unnamed American woman he'd fallen for more than a decade ago. Gavin planned on talking to Iain about that later. Maybe the guy needed a neutral party to kick him in the butt and encourage him to go after what he clearly wanted.

Over dessert, things got really interesting.

Jamie leaned close to whisper in his ear. "Should we tell them yet?"

"Sure. Want me to do it, or would you rather?"

"You should do it."

He laid a hand on her thigh under the table. "Anything for my girl."

Gavin pushed his chair back, rose, and tapped his fork on his wine glass.

All eyes focused on him.

"Jamie and I have an announcement," he said, rolling his shoulders back. "We're getting married on January twenty-sixth."

A round of clapping and a few whistles ensued.

Jamie beamed up at him.

He beamed right back at her.

"About bloody time," Lachlan said with a teasing quirk of his lips.

"Sure you're legal?" Aidan said. "Can't have the groom arrested at the altar."

"He's legal, Aidan," Rory said. "Can't say the same for you, though, after seeing your pickup in a no-parking zone in Loch Fairbairn."

"I didnae see the sign," Aidan replied with a tone and an expression of mock innocence.

While everyone else teased and joked, Gavin sat down again and spotted Lachlan and Erica engaged in a secret conversation several chairs away. After a moment, Erica tapped her wine glass with a fork. Once all gazes gravitated to her, she seemed to lose her nerve, biting her lower lip.

Lachlan hooked an arm around her shoulders and whispered something in her ear.

Erica shook her head. She sat up a little straighter and said, "I hope we aren't horning in on Jamie and Gavin's news, but we couldn't wait any longer to tell you guys. I'm pregnant again."

Cheers. Whoops. Glasses raised and clinked in a disorganized toast.

Aidan, seated next to Lachlan, grasped his brothers shoulder and shook it. "Good going, Lachie. Keep your woman by keeping her pregnant. She'll be too busy herding your bairns to get bored with you."

Calli elbowed her husband in his side. "You should talk."

Silence fell over the group as Gavin and apparently everyone else in the room wondered what Calli had meant. They needed to wait only a moment.

Aidan took his wife's hand and kissed it. "Tell them."

Calli bumped her shoulder against his and then faced the crowd. "I'm pregnant again too."

More cheers. More whoops. Another disorganized round of raised and clinked glasses.

"Jeez," Gavin said, shaking his head at Aidan, "let my sister have a break sometime, will you? She just had a baby and now you've got another bun in her oven."

"I am not an oven," Calli said. "Though Aidan is hot as an oven, and I can't stay out of the kitchen."

"Yuck," Gavin said, curling his lip in overly dramatic disgust. "I don't need to hear about your sex life, C."

Rory thumped his fist on the table, rattling the glasses and plates. Once everyone had quieted down and turned their attention to him, Rory said, "My wife has an announcement too."

Emery stared at him wide-eyed for a couple seconds, then her surprise melted into a brilliant smile. "Now is the time?"

"Yes, m'eudail. Can you think of a better time?"

Her grin widened. She clasped her husband's hand and told the group, "I'm pregnant. With twins."

The whoops and cheers that erupted deafened Gavin. The volume of joy for this announcement made the previous ones seem like nothing. Not that the family wasn't equally happy for Jamie and Gavin, Lachlan and Erica, and Aidan and Calli. They were, of course. But everybody knew how long Rory had waited to find the right woman and how long he'd wanted to have a family of his own. Emery had waited a long time too, though with a lot less trauma and angst than Rory had endured. Their love story was epic and fast becoming a legend in the village of Loch Fairbairn.

The other members of the American Wives Club, Calli and Erica, leaped out of their chairs to descend on Emery, encompassing her with their arms and babbling about how wonderful this was. Rory observed with an expression Gavin had never seen on the man before. He looked contented, completely and serenely. Adoration for his wife glowed in his eyes and in the smile that slowly overtook him.

Emery glowed too, even as the other MacTaggarts swarmed around her and Rory. Emery couldn't make it out of her chair while overrun with thrilled relatives, but Rory shot up from his seat before anyone could pin him down. His brothers hugged him and slapped his back, and even Iain hurried over to offer congratulations.

When Gavin finally pushed through the crowd to grasp Rory's hand, the room went silent. Everyone stopped moving.

Rory scowled at Gavin, his grip on Gavin's hand firm. "Did ye think ye'd get away with it?"

"Uh, get away with what?"

A grin broke across Rory's face. "Congratulating me with only a handshake."

That's when Rory did something Gavin never would have imagined in a million-billion years. Emery had assured him Rory never did this to anyone but her. Even his wife, apparently, didn't know everything about him because Rory did it.

He pulled Gavin into a hug.

"You're family now," Rory said. "Act like it."

The silence morphed into the sounds of a boisterous family gathering once again.

By the time the festivities petered out, and everyone had exchanged gifts, Gavin wanted nothing more than to get Jamie alone and give her the one present he'd withheld from public viewing. And yeah, he wanted to get her naked too. They had a lot to celebrate. Thankfully, Rory and Emery excused themselves as soon as the guests had departed, hurrying up to their top-floor sanctuary. Soon, they'd move into their new, smaller home. Not long after that, they'd have twin babies.

Rory might need some Xanax to deal with that chaos.

Gavin remembered what Emery had said earlier when he congratulated her on the baby news.

"My husband almost passed out," Emery told Gavin, "when he found out it's twins. Took him all day to recover from the shock."

"He seems really happy about it," Gavin had said.

"Oh, he is. And so am I." She'd turned to Jamie then and asked, "When will it be your turn?"

Jamie's eyes had flared wide. "We aren't even married yet."

"Erica got knocked up before she married Lachlan. So did Calli."

Luckily, Emery's sister, Hadley, had interrupted at that point, determined to discuss with Emery the challenges of having twins.

Gavin's thoughts returned to the present, and he drew Jamie close to murmur in her ear. "Meet me in the sitting room in ten minutes."

"Why ten minutes?"

"Need to prepare your surprise."

Her voice dropped to a throaty purr. "A sexy surprise?"

"You'll find out in ten minutes."

With a lot of effort, he tore himself away from her luscious body and ran to the sitting room.

Jamie counted the minutes and seconds on the old-fashioned clock on her bedside table. Her foot tapped the floor faster than the second hand ticked. Her pulse quickened too with an excitement that seemed out of proportion with what Gavin had promised her. A surprise. A sexy one, she'd wager. Why should the prospect make her knees weak and her body warm and wet in the best places? She'd been with Gavin many times, but this time felt different.

They'd celebrated their first Christmas as an engaged couple, and after so many months of wondering if they would stay together, they'd set a date for the wedding. No more wondering. No more fears about a man trampling her again. She controlled her own destiny.

She belonged with Gavin. Nothing would tear them apart again.

When precisely ten minutes had elapsed according to the clock, she raced down the hall to the sitting room. As the door clapped shut behind her, she froze a few feet inside the room, stunned by the sight before her.

Stunned in a wonderful and silkily warm way.

Gavin lay stretched out on a plush rug in front of the fireplace. He'd shut off all the lights, and the only illumination came from the flickering fire and the candles he'd placed on the mantle and the coffee table as well as the sills of the tall windows. Outside the window, snowflakes floated down toward the ground. The golden glow of the flames in the sitting room danced over Gavin's skin and the sculpted muscles of his chest and abdomen. The kilt Rory had given him covered Gavin from his hips down to his knees, though with one knee bent, the fabric had ridden up one thigh to expose nearly all the thick muscles of his leg.

Bod an Donais. He was beautiful—and hers.

He patted the rug beside him. "Come over here and unwrap your last present."

The sensual rumble of his voice made her skin tighten, her breasts too. She moved closer, anticipation tingling through her. As she lowered onto the rug, her legs tucked under her, she skimmed a hand along the center line of his abs until her fingers met the plaid. "I've never had a present gift-wrapped in a kilt."

"I've never worn a kilt before, so we're even." He took hold of her hand, shifting it down to cover the hard line of his erection. "Better unwrap me quick. I've been lying here thinking about what I want to do to you, and I'm about to lose it just having you this close."

She slipped a finger inside the waist of his kilt, only to discover he had done a slapdash job of securing it. Since he'd never worn a kilt before, she cut him some slack. Besides, his lack of finesse with the plaid made her job easier. She peeled the kilt away from his hips, letting it spill across the rug.

His rigid cock waved in front of her.

"I'm liking this gift," she said, and closed her hand around his shaft, pumping slowly.

"Ah," he hissed, his face pinched. "Jamie, I need—"

She released him and shed her clothes. Naked beside him, she laid a palm on his chest and gave it a little shove. "Lie back. This is my gift, and I mean to take full advantage of it."

"Yes, ma'am." He rolled onto his back and clasped his hands under his head. "I love a bossy Scottish lass."

"And I love a bossy American man." She straddled his lap, towering over him on her knees. "But I absolutely adore a man who lets me have my way with him."

"Guess you lucked out, because I give you both."

She bent to rasp her tongue over his nipple, delighted by his sharp intake of breath. His reaction spurred her to swirl her tongue around that nipple and then take it between her teeth and tug. When he choked back a gasp, she raked her nails down his chest, over those defined abs, until he groaned and wriggled.

"Still like a bossy Scottish lass?" she asked.

"Always." His voice was rough with a need that matched the throbbing heat in her sex. "But if you don't do me quick, I really will lose it—all over this nice, new kilt."

She grasped his shaft, positioning it for penetration, and sank down onto his length inch by inch, loving the sensation of his hardness gliding into her. When she'd taken his girth as deep inside as possible, she settled her palms on his chest and gazed into his gorgeous, golden-brown eyes.

He looked at her with such a potent combination of love and lust that her heart thudded and pleasure jolted through her. He groaned, his eyes drifting half closed. "You feel so good."

She lunged down to take his mouth in a tongue-tangling kiss that left them both breathing hard.

His eyes shot wide, and he grasped her hips as if to lift her off him. "Jamie, we forgot the condom."

"I was thinking…" She averted her focus to his chest, suddenly anxious about what he might say to her suggestion. "How would you feel about getting started on our family plans tonight?"

"Family plans?" He gazed at her with confusion.

"You want to have bairns, don't you?"

"With you, yeah, of course." His hold on her hips slackened, though his hands stayed in position. "You really want to start trying tonight?"

"If you do, I do." She placed her hands over his on her hips. "It's become a MacTaggart tradition, men getting their women up the duff before the wedding."

He laughed, the sound resonating in his chest. "I'm assuming 'up the duff' means pregnant."

"It does."

"Guess we shouldn't break the tradition, eh?"

She loved that naughty tone in his voice. She loved the feel of him inside her, the weight of his hands on her hips, the sensation of all that muscle beneath her and the thought of what that body could do to her. She loved *him*.

Keeping her hands over his, she began to move, rocking slowly, rising up and gliding back down his shaft, over and over in a sweetly erotic rhythm. He groaned and grasped her hips a little tighter, binding her to him while he bent his knees enough to get leverage and rock up every time she slid back down, melding their bodies in the most intimate and satisfying way. She let her head fall back, her hair cascading behind her and teasing her skin with feathery brushes. Her sensitized skin heightened every tiny sensation, from the caress of her own hair on her back and shoulders to the heat and firmness of his shaft and the flexing of his muscles as he met her movements with his own.

No more fear. No more barriers between them. This moment, this act, it united them completely in body and heart and soul.

"Oh Gavin," she moaned, eyes half closed, lost in the bliss of their joining, "we're making a baby tonight. I can feel it."

"Me too." He slung his arms around her and surged up to kneel on the plaid. Sitting back on his heels with her balanced on his lap, he rumbled, "Hook your legs around me, baby."

She locked her ankles behind his ass. With his hands on her back anchoring her, she leaned back farther, and together they moved. He thrust deeper, pulling her toward him. She moaned louder and flung her arms around his neck, her hands linked at his nape, her body still angled away from him. Her breasts bounced as he plunged in harder, faster, yanking her hips into him with each thrust. She lunged forward to cling to him, her arms tight around his neck, her breaths blustering against his ear. The pleasure escalated inside her like a spring coiling tighter and tighter, exerting a pressure that promised to blast her apart in the most incredible way.

He growled near her ear, his pace accelerating, plowing into her with unbelievable power and control. "Come for me, baby. Come for me now."

Those words, spoken in a voice roughened by passion, broke the coil. Her climax exploded through her, hot and strong and overwhelming in the ecstasy it unleashed. She clenched him so tightly with her legs and arms, with her whole body, that he gasped into her ear.

She threw her head back and let the pleasure erupt from her in wild cries.

Gavin rolled forward, pinning her to the plaid on her back, and punched into her with reckless need again and again. His release jetted into her deepest places, hot and powerful, branding her with the essence of him. He thrust once more, his cock pulsing deep within her. Spent, he rolled off her body to lie alongside her on the tartan kilt. They both breathed hard, struggling to regain their equilibrium after the world-tilting experience they'd shared. Sex had never been like this before, not even with him.

He spread a hand on her lower belly, his fingers over her womb. "I hope we did make a baby tonight. It seems right that we should. A baby would be the best Christmas present ever."

"Our bairn wouldn't be born on Christmas. Pregnancy lasts nine months, not twelve."

"But we'll know we made a baby on this night." He kissed her tummy and rested his chin above her navel. "I got everything I want for Christmas. What about you?"

The hint of anxiety in his expression made her chest ache—in a good way. She loved knowing he cared so much about her happiness, as much as she cared about his.

She threaded her fingers through his hair. "This is everything I wanted too."

He pulled the tartan over her like a blanket. "Gotta keep the mother of my child warm and safe."

Movement outside the window drew her attention, and she studied the big snowflakes swirling beyond the glass. Christmas. Snow. Gavin. A baby. What more could she want?

Nothing, she mused with a soft smile. Nothing at all.

"What's that smile for?" Gavin asked, cuddling closer, enclosing her with his body.

"Mm, I was thinking…" She ran a hand up and down his bicep. "If you want to keep me warm and make sure we made a baby, you'd better do that again. Maybe twice more. Just to be sure."

"Anything for my girl."

Epilogue

Iain
February 15

The door to Rory's office hung open, an invitation to enter. I paused on the threshold to take in the sight before me, the sight of my formerly uptight cousin's office in disarray. Cardboard boxes squatted on the floor in stacks, some taped shut, others open and awaiting more items. Rory hunched behind the large desk fiddling with a dispenser for packaging tape. A strip of the clear tape had gotten stuck on his shirt sleeve, and he yanked it off but fought to keep the stuff from clinging to his fingers.

I ambled inside the room, stopping at the nearest chair, laying my hand on its back. "The office doesn't want to let you go, eh, Rory?"

My younger cousin glanced up in surprise, the tape stuck to his thumb. "You're early."

"No, you've lost track of time." I pointed to the clock on the wall. "It's eleven o'clock."

Rory's eyebrows lifted as he followed my finger-pointing to the clock. "I did lose track of the time."

I took a seat in the chair in front of Rory's desk. "Did that ever happen to you before Emery?"

Rory ripped the tape off his thumb and tossed it onto the floor, then dropped into his leather chair. "You know it didn't. I was obsessed with timeliness and order."

"A good woman cured you of that." I propped my head on my hand, my elbow on the chair's arm. "I've been thinking about the changes in this family over the past few years. You, Lachlan, and Aidan took chances and came out the better for it. I admire the three of you for that. Even Jamie is happily married and pregnant. I have to admit I'm a bit jealous of my cousins."

"Jealous of what? You have more than enough money, you do what you want when you want, and you can have any woman you want."

Therein lay the problem but talking about it made my skin itch. I'd never told a soul about the event that drastically altered the course of my life and left me adrift for far too long. Aidan knew part of the story, the part about the woman I'd lost. I'd never told anyone more of the tale until I met Gavin Douglas. Somehow, his plight had inspired me to open up about the worst time in my life, though even Gavin didn't know the whole story.

I wouldn't tell all of it to Rory either. I couldn't. The shame of what I'd done still tainted me down to the core of my being.

"Aye, any woman I want," I said. "Except the only one who matters."

Rory leaned back in his chair, watching me with that analytical gaze I recognized as quintessentially Rory. "We all know something happened to you in America, but you've never wanted to talk about it."

Still didn't want to. I resisted the urge to fidget in my chair. Unlike Rory, I'd never repressed my fears or my feelings. I'd embraced them, if anything, a bit too fervently and earned the title of notorious. All that was in the past, though, and I needed a fresh start.

I needed *her*.

Rory toyed with a card lying on the table, a greeting card. He flipped it open, giving me a glimpse of glittery hearts on the front. "Is this about a woman? The MacTaggart grapevine has embellished the story over the years, but it all began with what Kevin Lister claimed he heard you say at a pub one night."

Damn that blethering drunkard. Not that I could complain since I'd been jaked at the time as well.

"Yes," I said calmly though my stomach had started to roil. "I lost a woman. No, that's not quite right. I gave her up without a fight, and I've regretted it ever since."

Rory raised the Valentine's card and turned it so I could see the words his wife had scrawled inside it, large and impossible to miss. *Love is a journey from pain to redemption. Never forget how far we've come.*

My throat grew tight and thick, but I managed an even tone when I said, "What am I meant to take away from your wife's effusive love for you? It's charming but—"

"Never give up. That's the lesson." Rory set down the card. "Tell me more about your woman."

Sighing, I resigned myself to the conversation I must have with my favorite solicitor. "Gavin keeps telling me it's not too late to try again. I ran away from the problem thirteen years ago. Let a family of bullies chase me out of America and away from the only woman I've ever loved, convinced myself she was better off without me. Every day since, I've regretted that mistake. When Gavin had a similar problem, he fought like the devil, with your help, and never gave up until he found his way back to Jamie. He has more courage than I ever did. Maybe I don't deserve a second chance, but I need to try."

"Of course you deserve a second chance, Iain. Everyone does."

"You have no idea of what I did to the girl." I couldn't suppress the urge anymore and squirmed in my seat. No amount of fidgeting could ease the discomfort, though, because it resided in my soul. "My only consolation was that she went on with her life. Maybe she married and had children. I'm certain she went on to the career in teaching she'd always wanted. She's clever and stubborn, beautiful and feisty, the sort of woman who makes a man want to hold on to her forever."

The smile that kinked Rory's lips conveyed humor but also compassion. "You loved her."

"I still do." I twisted my mouth in disgust. "I'm too old to be such an eejit about a girl I knew in the distant past. I'm a dinosaur, she's a butterfly."

Rory chuckled softly. "You are turning into a maudlin codger, aren't ye, Iain? Lachlan's six years younger than you. Does that make him a dinosaur? I must be approaching that status too since I'm forty now."

"I'm fifty." I leaned forward, determined for some odd reason to hammer into his mind that I was too old for this. "And she would be thirty-five now. I'm no stripling lad, I'm a dirty old man."

Rory laughed outright this time, shaking his head. "Bloody hell, you're determined to paint yourself that way. Lachlan thought he was a dirty old man for seducing Erica. She's fourteen years younger than he is. Your girl is fifteen years behind you. Not such an enormous difference, is it? Or do you think Lachlan had no right to marry Erica?"

"Lachlan never did what I did to—"

"For pity's sake, Iain." Rory bent forward, arms on the desk, his gaze sharpening on me. "Lachlan left Erica. He broke her heart, and for two months she refused to see or speak to him. And look what I did to Emery." He scoffed at himself. "A marriage of convenience, a bloody business arrangement with sex as a stipulation. I told her I'd never love her, and even when she was about to walk out on me, I couldn't admit I needed her. Why she took me back, I'll never know."

"What's your point? We MacTaggarts are a bunch of bloody fucking erses?"

Rory stared at me in the stone-cold way that intimidated many people, but not me. I'd known him since the day of his birth—I'd changed his dirty nappies, for Christ's sake—and it was hard to be intimidated by a man whose erse you'd wiped.

"You are not too old," Rory said in an even tone. "You deserve a second chance. If as you say you've learned a lesson from Gavin's experiences, then take this chance. Let's find your woman."

"That's why I came here. But, ah…" I squirmed again. "*Hosenscheisser*. It's more difficult than I expected. Thinking of doing a thing is easy, taking action is a bleeding terror."

"If you want to curse in German, you could at least inform me of the meaning."

"Trouser-shitter, literally. Cursing at myself. It means I'm a damn coward who's too afraid to take a risk."

Rory drew his head back as if my statement had shocked him. "Iain MacTaggart is admitting to being afraid? I should mark this day on my calendar, so we can commemorate the event every year."

"Have your fun with me, I deserve it." I set my hands on my knees. "But will you help me find her?"

"Of course I will." He cleared his throat in a sardonic manner. "But I will need to know the lassie's name first."

A name I hadn't spoken aloud in more than a decade. I thought her name every day, a hundred times or more, but I hadn't voiced it in far too long. "Rae Everhart."

Rory nodded, then retrieved a pad of paper and a pen from a drawer. He pushed the items across the desk toward me. "Write down everything you know about her."

I picked up the pen, my gaze trained on the blank sheet of paper. "Do you think we can find her?"

"With my legal connections and the help of an investigator I know in America, I'm certain we can. It might take time, but we will find her." Rory tapped a finger on the paper to gain my attention. "You know I never make a promise I can't keep."

"One of your most admirable traits." Unlike me. I'd broken too many vows to count, but now that I'd set my sights on tracking down Rae, I knew this would be one vow I'd keep—with Rory's help.

Pen in hand, I began to document every fact I remembered about Rae Everhart. Memories unreeled in my mind, memories of her auburn hair shining in the sunlight, of the way her sapphire-blue eyes sparkled and captivated me, the delicate melody of her laughter, her throaty moans when I'd made love to her.

My hand froze in the middle of writing a word. Dear God, was I really doing this?

Yes, I was.

To see Rae again after all this time…Would she want to see me? Not knowing the answer used to unnerve me. Today, after resolving to do this at last, I had a different reaction. A sort of excitement I hadn't experienced in years electrified me, and I dove into my writing task with a new fervor.

For the first time in thirteen years, I felt fully alive.

Iain MacTaggart returns in *Notorious in a Kilt*.

nna Durand is a bestselling, multi-award-winning author of contemporary and paranormal romance. Her books have earned best-seller status on every major retailer and wonderful reviews from readers around the world. But that's the boring spiel. Here are some really cool things you want to know about Anna!

Born on Lackland Air Force Base in Texas, Anna grew up moving here, there, and everywhere thanks to her dad's job as an instructor pilot. She's lived in Texas (twice), Mississippi, California (twice), Michigan (twice), and Alaska—and now Ohio.

As for her writing, Anna has always made up stories in her head, but she didn't write them down until her teen years. Those first awful books went into the trash can a few years later, though she learned a lot from those stories. Eventually, she would pen her first romance novel, the paranormal romance *Willpower*, and she's never looked back since.

Want even more details about Anna? Get access to her extended bio when you subscribe to her newsletter and download the free bonus ebook, *Hot Scots Confidential*. You'll also get hot deleted scenes, character interviews, fun facts, and more! You also get the short story *Tempted by a Kiss* and a bonus audio chapter narrated for you by Shane East. Visit AnnaDurand.com to sign up!

CPSIA information can be obtained
at www.ICGtesting.com
Printed in the USA
LVHW080428041022
729908LV00013B/833